SO-AKS-887

PRAISE FOR THE
SEBASTIAN ST. CYR MYSTERY SERIES

"This riveting historical tale of tragedy and triumph, with its sly nods to Jane Austen and her characters, will enthrall you."
—Sabrina Jeffries, *New York Times* bestselling author of
If the Viscount Falls

"Sebastian St. Cyr is everything you could want in a Regency-era nobleman-turned–death investigator: uncannily clever, unwaveringly reserved, and irresistibly sexy. The entire series is simply elegant."
—Lisa Gardner, #1 *New York Times* bestselling author of
Crash & Burn

"Thoroughly enjoyable . . . moody and atmospheric, exposing the dark underside of Regency London."
—Deanna Raybourn, *New York Times* bestselling
author of *A Curious Beginning*

"Filled with suspense, intrigue, and plot twists galore."
—Victoria Thompson, national bestselling author of
the Gaslight Mysteries

"A serial-killer thriller set two hundred years ago? . . . It works, thanks to Harris's pacing and fine eye for detail."
—*Entertainment Weekly*

"Harris melds mystery and history as seamlessly as she integrates developments in her lead's personal life into the plot." —*Publishers Weekly* (starred review)

continued . . .

"Harris combines all of the qualities of a solid Regency in the tradition of Georgette Heyer. . . . Anyone who likes Amanda Quick and/or is reading the reissued Heyer novels will love this series." —*Library Journal* (starred review)

"Perfect reading. . . . Harris crafts her story with the threat of danger, hints of humor, vivid sex scenes, and a conclusion that will make your pulse race. Impressive."
—*The New Orleans Times-Picayune*

Books in the Sebastian St. Cyr Mystery Series

WHO
BURIES
THE DEAD

A Sebastian St. Cyr Mystery

C. S. HARRIS

AN OBSIDIAN MYSTERY

OBSIDIAN
Published by New American Library,
an imprint of Penguin Random House LLC
375 Hudson Street, New York, New York 10014

This book is a publication of New American Library. Previously published in an
Obsidian hardcover edition.

First Obsidian Mass Market Printing, March 2016

ISBN 978-0-451-41812-8

Printed in the United States of America
10 9 8 7 6 5 4 3 2 1

Penguin
Random
House

For my own Aunt Henrietta:
Henrietta Wegmann Ecuyer
1909–2005
A grand and inspiring lady

Let the dead bury their dead.

LUKE 9:60

Chapter 1

Sunday, 21 March 1813

*T*hey called it Bloody Bridge.

It lay at the end of a dark, winding lane, far beyond the comforting flicker of the oil lamps of Sloane Square, beyond the last of the tumbledown cottages at the edge of a vast stretch of fields that showed only black in the moonless night. Narrow and hemmed in on both sides by high walls, the bridge was built of brick, worn and crumbling with age and slippery with moss where the elms edging the rivulet cast a deep, cold shade.

Cian O'Neal tried to avoid this place, even in daylight. It had been Molly's idea to come here, for on the far side of the bridge lay a deserted barn with a warm, soft hayloft that beckoned to young lovers in need. But now as the wind tossed the elms along the creek and brought the distant, mournful howl of a dog, Cian felt the hard, pulsing urgency that had driven him here begin to ebb.

"Maybe this ain't such a good idea, Molly," he said, his step lagging. "The barn, I mean."

She swung to face him, dark eyes shiny in a plump, merry face. "What's the matter, Cian?" She pressed her warm, yielding body against his, her voice husky. "You havin' second thoughts?"

"No. It's just . . ."

The wind gusted up stronger, banging a shutter somewhere in the night, and he jerked.

To his shame, he saw enlightenment dawn on her face, and she gave a trill of laughter. "You're scared."

"No, I ain't," he said, even though they both knew it for a lie. He was a big lad, eighteen next month and strong and hale. But at the moment, he felt like a wee tyke frightened by old Irish tales of the Dullahan.

She caught his hand in both of hers and backed down the lane ahead of him, pulling him toward the bridge. "Come on, then," she said. "How 'bout if I cross first?"

It had rained earlier in the evening, a brief but heavy downpour that left the newly budding leaves of the trees dripping moisture and the lane slippery with mud. He felt an icy tickle at the base of his neck and tried to think about the sweet warmth of the hayloft and the way Molly's soft, eager body would feel beneath his.

They were close enough to the bridge now that Cian could see it quite clearly, its single arch a deeper black against the roiling darkness of the sky. But something wasn't quite right, and he felt his scalp prickle, his breath catch, as the silhouette of a man's head loomed before them.

"What is it?" Molly asked, the laughter draining from her face as she whirled around and Cian started to scream.

Chapter 2

Monday, 22 March, the hours before dawn

The child lay curled on his side in a cradle near the hearth, his tiny pink lips parted with the slow, even breath of sleep. He had one tightly clenched fist tucked up beneath his chin, and in the firelight the translucent flesh of his closed eyelids looked so delicate and fragile that it terrified his father, who stood watching him. Someday this infant would be Viscount Devlin and then, in time, the Earl of Hendon. But now he was simply the Honorable Simon St. Cyr, barely seven weeks old and oblivious to the fact that he had no more real right to any of those titles than his father, Sebastian St. Cyr, the current Viscount Devlin.

Devlin rested the heel of one outthrust palm against the mantelpiece. His breath came harsh and ragged, and sweat sheened his naked flesh despite the air's chill. He'd been driven from his sleep by memories he generally chose not to revisit during daylight. But he could not stop the images that came to him in the quiet hours of darkness, visions of dancing flames, of a woman's tortured body writhing in helpless agony, of soft brown hair fluttering against the waxen flesh of a dead child's cheek.

The past never leaves us, he thought. We carry it with
us through our lives, a ghostly burden of bittersweet
nostalgia threaded with guilt and regret that wearies the
soul and whispers to us in the darkest hours of the night.
Only the youngest children are truly innocent, for their
consciences are still untroubled, their haunted days yet
to come.

He shuddered and bent to throw more coal on the fire,
moving carefully so as not to wake the sleeping babe or
his mother.

When Sebastian was a child, it had been the custom
for the infants of the aristocracy and the gentry to be
farmed out to wet nurses, often not returning to their
own families until they were two years of age. But it was
becoming more common now for even duchesses to
choose to nurse their own offspring, and Hero, the child's
mother and Sebastian's wife of eight months, had been
adamantly against hiring a wet nurse.

His gaze shifted to the blue silk–hung bed where she
slept, her rich dark hair spilling across the pillow. And
he felt it again, that nameless wash of apprehension for
this woman and this child that he dismissed as lingering
wisps from his dream and fear born of a guilt that could
never be assuaged.

A clatter of hooves and the rattle of carriage wheels
over granite paving stones carried clearly in the stillness
of the night. Sebastian raised his head, his body tensing
as the carriage jerked to a halt and a man's quick, heavy
tread ran up his front steps. He heard the distant peal of
his bell, then a gruff, questioning shout from his majordomo, Morey.

"Message for Lord Devlin," answered the unknown
visitor, his voice strained by a sense of urgency and what
sounded very much like horror. "From Sir Henry, of Bow
Street!"

Sebastian threw on his dressing gown and slipped quietly from the room.

Chapter 3

*T*he head had been positioned near the end of one of the low brick walls lining the old bridge, its sightless face turned as if to watch anyone unwary enough to approach. A man's head, it had thick, graying dark hair, heavy eyebrows, and a long, prominent nose.

"Nasty business, this," said the burly constable, the pine torch in his hand hissing and spitting as he held it aloft in the blustery wind.

Sir Henry Lovejoy, the newest of Bow Street's three stipendiary magistrates, watched the golden light dance over the pale features of that frozen, staring face and felt his stomach give an uncomfortable lurch.

The night was unusually cold and starless, the flaring torches of the constables fanning out along the banks of the small stream filling the air with the scent of burning pitch. They'd need to make a more thorough search of the area in the morning, of course. But this was a start.

Even in daylight, this rutted, muddy lane was seldom traveled, for beyond the winding rivulet spanned by the narrow, single-arched bridge lay a vast open area of market and nursery gardens known as the Five Fields. All were shrouded now in an eerie blackness so complete as to seem impenetrable.

Hunching his shoulders against the cold, Lovejoy moved to where the rest of the unfortunate gentleman's strong, solid body lay sprawled in the lane's grassy verge, his once neatly arranged linen cravat disordered and stained dark, the raw, hacked flesh of his neck too gruesome to bear close inspection. He'd been Lovejoy's age, in his fifties. That should not have bothered Lovejoy, but for some reason he didn't care to dwell on, it did. He drew a quick breath fouled with a heavy, coppery stench and groped for his handkerchief. "You're certain this is—was—Mr. Stanley Preston?"

"I'm afraid so, sir," said the constable. A stout young man with bulging eyes, he towered over Lovejoy, who was both short and slight. "Molly—the barmaid from the Rose and Crown—recognized the, er, head, sir. And I found his calling cards in his pocket."

Lovejoy pressed the folded handkerchief to his lips. Under any circumstances, such a gruesome murder would be cause for concern. But when the victim was cousin to Lord Sidmouth, a former prime minister who now served as Home Secretary, the ramifications had the potential to be serious indeed. The local magistrate had immediately called in Bow Street and then withdrawn from the investigation entirely.

The sound of an approaching carriage, driven fast, jerked Lovejoy's attention from the blood-drenched corpse at their feet. He watched as a sleek curricle drawn by a pair of fine chestnuts swung off Sloane Street to run along the north side of the square and enter the shadowy lane leading to the bridge.

The driver was a gentleman, tall and lean, wearing a caped coat and elegant beaver hat. At the sight of Lovejoy, he drew up, and the half-grown groom, or tiger, who clung to a perch at the rear of the carriage leapt down to run to the horses' heads. "Best walk them, Tom," said Devlin, jumping lightly from the curricle's high seat. "That's a nasty wind."

"Aye, gov'nor," said the boy.

"My lord," said Lovejoy, moving thankfully to meet him. "My apologies for calling you out in the middle of such a wretched night. But I fear this case is worrisome. Most worrisome."

"Sir Henry," said Devlin. Then his gaze shifted beyond Lovejoy, to the severed head perched at the end of the bridge, and he let out a harsh breath. "Good God."

The Viscount was some one score and five years younger than Lovejoy and stood at least a foot taller, with hair nearly as dark as a Gypsy's and strange amber eyes that gleamed a feral yellow in the torchlight as the two men turned to walk toward the stream. "Have you learned anything yet?" he asked.

"Nothing, really, beyond the victim's identity."

They had first met when Devlin was wanted for murder and Lovejoy had been determined to bring him in to trial. In the two years since that time, what had begun as respect had deepened into an unlikely friendship. In Devlin, Lovejoy had found an unexpected ally with a fierce passion for justice, a brilliant mind, and a rare genius for solving murders. But the young Viscount also possessed something no Bow Street magistrate or constable could ever hope to acquire: an innate understanding and knowledge of the rarified world of gentlemen's clubs and Society balls frequented by the likes of the man whose head now decorated this deserted bridge on the edge of Hans Town and Chelsea.

"Were you acquainted with Mr. Preston, my lord?" Lovejoy asked as Devlin paused to study the dead man's bloodless features. The wind shifted the graying hair in a way that, for one horrible moment, made the man seem almost alive.

"Only slightly."

Preston's fine beaver hat lay upside down at the base of the pier, and Devlin bent to pick it up, his face thoughtful as he felt the crown and brim.

Lovejoy said, "I fear Bow Street is going to come under tremendous pressure from both the Palace and Westminster to solve this. Quickly."

Devlin's gaze shifted to meet his. They both understood the ways in which that kind of pressure could lead to the hasty arrest and conviction of an innocent man. "You're asking for my help?"

"I am, yes, my lord."

Lovejoy waited anxiously for a response. But the Viscount simply stared off across the darkened fields, his face giving nothing away.

Lovejoy knew Devlin's own near-fatal encounter with the clumsy workings of the British legal system had much to do with his dedication to seeking justice for the victims of murder. But the magistrate had always suspected there was more to it than that. Something had happened to the Viscount—some dark but unknown incident in the past that had driven him to resign his commission in the Army and embark on a path of self-destruction from which he had only recently begun to recover.

The wind gusted up stronger, thrashing the limbs of the elms along the creek and sending a torn playbill scuttling across the bridge's worn brick paving. Devlin said, "The crown and upper brim of Preston's hat are wet, but not the underside. And since the hair on his head looks dry too, I'd say he was out walking in the rain but was killed after it let up. What time was that?"

"About half past ten," said Lovejoy, and let go a sigh of relief.

Chapter 4

Sebastian turned to where Preston's body lay on its back, arms flung out to the sides, one leg slightly bent, the wet grass dark with his blood. He'd seen many such sights—and worse—in the six years he'd spent in the Army. But he'd never become inured to carnage. He hesitated for the briefest moment, then hunkered down beside the headless corpse.

"Who found him?" he asked, resting a forearm on one knee.

"A barmaid and stableboy from the Rose and Crown," said Lovejoy. "Just after eleven. It was the barmaid—Molly Watson, I believe she's called—who alerted the local magistrate."

Sebastian twisted around to study the deserted lane. "What was she doing here at that time of night?"

"I haven't actually spoken to her. Sir Thomas—the local magistrate—told her she could go home before I arrived. But from what I understand, she couldn't seem to come up with a coherent explanation." Lovejoy's voice tightened with disapproval. "Sir Thomas says he suspects their destination was the hayloft of that barn over there."

Sebastian had to duck his head to hide a smile. A

staunch reformist, Lovejoy lived by a strict personal moral code and was therefore frequently shocked by the activities of those whose approach to life was considerably freer than his own.

"Was his greatcoat open like this when he was found?" asked Sebastian. He could see Preston's pocket watch lying on the ground beside his hip, still fastened to its gold chain.

"One of the constables said something about searching the man's pockets for his cards. I suspect he must have opened the greatcoat in the process."

Sebastian jerked off one glove and reached out to touch the blood-soaked waistcoat. His hand came away wet and sticky. "He's still faintly warm," he said, wiping his hand on his handkerchief. "Do you know when he was last seen?"

"According to his staff, he went out around nine. His house isn't far from here—just off Hans Place. I'm told he was a widower with two grown children—a son in Jamaica and an unmarried daughter. Unfortunately, the daughter spent the evening with friends and has no knowledge of her father's plans for the night."

Sebastian let his gaze drift over the darkened, grassy banks of the nearby stream. "I wonder what the devil he was doing here. Somehow I find it doubtful he was looking for a warm hayloft."

"I shouldn't think so, no," said Sir Henry, clearing his throat uncomfortably.

Sebastian pushed to his feet. "You'll be sending the body to Gibson?" he asked. A one-legged Irish surgeon with a dangerous opium addiction, Paul Gibson could read the secrets of a dead body better than anyone else in England.

Sir Henry nodded. "I doubt he'll be able to tell us anything beyond the obvious, but I suppose we ought to have him take a look."

Sebastian brought his gaze, again, to the head on the

bridge, the puddle of blood beneath it congealed in the cold. "Why cut off his head?" he said, half to himself. "Why display it on the bridge?" It had been the practice, once, to mount the heads of traitors on spikes set atop London Bridge. But that barbarity had been abandoned nearly a hundred and fifty years ago.

"As a warning, perhaps?" suggested Sir Henry.

"To whom?"

The magistrate shook his head. "I can't imagine."

"It takes a powerful hatred—or rage—to drive most people to mutilate the body of another human being."

"Rage, or madness," said Sir Henry.

"True."

Sebastian went to study the ground near the bridge's old brick footings. He carried no torch, but then, he didn't need one, for there was an animal-like acuity to his eyesight and hearing that enabled him to see great distances and in the dark, and to distinguish sounds he'd come to realize were inaudible to most of his fellow men.

"What is it?" asked Sir Henry as Sebastian slid down to the water's edge and bent to pick up an object perhaps a foot and a half in length and three or four inches wide, but very thin.

"It appears to be an old metal strap of some sort," said Sebastian, turning it over in his hands. "Probably lead. It's been freshly cut at both ends, and there's an inscription. It says—" He broke off.

"What? What does it say?"

He looked up. "It says, 'King Charles, 1648.'"

"Merciful heavens," whispered Sir Henry.

Every English schoolboy knew the story of King Charles I, grandson of Mary, Queen of Scots. Put on trial by Oliver Cromwell and his Puritan cohorts, he was beheaded on 30 January 1649. Only, because the old-style calendar reckoned the new year as beginning on 25 March rather than the first of January, chroniclers of the time recorded the execution date as 1648.

"Perhaps it's unrelated to the murder," said Sir Henry. "Who knows how long it's been here?"

"The top surface is dry, so it must have been dropped since the rain let up."

"But . . . what could a man like Stanley Preston possibly have to do with Charles I?"

"Aside from sharing the manner of his death, you mean?" said Sebastian.

The magistrate tightened his lips in a way that whitened the flesh beside his suddenly pinched nostrils. "There is that."

A church bell began to toll somewhere in the distance, then another. The mist was beginning to creep up from the river, cold and clammy; Sebastian watched as Sir Henry stared off down the lane to where the oil lamps of Sloane Square now showed as only a murky glow.

"It's frightening to think that the man who did this is out there right now," said the magistrate. "Living amongst us."

And he could do it again.

Neither Sir Henry nor Sebastian said it. But the words were there, carried on the cold, wild wind.

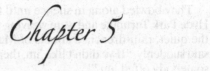

Chapter 5

*T*he smell of freshly spilled blood had spooked the horses so that Sebastian had his hands full as he turned the curricle toward home.

"Is that really an 'ead on the bridge?" Tom asked as they swung into Sloane Street. "A man's 'ead?"

"It is."

The tiger let out his breath in a rush of ghoulish excitement. "*Gor.*"

Small and sharp faced, the boy had been with Sebastian for more than two years now. Not even Tom knew his exact age or his last name. He'd been living alone on the streets when he'd tried to pick Sebastian's pocket—and ended up saving Sebastian's life.

More than once.

Sebastian said, "It belongs—or I suppose I should say belonged—to a Mr. Stanley Preston."

Tom must have caught the inflection in Sebastian's voice, because he said, "I take it ye didn't much care for the cove?"

"I barely knew him, actually. Although I must admit I have difficulties with men whose wealth comes from sugar plantations in the West Indies."

"Because they grow sugar?"

"Because their plantations are worked not by tenants, but by slaves—mostly Africans, although they also use transported Irish and Scottish rebels."

They bowled along in silence until they'd passed the Hyde Park Turnpike and were weaving their way through the quiet, rain-drenched streets of Mayfair. Then Tom said suddenly, "If ye didn't like 'im, then why ye care that somebody offed 'im?"

"Because even those who own West Indies plantations don't deserve to be brutally murdered. Apart from which, I find the idea of sharing my city with someone who goes around cutting off the heads of his enemies somewhat disconcerting."

"Discon-what?"

"Disconcerting. It makes me feel . . . uncomfortable."

"I reckon it was a Frenchman," said Tom, who had a profound suspicion of foreigners in general and the French in particular. "They're always cuttin' off folks' 'eads."

"An interesting theory that certainly merits consideration." Sebastian drew up before the front steps of his Brook Street town house. The oil lamps mounted on either side of the door cast a soft pool of golden light across the wet paving, but the house itself was dark and quiet, its inhabitants still sleeping. "Take care of the horses, then go to bed and stay there. It's nearly dawn."

Tom scrambled forward to take the reins as Sebastian dropped lightly to the pavement. "Ye gonna 'ave a lie-in?"

"No."

"Then I don't reckon I will," said Tom, his chin jutting forward mulishly.

Sebastian grunted. The lad's grasp of the concept of obedience was still rather shaky.

He watched Tom drive off toward the mews, then turned to enter the house. Moving quietly, he stripped off his clothes in the dressing room and slipped into bed beside Hero. He didn't want to wake her. But the need to feel her warm, vital body against his was too strong. He carefully slid one arm around her waist and pressed his chest against the long line of her back.

Her hand came up to rest on his, and in the darkness he saw her lips curve into a soft smile as she shifted so she could look at him over her shoulder. "You were a long time," she said. "Was it as bad as Sir Henry's message led you to expect?"

"Worse." He buried his face in the dark, fragrant fall of her hair. "Go back to sleep."

"Can you sleep?"

"In a while."

"I can help," she said huskily, her hand sliding low over his naked hip, his breath catching in his throat as she turned in his arms and covered his mouth with hers.

※

He came downstairs the next morning to find Hero in the entryway wearing a hunter green pelisse and velvet hat with three plumes. She was pulling on a pair of soft kid gloves but paused when she looked up and saw him.

"Well, good morning," she said, her eyes gently smiling at him. "I didn't expect to see you up this early."

"It's not early."

She shifted to adjust her hat in the looking glass over the console. "It is when you've been up most of the night."

She was an extraordinarily tall woman, nearly as tall as Sebastian, with hair of a rich medium brown and fine gray eyes that sparkled with an intelligence of almost frightening intensity. She had the kind of looks more often described as handsome than pretty, with a strong chin, a wide mouth, and an aquiline nose she had inherited from her father, Lord Jarvis, a distant cousin of the mad old King George and the real power behind the

Prince of Wales's fragile regency. Once, Jarvis had tried to have Sebastian killed—and undoubtedly still would, if he found it expedient.

"Another interview?" he asked, watching her tilt her hat just so. "What is it this time? Dustmen? Chimney sweeps? Flower girls?"

"Costermongers."

"Ah."

She was writing a series of articles on London's working poor that she intended to eventually gather together into a book. It was a project that disgusted her father, both because he considered such activities unsuitable for a female, and because the entire undertaking smacked of the kind of radicalism he abhorred. But then, Hero had never allowed her father's expectations or prejudices to constrain her.

She said, "Stanley Preston's murder is in all the morning papers. Was he truly decapitated?"

"He was."

She pivoted slowly to face him again, her eyes wide and still.

He said, "Do you have a moment? There's something I'd like you to see."

"Of course." Slipping off her pelisse, she followed him into the library, where he'd left the ancient metal strap on his desk.

"I found this not far from Preston's body." He handed her the length of lead and gave her a brief description of the scene at the bridge.

"'King Charles, 1648,'" she read, then looked up at him. "I don't understand. What is it?"

"I could be wrong, but I've seen strips of metal like this before, wrapped around old coffins."

"Surely you're not suggesting this came from the coffin of Charles I?"

"I don't know. But it's telling the inscription reads, 'King Charles' rather than 'Charles I,' and 1648 rather than 1649. Where exactly is Charles I buried? I've realized I have no idea."

"No one does. After the execution, there was talk of interring him in Westminster Abbey. But Cromwell refused to allow it, so the King's men took the body away at night and buried it in secret. There are conflicting reports about what they did with him. I've heard speculation he may be somewhere in St. George's Chapel in Windsor Castle. But no one knows for certain." She frowned. "What were Preston's politics?"

"I'd be surprised if he nourished any secret nostalgia for the Stuarts, if that's what you're thinking."

She ran her fingertips over the scrolled engraving, her features composed but thoughtful. "Do you mind if I show it to Jarvis?" she asked, reaching for her pelisse again.

"He's not going to like my involving you in another murder investigation."

"Don't worry," she said as Sebastian took the pelisse from her hands to help her with it. "I seriously doubt he could dislike you more than he already does."

He laughed at that. Then he turned her in his arms, his hands lingering on her shoulders, his laughter stilling.

"What?" she asked, watching him.

"Just that . . . whoever killed Stanley Preston was either driven by a rage bordering on madness, or he is mad. And of the two, I'm not certain which makes him more dangerous."

"Madness is always frightening, I suppose because it is so incomprehensible. Yet I think I'd fear more the man who is brutal but sane, and therefore capable of shrewd, cold calculation."

"Because he's clever?"

"That, and because he's less likely to make mistakes."

Chapter 6

*S*ebastian ordered his curricle brought round and came out of the house half an hour later to find Tom walking the grays up and down Brook Street. It had rained again sometime in the early-morning hours, leaving the pavement wet, with dull, heavy clouds that pressed down on the city's crowded rooftops and soaring chimneys. The horses' breath showed white in the cold.

"If you fall asleep and tumble off your perch," said Sebastian, taking the reins, "I won't stop and pick you up."

But Tom simply laughed and scrambled back to his place.

They headed south, curling around the edge of Hyde Park, where faint wisps of mist still drifted through the trees and the distant clumps of shrubs were no more than blurred shadows.

There'd been a time not so long ago when Knightsbridge and Hans Town were sleepy, pleasant villages lying several miles beyond the sprawl of London. Now, neat terrace houses of three and five stories—plus basements and attics—lined spacious squares and a broad thoroughfare called Sloane Street that stretched from Knightsbridge down toward Chelsea and the Thames. This was a district favored by prosperous barristers, physicians, and bankers, with a scattering of respectable lodging houses and workshops and a few more modest but comfortable homes for tradesmen.

Reluctant to disturb Preston's grieving daughter so early in the day, Sebastian went instead to the Rose and Crown. A well-tended inn built of brick in the last years of the eighteenth century, it had a freshly whitewashed arch leading to a bustling yard and a public room that smelled of bacon and wood smoke and hearty ale. A buxom, dark-haired, dark-eyed girl of perhaps sixteen was wiping the tables when Sebastian walked in.

"You're Molly?" he asked.

She turned, a smile lighting up her pretty face as she let her gaze rove over him in frank assessment. "I am. Who're you?"

"Devlin. I wonder if I might ask you a few questions about last night?"

The smile disappeared and she retreated behind the gleaming oak counter that stretched along one wall. "What you want t' know fer? You don't look like no beak t' me."

"I'm not." He laid a coin on the counter between them, the metal clicking softly against the polished wood. "I'm told you recognized Mr. Preston last night. Did he come here often?"

Her hand flashed out, and the coin disappeared. "Sometimes. Though he mostly favored the Monster."

"The Monster?"

She jerked her head toward the west. "It's just off Sloane Street." She wrinkled her little button of a nose. "The place is so old you have t' walk down a couple of steps to get in the front door."

Sebastian let his gaze wander around the taproom, with its neat round tables and straight-backed chairs and gleaming wainscoting. "Did Mr. Preston come in here last night?"

"Nah. Ain't seen him for a fortnight or more."

"When he would come in, what did he drink?"

"Ale, mostly. But he weren't no lush, if that's what you're askin'. Usually, he'd just pop in for a quick pint of an evenin', then leave."

Sebastian brought his gaze back to her pretty, expressive face. "I understand you're the one who told the magistrate what you'd found at the bridge. But someone else was with you, wasn't he? Someone from the stables?"

"Cian O'Neal." Her voice dripped scorn. "Took one look at that head sittin' up there and started screamin' like he weren't never gonna stop. When I said, 'We gotta go tell Sir Thomas,' he took t' shakin' all over, and his eyes got so big I thought they was gonna pop right out of his head. I grabbed hold of his arm, but he jerked away and run off. Never even looked back."

"Did you see anyone else near the bridge?"

She stared at him. "What're you thinkin'? That there was *two* heads there?"

"I was wondering if you might have seen someone running away as you walked up the lane."

"No. I remember laughin' at Cian because it was so dark and quiet, he was scared even before we seen the head."

"Can you think of any reason for Mr. Preston to have been at the bridge at that time of night?"

Her eyes widened slightly. "Never thought about that, but . . . Well, no. Truth is, most folks around here tend t' avoid Bloody Bridge after dark."

"Bloody Bridge?"

"That's what it's called, you know."

"No, I didn't know."

She sniffed, nearly as contemptuous of his ignorance as she was of poor Cian O'Neal's terror. "Folks say it's haunted by those who've died there over the years."

"Yet you weren't afraid to go there," said Sebastian.

She shrugged. "It's the quickest way t' get t' Five Fields, ain't it?"

"And why would you want to go to Five Fields at night?"

She gave him an impish smile and raised her eyebrows in a knowing look. "I won't be goin' there with Cian again, that's fer sure."

"Tell me, what did you think of Mr. Preston?"

She shrugged. "He never give me no trouble, the way some of 'em do, if that's what yer askin'."

"Have you heard anyone speculating about what they think might have happened to him?"

"Most folks're sayin' footpads must've done it, which just goes t' show what they know."

"What makes you so certain it wasn't footpads?"

She lifted her chin. "Why, I could see his pocket watch, couldn't I? Danglin' from its chain like he was just checkin' the time. Ain't no footpad gonna go t' all the trouble of cuttin' off a feller's head and then leave his watch like that."

"Mr. Preston's greatcoat was unbuttoned when you saw him?"

She frowned. "Well, I guess it musta been. Didn't really think about it, but, yeah, I reckon it was."

Sebastian made inquiries at the stables, but Cian O'Neal hadn't come to work that morning. He eventually tracked the lad to a tumbledown cottage off Wilderness Row, where he lived with his widowed mother and five younger siblings.

Sebastian's knock was answered by the lad's mother, a rail-thin, worn-down woman with gray-threaded hair who looked sixty but was probably younger than forty, judging by the squalling infant in her arms.

"Beggin' your pardon, me lord," she said, dropping a

curtsy when Sebastian explained who he was and the purpose of his visit, "but I'm afraid you won't be gettin' much sense out of Cian. He didn't sleep a wink all night—just sat in the corner by the fire and shivered. Some constable come by here from Bow Street and tried to talk to him a bit ago, and the poor lad started babblin' all sorts of nonsense about havin' seen the Dullahan."

Sebastian had heard of the Dullahan. A figure in Irish folklore said to be a horseman dressed all in black and astride a black, fire-breathing stallion, he rode the darkened lanes and byways, carrying his own head in his hand. According to legend, whenever the Dullahan stops, a man, woman, or child dies.

Sebastian said, "I'd like to try talking to him."

He knew by the worry pinching the woman's face that she'd rather have denied him. But she belonged to a class whose members had been trained since birth to obey their "betters."

She dropped a curtsy and stood back to let him enter.

The cottage was clean but wretchedly poor, with low, heavy beams, a swept dirt floor, and a worm-eaten old table with benches that looked as if they'd been knocked together from scrap wood picked up off the street. Of one room only, the place had a mattress in an alcove half-hidden behind a tattered curtain and a pegged, roughly hewn ladder that led up to a loft.

Cian O'Neal sat on a low, three-legged stool before the fire, his shoulders hunched forward, his hands thrust together between his tightly clasped knees. He was a fine-looking lad of seventeen or eighteen, big and strapping and startlingly handsome, with clear blue eyes and golden hair that curled softly against his lean cheeks. He kept his attention fixed on the fire, as if oblivious to Devlin's approach. But when his mother touched him on the shoulder, he jerked violently and looked up at her with wide, terrified eyes.

"Here's a lord come to talk to you, Cian," she said gently. "About last night."

The boy's gaze slid from her face to Sebastian. A spasm passed over his features, the chest beneath his thin smock jerking visibly with his quick, agitated breathing.

Sebastian said, "I just want to know if you saw anything—heard anything—that might help us figure out what happened last night."

The boy opened his mouth, the air rasping in his constricted throat as he drew a deep breath that came out in a high-pitched, terrified scream.

Sebastian pressed a coin into the poor woman's hand and left.

Chapter 7

"You aren't seriously suggesting that I might somehow know who killed Stanley, or why? Good God!"

Henry Addington, First Viscount Sidmouth and Home Secretary of the United Kingdom of Great Britain and Ireland, stood with his hands clenched at his sides, his gaze on the big man who sat at his ease in a tapestry-covered armchair beside the empty hearth of his Carlton House chambers.

Charles, Lord Jarvis, fingered the handle of a diamond-studded quizzing glass he'd lately taken to wearing on a riband around his neck. "You would have me believe you do not?"

"Of course not!"

Jarvis pursed his lips. He was an unusually large man, impressive in both height and breadth, his face fleshy, his lips full and unexpectedly sensual, the aquiline nose he'd bequeathed to his daughter, Hero, lending a harsh cast to his face. Addington might be Home Secretary while Jarvis carried no official title, but Jarvis was by far the more powerful man. He owed his preeminence not to his kinship with the King—which was distant—but to the brilliance of his mind and the unflinching ruthlessness of the methods he was willing to use to protect the power and prestige of the monarchy at home and the interests of Britain abroad. The only thing that had kept the Prince Regent from suffering the same fate meted out to his fellow royals across the Channel was Jarvis, and most people knew it.

Jarvis raised his quizzing glass to one eye and regarded the Home Secretary through it. "You would have me believe this murder has nothing to do with you?"

"Nothing."

"The man was your cousin."

A faint, telltale line of color appeared high on the Home Secretary's cheekbones. "We were not . . . close."

"And his death in no way involves any affairs of state?"

"No."

Jarvis let the quizzing glass fall. "You're quite certain of that?"

"Yes!"

Jarvis rose to his feet. "You relieve my mind. If you should, however, discover you are mistaken, you will of course alert me at once?"

Sidmouth's jaw tightened. He was in his mid-fifties now, his once dark hair turning silver, his waist grown thick, the flesh of his hands and face as soft and pale as any pampered gentlewoman's. But he had the jaw of a butcher or a prizefighter, strong and powerful and pugnacious. "Of course," he said.

"Good. That will be all."

Sidmouth bowed curtly and swept from the room.

A moment later, the tall, dark-haired former hussar major who had been waiting in the antechamber appeared in the doorway. His name was Peter Archer, and he was one of several former military officers in Jarvis's employ.

"Sidmouth is hiding something," said Jarvis. "And I want to know what it is."

A faint smile curled the major's lips as he bowed. "Yes, my lord."

Chapter 8

*H*oping that Paul Gibson had made some progress in the postmortem of Preston's body, Sebastian turned his horses toward the Tower of London, where the Irishman kept a small surgery in the shadow of the grim medieval fortress's soot-stained walls.

The friendship between Sebastian and the former regimental surgeon dated back nearly ten years, to the days when both men wore the King's Colors and fought the King's wars from Italy to the West Indies to the Peninsula. Then a cannonball took off the lower part of Gibson's left leg, leaving him racked with pain and tormented by an increasingly serious opium addiction. In the end, he'd left the Army and come here, to London, where he divided his time between his surgery and teaching anatomy at the city's hospitals. He knew more about the human body than anyone Sebastian had ever met, thanks in part to an ongoing series of illicit dissections performed on cadavers filched from the area's churchyards by resurrection men.

Until that January, Gibson had lived alone. But he now shared the small, ancient stone house beside his surgery with Alexi Sauvage, a beautiful, enigmatic, and unconventional Frenchwoman who was as damaged in her own way as Gibson.

Rather than chance an encounter with her, Sebastian cut through the narrow passage that ran along Gibson's house and led to the unkempt yard at the rear. Overgrown with weeds and a mute witness to the secrets buried there, the yard stretched down to a high stone wall that abutted the single-room outbuilding where Gibson performed both his legally sanctioned autopsies and his covert dissections. Through the open door, he could hear the Irishman singing softly under his breath, *"Ghile Mear 'sa seal faoi chumha, 'S Éire go léir faoi chlócaibh dubha. . . ."*

The headless, naked body of Stanley Preston lay on the high stone table in the center of the room. When Sebastian's shadow fell across it, Gibson broke off and looked up. "Ah, there you are, me lad," he said, exaggerating his brogue. "Thought I'd be seeing you soon enough."

He was only several years older than Sebastian, but chronic pain had already touched his dark hair with gray at the temples and dug deep lines in his face. His opium addiction hadn't helped either, although Sebastian noticed he didn't look quite as emaciated as he had lately.

Pausing in the doorway, Sebastian let his gaze drift around the cold room until he located Preston's head, cradled in an enameled basin on a long shelf. In the last twelve hours, the face seemed to have sunk in on itself, taking on a waxy, grayish tinge.

Sebastian swallowed and brought his gaze back to the rest of the cadaver. A small purple slit, clearly visible against the alabaster flesh, showed high on the man's chest.

"He was stabbed?" said Sebastian. "Why the hell didn't I see that?"

"Probably because he was so drenched in blood from

his head being taken off. And because he was stabbed in the back. What you're seeing is where the tip of the blade came all the way through his body—but not by much, I'd say. It just barely sliced his waistcoat. If you'll help me turn him over, I'll show you."

"That's quite all right; I'll take your word for it."

Gibson grinned.

"So that's what killed him?" said Sebastian.

"It might have, eventually. But not right away. I suspect he fell when he was stabbed, and his killer finished him off by slitting his throat." Gibson paused. "Obviously, he got a wee bit carried away and completely cut off the head."

"With what? Any idea?"

"My guess is a sword stick; the stab wound in the back is the right size. I'd say your killer ran him through with the sword stick, then used the same blade to slit his throat, slashing down as the poor man lay on the ground. Could be he wasn't intending to cut off the head—he was just trying to make sure Preston was dead."

"So why did he then pick up the head and put it on the bridge?"

"Ah. Nobody told me that part."

Sebastian studied the ragged, truncated flesh of the cadaver's neck. He'd lopped off more heads than he cared to remember with a heavy cavalry sword swung from the back of a horse. But to chop the head off a man lying on the ground with a slim sword stick must surely be considerably more difficult. "How easy is it to cut off a head like that?"

"Not easy at all, evidently. Took whoever did it at least a dozen blows, maybe more."

"Lovely." Sebastian turned to stare out at the yard. The cloud cover from last night's storm was beginning to show signs of breaking up, but the sunlight was still weak and fitful. As he watched, a woman came out of the house and paused for a moment on the back stoop.

She was small and slight, with a head of fiery red hair and the kind of pale skin more often seen in Scotland than in France. Her gaze met his, and he saw her nostrils flare, her lips tighten into a flat line as she picked up a basket and trowel and moved to where he realized someone was nurturing a small plot of sweet peas and forget-me-nots along the house's rear wall.

Sebastian said, "Does Madame Sauvage know you've spent the last few years planting this yard with the remains of your dissections?"

"Aye, I told her. She says all the more reason to clean it up."

Sebastian leaned one shoulder against the doorjamb and watched her. He knew some of her history, but not all of it. Born in Paris in the days before the Revolution, she'd trained as a physician in Italy. But because Britain refused to license female physicians, she was allowed to practice in London only as a midwife. Like Gibson, she was in her early thirties and by her own account had already gone through two husbands and two lovers.

All were now dead—one of them by Sebastian's hand.

Gibson said, "And how is young master Simon St. Cyr?"

"He's an angel—until the clock strikes six in the evening, at which point he starts screaming bloody murder and is impossible to console until nearly midnight."

"Colicky, is he? It'll soon pass."

"I sincerely hope so."

The surgeon grinned and limped over to stand beside him. Gibson's gaze rested, like Sebastian's, on the woman now working the rich black soil near the house. "I've asked Alexi to marry me a dozen times," he said with a sigh, "but she won't hear of it."

"Does she say why not?"

"She says all of her husbands have died."

So have her lovers, thought Sebastian, although he didn't say it.

He shifted to study his friend's lean, pain-lined face. "She said she could do something to help with the phantom pains from your missing leg." His pain—and his opium addiction. "Has she tried?"

"She keeps wanting to, but it sounds daft to me. How can a box with mirrors possibly do any good?"

"It's worth making the attempt, isn't it?"

The Irishman simply shook his head and turned back to his work. "I'll let you know if I find anything else."

Sebastian nodded and pushed away from the doorframe.

But as he followed the narrow path to the gate, he was aware of Alexi Sauvage's gaze on him, silent and watchful.

It often seemed to Sebastian that trying to solve a murder was somewhat akin to approaching a figure in the mist. At first an indistinct, insubstantial blur, the murdered man or woman began to take form and emerge in detail only as Sebastian came to see the victim through the eyes of the various people who had known, loved, or hated him.

At the moment, virtually all Sebastian knew about Stanley Preston was that the man was cousin to the Home Secretary, a widower and father of two who owned plantations in Jamaica and was not in the habit of trying to fondle the pretty young barmaid at the local pub. Before he approached the dead man's grief-stricken daughter, Sebastian felt the need to learn more. And so his next stop was the home of Henrietta, the Dowager Duchess of Claiborne.

One of the grandes dames of Society, the Duchess had long maintained a relentless interest in the personal lives and antecedents of everyone who was anyone. Since she also possessed an awe-inspiring memory that deemed few details too trivial not to be retained forever, he couldn't think of anyone in London better able to tell him what he needed to know about Mr. Stanley Preston.

Born Lady Henrietta St. Cyr, elder sister of the current Earl of Hendon, she was known to the world as Sebastian's aunt, although she was one of the few people aware of the fact that the relationship between them was in name only. She lived alone with an army of servants in a vast town house on Park Lane, in Mayfair. Technically, the house belonged to her son, the current Duke of Claiborne, who resided at a far more modest address in Half Moon Street. An amiable, somewhat weak-willed gentleman now of middle age, he was no match for the Dowager Duchess, who had every intention of dying in the house to which she had come as a bride some fifty-five years before. She was proud, nosy, perceptive, arrogant, judgmental, opinionated, and wise, and one of Sebastian's favorite people.

He found her ensconced in a comfortable chair beside her drawing room fire, an exquisite cashmere shawl draped about her stout shoulders and a slim, blue-bound book in her hands.

"Good heavens, Aunt Henrietta," he said, stooping to kiss one subtly rouged and powdered cheek. "Have I caught you reading a novel?"

Rather than put the book aside, she thrust one plump finger between the pages to mark her place. "I bought it to see what all the fuss is about—it has quite taken the ton by storm, you know. But I must confess to finding it unexpectedly diverting."

Sebastian went to stand before the fire. "Who wrote it?"

"No one knows. That's partly what makes it so delicious. It's simply ascribed to 'the author of *Sense and Sensibility*.' And no one has yet to discover who she is."

He reached to pick up one of the other two volumes resting on the table beside her and read the title. "*Pride and Prejudice*. Whoever it is obviously likes alliteration."

"And she has the most devastatingly wicked wit. Listen to this." She opened the book again. " 'They were in fact very fine ladies . . . had a fortune of twenty thousand pounds, were in the habit of spending more than they ought, and of associating with people of rank; and were therefore in every respect entitled to think well of themselves, and meanly of others. They were of a respectable family in the north of England, a circumstance more deeply impressed on their memories than that their brother's fortune and their own had been acquired by trade.' "

"Devastating, indeed. I wonder, could you tear yourself away from this delightful tale long enough to tell me what you know of Mr. Stanley Preston?"

"Stanley Preston?" she repeated, looking up at him. "Whatever for?"

"You haven't seen the morning papers?"

"No; I've been reading this book. Why? What's happened to him?"

"Someone cut off his head."

"Good heavens. How terribly gauche."

"Frightfully so. What do you know of him?"

She laid the book aside, open and facedown, although he noticed she gave it one or two reluctant glances before she brought her attention back to him. "Well, let's see. The family is old—he's from the Devonshire Prestons, you know, although his is a rather insignificant, cadet branch."

"Yet his cousin is Lord Sidmouth."

She waved a dismissive hand; obviously, the Home Secretary's antecedents did not impress her. "Yes, but Sidmouth himself was only recently raised to the peerage. His father was a mere physician."

"So where did Preston acquire his wealth?"

"His father married a merchant's daughter. The woman was dreadfully vulgar, I'm afraid, but quite an heiress. The elder Preston invested her inheritance in land in the West Indies and did very well for himself, as a result of which he was able to marry his own son— Stanley—to the daughter of an impoverished baron."

"Wealth acquired from trade being seen as something vile and shameful that can be magically cleansed by investment in land—even when that land happens to be worked by slaves?"

She frowned at him. "Really, Sebastian; it's not as if he were engaged in the slave trade. Slavery is perfectly legal in the West Indies. The French tried to do away with it, and look what happened to them. A bloodbath!"

"True," said Sebastian. "What was the name of this baron's daughter? I gather she's dead?"

"Mmm. Mary Pierce. Lovely young woman. In the end, the marriage was surprisingly successful; Preston positively doted on her. But she died in childbirth some seven or eight years ago. I've often wondered why he never remarried. He's still quite attractive and vigorous for his age."

"Not anymore."

"Don't be vulgar, Devlin."

He gave a soft huff of laughter. "Tell me about the daughter. What's her name?"

"Anne. She must be in her early twenties by now. Still unmarried, I'm afraid, and in serious danger of being left on the shelf. Not that anyone is exactly surprised."

"Why? Is she ill-favored?"

"Oh, she was pretty enough when she was young, I suppose. But Preston never did move in the highest circles, and Anne has a tendency to be rather quiet— and a tad strange, to be frank."

"Strange? In what way?"

"Let's just say she's more like her father than her mother. And of course it hasn't helped that her portion from her mother is not large."

"I was under the impression Preston's holdings in Jamaica are substantial."

"They are. But that will all go to the son."

"I assume the man was a Tory?"

"I should hope so. Although unlike Sidmouth, I don't believe he was overly interested in affairs of state. His passion was collecting."

"Collecting? What did he collect?"

"Curiosities of all sorts, although mainly antiquities. He had a special interest in items that once belonged to famous people. I'm told he has a bullet taken from the body of Lord Nelson after Trafalgar, a handkerchief some ghoulish soul dipped in Louis XVI's blood at the guillotine . . . that sort of thing. He even has heads."

Sebastian paused in the act of leaning down to throw more coal on the fire. "Heads? What sort of heads?"

"Those with historical significance."

"You mean, *people's* heads?"

"Mmm. I'm told he has Oliver Cromwell, amongst others. But don't ask me who else because I've never seen them. They say he keeps them displayed in glass cases and—" She broke off. "How did you say he died?"

"Someone cut off his head."

"Dear me." She readjusted her shawl. "I take it you've involved yourself in this murder investigation?"

"I have, yes."

"Amanda won't like it. That girl of hers is starting her second season, and Amanda blames you for Stephanie's failure to go off last year."

Sebastian's older sister, Amanda, was not one of his admirers. He said, "From what I observed, I'd say my niece was enjoying her first season far too much to settle down and bring it all to an end."

"Yes, I'm afraid she's your mother all over again."

When Sebastian remained silent, she picked up her book and said, "Now, go away. I want to get back to my reading."

He laughed and kissed her cheek again. "If you're

not careful, Aunt, people are going to start accusing you of being bookish."

"Never happen."

He turned toward the door. But before he reached it, she said, "Is it wise, involving yourself in this murder, Devlin? You've a wife and child to think of now."

He paused to look back at her. "I am thinking of them. Whoever did this is not someone I want roving the city."

"We pay constables and magistrates to take care of that sort of thing."

"I don't believe that means the rest of us can simply abdicate all responsibility for our own safety."

"Perhaps. Yet . . . why you, Devlin? Why?"

But he only shook his head and left her there, her attention once more captured by the pages of her book.

Chapter 9

"We costermongers is a proud lot," the wizened old woman told Hero. "Ain't no doubt about it. We all knows each other, and we keeps ourselves to ourselves."

Her name was Mattie Robinson, and she sat perched on a three-legged stool behind an apple stall formed by laying a flat wicker tray across two upended crates. She'd been born, she said, in the year they sent poor Dick Turpin up the ladder to bed, which Hero figured made her somewhere in her seventies. She wore a man's tattered greatcoat and had a plaid shawl knotted about her head, and still she shivered, as if the cold from all the decades spent sitting at her stall had irrevocably settled deep in her bones. She'd agreed to talk to Hero for two shillings—which was, she admitted, considerably more than an entire day's take.

"I've kept me stall here at the corner of St. Martin's Lane and Chandos Street e'er since me leg was crushed by a gentlewoman's carriage." She shook her head, as if the ways of the gentry were a puzzle to her. "Didn't even stop to see if I was alive or dead."

"When was that?"

"The year after me Gretta was born. Before that, I used t' work the Strand." Hero had learned enough by now to know what costermongers meant when they spoke of "working" a street or district.

"Me Nathan was alive then," said Mattie. "He had his own handbarrow, y'know. We was doin' grand, with two nice rooms and our own furniture." Her watery brown eyes clouded with memories of a loss that was now some half a century in the past. "We was even sendin' our boy, Jack, t' school. But after I was laid up fer the better part of a year, we had to pledge all the furniture and move to an attic room in Hemming's Row. And poor Jack, he had t' leave school and start t' work with his da."

"How old was Jack?"

"Six. Afore that, Nathan used t' hire a lad every mornin' at the market. A coster needs a lad, you see, t' help watch the barrow, else thieves'll steal him blind when his back is turned. And a boy's voice carries better'n a man's. All them years of shoutin' ruins a coster's throat real quick."

Hero checked her list of questions. "How many hours are you here, at your stall?"

"This time of year? I'm usually here from eight in the mornin' till ten at night. My Gretta, she gets up early and goes t' market t' get me apples and things. I don't know what I'd do without her. I can hobble down here by meself, but 'tain't no way I could haul me basket of apples from market."

"Is Gretta a coster as well?"

"Aye. She works Beaufort Wharfs with her da's barrow. Ain't many women can handle a barrow, but me Gretta's always been a strappin' lass. Course, she's gettin' on in years now herself; don't know how much longer she'll be able to keep it up. And then what's t' become of us?"

"She never married or had children?"

A gleam of amusement lit the older woman's eyes. "'Tain't one coster out of ten is married proper-like. Most

see it as a waste of money could be better spent buyin'
stock. No parson never said words o'er me and Nathan,
but it didn't make no difference t' us or t' anybody else."

"And Gretta?"

Mattie shook her head. "She always says costers treat
their wives worse'n cheap servants, and ain't no man
ever gonna beat her."

Hero suspected those sentiments spoke volumes
about the behavior of the late Nathan Robinson, but all
she said was, "What about your son, Jack? Is he a costermonger as well?"

The old woman turned her head to spit, as if needing
to clear a foul taste from her mouth before she could
speak. "Me Jack was impressed by His Majesty, back
in the American War. Ain't seen nor heard nothin' from
him since. I reckon he's dead, but ain't nobody ever told
us fer certain."

"I'm sorry," said Hero.

Again, that faint sparkle of amusement. "What fer?
Ye ain't His Majesty, now, is ye?"

Hero laughed out loud. "No." A donkey in the street
beside them began to bray loudly. "What do you normally have for breakfast and supper?"

The question obviously struck Mattie as rather daft,
but she answered readily enough. "Bread and butter, same
as everybody else. A few herrings now and then. Course,
if we've had too many days of wet weather, we don't eat
nothin'. Can't eat up our stock money, now, can we? Then
what would we do?"

Hero focused on recording the woman's answer, being
careful not to allow any emotion to show on her face.
She'd thought, when she first began this series of articles,
that she understood the plight of the city's poor. But she
knew now that she had never appreciated just how thin
the line between survival and starvation was for a vast
segment of London's population. A few pence a day could

make the difference between supper and a place to sleep, and a cold, hungry night spent huddled beneath the arches of the Adelphi.

Mattie said, "The nice thing about hunger is that while ye feel it at first, it goes off after a while if ye've nothin' t' eat. Don't know why, but I ain't one t' question the goodness of God."

"Do you go hungry often?"

"Mostly in the winter, when we've had a long spell of wet weather. And of course, in winter ye needs fire and candles, and they're so dear. There's many a night Gretta and I jist go t' bed. But I ain't complainin'. There's plenty worse off than us. Least we ain't got no little ones t' worry about."

Hero stared off down the street, to where a wagon loaded with lumber jolted heavily over the wet paving. There were more questions she'd intended to ask the old woman. But sometimes, the frank recitals of bad luck and loss and endless struggle threatened to overwhelm her.

"Thank you," she said, and gave Mattie another shilling before walking away.

After the squalor and desperation of St. Martin's Lane, there was something vaguely obscene about the opulence of the Prince of Wales's London residence on Pall Mall.

As Hero followed a liveried and powdered footman through the silk-hung marble corridors of Carlton House, she found she couldn't stop thinking about Mattie Robinson and Gretta and the boy, Jack, dragged away from his family to fight in one of His Majesty's wars so long ago.

The chambers set aside for the exclusive use of her father, Charles, Lord Jarvis, lay at the top of a sweeping grand staircase ornamented with exquisite plasterwork and copious gilding. She found him seated at a delicate

French desk that, like so much else in the palace, had been supplied to the Prince of Wales by the same Parisian *marchand-mercier* who'd served as interior decorator to the ill-fated Marie Antoinette.

Jarvis looked up at her entrance and dismissed the footman with a curt nod, his eyes narrowing as his gaze traveled over her. "You're looking surprisingly well—despite Devlin's insistence on using you as a milk cow for his son."

"The decision was mine and you know it," she said, slipping off her pelisse.

Jarvis simply grunted and set aside his quill. "I had hoped motherhood would have a domesticating effect on you. But I'm told you've undertaken to write a new article, this one on that blackguard tribe of costers infesting our streets."

"And who told you that, Papa?" she asked with a silken assumption of ignorance that brought an answering gleam of amusement to his intense gray eyes. Everyone in England knew Jarvis directed a vast network of spies and informants who reported not to the Prince or Downing Street, but to Jarvis alone.

The smile faded. He said, "No good can come of this project of yours, you know."

"I disagree." She unwrapped the brown paper parcel she had brought with her to reveal the thin strip of old inscribed lead. "I was wondering if you know what this is?"

He stood, taking the old metal band in his hands and carrying it to the window.

She watched him turn the upper surface to the light, his lips pursing as he ran his thumb over the scrollwork. Jarvis's face never betrayed his thoughts or emotions. But she knew him well, so that very lack of any of the traces of surprise or interest one would expect told her she'd come to the right place.

He said, "Where did you get this?"

"It was found last night at Bloody Bridge, near where Mr. Stanley Preston was murdered. You've seen it before, haven't you?"

He fingered one sliced end of the strap, then set it aside and reached for his handkerchief to carefully wipe his hands. "Devlin's involved you in this murder, has he?"

"I involved myself."

He tucked away his handkerchief.

She said, "It's always been my understanding that the final resting place of Charles I is unknown."

"It was—up until a week or so ago."

Jarvis clasped his hands behind his back and shifted his gaze out the window to the forecourt below. "Three years ago, after the death of the Princess Amelia, His Majesty decided to build an elaborate new royal vault at Windsor Castle, beneath the Wolsey Chapel at St. George's. As originally constructed, the vault could only be accessed from outside the chapel. But the Prince Regent recently decided to install a new entrance in the form of a sloping passage that opens from the quire of St. George's itself." He paused to glance over at her. "You know Princess Augusta is gravely ill and unlikely to recover?"

"Yes," said Hero. Princess Augusta, elder sister to King George III, was both aunt and mother-in-law to the Regent and had taken refuge in England after the death of her husband, the Duke of Brunswick, in battle against Napoléon.

"Because of her imminent death, the workers were urged to proceed quickly. Several days ago, they accidentally broke through a thin brick wall into the vault containing Henry VIII and Jane Seymour. The vault's general location was known, but over the years its exact placement had been forgotten." He slipped a delicate gold snuffbox inlaid with a swirl of seed pearls from his pocket and flicked open the lid with his thumbnail. "According to records, the vault should have contained only Henry and his favorite Queen. But in looking through the aperture they'd made, the workmen were surprised to see not two, but three adult-sized coffins."

"The third being that of Charles I?"

"As it happens, yes." He lifted a delicate pinch of snuff to one nostril and sniffed. "The Dean of the chapel immediately contacted Carlton House. Given the importance of the find, I personally made the journey out to Windsor to inspect the discovery on behalf of the Prince."

"And?"

"Henry VIII's coffin is in decidedly poor condition. You can see where a crude opening had at some point been cut in the wall of the vault immediately above it and then filled in. Frankly, I suspect the opening was made by the men who lowered the third coffin into the vault, and they accidentally dropped it on Henry. Jane Seymour, however, was off to one side and intact."

"And the third coffin?"

"The third coffin was still covered by its dusty black velvet pall, which, upon being raised, revealed a plain lead coffin encircled by a strap inscribed 'King Charles, 1648.'" He nodded to the metal scroll. "Like this."

"You had the coffin opened?"

"Not at all. Indeed, the Dean and Canons have strict instructions to guard the site well. The Prince is anxious to personally hold a formal examination of the contents of the third coffin as soon as the construction of the passage is complete—and Princess Augusta is dead and buried, of course."

"Why? I mean, why examine the remains of Charles but not the others?"

Jarvis tucked the snuffbox into his pocket. "I'm afraid His Highness has long maintained a rather morbid fascination with the Stuarts. He says he wishes to answer some historical questions, but I suspect he's mainly driven by a desire to look upon the mortal remains of a

British royal so unpopular as to lose his head at the hands of his subjects." His gaze returned to the metal fragment. "If this strap has indeed come from Charles's coffin, the Regent will not be pleased to learn that someone has interfered with the burial before he's had the chance to do so himself."

"Do you think there could be political implications to this?" asked Hero.

"Anything involving the Stuarts is always cause for concern—as is the relationship between Stanley Preston and the Home Secretary." He watched her fold the section of lead back into its brown paper wrapping, then said, "I don't like your involvement in this, Hero."

She looked over at him. "If it were up to you, I would neither write about the situation of London's poor nor investigate murders—or even nurse my own newborn son. Pray tell, how would you have me pass my days?"

"Shopping in Bond Street. Embarking on an endless round of morning calls. Reading the latest lurid romance . . . Surely you know better than I how women of your station spend their time."

She smiled. "I enjoy shopping and reading."

"Then you should do more of it."

"I'm not like that," she said, suddenly serious.

His lips flattened into a tight line. "You should have been born a boy."

"I like being a woman just fine." She kissed his cheek, then carefully readjusted the tilt of her hat. "Will you be sending someone out to Windsor?"

He declined to answer her question.

But later, as she was leaving Carlton House, she saw one of the tall former guardsmen in Jarvis's employ crossing the courtyard at a run.

Chapter 10

Once, years before, when Sebastian was a small boy in short coats, he befriended a tall, strapping young footman named Luge. Sebastian was the son of an earl, while Luge was in service to Sebastian's grandmother, the Dowager Countess of Hendon. But for a brief, shining moment out of time, man and boy had connected in a way that transcended such ordinary impediments as station, age, and race.

Afterward, Sebastian would wonder at the good-natured patience of the handsome, ebony-skinned footman who had indulged the boundless curiosity of a small boy who could listen for hours to Luge's tales of the sun-drenched sands and crystal-clear seas of Barbados, the island of his birth. Luge had been only eight years old when the Dowager Countess purchased him at a slave market in Bridgetown and brought the child back to England as her page. Once, he even showed Sebastian the brand on his shoulder and grinned as the boy reached out to trace the initials of the master who had marked Luge as his property the way Sebastian's father marked his own horses and cattle.

"Did it hurt?" Sebastian asked in awe.

"I reckon," said Luge. "But I don't remember. I was still little."

Sebastian had seen brands on ragged men and women in the streets—usually a "T" for "thief" or an "M" for "manslaughter." But the thought of anyone doing that to a small child horrified him so much that he stayed away from Luge for a few days. And the next time Sebastian visited his grandmother, he was told that Luge had taken off his powdered wig, set it atop his folded velvet livery, and simply walked off into the gathering dusk.

The Dowager advertised for his return, although no one paid much attention anymore to advertisements for runaway slaves. A succession of court cases had reinforced the popular belief that the air of England was "too pure for a slave to breathe."

But what was true of the air of England was not true of the air in England's colonies. Even those who supported the freeing of England's ten to fifteen thousand slaves often grew fainthearted at the thought of the financial havoc that would result from the emancipation of those who toiled to produce the sugar, tobacco, cotton, indigo, and rice that made England wealthy and powerful.

Some twenty years after Luge walked away to freedom, Sebastian had landed with his regiment in Barbados to find the island little changed from the colony Luge had described. A dazzling sun still soaked golden sands lapped by achingly blue waters, and vast weathered docks swarmed with ebony-skinned men in canvas trousers, their sweat-sheened backs crisscrossed with the scars of past floggings.

Such sights did not shock Sebastian, for the lash was applied with brutal frequency to the men who enlisted or were impressed into His Majesty's Army or Navy; even Englishwomen were still sometimes stripped naked to the waist and whipped at the cart's tail. But as he climbed through Bridgetown's dusty streets, past low buildings with long windows shaded by deep verandas and shuttered against the oppressive heat, he came upon an open square crowded with African men, women, and children of all ages. Some sat blankly staring into space, while others huddled together, mothers hugging infants to their breasts as solemn, wide-eyed toddlers clutched their skirts. A few planters, sun-reddened faces shadowed by broad-brimmed hats, circulated amongst them. The air was thick with the smell of cigar smoke and human sweat and wretched despair, and Sebastian drew up abruptly as the realization of what he was witnessing slammed into him.

A young woman and a good-looking boy of perhaps eight or ten were pushed up onto the block. Transfixed by fascination and horror, Sebastian could only watch as the auctioneer expressed a wish to sell mother and child together. But the woman had a withered right arm that discouraged buyers, whereas interest in her handsome son was strong. The auctioneer finally agreed to sell the two separately, and silent, helpless tears rolled down the woman's cheeks as a spirited bidding began for the child.

Then the hammer fell, and the successful bidder—a fat man with bad teeth and an egg-stained waistcoat—pushed forward to collect his new property.

"*No,*" the mother screamed, lunging forward as the boy was led away. "No! You can't take him. Oh, please don't take him. *Please.*"

Hands caught her, dragged her back. She fought wildly, uselessly, her face contorted with hopeless anguish. For one suspended moment, her frantic gaze met Sebastian's over the heads of the onlookers, and he felt a wash of helpless shame—for his nation, his race, his time, and his own inaction—that he'd known even then would never leave him.

Now, as Sebastian drew his curricle up before the impressive home of Stanley Preston, he found himself remembering both Luge and that nameless, frantic mother. This graceful half-timbered Elizabethan manor might be half a world away from the cane fields and slave markets of the West Indies, but those cruelties had helped pay for it.

Most of Hans Town's prosperous, up-and-coming residents were happy to occupy one of the newly constructed, identical brick terraces that lined Sloane Street and the new squares. But not Stanley Preston. He had chosen as his residence a grand relic of a bygone age. Known as Alford House, it stood in the well-tended remnants of what must originally have been a much larger garden, its brick walkways now gently sunken and mossy, its climbing roses twisted and knotty with the passage of the years. There were other such once grand houses in the area, but most had been turned into schools or hospitals, their noble owners having long ago fled to the likes of Berkeley Square or Mount Street.

Sebastian half expected to find the murdered man's daughter, Anne, too prostrate with grief and shock to receive him. But she appeared after only a few moments, a slim figure in a simple black mourning gown, looking pale and shaken but admirably self-possessed.

She accepted his condolences and his apologies for disturbing her with a graciousness he couldn't help but admire, and showed him into an elegant sixteenth-century drawing room with an elaborately molded plaster ceiling and dark paneled walls hung with a collection of old-fashioned dueling pistols and swords.

"Father loved this house," she said, sinking onto a tapestry-covered settee near the room's massive stone fireplace. "It's old and drafty and frightfully unfashionable, but he didn't care. It's rumored Charles II actually hid here once during the Civil War, you know. There's even supposed to be a secret passage somewhere, although Father never could find it."

"Your father was interested in the Stuarts?" asked Sebastian, adjusting the tails of his morning coat as he settled in a nearby chair.

"He was interested in anyone famous—or infamous. In fact, the more infamous or tragic, the more interested Father was."

She was more attractive than his aunt's words had led him to expect, although undoubtedly shy, even nervous, in his presence. Her hair was the color of sun-warmed oak, cut short so that it curled softly around her face, her eyes wide set and deep and swollen from her tears. She said, "I keep thinking, if only Father had come with us last night to Lady Farningham's musical evening, he'd still be alive."

"Do you know why he chose not to attend?"

An unexpected smile lit up the depths of her mossy green eyes. "Father loathed musical evenings. He used to say that if he ended up in hell, the devil would torment him by forcing him to spend the rest of eternity listening to young ladies play harps." Her smile faded, became something painful. "I had the impression he was planning a quiet evening at home. I can't imagine what would have taken him to Bloody Bridge."

"So it really is called that?"

"It is, yes. I've heard it's a corruption of 'Blandel Bridge,' but its history is certainly bloody enough. Several people were killed there by footpads at the end of the last century, and it was the scene of repeated skirmishes during the Civil War. Father was always poking around there, finding rusty old spurs and bridle bits he said must have been lost in the fighting. But obviously he wouldn't have been doing that at night."

"I understand he was something of a collector."

Again, that soft glow of remembered affection warmed

her features. "I sometimes think Father would have been happiest as a wizened old eccentric charging the public a shilling to gawk at his cabinet of curiosities. He loved nothing more than showing off his collection. Mama always insisted he keep all but the most decorative items out of her drawing room, and he's honored her memory by continuing to respect her wishes in that. But I'm afraid the rest of the house is overflowing with his various collections."

"You say he was interested in relics of the Stuarts?"

"The Stuarts and the Tudors. They were his particular obsession. In fact, he has an entire gallery devoted to them."

"May I see it?"

If she was surprised by the request, she was too well-bred to show it. "Yes, of course."

She led the way to a long paneled room lined with glass cases filled with everything from daggers and maces to snuffboxes and opera glasses. Peering into the nearest case, he could see a dagger said to have belonged to James I, a carved and gilded angel from the reredos of a vanished monastery, and a faded silk pincushion with a neatly printed label that read GIVEN BY MARY, QUEEN OF SCOTS, TO HER LADY-IN-WAITING THE MORNING OF HER EXECUTION.

She said, "When Father was a boy, an aged cousin gave him a stirrup said to have been used by Richard III at Bosworth Field. He was so taken with the idea of possessing something that had once belonged to such an illustrious historical figure that it became his lifelong passion."

Sebastian let his gaze drift along rows of cases, to where a blue velvet curtain hung at the far end of the room. He didn't see any heads.

He said, "I'm told your father had certain relics of Oliver Cromwell."

"Only this." She moved to the end of the gallery to

draw back the long fall of velvet. "He had the curtain installed after a dinner guest wandered in here by mistake, saw them, and fainted."

The curtain opened to reveal three small glass and mahogany display cases mounted on pedestals. Each contained a severed human head resting in artfully arranged folds of the same blue velvet.

"That's Cromwell," she said, indicating the case on the right.

The head was unexpectedly small, as if it had shrunk as it dried, the flesh so darkened as to look almost black, the cheeks sunken, the eyes reduced to mere slits. Yet there was something about the slope of the forehead, the curve of the skull, that eerily echoed the paintings Sebastian had seen of the Lord Protector.

She said, "Most of the traitors' heads that were displayed on pikes eventually rotted. But Cromwell died a natural death and was embalmed—it wasn't until after the Restoration that his body was dragged from Westminster Abbey and hung in chains at Tyburn. Then the head was impaled along with those of two other regicides on spikes and mounted above Westminster."

"Not London Bridge?"

"No. I suppose Westminster was chosen since it was the scene of their crime. The three heads were up there for decades, as a warning to anyone who might be tempted to imitate their deeds."

Sebastian shifted his gaze to the young woman beside him. She was utterly unperturbed by a ghoulish sight the likes of which would cause many gentlewomen to fall into strong hysterics. But then, he realized, she had grown up surrounded by her father's bizarre collection. It was a side of Miss Anne Preston that was both unexpected and more than a little thought provoking.

He brought his attention back to the remnants of the man who had once butchered men, women, and children the length of England, Scotland, and Ireland. Traces of hair and the mustache remained, but the ears and part of the nose were gone. He said, "All those years on a spike above Westminster Hall appear to have taken quite a toll."

"Actually, much of the damage is fairly recent. The head was owned for a time by the actor Samuel Russell, and he was said to be in the habit of getting foxed and passing it around at his dinner parties. I gather he and his guests dropped it a few times."

"So how did the Lord Protector go from being on a spike above Westminster to being an object of conversation at an actor's drunken dinner parties?"

"Sometime during the reign of James II, there was a violent storm. The high winds broke the spike, and the head fell down."

"I'm surprised it didn't smash."

"I suspect it would have, had it hit the pavement. But it was caught by a guard who happened to be patrolling below. Evidently his sympathies still lay with the Puritans, because he took the head home and hid it. There was quite a hue and cry when its loss was discovered in the morning—they even offered a reward for the head's return."

"Why? I mean, why would they care at that point?"

"I can't imagine. Perhaps they feared it might become a relic. But the reward wasn't enough to tempt the guard, and he kept it hidden. Father could have told you how it got from the guard to Russell, but I've forgotten."

Sebastian shifted to the next pedestal. This head was more gruesome than the last, being light brown in color rather than black and less shrunken, with its nearly toothless mouth gaping open in a frightful grin. The neatly engraved brass plaque on the front of the case said simply, HENRI IV.

Sebastian stared at it. "That's Henri IV? The French king?"

"Yes."

"How did your father get him? I thought he was buried along with the rest of France's royals at the basilica of Saint-Denis in Paris."

"He was. But when the revolutionaries broke open all the royal tombs and tossed the contents into a common grave, someone with a fondness for 'Good King Henri' saved his head and smuggled it out of the country."

"Why?"

Her face lit up with silent laughter. "You obviously don't understand the mentality of collectors."

"Do you?"

"Not entirely. But after years of observing Father, I'd say much of the fascination comes from the way old items can make us feel closer to the past."

Sebastian thought he was beginning to understand why Anne Preston was generally regarded as being both quiet and a bit strange. She must have learned long ago that this sort of conversation didn't play out well in London's drawing rooms.

They shifted to the third pedestal. This head was both the best preserved and the most gruesome of the three, its eyelids half-closed, its lips pulled away from the teeth as if frozen in a rictus of agony. At the back of the neck, Sebastian could see quite clearly a deep cut above the one that had severed the head from the body, where the executioner's first stroke had obviously failed in its object.

The case was unlabeled.

"Who is this?" asked Sebastian.

"This was Father's most recent acquisition. It's believed to be the Duke of Suffolk—father to Lady Jane Grey. He was executed by Queen Mary in the Tower of London."

"So were a lot of other people. One would think you could fill a room with the heads of Elizabeth's victims alone."

"True. But their heads didn't usually survive. They were typically parboiled, set up on pikes above London Bridge, and then eventually thrown into the river."

"But not Suffolk?"

"No. His head was buried with the rest of his body at Holy Trinity in the Minories. Father said it probably survived so well because it fell into a box of sawdust, and the tannins preserved it."

Sebastian let his gaze drift, again, around that macabre cabinet of curiosities, but he didn't see anything similar to the metal band he'd found at Bloody Bridge.

He said, "What do you know of an old piece of thin lead, perhaps a foot and a half in length and three or four inches wide, bearing the inscription 'King Charles, 1648'?"

She looked puzzled. "I've never heard of such a thing. Why?"

"It was found near where your father was killed."

She was reaching to draw the curtain across the display pedestals. But at his words, she paused, her fist clenching on the rich velvet cloth. "Is it true, what they're saying—that whoever killed Father also cut off his head?"

"I'm afraid so."

"Who would do such a thing?"

"Can you think of anyone with whom your father might have quarreled recently?"

"No. No one," she said quickly.

Too quickly.

"You're certain?" he asked, watching her closely.

"Yes. Of course."

"If you think of anyone, you will let me know?"

"If I think of anyone."

She busied herself with closing the curtain. But he noticed that her hand was no longer steady, and it was obvious that the nervousness he'd glimpsed earlier had returned, tightening the features of her face and agitating her breathing. At first, he had mistaken her nervousness for the shyness of a young woman who felt ill at ease in company. Now he realized it was because she was afraid—afraid of *him*.

And of what he might learn.

Chapter 11

"*H*e collected *heads*?" Sir Henry Lovejoy's already high-pitched voice rose to a shrill squeak. "Men should be buried—not put on display as if they were in the same category as hunting trophies!"

"I suspect he didn't see the heads as all that different from the daggers and pincushions he also collected," said Sebastian.

The two men were walking up Bow Street toward the public office. The footpaths were still dark and wet from the latest rain, with gray clouds pressing low on the city and promising more. Lovejoy was silent for a moment, as if trying—and failing—to understand such a mentality. "It's a disturbing coincidence—that the man should collect the heads of historical figures, only to have someone cut off his own."

"If it is a coincidence."

Sir Henry hunched his shoulders against the damp, blustery wind. "Most of Preston's servants had a half day off on Sunday. But according to the butler, Preston went out for some hours on the day of his death. Unfortunately, he took a hackney rather than his own carriage, so unless we can trace the jarvey, we're unlikely to know where he went. He returned at approximately four in the afternoon and spent some time puttering around with his collections until dining with his daughter at seven. Then, at something like nine in the evening—or perhaps half past—he went out again, walking this time, and stopped in an old public house just off Sloane Street."

"The Monster?"

"As it happens, yes. You've heard of it?"

"Molly Watson told me he went there regularly. It sounds like the sort of place likely to appeal to someone with Preston's interests."

Sir Henry nodded. "It dates back to the days of the Dissolution. They say the name is actually a corruption of 'the Monastery.'"

"How long was he there?"

"Not long. According to the barman, he fell into an argument with another gentleman in the taproom and stormed off shortly after ten. Fortunately, the gentleman in question is a regular patron of the establishment, so the barman was able to identify him as a banker by the name of Austen. Henry Austen."

The name was unfamiliar to Sebastian. "What do you know of him?"

"I've had one of the lads looking into him. He's the son of a Hampshire clergyman. Originally trained for the church himself, but joined the militia at the beginning of the war with France. Served a number of years, although he only saw action in Ireland. I gather he was involved in handling payroll and got caught up in the Duke of York scandal. That's when he resigned his commission and went into banking. He's done quite well for himself; his main bank is in Henrietta Street, here in the City, but he also has branches in various country towns such as Alton and Hythe."

"What's his connection with Preston?"

"That I don't know. He seems a rather good-humored, even-tempered chap from all we've been able to discover.

But I've kept the constables away from him so far—thought it might be better to let you have a go at him first." The bells of the city's churches began to toll, counting out the hour in a rolling cascade of sound as they drew up before the Bow Street Public Office. Lovejoy said, "There is one thing about Austen that may or may not be pertinent, but is nonetheless rather disturbing."

"Oh?"

"His wife is the widow of a French count."

"Please don't tell me *he* lost his head as well?"

"I'm afraid so. He was guillotined in 1794. I gather she's been ill for quite some time and may even be dying; Austen has his sister up from Hampshire to stay with them and help."

"What do you know about her?"

"The sister? I gather she's quite unremarkable. A spinster by the name of Jane. Miss Jane Austen."

⚜

Sebastian went first to the Austen bank on Henrietta Street in Covent Garden, only to be told by a plump, supercilious clerk with heavily oiled, sandy hair that Mr. Austen was "currently unavailable."

"Is he out, or simply not receiving?" asked Sebastian.

The clerk sniffed. "I'm afraid I really can't say." He started to turn away, a sheaf of papers in his hands.

"Can't, or won't?"

The icy menace in Sebastian's voice brought the clerk to an abrupt halt, his chin sagging in a way that caused his mouth to gape open, his pale blue eyes widening as his gaze met Sebastian's.

Sebastian said, "Consider your response very carefully."

"He . . . he is not in today. Truly. He was scheduled to visit one of our branches down in Hampshire this morning, and I—I can only assume he went."

"Where does he live?"

The man swallowed hard enough to bob his Adam's apple visibly up and down. "I don't think I should answer that."

Sebastian gave the young man a smile that showed his teeth. "Actually, I think you should."

The papers the clerk had been holding slipped from his fingers to flutter to the floor. "Sloane Street. Number sixty-four Sloane Street."

"The keeper o' the Hyde Park Turnpike is gonna think we're up to somethin' 'avey-cavey," said Tom as Sebastian turned his horses toward Hans Town for the third time that day.

"Very likely," agreed Sebastian, guiding his pair around a slow collier's wagon.

The Austen house lay halfway down Sloane Street, not far from Sloane Square and the narrow, haunted lane that led to Bloody Bridge. One of a long line of terraces built late in the previous century, it had neat, white-framed windows and a shiny front door and was in every respect what one might expect of a prosperous, up-and-coming banker.

The door was opened by a young and rather inexperienced housemaid who confirmed the bank clerk's information, saying breathlessly, "I'm sorry, me lord, but the master left at the crack o' dawn, he did." When Sebastian then asked to see Mr. Austen's sister instead, the girl grew so flustered she dropped the card he'd handed her.

She retrieved the card with a stammered apology and hurried away, only to return a moment later and escort him up to an elegant octagonal drawing room. The salon was expensively furnished in the latest style, with Egyptian-inspired settees covered in peach- and lime-striped silk, ornately carved gilt mirrors, and an exquisite collection of French porcelains. The only odd note came from a small, rather plain writing desk that rested on a round, inlaid rosewood table positioned before the windows so that it overlooked the garden. At Sebastian's entrance, the woman seated beside it thrust whatever she'd been working on beneath the desk's slanted lid so quickly that the corners of some of the pages were left protruding.

"Lord Devlin," she said, rising from her chair to come forward and greet him.

Like the plain writing desk, Miss Jane Austen looked vaguely out of place in the room, both more comfortable and less ostentatious than her surroundings. Somewhere in her mid- to late thirties, she had an attractive, pixie face framed by short dark hair that curled from beneath a spinster's crisp white cap. Her cheeks were abnormally ruddy, her dress neat but not particularly fashionable, her dark eyes calm and assessing in a way that told him this was a woman accustomed to observing and analyzing her fellow men.

"I'm sorry my brother isn't here to meet with you," she said, "but he left for Alton this morning and isn't expected back until tomorrow evening."

"I appreciate your taking the time to speak to me instead," said Sebastian, settling in the chair she indicated. "I understand your brother was acquainted with Stanley Preston."

She sank onto the edge of a nearby settee, her hands nestled together in her lap. "Yes. My sister-in-law was great friends with the late Mrs. Preston, you see."

"She died in childbirth?"

"She did, yes. It was quite tragic. Their daughter, Anne, was only fifteen at the time. It's a difficult age for a young girl to be without a mother, and my cousin has attempted in the years since to stand in her friend's stead."

"Your cousin?"

"I beg your pardon; I should have explained. My

sister-in-law, Eliza, is also my cousin. Her mother and my father were sister and brother."

Sebastian studied Miss Jane Austen's small, expressive face. It was difficult to think of this quiet, provincial vicar's daughter as someone whose first cousin had been married to a French count guillotined in the Revolution. He said, "You've met Mr. Preston yourself?"

"At various times over the years, yes."

"What manner of man was he?"

"Mr. Preston?" She reached for a nearby embroidery frame, using the movement, he suspected, to give herself time to consider her response. "I would say his character was very much that of a devout and honest man. In truth, he had many admirable qualities. He was utterly devoted to his children and the memory of his dead wife. He was extraordinarily well-read on a number of subjects, particularly history. And he was responsible and moderate in most things—with one notable exception, of course."

"You mean, his passion for collecting?"

Her eyes crinkled in quiet amusement. "Yes; that is what I was referring to."

Sebastian found himself smiling. "Now that you've satisfied the proprieties by listing his admirable qualities, perhaps you could tell me some of his less admirable traits."

She took up her needle. "We all have our imperfections and idiosyncrasies, Lord Devlin. But I hope I am neither so unjust as to fault a man for falling short of perfection, nor so uncharitable as to catalogue his minor failings after his death."

"Yet if everyone persists in painting Stanley Preston as a saint, I am unlikely to ever discover who killed him."

She focused her attention on the neat stitches she was laying in her embroidery. "Well . . . I suppose you could say he had a tendency to be quarrelsome. He was also proud and socially ambitious. But in that I suspect he was not so different from most other men of his station."

"A lowering reflection, but sadly true, I fear."

He saw, again, that answering gleam of amusement in her eyes. She said, "The truth is, he was still a likeable man, for all that. There was no real malice in him."

Sebastian wondered if the slaves on Preston's Jamaican plantations would agree with that assessment. But all he said was, "Have you seen his collection of heads?" He could not imagine someone as prosaic and sensible as Miss Jane Austen fainting at such a sight.

"I have, yes. I've often pondered why he kept them. At first, I assumed he was driven by philosophical motives—that he derived some sort of salutary lesson from the contemplation of such tangible evidence that even the world's most powerful men are eventually reduced to nothing but shriveled flesh and bone. But I finally came to realize that he actually collected them for essentially the same reason rustics will travel miles to see a two-headed calf, or pay a sixpence to gawk at a hairy woman displaying herself at a fair."

"And why is that?"

"So that they may afterward boast of it to their friends— as if they are somehow rendered special by having seen something interesting. In Stanley Preston's case, it was as if he felt his stature was enhanced by the possession of relics of important figures from the past."

"He was impressed by wealth and power?"

"I would say there are few in our society who are not. Wouldn't you?"

"I suspect you are right." He let his gaze drift, again, around that fashionable, expensively furnished drawing room. "Tell me, does your brother's opinion of Stanley Preston match your own?"

"Oh, Henry is far more charitable than I when it comes to the foibles and vanities of his fellow men. He really should have been a vicar, you know, rather than a banker."

"So why did he quarrel with Preston at the Monster last night?"

She jerked ever so slightly, her thread snarling beneath her hands.

He said, "You do know, don't you." It was more of a statement than a question.

She rested the embroidery frame on her lap, her hands idle, her gaze meeting his. "It's a difficult subject to speak of, I'm afraid."

"Why's that?"

"It . . . it involves Anne."

"Yet it will come out eventually, whatever it is."

Miss Austen drew a troubled breath and nodded, obviously choosing her words with care. "Some years ago, when Anne was just seventeen, she formed an attachment to a certain hussar cornet. The man himself was also quite young—only a year or so older, I believe—and utterly penniless."

"But very dashing in his regimentals?"

"Devastatingly so, I'm afraid."

"Her father objected to the match?"

"What father would not? She was so very young. Even my cousin Eliza agreed that to allow a girl to attach herself at such a young age to a man with nothing but himself to recommend him would be folly."

"So what happened?"

"The young man's suit was denied. Fortunately for all concerned, his regiment was sent abroad not long afterward, and that was the end of it—or so everyone supposed. It was assumed by all who knew her that Anne had forgotten him—indeed, she lately seemed to be on the verge of contracting a promising alliance. But then, a month or so ago, the young man reappeared in London—a captain now, but still virtually penniless, I'm afraid."

"He's sold out?"

"Oh, no. He was badly wounded in the Peninsula and has been sent home to recuperate further."

"I take it Mr. Preston was still not inclined to favor such a match?"

She shook her head. "If anything, I'd say he was more opposed to it than ever before."

"And Miss Anne Preston?"

Jane Austen began to pick at her snarled thread. "I'm afraid I can't speak for another woman's heart."

Sebastian studied her carefully bowed head. "I still don't precisely understand how your brother came to fall into a quarrel with Preston last night."

Miss Austen kept her attention on her work. "Now that Eliza's illness has confined her to her rooms, Anne comes nearly every day to sit and read to her or, when my cousin feels up to it, simply to talk. It was during one of Anne's recent visits that Eliza confided that she'd decided she made a mistake six years ago in counseling Stanley Preston to refuse the young man's offer, and that she regrets having played a part in denying Anne the happiness she might otherwise have found with someone she loved."

"I take it Anne was unwise enough to repeat her friend's words to her father?"

"Yes. And since he couldn't confront poor Eliza about it, he shouted at Henry instead."

Sebastian thought he understood now why Jane Austen had mentioned Stanley Preston's quarrelsome tendency as one of his less admirable traits. "What is the name of this unsuitable young man?"

"Wyeth. Captain Hugh Wyeth."

"And where might I find Captain Wyeth?"

"I believe he has taken a room in the vicinity of the Life Guards barracks. But I'm afraid I can't give you his precise direction."

"Do you know his regiment?"

"No; I'm sorry."

"Thank you," said Sebastian, pushing to his feet. "You've been very helpful."

"Perhaps my brother will be able to tell you more when he returns to town," she said, rising with him, her expression one of earnest concern.

"Hopefully," said Sebastian. Although when he looked into those dark, intelligent eyes, he couldn't shake the conviction that this self-contained, quietly watchful woman actually knew considerably more than she'd been willing to divulge.

Sebastian spent the better part of the next hour making inquiries about Captain Hugh Wyeth at the various inns and taverns in the lanes and courts around the Life Guards barracks in Knightsbridge. But when the bells of the city's church towers began to chime six, he abandoned the search and turned his horses toward home.

"Ye thinkin' this hussar cap'n might be the one done for the cove at Bloody Bridge?" asked Tom as they rounded the corner onto Brook Street.

"I'd say he's certainly a likely suspect." The heavy cloud cover had already robbed most of the light from the day, so that the reflected glow of the newly lit streetlamps spilled like liquid gold across the dark, wet pavement. Sebastian guided his horses around a dowager's cabriole drawn up at the front steps of a nearby town house. And then, for reasons he could not have explained, he was suddenly, intensely aware of the solid length of the leather reins running through his hands, of the throbbing of the sparrows coming in to roost on the housetops above, and of the scattered drops of cold rain blown by a gust of wind against his face as he lifted his head to study the jagged line of roofs looming above.

"What?" asked Tom, watching him.

"Something doesn't feel right," he said, reining in hard just as an unseen force knocked the top hat from his head, and a rifle shot cracked from somewhere in the gathering gloom.

Chapter 12

"*Get down*," Sebastian shouted at Tom.

"'Oly 'ell," yelped the tiger, tumbling from his perch as Sebastian fought to bring the squealing, plunging pair under control. Then, rather than duck for cover down the nearest area steps, the boy leapt to the frantic horses' heads.

"God damn it!" swore Sebastian. "Are you trying to get yourself shot? Get out of here!"

"Easy lads, easy," crooned the tiger.

The whirl of a watchman's rattle sounded over the horses' frightened snorts and pounding hooves. "I say, I say," blustered an aging, fleshy man in a bulky great-coat as he trotted up, his lantern swaying wildly, one arm thrust straight above his head as he spun his wooden rattle furiously round and round. "Was that a shot? That was a shot, yes?"

"That was a shot," said Sebastian.

More people were spilling into the street—slack-faced butlers and elegant gentlemen in tails and one grimly determined footman brandishing a blunderbuss.

"Merciful heavens," said the watchman, swallowing hard. "Whoever heard of such a thing? In Brook Street, of all places! Where did it come from?" He turned in a slow circle with his lantern held high, as if its feeble light might somehow illuminate the would-be assassin.

Sebastian finally brought his frightened horses to a stand. "It came from the roof of that row of houses. But I suspect the shooter is long gone by now."

"Look at this!" said a skinny youth in silken breeches as he held up Sebastian's beaver hat with one white-gloved finger thrust through a neat hole in the crown. "That was close!"

" 'Oly 'ell," whispered Tom again, his hand sliding slowly down the nearest horse's quivering hide.

Sebastian could hear Simon's colicky wails even before he reached number forty-one Brook Street.

"At it again, is he?" said Sebastian, handing Morey his hat and driving coat.

A harassed expression drifted across the majordo-mo's normally carefully controlled countenance. At close range, the child's screams were painful. "I'm afraid so, my lord." He laid the driving coat over one arm, then froze when he got a better look at the elegant, high-crowned beaver hat in his hands. "Is that a bullet hole, my lord?"

Sebastian yanked off his driving gloves. "It is. And it was a new hat too. Calhoun is going to be devastated." He glanced up as another howl drifted down from above. "How long has he been at it?"

"A good while, I'm afraid. He started early this evening."

"Well, at least we know there's nothing wrong with his lungs," said Sebastian, taking the stairs to the nursery two at a time.

He was halfway to the third floor when he met Claire Bisette on her way down to make a fresh bottle of sweetened dill and fennel water. Hero might have refused to employ a wet nurse, but she'd welcomed Claire into their household with relief. An impoverished French *émigrée* in her early thirties, Claire was both older and considerably better educated than the young, ignorant country girls who typically served as nursemaids.

"What set him off?" he asked Claire.

She paused to push a stray lock of light brown hair out of her face with the back of one delicate wrist. "Who knows? Believe it or not, he's better now than he was."

Climbing to the top of the stairs, Sebastian found Hero walking back and forth before the nursery fire, the child's rigid body held so that her shoulder pressed against his stomach, his little fists clenched tight, his face red and distorted with his howls. At the sound of Sebastian's step, she turned, her quietly exasperated gaze meeting his.

"Here," said Sebastian, and walked forward to take his screaming son into his arms.

"I showed the section of inscribed lead to my father," Hero said sometime later, in a quiet moment when Simon dozed fitfully against her.

Sebastian had settled on the hearthrug beside her, his back propped against the side of her chair, a glass of wine in one hand. "And?" he asked, looking up at her.

"He says the tomb of Charles I was discovered just last week in St. George's in Windsor Castle, when the workmen constructing a new passage to the royal vault accidentally stumbled upon it. Needless to say, he was not at all pleased by the possibility that someone might have made off with the royal coffin strap."

Sebastian took a slow sip of his wine. "Interesting. Especially when you consider that Stanley Preston was an avid collector with a special interest in items from the Tudor and Stuart periods. He even has Oliver Cromwell's head."

"His actual *head*?"

"The actual head—along with those of Henri IV and the Duke of Suffolk."

"How ghoulish—not to mention suggestive, given how Preston died." She cautiously readjusted the sleeping child's weight. "What manner of man was he?"

"Preston? Proud. Socially ambitious. Quarrelsome. Although, according to a rather interesting spinster I met, he was also a devout and devoted family man. The sort, she says, one could like in spite of himself."

"If one could overlook the fact that he owned hundreds of slaves," said Hero.

"Yes. But it never ceases to amaze me the number of otherwise decent members of our society who can overlook it without any difficulty at all. I suppose it's because the institution is both legal and biblical—not to mention highly profitable. So it never occurs to most people to question the custom any further."

He realized she was staring at him with an oddly intent, unreadable gaze. "What is it you're not telling me?" she said.

He paused in the act of raising his wineglass to his lips. "What do you mean?"

"There's a trickle of dried blood on your left temple."

"There is?" He pushed to his feet and went to inspect his forehead in the mirror over the washstand. "So there is. That shot obviously came closer than I realized."

"Someone shot at you? *Tonight?*"

He wet a cloth and dabbed at the cut. "Just as I was turning onto Brook Street. They must have been lying in wait for me."

"And it didn't occur to you to mention it to me?"

"They missed."

"No, they didn't."

He dabbed at the dried blood again, his gaze still on his reflection in the mirror. "I've obviously stirred someone up. The problem is, I haven't the slightest notion whom. The only vaguely possible suspects I've found so far are a hussar captain who's been showing an unwelcome interest in Preston's daughter—unwelcome to Preston, that is—and a banker who publicly quarreled with Preston the night he died. But the banker is by all reports out of town, and I haven't even tracked down the captain yet."

"Someone must see you as a threat," said Hero, her voice oddly tight. "They tried to kill you."

"It could have been meant as a warning." The babe stirred and let out a soft cry, and Sebastian set aside the bloodstained cloth and turned to reach for the child. "Here; let me have him for a while."

She hesitated, and he saw something flare in her eyes, something that was there and then gone, as if quickly hidden away from him. They'd grown so much closer in the months since their marriage, yet he knew she still kept many of her thoughts and feelings from him.

"What?" he said.

"Just . . . be careful, Sebastian. I don't understand what's happening. But whatever it is, it's ugly. Very ugly."

"My dear Lady Devlin," he said teasingly as he eased the now squalling infant from her grasp. "Are you worried?"

He expected her to answer with one of her typically wry, flippant responses.

Instead, she reached up to touch her fingertips to the flesh beside the still raw wound on his forehead and said, "Yes."

Chapter 13

The royal residence of Windsor Castle lay in the provincial town of Windsor, some twenty miles to the west
of London on the southern bank of the river Thames.
Jarvis had dispatched one of his men that morning with
a message warning the Dean to prepare for a visit to the
royal vault. But by the time he arrived, the sun had long
since slipped below the western walls of the castle.

The Honorable and Right Reverend Edward Legge,
who served in the prestigious position of Dean of St.
George's Chapel, waited in the lower court to meet him,
the ancient medieval battlements looming dark against a
black sky. A ferociously ambitious cleric who'd long ago
perfected the art of flattering and pleasing those in power,
Legge was ponderous and fleshy, with startlingly dark,
heavy brows and a weak chin. Now his jowly face showed
slick with a nervous sweat despite the cold wind that
whipped at his cassock and sent dried leaves scuttling
across the castle's wide, sloping lawns. At his side stood
the chapel's virger, Rowan Toop, with a horn lantern
gripped tightly in one hand. The Dean might be in charge
of the day-to-day affairs of the chapel, but it was the virger
who oversaw the care and maintenance of the venerable
old buildings and supervised the burial of the dead.

"My lord," said the Dean, both men bowing low as a castle guard leapt forward to open the carriage door. "We are truly honored to—"

Jarvis stepped down with an agility surprising for one of his size and cut off the Dean with a curt, "I trust all is ready?"

"Yes, my lord. If I might be so bold as to offer your lordship a nice hot cup of tea? Or perhaps a glass of wine before we—"

"No."

The Dean bowed again, his habitual bland smile still firmly in place as he held out a hand toward the chapel's ornate western front. "If you'll come this way, my lord?"

They followed the lantern-bearing virger into the medieval church's vast, soaring nave, with its ancient stained-glass windows and elaborately carved ceiling and stately alabaster monuments. St. George's was second only to Westminster Abbey as the burial place of kings and queens, princes and princesses—although over the years the precise location of certain royals had become somewhat fuzzy.

The entrance to the Prince of Wales's new passage lay in the quire, guarded by a recently installed iron gate wrapped with a heavy padlock and chain. "Excuse me, my lord," said the Dean, producing a large key. "This will take but a moment."

Jarvis grunted, his gaze drifting over the colorful rows of helms and banners that hung above the intricately carved wooden quire stalls, for the chapel also served as home to the Knights of the Garter.

"As you can see, my lord," said the Dean as he fumbled with the lock, "we've taken every precaution to ensure that there will be no repeat of the unfortunate scenes that followed the discovery of King Edward's remains."

"I should hope so," said Jarvis. When workmen repaving the chapel late in the previous century had accidentally broken into the vault containing the seven-foot

coffin of Edward IV, so many gawkers and relic seekers
had managed to find their way into the crypt that they'd
carried off much of what was left of Edward—one tooth,
lock of hair, and finger bone at a time—before anyone
thought to put a stop to it.

The chain rattled as the Dean unwrapped the heavy
links, his breath forming a white vapor cloud in the cold.
"There," he said, swinging open the gate and stepping
back to allow the lantern-bearing virger to precede them.

The narrow, nearly complete passage sloped steeply
downward, so that they descended rapidly, their footsteps echoing hollowly, the cold air heavy with the smell
of dank earth and old death. The small vault that had
originally been intended as only a temporary repository
for Henry VIII's favorite Queen lay roughly halfway
between the high altar and the sovereign's garter stall,
on the western side of the passage. Three days before,
when Jarvis had last visited the crypt, the workmen had
expanded their original, accidental aperture into an
opening large enough to allow him to enter. Now all
the rubble from that effort had been cleared away and
a screen discreetly placed before the opening.

Jarvis waited, hands clasped behind his back, while
the Dean shifted the screen to one side.

"Not exactly what you'd expect as the final resting
place of Henry VIII and Jane Seymour, now, is it?" said
the virger, ducking inside with his lamp held before him.

The light danced around a crudely constructed vault
faced with rough brick and measuring no more than
seven or eight feet wide and ten feet long. The arched
ceiling was so low, Jarvis had to stoop considerably as
he entered.

The three coffins lay precisely as they had when he'd
last seen them, with Henry VIII's bones and bits of cloth
showing quite clearly amidst the decayed wood and
warped lead of his shattered casket. Beside him, Jane
Seymour's better-preserved casket rested at an odd

angle against the far wall, as if it had been hastily shoved aside by frightened men working stealthily to bury a murdered king.

The coffin of the unlucky Charles I lay to the left of his predecessors, still covered with the original black velvet pall, which had been carefully replaced after Jarvis's last visit.

The Dean said, "As you can see, my lord, nothing has been disturbed."

"Remove the pall," said Jarvis.

The Dean's smile of gentle complaisance faltered. "My lord?"

"You heard me."

The Dean nodded to the virger, who glanced around helplessly for someplace to set his lantern.

"Here, give it to me," snapped the Dean, taking the lantern from the man's grasp.

The virger swiped the palms of both hands down the sides of his cassock, as if reluctant to touch the dusty, threadbare old cloth before them. He was a skinny man well into his thirties, with straight, straw-colored hair and a long, bony face dominated by a protuberant mouth full of large, crooked teeth. Unlike the Dean, who was the seventh son of an earl and probably destined for a bishopric, the virger was a layman of far more ordinary origins. Moving slowly, he carefully folded back the pall to reveal Charles I's lead coffin, white and chalky with age.

On his last visit to the vault, Jarvis had left strict instructions that the coffin was not to be touched; its lid was to remain soldered tight and the leaden scroll that encircled it kept in place to await the Prince's formal examination. Now the scroll gaped open, its cut edges showing clearly where the section bearing the inscription KING CHARLES, 1648 had been removed. But rather than tackle the solder, the thieves had simply cut a large, square opening in the upper part of the lid—easy enough

to do since the outer lead coffin was only a thin sheet
and its wooden lining much decayed.

"Give me the lantern," said Jarvis.

The Dean stood frozen, eyes wide, jaw slack with
horror.

"Hand it to me, damn you."

The Dean gave a start and held it out to him.

Jarvis raised the lantern high, so that the golden light
played over the coffin's interior. An unctuous, foul-
smelling matter glistened from the cerecloth where it
had been pulled back to reveal a large bowl-like depression, of the size and shape of a head. But only a few
darkened wisps of hair now clung to the stained, waxy
shroud. The torso ended abruptly at the neck.

"Merciful heavens," said the Dean, one hand cupped
over his nose and mouth. "Someone's stolen the King's
head."

Chapter 14

Tuesday, 23 March

*H*ero cradled her infant son in her arms and watched in the glow from the fire as his tiny fist opened and closed against her bare skin.

She'd discovered a rare peace in the quiet hours before dawn, when the world still sleeps and the only sounds are the whispered fall of ash on the hearth and the soft suckling of a babe at his mother's breast. Smiling, she breathed in the child's sweet scent and let the quiet joy of the moment flow through her. She was still awed by the ability of her body to supply him with nourishment and had become fiercely protective of this time they shared. Her determination to nurse her own child was not the sacrifice Jarvis envisioned—not a selfless act at all, but something *selfish*. Something that brought her pleasure and a trembling awareness of the powerful depths of her love for both her son and the man who had given him to her.

Through all her growing-up years, she'd been determined never to marry, determined never to subject herself to the state of subordination to which England's laws reduced any woman unwise enough to become a wife. Yet even then, she had wanted this, wanted to have a child of her own.

The babe looked up, his gaze locking with hers. She smiled at him, and he gave her in return a big, toothless grin that sent a trickle of milk running down his chin. And she felt a swift, unexpected sting of tears in her eyes, for life's greatest joys contain within them a yawning sadness. A bittersweet awareness that even as we savor a cherished instant it is passing and will all too soon be but a memory.

A hushed murmur drew her gaze to where Devlin slept, his dark head moving restlessly against the pillow. She thought of the bullet that had come so close to taking him from her last night, and her arms tightened around the child's small, warm body. She was not a woman who was accustomed to fear; she'd always despised those who obsessed anxiously about the future. Yet with great love comes great fear—the fear of loss. And in that moment, she knew its cold grip.

She pushed it away, both ashamed of her weakness and appalled by it.

"It's your fault," she whispered to the now contented babe. "You've done this to me."

He smiled again, his suckling ceased, his eyes drifting closed.

She felt his small body relax against hers, heard his breathing ease into sleep. And still she sat beside the fire, hugging him close and savoring the moment.

She left Brook Street an hour later, the clatter of her horses' hooves echoing through the still, empty streets of Mayfair as her coachman turned the team toward the City. She'd been told that to truly understand the costermongers of London, she needed to attend one of the great central markets where they purchased their stock.

And so she had chosen to visit the grandest market of them all: Covent Garden.

The rising sun was just beginning to send streaks of gold and fiery orange across a pale sky when she reached the site of the city's largest produce and flower market. Yet already the vast square before the old temple-like church of St. Paul's was thronged with a shouting, shoving, laughing crowd that surged around stalls piled high with everything from mud-encrusted onions and potatoes to bundles of white leeks and dark purple pickling cabbages.

She had hired a skinny, fourteen-year-old boy named Lucky Liam Gordon to serve as her guide to the wonders of the market. He had a thatch of rusty brown hair and a scattering of freckles across a pug nose, and he was the son, grandson, and great-grandson of costermongers. Hero was only just beginning to understand how closely knit—and hereditary—the trade was.

"Them's the growers' wagons," said Lucky, nodding to the lines of empty covered wagons and carts pulling away from the square. "They start rollin' in from the farms about three. I hear tell they load 'em at sunset, then leave for the City anywhere between ten and one, dependin' on how far they've got to come." He had to shout to be heard over the roar of hundreds of haggling voices, the cracking of whips and the braying of donkeys and the rattle of iron-rimmed wheels bouncing over uneven paving stones.

Hero let her gaze drift over the crush of gaily painted handbarrows, the rows of donkey carts with cracked harnesses so old they were often held together with wire or rope. The crisp morning air was heavy with the scents of charcoal smoke and dung and earthy vegetables, the pungent aromas from the herb stalls mingling with the sweet fragrance of potted laurels and myrtles and boxes. She smiled at the sight of two little boys chasing each other across cobbles smeared green with discarded leaves. Then one of the boys slipped and nearly collided with a market woman staggering beneath a heavy basket balanced on her head, before careening into Hero.

"Careful," said Hero, keeping a strong grip on her reticule as she steadied the boy.

He threw her a cocky grin and darted off again.

The number of young children at the market, most of them boys, surprised her. Shrieks rose from a clutch of children washing at the pump, while more could be seen crowding around the fires of the coffee and tea stalls beneath the arcades, or congregating near the narrow lanes leading out of the square. Some looked no older than four or five.

"Why are they queuing?" asked Hero, watching the boys push and shove as they lined up.

"They're 'opin' some costermonger without a boy of 'is own will 'ire 'em for the day," said Lucky. "Some 'as parents what send 'em 'ere to look for work. But a good many of 'em are orphans. They sleeps under the stalls at night and eats mainly specks."

Hero brought her gaze back to his freckled face. "They eat what?"

"Specks. That's what we call anything that's overripe or shriveled, or that the wasps 'ave been at. They're set aside, ye see, then sold for a quarter the price o' the rest. Me da always says, if somethin' won't fetch a good price, then it must fetch a bad one."

Hero drew her notebook and pencil from her reticule and began scribbling notes.

Officially, Covent Garden Market was devoted to the sale of fruits, vegetables, and flowers. But she could also see old iron sellers and crockery stalls scattered amidst the produce, as well as countrymen peddling wild ducks and rabbits. Rows of baskets and slippers dangled against the railings of St. Paul's churchyard, while men and women with rusty trays slung from straps around their necks pushed their way through the crowd, hawking seedcakes and sweetmeats, razors and knives, ribbons and combs.

She was watching a lark at the bird catcher's stall beat its wings against the bars of its cage when Lucky said, "Ye know that feller?"

"Who?" asked Hero, her gaze scanning the surging, raucous mass of humanity.

"That queer-lookin' cove up there by the Piazza Hotel—the one with the fancy black boots. 'E's been staring at ye ever so long. At first, I thought maybe 'e was jist puzzlin' over what such a bang-up lady's doin' at Covent Garden Market. But 'e ain't no coster, and 'e ain't no grower neither, from the looks of 'im. So what's 'e doin' 'ere?"

Hero could see him now, a slope-shouldered man of medium height, lanky except for a small, slightly protuberant belly. He had a slouch hat tipped back on his head and was leaning against one of the granite pillars of the elevated north piazza, a tin cup from a nearby coffee stall cradled in one hand, the other resting negligently in his pocket.

"How do you know he's not a costermonger?" she asked.

Lucky laughed. "I know."

The man took a slow sip of his coffee. He wore neither the blue apron of the greengrocers nor the straw hat, smock frock, and dusty shoes of the countrymen, although his coat and breeches had never been of particularly good quality and were now worn and rumpled and greasy. Only his well-polished, high-topped boots struck a discordant note.

For one long, intense moment, the man's gaze met hers across the square, and Hero felt her mouth go dry and an unpleasant sensation crawl across her skin. He had an oddly uneven face, with a full-lipped, crooked mouth and one eye that seemed slightly larger than the other. The sun was just cresting the rooftops of the decrepit seventeenth-century houses that lined the square and spilling golden light across the ragged, raucous crowd. The slanting sunlight caught the smoke from the charcoal fires so that, for one eerie moment, the air took on a hellish glow. Then the sun inched higher, and the illusion was broken.

"How long has he been watching us?" she asked Lucky. To her knowledge, she had never seen the man before and could not imagine who he might be.

"I can't say fer sure," said Lucky. "But I noticed 'im right after we got 'ere."

She studied the unknown man's strange profile. He was perhaps thirty-five or more years of age, his straight black hair worn long enough to hang over his collar, and a two- or three-days' growth of beard shadowed his face. He kept his head deliberately turned away. But she had no doubt that he was still aware of her, that she was the reason he was here, now.

"If I didn't know better, I'd think 'e followed ye 'ere," said Lucky. "Only, why would some feller be followin' ye?"

"I don't know," said Hero, shoving her notebook and pencil back into her reticule. "But I intend to ask him."

Gathering her carriage gown in both fists to lift the hem clear of the muck-strewn paving stones, Hero strode across the square, weaving around weathered, half-rotten stalls and plowing determinedly through the throngs of earnestly haggling purchasers and sellers. She had almost reached the step up to the piazza when the black-booted man pushed away from the pillar and melted into the crowd.

She tried to follow him, shoving past sieves piled high with apples and a thick mass of gawkers gathered around what looked like an upside-down umbrella filled with ribald prints. But by the time she reached the corner of James Street, he had disappeared.

She stared out over the noisy sea of donkeys and

barrows and ragged men and women clogging the lane. *"Blast,"* she whispered beneath her breath.

"Who was he?" asked Lucky as he caught up with her.

But Hero only shook her head, conscious of an unpleasant tingling in her fingertips and a sensation of disquiet that would not be stilled.

Chapter 15

Sebastian was sitting down to a solitary breakfast after a hard ride in the park when he heard the distant peal of the front bell, followed by a young woman's voice in the hall.

"A Miss Anne Preston to see you, my lord," said Morey, appearing in the doorway. "She says it's urgent."

"Please, show her in."

Stanley Preston's daughter came in with a quick step and a determined, almost fierce expression that faded to chagrin as she drew up just inside the doorway. "I've interrupted your breakfast. I do beg your pardon. I'll go—"

He pushed to his feet. "No. Please, come in and sit down. May I offer you some tea? Toast, perhaps?"

"Nothing, thank you." She took the seat he indicated, both hands gripping her reticule in her lap as she leaned forward. "I'm sorry for coming so early, but I spoke to Jane Austen last night, and she says she told you about Hugh—I mean, Captain Wyeth. I . . . I don't think she realized that when you heard about Father's argument with Mr. Austen, you might leap to some unfortunate conclusions."

Sebastian suspected that Jane Austen had been

perfectly aware of the implications of what she'd told him. But all he said was, "Conclusions about what?"

"About H—Captain Wyeth, and Father."

Sebastian reached for his tankard and calmly took a sip of ale, his gaze one of polite interest.

When he remained silent, she said in a rush, "I won't deny that Father was displeased when he learned Captain Wyeth had returned to London. But there was never any confrontation between them. Truly there wasn't." She looked at him with a pinched, earnest face, as if she could somehow will him to believe her.

She was an appallingly bad liar.

Sebastian cut himself a slice of ham. "Yet your father quarreled with Mr. Austen over a simple statement of regret voiced by the man's wife from her sickbed?"

"Father never could abide having his judgments questioned or being told he was wrong—about anything."

"Oh? And what, precisely, led your friend to change her mind about Captain Wyeth?"

Anne Preston threaded her reticule strings between her fingers. "When she opposed the match between Hugh and me six years ago, Eliza was very much governed by material considerations. She thought at the time she had my best interests at heart. But . . ."

"Yes?" prompted Sebastian.

"She says her illness has altered her perception, that she now sincerely regrets the part she once played in helping to deprive me of the happiness I could have enjoyed all these years."

"Your father found that objectionable?"

"Father always hoped to see us—that is, my brother and me—marry well. It was extraordinarily important to him."

"So Captain Wyeth has renewed his quest for your hand?

"Oh, no. No. We . . . we've only met a few times since his return to London—as old acquaintances. Nothing more."

Sebastian noted the telltale stain of color on her cheeks. But all he said was, "I understand Captain Wyeth has taken a room in Knightsbridge. Where, precisely?"

She stared at him. "But . . . I've just explained there is no reason to involve him in any way."

"Nevertheless, I would like to speak with him."

He watched her nostrils flare in panic as she realized her bold attempt to shield the captain from suspicion had failed utterly. She dropped her gaze to her clenched hands and said quietly, "He's at the Shepherd's Rest, in Middle Row."

"Thank you," said Sebastian.

She fiddled again with the strings of her reticule. "You asked yesterday if there was anyone with whom Father had quarreled recently."

"Yes?"

"I've been giving your question some thought, and it occurs to me that there is someone. I don't know if you could say Father *quarreled* with him precisely, but Father was definitely afraid of him. His name is Oliphant. Sinclair Oliphant."

In the silence that followed her words, Sebastian could hear himself breathing, feel the slow and steady beat of his own pulse. He cleared his throat and somehow managed to say, "You mean, Colonel Sinclair Oliphant?"

"Yes, although he's Lord Oliphant now. He inherited his brother's title and estates, you know."

"Yes; I did know. Although it was my understanding he'd been posted as governor of Jamaica."

"He was, yes. But he recently surrendered his position and returned to England. He's taken a town house in Mount Street for the Season."

Sebastian reached for his ale and wrapped both hands around the tankard. Three years before, in the mountains of Portugal, Sinclair Oliphant had deliberately betrayed Sebastian to a French major known for his inventive and painful ways of inflicting death. Sebastian had survived. But what the French major had done after that would haunt Sebastian for the rest of his life.

He took a long, slow swallow of the ale, then set the tankard aside with a hand that was not quite steady. "Why was your father afraid of Oliphant?"

"I don't know, exactly. I mean, I know Father was furious with Oliphant's behavior as governor. In fact, Father went out there last year precisely to try to do something about him."

"Your father was in Jamaica last year?"

"Yes."

"Did you go with him?"

"Oh, no; I stayed with the Austens. I've never actually been to Jamaica at all. Father always said it wasn't a healthy place for a woman."

"It isn't a healthy place for anyone."

He studied her smooth, seemingly guileless young face. He wanted to ask if it bothered her to know that the clothes on her back, like the pearl drops in her ears and the food she ate every day, were paid for by the labor of enslaved men, women, and children. But all he said was, "Do you know if your father had anything to do with Oliphant's decision to return to England?"

"No; Father never discussed such things with me. But last Friday, he was out for several hours in the afternoon, and when he returned home, he looked positively *stricken*. I asked what was wrong, and he said that he was afraid he'd made a mistake—that Oliphant is far more dangerous than he'd realized."

"Your father was right. Oliphant is dangerous. Very dangerous."

Something in his voice must have given him away, for she looked at him strangely, her lips parting, a faint frown line creasing her forehead. "You know him?"

"I did. Once," said Sebastian, and left it at that.

After she had gone, he went to stand before the long windows overlooking the terrace and the gardens below. The neatly edged parterres showed a vibrant green in the fitful sunshine, the newly turned earth a warm brown. But he saw only ancient stone walls burned black and a child's doll lost in a drift of orange blossoms.

There are moments in the course of a man's life that can irrevocably alter its path and sear his soul forever. Sebastian had encountered such a pivotal moment one cold spring in the mountains of Portugal, when he had obeyed the orders of a colonel he knew to be both vicious and deceitful, and dozens of innocent women and children had paid with their lives for his gullibility. Another man might have sought refuge in a string of excuses: *I didn't know. . . . I was simply obeying orders. . . . I was too late to save them.* But not Sebastian. Their spilled blood had irrevocably colored his sense of who and what he was.

Once, he had sworn to avenge their deaths, sworn to kill Oliphant even if it meant he had to die for it himself. But, with time, he had come to realize that the drive for vengeance was his own, that it was his own pain he sought to ease, his own guilt he hoped to redeem. Those gentle, religious women who had dedicated their lives to the care of others, and died because of it, would have prayed for Sinclair Oliphant's salvation. Not for his death.

Sebastian would not violate their memory by killing in their name. But there was a difference between vengeance and justice, and he was determined that the innocents of Santa Iria would have justice.

One way or another.

The elegant house on Mount Street so recently hired by Sinclair Oliphant for his gently bred wife and their five children rose five stories tall, its shiny black door flanked by polished brass lanterns, its marble front steps freshly scrubbed. Sebastian stood for a time on the footpath, his gaze on that stately facade, his thoughts on the man he'd last seen in a rough campaign tent in the mountains of Portugal. Colonial governorships were coveted, lucrative positions seldom surrendered voluntarily. If Stanley Preston was, in fact, behind Oliphant's sudden, unexpected return to London, then Preston had made himself a dangerous enemy indeed.

Still thoughtful, Sebastian mounted the house's front steps. His knock was answered by a somber butler who provided the information that his lordship was breakfasting that morning at White's. But Sebastian had to trail Oliphant from the clubs of St. James's through several exclusive shops in Bond Street before he finally came upon his former colonel at Manton's shooting gallery in Davies Street.

Leaning against a nearby wall, Sebastian crossed his arms at his chest and waited while Oliphant methodically culped wafers with one of Manton's sleek new flintlock pistols. The man looked much as Sebastian remembered him. In his mid-forties now, he was trim, broad shouldered, and tall, with the erect carriage typical of a career military officer. His jaw was strong and square, his cheeks lean, his lips habitually curled into a smile that hid a capacity for self-interest that was brutal in its intensity.

Sebastian had no doubt that Oliphant was aware of his presence. But the colonel simply went on calmly hitting the rows of paper targets attached to an iron frame at the far end of the long, narrow room. After each shot, he paused, reloaded his pistol, and fired again, the acrid smoke billowing around them, until the last wafer went down. Only then did he turn to face Sebastian, his movements graceful and untroubled, almost bored.

It was the first time Sebastian had seen the colonel

since he'd sent Sebastian on a mission deliberately calculated to end in so much innocent death. Now Sebastian searched the man's clear blue eyes for some sign of guilt or regret or even discomfort. But he saw only the familiar self-satisfaction edged faintly with contempt. And he knew then that the events of that faraway spring—the deaths that had shattered Sebastian's soul and marked him for life—had troubled the man who caused them not at all.

Sebastian felt a powerful surge of rage pulse through him. He wanted to smash his fist into that complacently smiling face. He wanted to feel flesh split and bone shatter beneath his driving knuckles. He wanted to wrap his hands around the man's throat and crush it until he saw the life ebb from those hated eyes. And he had to clench his hands at his sides and force himself to take a deep, steadying breath before he could bring the surging bloodlust under control.

"I didn't realize shooting had become a spectator sport," said Oliphant, calmly passing the pistol to a waiting attendant.

Sebastian held himself very still. "Practicing in case someone should challenge you to a duel?"

Oliphant's smile never slipped. "I like to keep my hand in." He stripped off the leather sleeves he wore to protect his starched white cuffs and went to wash his hands at the basin. "You're not here to shoot?"

"Not today." Sebastian watched him splash warm water over his face and reach for the towel. "How long have you been back from Jamaica?"

"Not long," said Oliphant, his attention seemingly all for the task of drying his hands.

"I understand you knew a man named Preston. Stanley Preston."

Oliphant glanced over at him. "As it happens, I did. Why do you ask?"

"Someone cut off his head and used it to decorate a bridge near Five Fields."

"So I had heard."

"I'm told he was afraid of you. Why?"

"Who told you that?"

"Are you saying he wasn't?"

Oliphant tossed the towel at the washstand and turned away to ease his coat up over his shoulders with the attendant's help. "Some people frighten easily." He adjusted his cuffs. "They say you came down from the hills in Portugal swearing to kill me on sight." He pivoted to face Sebastian, his arms spread wide, his eyebrows lifted as if in inquiry—or challenge. "Change your mind?"

"Not exactly."

The man's handsome smile slipped ever so slightly, then broadened. "What do you have in mind? Pistols at dawn? Or a knife wielded in darkness from a fetid alley?"

Sebastian shook his head. "Three years ago, an innocent Portuguese nun was raped and tortured to death because of you, while thirty-two children and the simple, pious women who cared for them were put to the sword or burned alive. No English court will ever convict you for what you did to the convent of Santa Iria. But if you murdered Stanley Preston, I'm going to personally watch you hang for it."

Then he turned and strode from the room, before the urge to kill the man with his bare hands overwhelmed him.

Chapter 16

*H*ero arrived home from her early expedition to Covent Garden to find Devlin seated at his desk, fitting a new flint into his small, double-barreled pistol.

"The strangest thing happened at the market this morning," she said, yanking off her yellow kid gloves as she walked into the library. "There was this man—" She broke off as Devlin looked up and she saw his face.

The room was filled with shadows, for the day had grown overcast and he had no need to kindle a candle to light his work. Yet even in the gloom, she could sense the taut, hard set of his features, see the lethal gleam in the strange yellow luminosity of his eyes. "What is it?" she said.

"Sinclair Oliphant is in London."

She was suddenly, acutely aware of the ticking of the mantel clock, of the lean strength of his fingers as he worked on the gun. He had told her some of the events of that blood-soaked Portuguese spring. She knew of Oliphant's betrayal and the hideous carnage that flowed from it. But she'd always suspected that Devlin hadn't told her everything. That he was holding back some crucial component of the events of that day. And that what he hugged quietly to himself was the part that most lacerated his soul and drove him on a path to destruction.

She set aside her gloves. "You've seen him?"

He nodded. "Anne Preston came to me this morning. I think her main purpose was to try to convince me of Captain Wyeth's innocence, but she also told me her father was afraid of Oliphant. It seems Preston objected to Oliphant's actions as governor of Jamaica, and I wouldn't be surprised if he used his influence with his cousin the Home Secretary to have Oliphant recalled."

"You're suggesting Oliphant might have hacked off Preston's head and set it up on Bloody Bridge in revenge?"

"Personally? Probably not. Sinclair Oliphant has always preferred to let other people do his dirty work."

She watched him square the flint to the frizzen and begin to tighten down. He was a man comfortable with violence, willing to use it when necessary and perhaps sometimes even welcoming it. But she did not believe he would take it upon himself to simply execute Oliphant, as he might once have done.

Then she wondered if he sensed the drift of her thoughts, because he said, "I'm not going to kill him out of hand and hang for it, if that's what you're worried about. But I wouldn't be surprised if he has already tried to have me killed."

She stared at him. "You think he was behind last night's shooter? But . . . you didn't even know about his involvement with Preston until this morning."

Devlin closed the frizzen and brought the flint gently down on it. "If Oliphant sent that shooter, it was because of Santa Iria, not because of Preston. As soon as Oliphant made the decision to return to London, he knew he was going to need to deal with me. And the people Oliphant deals with generally end up dead."

"Then perhaps you should kill him," she said. "As

long as you can be certain you won't hang for it, of course."

His eyes crinkled with amusement, for he thought she spoke in jest. Except that she hadn't. She loved him with a fierceness that could steal her breath and freeze her heart with the fear of losing him. But while she admired Devlin's moral code, she did not completely share it. In many ways, she was still very much her father's daughter.

He slipped the pistol into his pocket and rose to his feet. "If Oliphant was behind Stanley Preston's murder, I'm going to see him hang for it."

"And if he didn't have Preston murdered?"

Devlin smiled again, this time with lethal purpose-fulness. "Then I'll kill him when he comes to kill me."

Chapter 17

Half an hour later, Sebastian was walking out of the house toward his waiting curricle when a stylish barouche drawn by a team of blood bays and emblazoned with the Jarvis crest rounded the corner and drew up close to the kerb.

The carriage's near window came down with a snap. "Ride with me around the block," said Jarvis as one of his liveried footmen rushed to open the carriage door.

Sebastian paused at the base of the house steps. "Why?"

"Do you seriously expect me to discuss it in the street?"

Sebastian exchanged looks with Tom, who was standing nearby at the chestnuts' heads. Then he leapt up into Jarvis's carriage and took the forward bench.

"What you are about to hear is told in the strictest confidence," said Jarvis as his team moved forward with a jerk.

Sebastian studied his father-in-law's full, complaisant face. "Sent one of your minions out to Windsor Castle, did you?"

The other man's eyes glittered with an animosity he made no attempt to disguise. "As it happens, I went myself."

"And?"

"Charles's I's burial vault has been violated. The inscribed section of the lead band that once encircled the coffin has been removed, as has the King's head."

"The head?" Sebastian stared at him, his attention well and truly caught. "Was anything else taken from the crypt?"

"That has not yet been determined, although I have instructed the Dean and his virger to make a thorough investigation."

"Did you open Charles's coffin when you first inspected the vault for the Prince Regent?"

"I did not." The carriage swung onto Bond Street, and Jarvis reached up to grasp the strap that dangled beside him. "It is the Prince's wish that he be present at the coffin's opening, with the contents to be inspected not only by himself, but by a number of other important individuals."

"So if you never actually opened the coffin, before, how can you be certain the head was ever there? King Charles might have been buried without it."

"The depression where the head once rested within the folds of the cerecloth is quite obvious. Apart from which, all the accounts we have of the events that occurred immediately after the execution state quite clearly that Charles's head was sewn back onto the body before the dead King's remains were put on display."

"Was he put on display?"

"Of course he was. It would have been vitally important to the usurpers that the populace be convinced their King was indeed dead."

Sebastian stared thoughtfully out the window at a costermonger with a gaily painted donkey cart, the boy beside him shouting, "Turnips, penny a bunch!"

"The princess Augusta is not expected to live out the day," Jarvis was saying. "Her funeral will doubtless take place sometime next week, and the Regent is determined to hold the formal opening of Charles's tomb immediately thereafter."

Sebastian brought his gaze back to his father-in-law's face. "I take it no one has told His Highness that someone already beat him to it? No wonder you didn't want to discuss this in the street."

Jarvis tightened his grip on the strap. "It's conceivable the theft has political implications. Was Stanley Preston an admirer of the Stuarts?"

"The Stuarts certainly interested him. But I don't know if you could say he admired them."

"You're certain?"

"No. At this point, I'm not certain of anything."

"And you've learned nothing that might suggest who was behind the violation of the royal vault?"

Sebastian found himself faintly smiling. "No."

Jarvis studied him through hard, narrowed eyes. "You find my question amusing?"

"Amusing? Not exactly. Two days ago, a man was murdered in a particularly brutal fashion by someone who is still out there, walking our streets. Yet your only concern in all this is how it might lead to the recovery of some moldering old head?"

"This is not simply some random 'moldering old head' we're talking about," snapped Jarvis in a rare show of irritation. "And as for whatever fears have been aroused amongst the populace by the grisly manner of this murder, they will be easy enough to assuage with a swift public hanging."

"Whether the hanged man is actually guilty of the murder or not?"

"Fortunately, we don't all share your maudlin obsession with guilt and innocence."

Sebastian met his father-in-law's hard, ruthless gaze and wondered why it had never occurred to him just how much Jarvis and Oliphant had in common.

The carriage swung back onto Brook Street, and

Jarvis signaled his coachman to pull up. "I want that head."

"If I should happen to come across it, I'll see it's returned to you." Sebastian opened the door without waiting for the footman. Then he paused on the step to look back and say, "What do you know of Sinclair, Lord Oliphant?"

"The man who was until recently governor of Jamaica?" Jarvis frowned. "Very little. Why?"

"Colonial governors are appointed by the Crown, are they not?"

"Officially. But they're handled by the Home Office."

"That's what I thought," said Sebastian, stepping down.

Jarvis leaned forward, his hand coming up to stay the footman who had moved to close the door. "I don't like Hero's involvement in this affair; it's too dangerous."

"Hero lives her own life as she sees fit—as well you know."

Something flared in the powerful man's eyes. "If anything should happen to either my daughter or my grandson because of this ridiculous obsession of yours, you won't live long enough to mourn them."

Then he settled back, turned his face away, and signaled his coachman to drive on.

Sebastian drove his curricle to the Home Office, where he learned from a helpful clerk that Lord Sidmouth was in Downing Street and would surely be closeted with the Prime Minister for the rest of the day on a matter of supreme urgency that the clerk refused to particularize.

"Think 'e's avoiding ye?" asked Tom when Sebastian took the reins again, then paused to stare thoughtfully toward the river.

"Perhaps. But perhaps not."

The discovery that an undetermined number of royal relics—including the head of King Charles I—were missing from the chapel at Windsor Castle had added a bizarre new twist to the murder of Stanley Preston. It seemed probable that whoever stole the relics did so with the intent of selling them to Preston, either directly or—more likely—through some unknown middleman. Could that explain Preston's presence at the bridge on such a cold, wet night? Was he there to take possession of the stolen relics?

The problem with that theory was that such items were typically delivered to their wealthy purchasers' doorsteps, discreetly hidden inside straw-filled tea chests. Not handed over under cloak of darkness at the end of a deserted lane. Yet the presence of Charles I's coffin strap at the murder scene suggested an undeniable link. Had the relics been dangled before Preston as clever bait to lure him to some out-of-the-way spot where he could be murdered? Why was the engraved strap left at the scene? Deliberately? Or by accident?

And where was the King's purloined head?

Still pondering these questions and more, Sebastian turned his horses toward Knightsbridge and a ramshackle hostelry called the Shepherd's Rest.

Chapter 18

*C*aptain Hugh Wyeth was playing solitaire at a table in the crowded taproom, a half-empty tankard of ale at his elbow, a deck of cards held in his left hand, his right arm resting in a sling. He looked up when Sebastian approached his table, his gaze assessing, guarded.

"You're Devlin?" he asked.

"Yes."

Wyeth set his deck of cards upside down amidst the ruins of his game. "I've been expecting you."

Six years of war coupled with the pain of a severe injury and long recovery had etched lines in the captain's once boyish face. But he was still, as Jane Austen had noted, devastatingly handsome in his regimentals, with black hair and blue eyes and lean, sun-darkened features. He gaze never left Sebastian's. "I didn't kill Stanley Preston."

"I imagine it would be rather difficult to cut off a man's head with your arm incapacitated," said Sebastian, nodding to the sling.

"So it would—if I were right-handed. As it happens, I am not."

"Ah."

A group of laughing officers, some on crutches, others

looking more hale, crowded into the taproom. Sebastian said, "Are you capable of walking?"

The captain rose to his feet. "Of course. It's mainly my arm that's still not working right. But I hope to be able to rejoin my regiment soon."

"Where were you wounded?" Sebastian asked as they left the inn and cut across Knightsbridge toward the Life Guards barracks and the park beyond.

Wyeth stumbled as he stepped off the kerb, his lips tightening in a fleeting grimace as he regained his balance. "San Muñoz, last fall."

"You're certain you're up to walking?" asked Sebastian, watching him.

"My leg gets stiff if I sit for too long, that's all."

They cut between the officers' stables and the riding school, the tall brick buildings casting cold, dark shadows across the ground.

Sebastian said, "I take it Miss Preston warned you to expect me?"

"She did, yes. She's terrified I'm going to be blamed for her father's death."

"Because Preston objected to your friendship?"

A gleam of self-deprecating amusement showed in the captain's pain-shadowed face. "Oh, I don't think he'd have had too much difficulty with our *friendship*. It was the prospect of something more serious that he found intolerable." He watched a troop of new recruits leading their horses from the stables to the riding school, his smile fading as the clatter of shod hooves over cobbles echoed between the crowded buildings. "Look—I understand now just how presumptuous it was of me all those years ago to ask someone as young as Anne was then to share my life; to expect her to follow the drum and face all the hardships and dangers that come with being an Army wife. But at the time . . ." He hesitated, then shrugged. "We were both so young, and I was so very proud of my new colors—proud and utterly blind to how foolish it would have been for a woman with her prospects to throw herself away on a poor vicar's son from the fens of East Anglia."

The words were right: contrite, respectful of conventions, resigned. And yet . . .

And yet, Sebastian could sense the anger thrumming through the captain's lean, battle-hardened frame. Anger at himself, for his lack of major advancement in the Army. Anger at the fates, for the impoverished birth that was none of his doing. Anger at society, for the barriers it had thrown up to keep him from marrying the woman he loved. He hid it well, but the anger was there, deep-seated and powerful.

Powerful enough to drive him to cut off a man's head while in the grip of a murderous rage?

Perhaps.

"Your parents are still there?" asked Sebastian. "In East Anglia?"

"No. My mother died not long after I was sent overseas, and my father passed away six months ago."

"I'm sorry."

"I've an older sister living here, in Knightsbridge. That's why I came to London. She hasn't the room to put me up in her house, but it's good to at least have her nearby." He cast Sebastian a sideways glance. "I didn't come to London expecting to see Anne again, if that's what you're thinking. To be honest, I imagined she must have married someone else years ago."

"But you did see her."

"We encountered each other—quite by chance—in Bond Street one morning." He swallowed hard, as if he found it necessary to choke back an upsurge of emotion before he could continue. "I thought I'd managed to forget her; truly, I did. But then I saw her, and it was as if all those years just . . . melted away."

Sebastian stared off across the park to where a nursemaid was playing catch with her two young charges. He himself had loved passionately and unwisely as a very young man, and come home from war to discover his love for the beautiful, brilliant actress Kat Boleyn still as intense—and still as hopelessly, impossibly wrong in the eyes of society. It was a love that had come close to destroying him.

That might well have destroyed him, if it hadn't been for Hero.

He said, "How did Preston find out you were in London again?"

"Some busybody spied Anne walking with me in the park last week and told him. He confronted Anne, and she confessed the truth."

"Which is?"

"That our feelings have not changed."

Sebastian watched one of the little boys catch the ball, then tumble over backward, his delighted laughter carrying on the breeze. Captain Wyeth's frank confession gave the lie to what Anne Preston had told him just that morning. Was Wyeth more honest? Sebastian wondered. Or simply clever enough to realize that claims of mere friendship were unlikely to be believed?

He said, "I take it Preston was no more inclined to favor a match between you now than he was six years ago?"

Wyeth pulled a face. "Hardly. He had high hopes of Anne agreeing to marry some baronet who's been courting her. Anne's grandfather married a rich merchant's daughter, you know, and then Stanley Preston himself improved the family's social standing by marrying the daughter of an impoverished lord. It was his ambition to see Anne marry both a title *and* money. And he was not a man who liked to have his ambitions thwarted."

"When did you last see him?"

Wyeth's gaze slid away, his jaw hardening.

Sebastian said, "Recently, I take it?"

The other man nodded.

"Why?" asked Sebastian.

Captain Wyeth looked confused. "I don't understand."

"I mean, why, exactly, did you see him?"

"If you must know, he came barging into the taproom of the Shepherd's Rest last Saturday evening. Threatened to horsewhip me if he ever found out I'd been near his daughter again."

"And how did you respond?"

"I told him I'm not some slave on one of his plantations, and that if he ever tried it, I'd—" He broke off.

"You'd—what?"

Wyeth let out his breath in an odd expulsion that sounded like a laugh, but wasn't. "I said I'd take the whip away and use it on him myself. But I didn't kill him. I swear to God, I didn't kill him."

"Where were you Sunday night?"

"At a musical evening given by Lady Farningham."

"The same event attended by Miss Preston?"

"As it happens, yes."

"Did Stanley Preston know you were going to be there?"

"Good God, no."

"So certain?"

"Yes. If he'd known, he wouldn't have allowed her to attend."

"What time did this musical evening end?"

"I couldn't say. I myself left early."

"And went where?"

"For a walk."

"Alone? In the rain?"

"Yes, damn you."

"You do realize Preston was killed sometime between half past ten and eleven?"

Wyeth was silent for a moment, his gaze narrowing as he watched a duck come in low to land on the shiny stretch of ornamental water beside them. Then he said again, more quietly this time, "I tell you, I didn't kill him."

"So who do you think did?"

"I don't know! You think that if I had any idea, I wouldn't tell you?" He put up his left hand to massage the shoulder of his wounded arm. "The truth is, Stanley Preston could become damnably abusive when in a passion. He could have tangled with anyone. I know he had a row recently with Thistlewood that nearly ended in blows."

"Who?"

"Basil Thistlewood III. He keeps a cabinet of curiosities down on Cheyne Walk, in Chelsea. I'm told it's been there forever—his grandfather actually started it."

"I've heard of it," said Sebastian.

Wyeth nodded. "I remember my sister taking me to see it when I came to visit her one time as a lad."

"Do you know why Preston and Thistlewood quarreled?"

"From what I understand, Thistlewood was in a rage over Preston's acquisition of the Duke of Suffolk's head. Claimed it should've been his by rights, only Preston cheated him out of it."

"Thistlewood also collects heads?"

"He collects anything and everything."

Sebastian studied the captain's open, seemingly guileless face. He came across as an essentially pleasant young man—troubled and bitter, perhaps, but basically honest and straightforward and unaffected. And yet . . .

And yet, Wyeth and Anne Preston had just sent Sebastian in two very different directions, with Miss Preston pointing a subtle finger toward Oliphant, while Wyeth implicated the keeper of a Chelsea cabinet of curiosities.

And Sebastian couldn't get past the suspicion that both helpful suggestions were as deliberate as they were coordinated.

Chapter 19

There was nothing in London quite like Basil Thistlewood's coffeehouse, built overlooking the broad waters of the Thames at Chelsea. It had been in existence for nearly a century, with new and exotic items added to its overstuffed rooms every year. Admission was free for the price of a cup of coffee or the purchase of a catalogue.

"You'd like a catalogue, my lord?" asked Thistlewood, bustling forward as soon as he heard Sebastian talking to the barman. "Tuppence each. Three for fivepence, and a tanner will get you a personal guided tour."

The coffeehouse owner was a wiry, gaunt-faced man, probably somewhere in his early fifties, with watery, bloodshot eyes, beard-stubbled cheeks, and unruly gray eyebrows that met over the bridge of a ponderous nose. A stale, musty odor rose from his old-fashioned frock coat and yellowed, ruffle-fronted shirt, as if he'd borrowed his clothes from one of the cases in his exhibit.

"A personal tour, please," said Sebastian, duly handing over his sixpence.

Thistlewood swept a courtly bow. "Right this way, your lordship."

He ushered Sebastian into a chamber jammed with

dusty, glass-topped cases and walls crowded close with everything from curious pieces of driftwood and giant turtle shells to primitive spears and antique swords. Items too large for the cases or walls—a stuffed alligator, giant elephants' tusks, even a canoe fashioned from a hollowed-out log—hung from the ceiling.

Pausing in the center of the room, Thistlewood sucked in a deep breath and launched into what was obviously a well-rehearsed spiel, delivered in a singsong voice. "In this case here, you'll see a Roman bishop's crosier, antique coins found when they were laying down new water pipes in Bath, and a set of prayer beads made from the bones of St. Anthony of Padua."

"Really?" said Sebastian, peering at the rosary. The beads certainly appeared to have been made from someone's bones.

Thistlewood squared his shoulders and looked affronted. "Surely you are not questioning their authenticity?"

"No; of course not."

They moved to the next case. "The most notable items here are a piece of sandstone bearing the fossilized imprints of ancient ferns, and a giant frog found on the Isle of Dogs."

Sebastian studied the stuffed amphibian, which looked to be a good fourteen inches long. "Somehow, I suspect he was not native to fair England."

"No," agreed Thistlewood. "Most likely a stowaway hopped off one of the ships docked there, I always thought." He raised a hand toward the wall above the case. "The sword you see hanging here was used in the coronation of King Charles himself. And—"

"First, or Second?" asked Sebastian, his interest caught.

"First." Thistlewood nodded to the next case. "And here we have Queen Elizabeth's prayer book and strawberry dish."

"Where did you get all these"—Sebastian paused,

searching for an appropriate word, and finally settled on—"objects?"

"The original collection was begun by my grandfather, the first Basil Thistlewood. He was valet to none other than Sir Hans Sloane himself, before Sir Hans bequeathed most of his collection to the nation. When my grandfather left his service in 1725 to open a coffeehouse on these premises, Sir Hans most graciously gave him a number of items to put on display. My grandfather himself increased the collection considerably, as did my father after him, and I have continued the tradition. Fortunately, we are quite popular with sea captains, who every year bring us a variety of new, interesting specimens from their worldwide voyages."

Sebastian leaned over a nearby case to study the array of stone projectile points displayed there. "I've heard you were recently frustrated in your attempts to acquire the Duke of Suffolk's head."

Thistlewood worked his jaw back and forth, as if so overcome with fury as to find it difficult to spit out his words. "It should have been mine. I'm the one who heard about it first and identified it."

"Oh?"

"I've long suspected Suffolk was buried at Holy Trinity. So when the sexton told me they'd found a small box containing a head while in the process of setting the crypt in order, it took only one look for me to know right away whose it was."

"You recognized him?"

"Instantly! The resemblance to his portraits is striking."

"I'd always heard Suffolk was beheaded with one clean stroke."

"A tale, I'm afraid, put about to quiet the murmurs of the populace." He nodded to a long-handled sword hanging near the doorway to the next room. "See that? It's an executioner's sword. They were typically between three and four feet long, and about two inches wide. The handle was made like that so the executioner could grip it in both fists to get a good leverage."

Sebastian studied the plain, heavy blade. According to family tradition, two of his mother's ancestors had lost their heads on Tower Hill. But until now, Sebastian had never given much thought to the particulars of their executions.

"There were two different types of blocks used, you know," said Thistlewood, warming to what was obviously a favorite topic. "With a high block, like this one here"—he paused to put his hand on a worn chunk of wood several feet high, with a large, polished scoop on one side and a slight indentation on the other—"the prisoners would kneel and bend forward so that their heads rested over the top of the block. But with the low block, the poor condemned souls had to lie down flat with their necks on this little thing here—" He pointed to a long, narrow length of wood resting atop a nearby case. "That put their heads at all the wrong angle for the job, I'm afraid."

Sebastian tried to ignore an unpleasant tickling sensation along the base of his skull.

"Of course," Thistlewood was saying, "the block was only used when the executioner employed an axe, rather than the sword. Here in England, we tended to favor the style of axe you see here—" He pointed to a massive specimen hanging precariously from the ceiling. "It's basically modeled after a woodsman's axe."

"Looks nasty," said Sebastian, squinting up at it.

"It is indeed. The handle is a full five feet long, while the blade is ten inches. In Germany, they used something quite different—essentially a giant butcher's cleaver, except with a longer handle. Unfortunately, I don't have one of those, so I can't show it to you."

"That's quite all right," said Sebastian. "How many blows did it take to cut off the head of Charles I?"

"Just one; all the reports agree on that. Whoever did

it obviously knew his craft, which wasn't usually the case, I'm afraid. The executioner who did for Anne Boleyn used a sword and did it in one stroke too; but then, he was brought over from France special, at her request, because he was so good. The thing is, beheadings weren't all that common, and they were typically done by the hangman, who botched the job more often than not. Took three blows to get the head off Mary, Queen of Scots. And the idiot who did for the Countess of Salisbury struck the poor old woman *eleven times* before he got the job done."

Sebastian found his gaze drawn, again, to the executioner's sword. "So how did Preston end up with Suffolk's head, if you're the one who first identified it?"

"Pure greed on the part of the sexton, I'm afraid. Once he knew what he had, he went trotting off to Preston and offered to sell it to him."

"It must have been infuriating to discover that Preston had managed to buy Suffolk's head away from you."

"Wasn't it just!" agreed Thistlewood. "Why, I—" He broke off, eyes widening as he suddenly became aware of the dangerous trap yawning before him. Clearing his throat, he turned away to rub the sleeve of his coat across the top of the nearest case, as if wiping at a smudge. "But then, happens all the time. I'm used to it."

"You didn't quarrel with Preston because of it?"

"Well . . . we may've had words when we met by chance in Sloane Square one day. But nothing serious. No, no; I'm a humble man; can't expect to compete with those blessed with deep pockets."

"What is the going price for a head?"

"Depends on who the head originally belonged to, I suppose. But I couldn't really say. Virtually everything here was given to me—or my father or grandfather—to be put on display for all to see."

"I take it Preston bought many of the objects he collected?"

"He did, yes. But then, he could afford to, couldn't he?"

"And you're saying the sexton who found Suffolk's head took it to Preston?"

Thistlewood's enormous nose quivered with a renewed rush of indignation. "The very day I identified it!"

"Did he actually take the head to Alford House and offer it to Preston himself?"

"I suppose. I mean, he must've, right?"

Rather than answer, Sebastian let his gaze wander, again, around that extraordinary collection. "Who would one contact, if he were interested in trafficking in rare objects of an historical nature?"

"Well, there's Christie's, of course."

"What if one were interested in something a little more . . . illicit?"

Thistlewood gave a quick look around, as if to make certain no one was listening, then leaned in close to whisper, "There's a shop in Houndsditch, kept by an Irishwoman name of Priss Mulligan. She carries all sorts of things. Some of her stock comes from émigrés and others down on their luck, but not all. Or so I'm told."

"Provides a market for stolen goods, does she?"

Thistlewood nodded solemnly. "Works with smugglers bringing items in from the Continent too. Only, you didn't hear that from me, if you get my drift. She's not someone you want to get riled at you. Folks who cross Priss Mulligan have a nasty habit of disappearing— or turning up dead in horrible ways." He closed his eyes and gave a little shudder. "Horrible ways."

"Do you think Stanley Preston could have run afoul of her?"

"Could've. Hadn't thought about it, but there's no denying he definitely could've. Heard he bought a Spanish reliquary from her a month or so ago. Some saint's foot, although I can't recall precisely whose, at the moment. Thing is, Preston had a temper—hot enough to override his sense, when he was in a passion. And anyone who deals with Priss Mulligan had best keep their wits about them at all times." Thistlewood paused, his tongue flicking out to lick his dry lips. "You . . . you won't be telling her where you heard any of this, will you?"

"I can be very discreet," said Sebastian. "Tell me this: What do you think Preston was doing at Bloody Bridge that night?"

Thistlewood's eyes went wide. "Don't know. Does seem a queer place for him to be, don't it?"

"Any chance he might have been taking possession of some new object for his collection?"

"At Bloody Bridge? In the middle of the night? Whatever for?"

"Perhaps the object—or objects—were illicitly acquired by the seller."

"But . . . why Bloody Bridge?"

Sebastian had no answer for that.

He studied the curiosity collector's slack, seemingly innocent face. "Where were you Sunday night?"

"Me?" Thistlewood's gaze faltered beneath Sebastian's scrutiny and drifted away. "Same place I am every night: here."

"Never left?"

"Not for a moment, from noon till past midnight." He cleared his throat. "Now; shall we move on to the next room?"

"Please."

Sebastian continued to listen with only half his attention while Thistlewood droned on about Roman pitchers and Pacific dart guns. He figured it was at most a mile— probably less—from the coffeehouse to Bloody Bridge. It would have been easy enough for Thistlewood to walk there, whack off Preston's head with one of the many swords in his collection, and hurry back, all within half an hour.

It was certainly a possibility; from the sound of things,

Thistlewood was angry enough about Preston's purchase of Suffolk's head to have decided to exact such a ghoulish revenge.

Except, how would Thistlewood have known to seek his victim that night at Bloody Bridge?

Chapter 20

"*Ni-ew mackerel, six a shilling!*"

Sebastian pushed his way through the ragged crowd of rough men, desperate-looking women, and sharp-faced, grimy urchins clogging the narrow lane known as Houndsditch. The decaying, centuries-old buildings rising from the pavement cast the lane in deep shadow, their upper stories leaning precariously toward one another until it seemed they might almost touch overhead.

"*Wi-ild Hampshire rabbits, two a shilling.*"

"*Buy my trap, my rat trap!*"

Once, Houndsditch had been nothing more than a defensive trench dug along the western edge of London's city walls. Running southeast from Bishopsgate to Aldgate, it eventually grew so foul with refuse and offal and the bloated carcasses of dead dogs that city officials ordered it filled in. Never a fashionable area, it was occupied today mainly by immigrants and their descendants, particularly Huguenots from France, Jews from the Netherlands, Germany, and Poland, and, increasingly, the Irish. The poverty of the residents made it a center for rag fairs and secondhand shops.

Crude stalls piled with everything from battered tin saucepans and worn-out boots to cheap tallow candles lined the street, while bellowing vendors dispensed hot tea from cans and guarded piles of sliced bread and butter from the hordes of ragged, starving children. The air was thick with the smells of herring, smoke, effluvia, and despair.

Priss Mulligan's establishment stood on the corner of Houndsditch and a dark, narrow alley that curled toward Devonshire Square. Only two stories tall, with filthy, small-paned windows and sagging lintels, the structure looked to be in the final stages of dilapidation, its walls so darkened by grime as to appear almost black. Sebastian had to lean hard against the battered, warped door; a small brass bell jangled as it swung open.

He'd been expecting something similar to Basil Thistlewood's eclectic collection of rare treasures mixed indiscriminately with the curious or merely odd. But this was more like a thieves' den from a child's fable, with exquisitely painted porcelain vases, snuffboxes with intricate filigreed lids, willowy Chinese maidens carved from ivory, gilded saints' images, even a life-sized winged horse of glistening white marble.

He turned in a slow circle, trying to take it all in. When he came back around, he found himself being studied by a pair of beady black eyes.

"Who might you be, then?" demanded Priss Mulligan.

She couldn't have stood more than four foot ten and was nearly as broad as she was tall, with thick dark hair and creamy white skin and puffy round arms that ended in incredibly small, childlike hands.

"A potential customer?" Sebastian suggested.

She gave a disbelieving grunt. "'Tis possible, I'm supposing. But is it likely?" She pursed her lips and shot a stream of tobacco juice into a nearby can. "Nah."

In age, she could have been anywhere between thirty-five and fifty, her massive hips churning beneath her high-waisted, brown bombazine gown as she came forward, her gaze never leaving his face. "You ain't a beak; that I can tell, just looking at you."

"No," agreed Sebastian.

She sniffed and wiped her lips with the back of one hand.

Sebastian said, "I understand you recently sold a Spanish reliquary to a friend of mine."

"Oh? And who might your friend be?"

"Stanley Preston."

"Him as just got his head cut off?"

"So you did know him?"

"Sure, then, but any fool on the street would recognize that name. Ain't often a body gets his head lopped off in London—leastways, not these days."

"You didn't sell him a reliquary?" Sebastian nodded to a gilded bronze receptacle molded in the shape of an arm—presumably because that's what it contained. "Rather like that, except a foot."

"Came out of a church in Italy, that one did."

"How did it end up here?"

"Émigré sold it to me, just last week. Always coming in here, they are, looking to unload all manner of things. Need the money, you see."

Sebastian caught the faint sound of a man's hushed breathing coming from behind the curtained doorway at the rear of the shop. Someone was there, watching and listening.

He kept his gaze fixed on the woman before him. "Seems a curious item to pack when you're fleeing for your life," he said.

Priss Mulligan's lips pulled back in a smile that showed small, sharp teeth stained brown by tobacco. "Some people have no sense."

"When was the last time you saw Mr. Preston?"

"Didn't say I had seen him, me."

Sebastian studied the woman's plump, creamy face and small, still faintly smiling mouth. Like most people who made their livings by buying and selling, she was shrewd and crafty and doubtless far from honest. But there was something else about her, something that went beyond mere venality. She was a woman whom even cocksure young boys would cross the street to avoid; whose presence made horses snort nervously and dogs slink, bellies to the ground. The degree of malevolence in her was palpable.

She was looking at him with narrowed eyes. "Have I seen you before?"

"Not to my knowledge."

She smiled wider and pointed one fat, stubby finger at him. "I know what it is. You look more'n a bit like that rifleman keeps a tavern just off Bishopsgate. Got those same nasty yellow eyes, he does."

"Interesting," said Sebastian, careful to keep his voice bland, almost bored, although in truth he was fully aware of the existence of a Bishopsgate tavern keeper who looked enough like him to be his brother—or at least a half brother. "You essentially have two choices: You can either answer my questions, or I can suggest to Bow Street that an inspection of your premises might yield some interesting results."

Her breath was coming fast now, in angry little pants. "Folks around here'll tell you, it ain't a good idea t' mess with Priss Mulligan."

"So I've heard." Sebastian let his gaze drift around the crowded shop. "I don't see any human heads."

"Only heads I ever sell are saints' heads, covered with silver or gilt bronze. Like that arm there."

"When was the last time you saw Stanley Preston?"

"Never said I did; never said I didn't."

"So when was it?"

Her smile shifted subtly, became something reflecting true humor, although the source of her amusement escaped him. "A month or more ago it was, to be sure."

"Who do you think killed him?"

"Someone who wanted him dead, I expect."

"Know anyone who falls into that category?"

"Not so's I can think of, offhand."

"You had no disagreements with him?"

Her eyes widened with a practiced intensity and semblance of earnest honesty that almost—but not quite—struck him as comical. "I did not," she said.

"How often would he buy from you?"

"Now and then."

"Did he ever put in a request for anything special?"

"On occasion."

"Such as?"

"Och, this 'n' that."

The breathing from the far side of the curtain grew harsher. Faster.

Sebastian said, "Must be something of a disappointment, to lose one of your best customers."

Priss Mulligan worked the wad of tobacco in her jaw. "I got others."

He touched his hand to his hat. "Thank you for your help."

"Anytime, yer lordship. Anytime."

He didn't bother to ask how she knew he was a lord. The truth was, asking any question of the Irishwoman was unlikely to elicit either a direct or an honest response. People like Priss Mulligan lived their lives behind a miasma of subterfuge and deliberately generated fear. It said something about Stanley Preston that he had done business with the woman. Repeatedly.

Sebastian walked out of the shop into the ragged crush of Houndsditch's overcrowded, desperately poor residents. The light was beginning to fade from the sky;

whatever warmth there might once have been was gone from the day.

As he turned toward Bishopsgate, where he'd left Tom with the curricle, he was aware of a nondescript, slope-shouldered man slipping from the noisome alley alongside the shop to fall into step behind him.

Chapter 21

With the approach of evening, a fierce bank of clouds had scuttled in from the east, their roiling dark underbellies tinged with a strange, coppery green glow. Billowing gusts of wind sent handbills fluttering over the uneven paving stones and flapped the worn black shawl of a stooped old woman hawking nuts from a rusty tray. The knots of dirty, pinch-faced children huddled closer to the braziers of the coffee stalls and hot-potato sellers, their hollow eyes following Sebastian without curiosity or comprehension as he passed.

He paused as if to study the colorful caricatures displayed in a print shop's dusty window, being careful not to glance toward the slope-shouldered man in polished black boots who drew up abruptly and started fumbling in his pockets as if in search of a handkerchief. When Sebastian walked on, the *click-click* of the man's bootheels was just audible above the din of rattling cartwheels and the shouts of the children and the singsong cries of the street sellers.

Sebastian quickened his pace and heard that distinctive *click-click* speed up. When he slowed, so did his shadow. Then, as they neared the end of the lane, Sebastian turned abruptly and strode back toward Priss Mulligan's shop.

The slope-shouldered man paused, his eyes widening ever so subtly. Of medium height and lanky despite his small potbelly, he had stringy black hair worn long enough to hang over his collar and a noticeably asymmetrical face with a bulbous nose and crooked mouth. But he was obviously convinced that Sebastian remained oblivious to him, because he simply turned as if to watch a brewer's wagon full of empty casks that was rattling up the street, its tired horses hanging their shaggy heads, the malty aroma of ale mingling with the smell of roasted nuts and hot coffee and dung.

"Who are you?" demanded Sebastian, walking right up to him. "And why the devil are you following me?"

He expected the man to run, or at least to deny following him. Instead, the man laughed, his face instantly transforming from bland abstraction into a mask of glee. "I'd heard you were good," he said. "But I didn't credit it, meself."

"Your mistake."

"Ain't it just?"

Sebastian studied the man's beard-shadowed face, the grimy collar and filthy hair. His clothes were those of a workman down on his luck—or someone who had other reasons for doing his shopping at the rag fairs of Rosemary Lane.

"Who are you?" said Sebastian again.

The man tipped his hat and bobbed his head, as if making an introduction. "Name's Flynn. Diggory Flynn."

"Why were you following me?"

Diggory Flynn's eyes slid away, his tongue flicking out to wet his full, oddly misshapen lips. "Didn't mean you no harm."

"And why should I believe you?"

"Never did you nothing, now, did I?"

"Maybe. Maybe not. Someone took a shot at me, just last night. Could have been you."

"I don't know nothin' about that."

"Who set you after me?"

"What makes you think anybody did?"

"Who told you I'm 'good'?"

A strange quiver passed over the man's lopsided face, then was gone. "You've got a reputation, you do."

Sebastian resisted the urge to grab the man by the front of his coat and shove him up against the dirty brick wall of the wretched shop beside them. "Why were you following me?"

"You got some folks worried, you do."

"Who?"

The man had the strangest eyes, one a pale blue that burned with a fierce intensity, as if lit from within by a fire bordering on madness; the other was light brown. "You think on it, you'll know."

"Where'd you get the boots?"

"The boots?" He cast an admiring glance down at them. "Won 'em off a hussar captain, I did. Ain't they grand?"

"I knew exploring officers in the Army who had no trouble rubbing grease in their hair or dressing themselves in filthy rags, but for some reason they really, really hated wearing anything but their own boots. It got them killed sometimes."

Diggory Flynn's face shone with merriment. But all he said was, "I wouldn't know nothin' about that. Weren't ever in the Army, meself."

Sebastian took a step back, then another, his gaze never leaving Flynn's face. "Turn around and walk back the way you came."

"What?"

"You heard me."

Flynn touched a hand to his battered slouch hat. "Yes, sir," he said, his grin never slipping. Then he thrust his hands in the sagging pockets of his worn-out coat and sauntered back up the lane, whistling "Bonny Light Horseman" softly beneath his breath.

⁕

"I assume this Diggory Flynn is the man you heard behind the curtain in Priss Mulligan's shop?" said Hero.

She was seated in the armchair beside the bedroom fireplace, one hand trailing lightly over the back of the big, long-haired black cat stretched out beside her. The cat had adopted them some months before, although they'd yet to come up with a name that seemed right for him. It was nearly midnight; the fire on the hearth filled the room with a warm golden glow, while outside, a howling wind buffeted the house and sent the rain clattering against the windowpanes.

"It's possible," said Sebastian, holding his dozing son against his shoulder, his palm splayed against the child's tiny body as he walked back and forth.

"Yet you don't sound convinced. Why?"

He found himself reluctant to put his suspicions into words. "She certainly has a nasty reputation. And I suspect it's well earned."

"It's odd, but he sounds rather like the man I saw at Covent Garden Market this morning."

Sebastian turned to look at her. "What man in Covent Garden?"

"I thought I told you about him. It was my coster guide, Lucky Gordon, who noticed him first. He was simply standing there, staring at me. But when I tried to approach and ask what he wanted, he disappeared."

Sebastian went to lay the sleeping babe in his cradle, then stood for a moment, watching the firelight dance over the child's soft cheeks and the gentle curve of his dusky lashes. And he knew it again, that chilling whisper of fear, that shuddering awareness of how fragile and vulnerable were the lives of those he loved.

"What?" asked Hero, watching him.

"As of dawn this morning, I had never heard of Priss

Mulligan. So why would she have set someone to follow my wife?"

"Why would anyone?"

When he remained silent, she said, "You think Diggory Flynn works for Oliphant, don't you?"

"Yes."

She tilted her head to one side, and he knew what she was thinking—that his history with Oliphant was tempting him to see connections where they didn't necessarily exist. He acknowledged that she might even be right.

But he didn't think so.

She said, "Why would Oliphant set someone to watch me? Not you, but me?"

Sebastian went to where a decanter stood warming on a table before the fire and poured himself a glass of brandy. "It's a game he plays; a game of intimidation. He wants people to know they're being watched—and that the people they love are vulnerable. He enjoys making them afraid."

"I would think he'd know you better than that—know that you don't frighten easily."

He watched her head bend as she stroked the cat, watched the firelight catch the subtle auburn glints in the heavy fall of her hair and glaze the angle of her cheekbone. He wanted to tell her that there were things Oliphant knew that she did not, and that sometimes the innocent are made to pay for the sins of the guilty. But all he said was, "The thought of anything happening to you or Simon scares the hell out of me."

She lifted her head to meet his gaze, her features calm and still. "Nothing is going to happen to us."

He took a long pull of his brandy and felt it burn deep in his chest. "Your father thinks I'm putting you at risk simply by looking into Preston's murder."

"Well, that's something you two have in common, then—needlessly worrying about Simon and me, I mean." She shifted her hand to scratch the cat beneath his chin, the feline's eyes slitting with pleasure as he lifted his head. "Jarvis tells me Charles I's head is missing, as well as the coffin strap."

Sebastian went to stand before the fire. "Saw him, did you?"

"This afternoon, when Simon and I were visiting my mother. He's not exactly pleased with you, is he?"

"Is he ever?"

A gleam of amusement showed in the gray eyes that were so much like her father's. "No." The amusement faded. "Do you have any idea yet how the theft from the royal vault figures into Preston's murder?"

"Oh, I've plenty of ideas. And not a bloody clue which—if any—of them are right. I don't even know who brought the coffin strap to the bridge that night. It could have been the original thief, or a dealer, or the killer—assuming that the thief or dealer *isn't* the killer. Or even Preston himself."

"Why would Preston be carrying it?"

Sebastian shrugged. "Perhaps he was taking it to show someone. Or perhaps he'd just purchased it." He tilted his head back and moved it slowly from side to side in a futile attempt to loosen some of the tension he carried in his neck. "If the strap had been left beside the body, I might think the killer intended it as some sort of statement or warning. But it wasn't; it was lying in weeds down near the creek, as if someone had simply dropped it."

"Perhaps the killer did leave it with the body. Only, someone else came along and picked it up. Someone who then dropped it in fright. Or perhaps the killer was stealing it and *he* dropped it."

"I can see Thistlewood or Priss Mulligan taking the coffin strap. But not Oliphant or Wyeth."

She smiled. "You complained last night that you had almost no suspects. Now you have almost too many: the unknown relic thief; a vindictive ex-governor; a scorned Army captain; a rival curiosity collector; and a nasty secondhand dealer."

"Don't forget the banker who quarreled with Preston right before he was killed. I haven't even been able to speak with him yet."

"What's his name? Do you know?"

Sebastian nodded. "Henry Austen. I spoke to his sister."

"You mean, Jane Austen?"

"Yes. You know her?"

"I met her a few times at a friend's salon last year. She's a deceptively clever woman with a devastating wit."

"She is indeed. She tells me Preston was angry with her brother over something Austen's wife said."

"Sounds like a rather silly argument over which to kill someone."

"True. Yet men have killed for less. And he is the last person known to have seen Preston alive." Sebastian drained his glass and set it aside. Then his gaze fell on the set of three slim blue volumes that rested on the table beside her chair, and he said, "Don't tell me you're reading this new anonymous novel as well?"

"My mother gave it to me. It's quite entertaining." She scooped the cat up into her arms and laughed out loud when he stiffened and widened his eyes in indignation. "And I've found the perfect name for you," she told the cat. "It precisely captures your charming blend of arrogance and aloofness—*and* your impressive handsomeness, of course."

"Oh? What's that?"

"Mr. Darcy."

Sebastian shook his head. "I don't understand."

She let the cat go and smiled as he jumped down in disgust. "Then you must read the book."

Chapter 22

*T*he next morning, Sebastian was standing on the corner of Henrietta Street, his gaze drifting over the facade of Henry Austen's bank, when a tall, slim man in a neatly tailored blue coat and high-crowned beaver hat emerged from the bank's entrance and walked across the street toward him.

He looked to be in his early forties, with a long face and aristocratic nose and a military carriage that lingered still. His small, thin mouth curled up in a pleasant smile that was probably habitual, and he looked enough like his sister that Sebastian had no difficulty identifying him.

"I thought I'd save my clerk the trauma of another visit from you and simply come out," said Henry Austen, drawing up before him.

"Was he traumatized?" asked Sebastian as the two men turned to walk along Bedford Street, toward the Strand and Fleet Street.

"He likes to pretend he is, at any rate." Austen threw him a swift, sideways glance. "My sister warned me to expect a visit from either you or Bow Street. Am I a suspect?"

"Bow Street thinks you are."

Austen pressed his lips together and drew in a deep breath that flared his nostrils. "It's because of that blasted incident in the pub the other night, is it?"

"Is there another reason Bow Street should suspect you?"

"Good God, no."

They paused at a side street to allow a collier's wagon to lumber past.

"Why, precisely, did you quarrel?" Sebastian asked. He'd already listened to Jane Austen's explanation, but he wanted to hear her brother's version.

"I don't know if I'd describe it as a quarrel, exactly. Preston was already furious when he walked into the pub. If you ask me, he was looking for someone on whom to unload some spleen, and I was simply there."

"What was he angry about?"

"The crushing of his grand ambition of seeing his daughter married to a title, I suppose. Jane told you about Anne, didn't she?"

"She did. Although I must admit I find it hard to believe Preston would be so enraged simply because your wife expressed regrets over something she said six years ago."

"Yes, well . . ." Austen put up a hand to scratch his ear. "The thing is, I didn't exactly tell my sister everything. I mean, Preston was angry because of what Eliza had said. But he was also furious with Jane."

"For what?"

"For 'encouraging Anne's romantic notions,' was the way he put it. You see, before Captain Wyeth reappeared in town, Anne was on the verge of accepting an offer from Sir Galen Knightly."

Sebastian was familiar with Sir Galen. A prosperous if somewhat lackluster baronet, he was ten years older than Sebastian—which would make him nearly twenty years older than Anne Preston. "And your sister discouraged the match?"

"Oh, no—at least, not intentionally. It's just that Anne likes to read romance novels."

"And Miss Austen gave her novels?"

The banker drew his chin back into his cravat and fiddled self-consciously with the buttons of his coat. "Well . . . yes."

Sebastian watched Austen's gaze slide away. The man obviously needed to take lessons in lying from someone with Priss Mulligan's talents. Although why he should be anything less than honest about his sister's involvement in Anne Preston's reading material escaped Sebastian entirely.

Sebastian said, "How well did you know Preston?"

"I've known him for years, although the real friendship was between our wives."

"Any idea what he might have been doing at Bloody Bridge on a rainy Sunday night?"

"I suppose it's possible he decided to go for a walk after leaving the pub. He'd worked himself up into quite a rage. Perhaps he realized he needed to cool off."

"I understand he had something of a temper."

"He did, yes. Although I've known worse. Much worse, actually. He was a man of strong passions who sometimes allowed his emotions to override his sense. But there was no real harm in him."

There was no real harm in him. Austen's words almost exactly echoed those of his sister. And Sebastian found himself wondering why both Austens had felt compelled to make such similar observations.

He said, "Can you think of anyone who might have wanted to kill him?"

"No. But then, as I said, we weren't exactly intimates."

"Did you ever hear him mention a man named Oliphant?"

"Who?"

"Sinclair, Lord Oliphant. He was until recently the governor of Jamaica."

Austen thought about it, but shook his head. "Sorry. You might try talking to Sir Galen Knightly. He owns plantations in Jamaica too, you know. And unlike Preston, he's quite a steady fellow. My sister Jane calls him Colonel Brandon."

"Colonel Brandon? Why?"

Austen glanced down, his eyes crinkling as if at a private joke. "I suppose you've never read *Sense and Sensibility*?"

"By the author of this new novel everyone is talking about? No."

"Ah. Well, there's a character in it—a Colonel Brandon—a staid, older man in love with a much younger woman, who herself prefers a younger, more romantic figure."

"And Sir Galen Knightly reminds your sister of this character?"

"He does, yes. I don't think Sir Galen was ever dashing, even when young."

"Unlike Captain Wyeth."

The amusement faded from Austen's face, leaving him looking serious and troubled. "Jane worries that Wyeth may well be another Willoughby or Wickham."

"Excuse me?" said Sebastian.

"The dastardly fellows in *Sense and Sensibility* and *Pride and Prejudice*."

"She thinks Wyeth is dastardly?"

"Not exactly; it's more that she worries he could be. Have you met him? He's quite handsome and charming."

"I didn't realize such attributes were considered a bad thing."

Austen gave a soft laugh. "Jane would tell you that handsome, charming young men without fortune should always be considered suspect, particularly when showering attentions on fair maidens of good family."

"I'm told Miss Preston is not well dowered."

"I suppose that depends on your standards. She's no great heiress, certainly. But she has a small portion from her mother in addition to what she'll get from Preston."

"I was under the impression Preston had entailed his estates to the male line."

"He did, yes; but I believe Anne stands to inherit some five thousand pounds invested in the Funds."

"Now that Preston is dead," said Sebastian.

Austen drew up and swung to face him. "Surely you don't think Wyeth—" He broke off, as if unwilling to put the suggestion into words.

Sebastian paused beside him. "If not Wyeth, then who? Who do you think killed Preston?"

Austen shook his head. "I would hope I don't number amongst my acquaintances anyone capable of such barbarity."

"Yet Preston obviously did. Whether he realized it or not."

Austen puffed out his cheeks as he exhaled a long breath. "You're right, of course. Although I must admit, it's troubling even to think about." He looked out over the wide gray expanse of the river cut by the newly constructed arches of what would eventually be the Strand Bridge. "Try talking to Sir Galen. They'd been friends since Knightly was a lad. He'd be far more likely to know if the man had recently acquired a dangerous enemy. You'll find him in his club's reading room, this time of day."

"Which club?"

"White's, of course. He's there every day from four until five. And he dines at Stevens every Wednesday and Sunday at half past six. He's quite the creature of habit."

Sebastian studied the banker's long, scholarly face.

That gentle, good-humored smile was firmly back in place. Yet there was an evasiveness, a lack of directness to his gaze, that was hard to miss. And Sebastian couldn't escape the feeling that, like his sister, Henry Austen was hiding something.

He thanked the banker and started to turn away, only to pause and say, "Was Preston carrying anything when he came into the pub that night?"

Austen looked puzzled. "Such as what?"

"A strip of thin, old lead, about eighteen inches long. Or perhaps a larger, wrapped package or satchel of some kind?"

Austen thought about it a moment, then shook his head. "No, he couldn't have been."

"You're certain?"

"Yes. I remember quite clearly; he came in with his arms held stiffly at his sides and his fists clenched. He couldn't have been carrying anything."

Chapter 23

Sir Galen Knightly was seated in one of the red bucket chairs in White's reading room when Sebastian walked up to him. A cup of tea rested on the table beside him, and he was engrossed in his newspaper's account of the previous evening's session at the House of Lords.

Sebastian doubted anyone had ever described Sir Galen as dashing, or even handsome. But he was not an unattractive man, despite his angular, somewhat blade-like features. Although he was now in his early forties, his frame was still strong and solid, his dark hair little touched by gray. His clothes were those of a prosperous country gentleman, tailored for comfort rather than style, as sober and serious as the man himself.

According to gossip, Knightly's father had been a notorious rake, a member of the infamous Hellfire Club well-known about London for his drunken excesses and addiction to deep play. It often seemed to Sebastian that Sir Galen lived his life as if determined to prove to the world that his character was not that of his scandalous father. Where the father had been profligate and intemperate, boisterous and careless, the son was steady, sober, and serious. Eschewing gaming hells, the track, and London's ruinously expensive highfliers, he devoted himself to scholarship and the careful management of his estates, in both Hertfordshire and Jamaica. He had married, once, when young. But his wife died in childbirth, leaving him heartbroken and—if possible—more serious than ever.

At Sebastian's approach, he looked up, his features set in grave lines.

"Do you mind?" asked Sebastian, indicating the nearby chair.

"No; not at all." Sir Galen folded his newspaper and set it aside. "I take it you're here about Preston?"

Sebastian settled into the chair and ordered a glass of burgundy. "I'm told you knew him well."

"I did, yes. His largest plantation in Jamaica lies between the land I inherited from my great-uncle and that of my mother's family."

"Have you spent much time there? In Jamaica, I mean."

Sir Galen reached for his tea and took a small sip. "I have, yes. After the death of my grandfather, I was sent to the island to live with my uncle. I find I miss it if I'm away from it too long."

Something of Sebastian's thoughts must have shown on his face, because Sir Galen said, "I'm told you're a rather outspoken abolitionist."

"Yes."

Sir Galen stared down at the delicately patterned china cup in his hands, then set it aside. "It's a dreadful institution. I don't care what the Bible says; I can't believe we were meant to own our fellow beings as if they were nothing more than cattle and horses."

"Yet you do."

"I do, yes; by the hundreds. I inherited them, the same way I inherited Knightly Hall in Hertfordshire and the money my grandfather invested in the Funds. I suppose I could sell them, but while that might soothe my conscience, it wouldn't do anything to improve their situation, now, would it? At least while they're under my care, I can see they're treated well."

"You could always free them."

"And so I would—if I could. But the law requires me to post bond guaranteeing their support for the rest of their lives. All five hundred of them. It would bankrupt me. If I were a better man, I suppose I'd do it anyway. But . . ." He shrugged and shook his head.

Sebastian studied the Baronet's sun-darkened, broad-featured face. Sebastian had heard of a woman who, upon inheriting an estate in the West Indies, loaded all of the plantation's slaves on a ship and transported them to Philadelphia, where she was able to set them free without posting a bond. But all he said was, "Did Preston feel the same way?"

"Stanley? Good God, no. He was convinced slavery was instituted by God to enable the superior European race to care for and shepherd the benighted souls of Africa. He genuinely believed that manumission was a misguided evil and contrary to God's plan."

"How often did he visit Jamaica?"

"He used to go out there quite regularly. But since his son, James, has taken over the management of the plantations, he's been more content to adopt the role of an absentee landlord."

"What can you tell me about his dealings with Governor Oliphant?"

"Oliphant?" Knightly pressed his lips together in disgust, as if the name tasted foul on his tongue. "He was extraordinarily unpopular with the planters, you know. Governors frequently are, but . . . Let's just say that Oliphant went far beyond what was proper."

"Care to elaborate?"

"Not really. Anything I could say would be all speculation and hearsay, and I have a healthy respect for England's slander laws—and no desire to fall afoul of them."

"Could Preston have had something to do with Oliphant's rather sudden, unexpected return to London?"

"He never boasted of it, if that's what you're asking. But—" Sir Galen cast a quick glance around and grimaced suggestively. "Well, his cousin is the Home Secretary, now, isn't he?"

"Miss Preston tells me her father was afraid of Oliphant."

"I've heard he has a reputation for being someone you don't want to cross. Unfortunately, Stanley Preston wasn't the kind of man to let that stop him." Knightly shook his head. "He was a brilliant man, well educated and learned in a number of subjects. But he was not always wise."

The waiter delivered Sebastian's wine, and he paused to take a deliberate sip before saying, "I understand Preston was also upset because of his daughter."

A faint band of color appeared high on the older man's cheekbones. "I don't know what you mean."

"He was disturbed, was he not, by the reappearance in London of a certain hussar captain?"

"I take it you mean Wyeth?"

"Yes."

Sir Galen shifted his gaze to the large, gilt-framed battle scene on the far wall. "I'm afraid Anne—Miss Preston—has a generous nature, which combined with a warm and trusting heart can sometimes lead her to misjudge those she meets, especially when a friendly manner and a graceful address create the appearance of amiability."

"You believe Wyeth's amiability to be merely an appearance?"

"I fear it may be. But then, as you are doubtless aware, I am not exactly a disinterested party. When she was younger, the difference in our ages seemed insurmountable. It was only recently I'd begun to think perhaps I might have some chance, but then—" He broke off and shifted uncomfortably with all the embarrassment of a painfully reserved man in love with a younger woman who has given her heart to another.

"Do you think Preston would have forbidden a match between his daughter and Captain Wyeth?"

"He was certainly determined to do all within his power to prevent them from marrying. He had a younger sister, you know, who married an Army officer and died a hideous death at the hands of the natives at a fort in the wilds of America."

"No, I didn't know that. Yet Anne Preston is of age, is she not?"

"She is, yes."

"Would she have married without her father's blessing, do you think?"

"If she believed his blessing unfairly withheld, I suspect she would, yes."

"And would he have disinherited her, if she married against his wishes?"

"He certainly swore he intended to do so. But would he have actually carried through with the threat?" Knightly tipped his head to one side, then shrugged. "I honestly don't know."

Sebastian stared at him. "You're saying Preston threatened to disinherit Anne if she married Captain Wyeth?"

"He told me the day before he was killed that he would cut her off without a farthing if she did. But I can't say whether or not he ever threatened Anne herself. He was like that, you know—full of bluster and passion, saying he was going to do things he would later realize were folly—once he calmed down."

"Men of that nature frequently accumulate enemies."

"Unfortunately, yes."

"Can you think of any—apart from Oliphant and Wyeth?"

Sir Galen studied his empty teacup, as if lost for a

moment in thought. Then he shook his head. "I'm afraid I can't, no. As I said, his passions sometimes ran away with him, leading him into careless or hasty speech better left unsaid. He doubtless alienated more people than he realized. But can I think of anyone else angry enough to kill him and cut off his head? No."

"Any idea what Stanley Preston might have been doing at Bloody Bridge that night?"

"No. I hadn't actually given it much thought, but you're right; it is odd for him to have been there so late, is it not?"

"He didn't often walk at night?"

"Only to the pub and back. There was a time not so long ago when Bloody Bridge had a well-deserved reputation for violence. I can't imagine him going there alone, at night."

"Did he say anything to you about some Stuart relics he was considering buying?"

Knightly shook his head. "Not that I recall, no. But then, I'm afraid I sometimes didn't pay a great deal of attention when Stanley would start prattling on about his collection."

Sebastian set aside his wineglass and rose to his feet. "Thank you. You've been very helpful."

Sir Galen rose with him and tucked his paper under one arm in an awkward, self-conscious gesture. "He was a good man, you know. My uncle died the summer I was fourteen, when we were in Jamaica. I had already lost my grandfather, and my parents long before that. Stanley Preston took me under his wing. I was nothing more than a tiresome adolescent, but he treated me like a man grown. You couldn't ask for a truer, more loyal friend. Whoever killed him—" He broke off, as if fearing the intensity of his emotions might lead him into the kind of intemperate speech he'd just credited to Stanley Preston. He pressed his lips together and shook his head, then said, "Whoever killed him left the world a poorer place."

"Who do you think did it?"

The question seemed to surprise Knightly. "Me?" He paused. "If it were me, I suppose I would look into Captain Wyeth's movements." A self-deprecating smile touched his lips. "But then, as I said, I'm not exactly disinterested in that quarter."

"It sounds to me as if this Captain Wyeth may well be our man," said Lovejoy as he and Sebastian stood on the terrace of the vast pile of government offices known as Somerset House, looking out over the sullen gray waters of the Thames. "He readily admits he has no alibi for the time of the murder, and given that Preston was opposing the captain's ambitions of marrying Miss Preston and had promised to disinherit her if she wed against his wishes, he also possessed a powerful motive."

"Just because he had a motive and no alibi doesn't mean he did it," said Sebastian, watching a crane fit into place a large stone on the new Strand Bridge. "I'm still not convinced Henry Austen is being entirely honest about his quarrel that night with Preston. It might be worthwhile to send a constable to talk to the Monster's regular patrons; one of them may have overheard something interesting."

Lovejoy nodded. "Good idea. We've recently discovered Preston received a visitor on Sunday morning, by the way—a physician named Sterling. Douglas Sterling."

"Preston was unwell?"

Lovejoy shook his head. "According to Miss Preston, her father was in the best of health—at least, as far as she knows."

"What does this Dr. Sterling say?"

"Very little, unfortunately. I sent one of my best

lads—a Constable Hart—to speak with him, but Sterling claims the visit was medical in nature and refuses to discuss it further. When Constable Hart tried to press the matter, the good doctor became quite agitated and stormed off. Hart thinks he's hiding something."

"Interesting. I'll have to have a go at him."

Lovejoy cleared his throat. "I should perhaps have mentioned this Dr. Sterling is quite aged."

"How aged?"

"Nearly eighty. He's been retired for years."

"So why was he treating Preston?"

"He claims he saw him as a favor."

"They were friends?"

"Miss Preston says he's the former colleague of some relative—a cousin of her grandfather, I believe."

Sebastian turned to stare at him. "Lord Sidmouth's father was a physician—and her grandfather's cousin."

"Was he? Then perhaps that's the connection."

"Where does this Dr. Sterling live?"

"Number fourteen Chatham Place. But I gather he spends most of his time at a coffeehouse near the bridge-head. He sounds like a crusty old gentleman. I suspect you'll not find him easy to coerce into talking, if he's made up his mind not to."

"Perhaps I can appeal to his better nature."

"After listening to Constable Hart," said Lovejoy, turning away from the river, "I'm not convinced he has one."

Chapter 24

Douglas Sterling proved to be one of those aged gentlemen who still clung to the powdered wigs considered de rigueur for men of birth and education when they were in their prime.

Sebastian found him in a coffeehouse on the east side of Chatham Place, seated near the bowed front window where he could watch the steady stream of traffic passing back and forth on Blackfriars Bridge. He was hunched over a medical journal that lay open on the table before him, but looked up and frowned when Sebastian paused beside him.

His face was heavily lined with age, the skin sallow and blotched with liver spots. But his frame was still lean, his hands unpalsied, his dark eyes shiny with a belligerent intelligence. "You're obviously not from Bow Street," he said, his voice raspy but strong. "So what in blazes do you want with me?"

"Mind if I have a seat?"

"As a matter of fact, I do," said the old man, and returned pointedly to his reading.

Sebastian leaned one shoulder against a nearby wall, his arms crossed at his chest. Through the window he could see a massive farm wagon heavily laden with hay jolting and swaying as it came down off the bridge's span. "Nice view," he said.

"Yes."

"Come here often, do you?"

"You must know I do; otherwise, you wouldn't have found me here, now, would you?"

"I understand you've retired from the practice of medicine."

"Pretty much."

"Yet you consulted with Stanley Preston the very day he died?"

"I like to keep my hand in, now and then."

"Now and then?"

"Yes." The aged physician gave up all pretense of reading and leaned back in his chair. "Who are you?"

"The name's Devlin."

Sterling's eyes narrowed. "The Earl of Hendon's son?"

"Yes."

"I hear you've taken a fancy to solving murders. In my day, gentlemen left that sort of thing to the constables and magistrates."

"Like Constable Hart?"

Sterling grunted. "The man is beyond impudent."

Sebastian studied the old doctor's watery, nearly lashless dark eyes. "He thinks you're hiding something."

Rather than become flustered, Sterling simply returned Sebastian's steady gaze and said, "He's welcome to think what he likes."

"It doesn't disturb you that someone lopped off Stanley Preston's head less than twelve hours after you saw him?"

"Of course it disturbs me—as it would any right-minded gentleman."

"Yet you refuse to divulge information which could conceivably lead to the apprehension of his killer."

"It is only your assumption—and that of the ridiculous Constable Hart—that I possess any such information."

"Are you by chance acquainted with the Home Secretary, Lord Sidmouth?"

"Huh. Knew him before he was even breeched, I did—although I doubt he'd acknowledge the likes of me now that he's become so fine. Lord Sidmouth, indeed. And his father no more than a simple physician, like me."

"You were colleagues?"

"We were. Although it was years ago, now."

"Yet you still maintained an acquaintance with Stanley Preston?"

"That strike you as odd?"

"I suppose not. Tell me this: Did Preston seem at all anxious when you last saw him? Frightened?"

"Hardly."

"How often would you see him?"

"Not often."

"Yet he consulted with you over a medical problem his own daughter didn't know he had?"

"I don't discuss my health with my daughters. Do you?"

"I don't have a daughter."

"A son?"

"Yes."

The old physician gave a throaty grunt. "Strapping young man like yourself, bet you think you want sons— carry on the name, make you proud at Oxford and on the hunting field, and all that rot. But mark my words: You get to be my age, it's a daughter you'll be wanting."

Outside in the square, the hay wagon had caught a wheel in a rut and shuddered to a halt. Someone shouted as the driver cracked his whip.

Sebastian said, "What did you think of Preston's interest in collecting the heads of famous men?"

The old physician thrust out his upper lip and shrugged. "Ever see the collection of anatomical specimens amassed by the late John Hunter? They're in the care of the Royal College of Surgeons these days."

"Can't say that I have."

"Mind you, Hunter's collection was based on anatomical peculiarities rather than whatever fame or infamy the individuals may have managed to acquire in life. But his point was the same."

"Was it? I'd have said the impetus behind Hunter's collection was education and research."

"He liked to think it was. Could even have started out that way. But if you'd ever observed his pride in his specimens, you'd know better."

Sebastian studied the aged doctor's sallow, wrinkled face. "Can you think of anything that might have taken Stanley Preston to Bloody Bridge last Sunday night?"

"No."

"Ever hear of a man named Sinclair Oliphant?"

"No," said Sterling again. Although this time he blinked, and his gaze skittered away.

"You're certain of that?"

"Course I'm certain," Sterling snapped and glared defiantly back at Sebastian again, as if determined to stare him down.

"Who do you think killed Stanley Preston?"

"I've no idea."

"None?"

"None."

"Then why your reluctance to discuss your last meeting with him?"

For one brief moment, Sterling's jaw sagged, and Sebastian caught a glimpse of uncertainty and what might even have been fear in the old man's eyes.

Then the aged physician clenched his teeth together.

"My meeting with Stanley Preston last Sunday was private, and I intend for it to remain that way. You can stand there for the rest of the day as far as I'm concerned, but I've told you all you need to know."

He hunched a shoulder and returned pointedly to his reading.

"Telling me what you think I need to know is not the same as telling me all you know," said Sebastian.

But Sterling kept his stare fixed on the page before him, the powder from his old-fashioned wig dusting the shoulders of his worn coat.

Frustrated, Sebastian went next to the Home Office, where his second attempt to speak to Viscount Sidmouth was no more successful than the first. This time, the clerk insisted that his lordship was at Carlton House in consultation with the Regent and was not expected to return that day.

Sebastian studied the clerk's pasty white face. He was a short, gently rounded man with a balding pate and a small, puckered mouth that curled up into what looked like a habitual condescending smile. "At Carlton House, you say?"

The smirk deepened. "That is correct."

"You're certain of that?" Sebastian could quite clearly hear the Home Secretary in conversation with a fellow cabinet member behind a nearby closed door. But the clerk had no way of knowing that.

"Of course I am certain," said the little man with a sniff.

"It's the oddest thing, but I'm beginning to get the impression the Secretary is deliberately avoiding me."

The clerk stared back at Sebastian, pale eyes blinking rapidly.

If Sidmouth had been closeted with anyone else,

Sebastian would have been tempted to set the supercilious clerk aside and open the door to the Home Secretary's office. But Sebastian recognized the voice of the nobleman whose low, measured tones alternated with Sidmouth's higher ranges: It was the Earl of Hendon, the man Sebastian had called Father until a short time ago.

Sebastian nodded to the closed door. "When the Secretary finishes his meeting with Lord Hendon, you can tell him that I'll be back."

The clerk gave a nervous titter. "When? When will you be back?"

"When will he be available?"

"I'm afraid I can't really say. He's busy. Very busy."

"Then I suppose I'll simply need to catch him when he's not busy."

The clerk's smile slid into something less confident. "What does that mean?"

But Sebastian simply smiled and walked away, leaving the clerk bleating behind him, "But what does that mean? What does it mean?"

That night, Sebastian donned silk knee breeches, buckled dress shoes, and a chapeaux bras and took his wife to a ball.

The ball was given by Countess Lieven, the Russian Ambassador's wife. Her husband had only recently been posted to the Court of St. James, yet the young Countess had already managed to make herself one of Society's leaders. She was politically astute, totally unscrupulous, breathtakingly snobbish, charismatic, and brilliant. Her invitations were amongst the most sought after in London, and her approval was critical to any young lady making her debut into Society.

"If he's that desperate to avoid you," Hero said to

Sebastian as their carriage joined the crush of fashionable vehicles making their way toward the Lievens' town house, "maybe he won't be there."

"His daughter is making her come out this Season. He'll be there."

Chapter 25

*H*enry Addington, First Viscount Sidmouth, stood at the edge of the crowded dance floor, an indulgent smile on his face as he watched his pretty, dark-haired daughter advancing through the movements of an energetic Scottish reel. Overhead, massive crystal chandeliers sparkled in the flickering light of a sea of candles. The air was thick with the smell of hot wax and expensive perfume and copious perspiration from the laughing, chattering, jewel-bedecked members of the ton. Sidmouth himself was looking more than a little damp.

So intent was the Home Secretary on watching his daughter's progress that he remained oblivious to Sebastian's approach until Sebastian said, "Ah; there you are."

Sidmouth gave an uncomfortable start and glanced around as if looking for someplace to hide.

"I've been wanting to speak to you," said Sebastian.

The Home Secretary's jaw sagged, his eyes bulging. "Yes, I know. But . . . *here*?"

"We could step into one of the withdrawing rooms, if you'd prefer."

"Perhaps you could come by my office tomorrow morning and—"

"No," said Sebastian.

Sidmouth cleared his throat uncomfortably. "One of the withdrawing rooms, yes." He led the way to a small alcove near the head of the stairs, then swung about to clear his throat and say in a low voice, "I'm told you're working with Bow Street to solve this ghastly murder of my poor cousin."

"I am, yes."

"We weren't close, you know," said Sidmouth. "First cousins once removed."

"But you did know him."

"Yes, of course. Just not . . . well."

"When was the last time you saw him?"

The Home Secretary blinked rapidly. "Can't really say, I'm afraid. But it's been weeks. Yes, surely weeks— if not months."

"Know anyone who might have wanted to kill him?"

Sidmouth looked shocked and vaguely offended by the suggestion. "Good gracious, no."

Sebastian studied the other man's long, pale face, with its patrician nose and incongruously heavy jaw. "I understand you know an elderly physician named Douglas Sterling."

"Sterling?" Sidmouth gave a nervous laugh. "He was an early colleague of my father. What has he to do with anything?"

"When did you last see him?"

"Good gracious; I've no idea. Why?"

Rather than answer him, Sebastian said, "Tell me about Sinclair Oliphant."

Sidmouth's face went slack. "What?"

"Why was he recalled from Jamaica?"

The Secretary drew back his shoulders and affected a haughty, ministerial air. "I'm afraid I am not at liberty to discuss Home Office affairs."

"But he was recalled."

"The decision to return to England was Lord Oliphant's own."

"That's not what I'm hearing."

Sidmouth waved one white-gloved hand in a dismissive gesture. "Rumor. Nothing but rumor."

"So you're saying your cousin had nothing to do with it?"

The Home Secretary's nostrils flared with the intensity of his indignation. "I beg your pardon?"

Sebastian met the man's angry gaze and held it. "It has occurred to you, surely, that Oliphant might be responsible for Stanley Preston's head ending up on Bloody Bridge? And that if he is, then you might be his next victim?"

Sidmouth's eyes went wide, his assumption of ministerial magnificence slipping. "Good God; you aren't seriously suggesting that *Oliphant* did that to Stanley?" Then he shook his head so vigorously he reminded Sebastian of a man coming in out of the rain. "No; I can't believe it."

"But something did happen between the two men."

"I didn't say that."

"From what I'm hearing, there were few people with whom Stanley Preston didn't quarrel at one time or another. Yet you would have me believe he never clashed with Oliphant while he was governor?"

"Yes, well . . . disputes between colonial governors and prominent local landowners are unfortunately all too frequent, you know."

"And Stanley Preston had the advantage of being first cousin—once removed—to the Home Secretary."

Rather than respond, Sidmouth kept his features composed into a politician's practiced mask.

"If I were you, I'd be very careful," said Sebastian, glancing significantly to where Sidmouth's daughter was now skipping down the line of dancers on her partner's arm.

He started to turn away, but Sidmouth's hand flashed

out, stopping him. "Surely you're not suggesting that Oliph—that someone might threaten my daughter?"

Sebastian studied the Home Secretary's twitchy, sweat-slicked face. "Look into what happened to the nuns and orphans of Santa Iria, then make up your own mind," he said, and left Sidmouth standing at the entrance to the alcove, his long, normally self-satisfied face now pale and haggard.

Hero was sipping a glass of lemonade, her gaze on Devlin's stunningly beautiful young niece, Miss Stephanie Wilcox, when a deep male voice behind her said, "Lady Devlin? It is Lady Devlin, is it not?"

She turned to find herself being addressed by a tall, fit-looking man in his forties with handsome, chiseled features, clear blue eyes, and a wide, even smile.

"I hope you'll forgive my boldness in approaching you without an introduction, but I knew your husband in the Peninsula." He swept an elegant bow. "I am Oliphant. Sinclair, Colonel Lord Oliphant."

Hero felt a hot, tingling sensation in her hands as a surge of primitive rage swept through her. For one blindingly intense moment, all she could think was that if this smiling, urbane man had had his way, Devlin would long ago have been consigned to a lonely, forgotten grave in the mountains of Portugal.

"Lord Oliphant," she said, her voice as coldly polite as her smile. "I have heard Devlin . . . speak of you."

A gleam of amusement showed in the colonel's eyes. But all he said was, "You're here without your husband?"

"Oh, no; Devlin is here." She studied Oliphant's even, patrician features, searching for some trace of the brutal, single-minded determination that could deliberately send a subordinate officer into the hands of the enemy and cause the deaths of dozens of innocent women and

children. But his mask of good humor and gentle benev-
olence was firmly in place.

He said, "I can't tell you how relieved I was to hear
that Devlin has finally settled down and married. The
responsibilities of family tend to exert such a—shall we
say—steadying influence on our wilder youths."

"Some more than others," Hero said dryly. She took
a slow sip of her lemonade. "I understand you've only
recently returned from Jamaica."

"I have, yes. It's a lovely place. Have you ever been?"

"Unfortunately, no. I've never visited any of the
islands."

"Pity. You must try to make it out there sometime.
I've no doubt you'll be charmed." He bowed again. "Do
give my regards to your husband." And he walked away,
leaving her wondering why he had approached her in
the first place.

She was still staring after him when she became aware
of Devlin coming up beside her. She could feel the aura
of lethal animosity radiating from him, see the cold,
deadly purposefulness in his face.

"What did he say?" he asked, his gaze, like hers, on
the retreating figure.

Hero shook her head. "Polite nothings. I don't understand why he bothered."

"To assess what you know. And to decide how easy
you are to intimidate."

"Unfortunately, one can't shoot a man in the middle
of a ball," said Hero. "Particularly not at one of Countess Lieven's balls. It's bad form."

Devlin smiled then, a smile that seemed to banish the
tortured memories and dark urges provoked by Oliphant's presence. But she knew they weren't really gone,
only tucked away out of sight.

Out of her sight.

She was suddenly, unnaturally aware of the roar of
well-bred voices and genteel laughter around them, of

the crush of bodies clothed in satin and silk, and the gleam of endless tiers of candles reflected in soaring, gilded mirrors. Theirs was a rarified world of manners and careful calculations ruled by the dictates of taste and fashion, a world where extremes of emotion were outré, where all was controlled and measured. An artificial hothouse where everyone pretended that civilization was more than just a thin, brittle veneer all too easily and frequently shattered.

She wanted to say, *We need to talk about this, Devlin. We can't keep shying away from acknowledging—and confronting—the darkest urges of our souls.* She wanted to tell him of her fears and share with him the tumult of feelings she could barely admit even to herself.

But as the music ended and new sets began to form for an old-fashioned court dance, what she said was, "When was the last time we danced?"

She saw the flicker of surprise in those strange yellow eyes as he turned toward her. He knew she loved to dance, but he also knew she'd been reluctant to come tonight, worried about how Simon would fare without her and anxious not to stay away too long.

"Before Christmas, at least," he said.

She smiled. "Long before Christmas."

He tipped his head to one side. "And Simon?"

"I think Claire can handle him a little longer—with the assistance, of course, of the parlor maid, the cook, Calhoun, and probably even Morey."

"Not Morey, I'm afraid. Simon's screams completely unman the poor fellow." His smiling gaze locked with hers; he swept a low, formal bow. "May I have the pleasure of this dance, my lady?"

She sank into a deep curtsy and rested her fingertips on his proffered arm. "I would be honored, my lord."

They moved into place as the music began. Together, they wove through the stately patterns of the dance, *pas simples* alternating with *pas doubles*, feet gliding, hands

touching and releasing, bodies dipping and swaying in
an age-old allegory of advance and retreat. She surrendered herself to the music and the all-too-fleeting pressure of his palm against hers.

And then the music ended and, with it, the moment.

They arrived back at Brook Street sometime later to
find a sealed billet addressed by an unfamiliar hand.
While Hero hurried upstairs to Simon, Sebastian tore
open the seal and glanced through the brief note.

> *There is something I must tell you. I shall be at*
> *home this evening, awaiting your visit.*
>
> *Sterling*

"When did this come?" he asked Morey.

"Only moments after you left, my lord. I asked the
lad who brought it if it was urgent, but he assured me
it was not."

Sebastian glanced at the clock and said, "Damn."

Chapter 26

Thursday, 25 March

*T*he next morning, Sebastian was preparing to leave for Chatham Place when an angry peal sounded at the front door.

"Who's that?" he asked, settling a length of starched cravat around his neck.

His valet—a slim, fair-haired, dapper man in his thirties named Jules Calhoun—glanced out the window. "Judging by the crest on the carriage door, I'd say it's your lordship's sister, Lady Wilcox."

Sebastian kept his attention on the delicate task of tying his cravat.

Calhoun said, "Shall I tell Morey to deny you?"

A woman's determined tread sounded on the stairs.

"I don't think Lady Wilcox intends to allow herself to be denied." Sebastian reached for his coat. "There's a hussar captain named Hugh Wyeth staying at the Shepherd's Rest in Knightsbridge. He was wounded in Spain last November and is still recuperating, although he could be exaggerating the lingering effects of his injuries for my benefit. He presents himself as genial, uncalculating, and even tempered; I'd be interested to know if he truly is."

The valet smoothed the set of the coat across Sebastian's shoulders. Calhoun was a genius at repairing the ravages that the pursuit of murderers could sometimes wreak on Sebastian's wardrobe. But he also possessed other, considerably more unusual talents that made him especially valuable to a gentleman with Sebastian's interests.

Amanda's footsteps sounded in the hall.

"If he's not," said Calhoun, "the staff at the inn should know it. I'll see what they have to say."

"I'd also be interested in learning more about his movements last Sunday. But be careful," Sebastian warned as Calhoun moved to open the door. "If Wyeth is our killer, the man is dangerous."

A roguish gleam showed in the valet's eyes. "He'll never know I've been asking about him; never you fear." He opened the door and bowed as Amanda swept past him. "Lady Wilcox."

Amanda ignored him.

"Dear Amanda," said Sebastian, reaching for his driving gloves as Calhoun quietly withdrew. "What a distinctly unfashionable hour for a social visit."

Amanda's nose quivered with the intensity of her dislike. "This isn't a social visit."

The eldest of four children born to the Countess of Hendon, Amanda was twelve years Sebastian's senior. She'd been blessed with their mother's slim, elegant figure and glorious golden hair. But she had inherited the Earl's rather blunt features instead of the Countess's famous beauty, and a lifetime of angry resentment had by now etched a permanently sour expression on her face.

"You're at it again, I hear," she snapped. "Dabbling in a murder investigation like some common Bow Street Runner."

"I don't know if I'd use the word 'dabbling,' exactly."

"You know this is the beginning of Stephanie's second season, yet you accost the Home Secretary in the middle of Countess Lieven's ball? *Countess Lieven*, of all people? One might almost suspect you of deliberately attempting to ruin my daughter's chances of securing an advantageous alliance."

Sebastian studied his half sister's haughty, angry face. She had never made a secret of her dislike of him, even when they were children. But it was only recently that he'd come to understand why.

Had she been born male, the title of Viscount Devlin, heir to all the Earl of Hendon's vast estates, would have been hers. But because she was a girl, that coveted position had gone instead to Hendon's firstborn son, Richard. After Richard's death, Hendon's second son, Cecil, had become Viscount Devlin. And with Cecil's death, the mantle had passed to Sebastian—the boy child who was not even Hendon's own son, but a by-blow produced by an illicit liaison between the Earl's lovely Countess and some nameless, unknown lover.

"As it happens, I like Stephanie," said Sebastian, drawing on his gloves.

"Then one can only assume you are doing this in some vicious attempt to harm me."

The extent of his sister's capacity for self-absorption still had the power to stun him, even after all these years. "Actually, Amanda, I am 'doing this' because somewhere out there, walking the same streets as you and I, is a very brutal, dangerous killer."

"You are Viscount Devlin," she said through gritted teeth. "However unfit you may be to occupy such an exalted station, it is nonetheless yours, and one might hope you would at least attempt to exert yourself to behave accordingly."

He flexed his hands in the tight leather gloves, then reached for his high-crowned hat. "You could try consoling yourself with the thought that I am not being paid for my efforts, so at least our exalted name remains unsullied by the stench of trade."

A flare of raw hatred glittered in the depths of her eyes—those blue St. Cyr eyes that were so unlike Sebastian's own yellow ones. "I should have known better than to try to talk to you," she said.

"Yes, you really should have." He glanced at the mantel clock. "And now you must excuse me, Amanda. I've someone to meet."

"You still intend to continue this nonsense? Despite everything I've said?"

"Yes."

"You bastard."

"Yes," he said again, and watched her sweep from the room.

⁕

Dr. Douglas Sterling's rooms lay on the second floor of a late-eighteenth-century brick building near the northwestern corner of Chatham Place. The address was not fashionable, but it was respectable, the street door shiny with a fresh coat of green paint, the banister of the grand staircase fragrant with beeswax, the carpet underfoot worn but not threadbare. Sebastian could hear a woman singing sweetly in the rooms overhead. But when he reached the upper corridor and rapped on Sterling's door, the knock went unanswered.

He had already checked the physician's favorite coffeehouse across the place, only to be told that the old man had yet to put in an appearance.

"Ain't like him not to be here," the coffeehouse owner had said in response to Sebastian's inquiries. "In fact, I was about to send one of my lads over to check and see if he's all right. He's always here five minutes after I open, every morning. You could set your watch by him, you could."

Sebastian knocked again at the old doctor's door, aware of a rising sense of disquiet.

"Dr. Sterling?" he called.

An eerie, oppressive stillness hung in the air. Even the singing woman upstairs had quieted.

Sebastian tried the knob and felt it turn in his hand. Hesitating, he reached for the dagger he kept in his boot, then slowly pushed open the door.

The panel creaked inward on its hinges, revealing a room still in heavy shadow and crowded with furniture, as if the resident had moved here from more expansive quarters yet been loath to part with any of his belongings.

"Dr. Sterling?" he called again, even though the silence in the rooms was absolute, the drapes at the front windows overlooking the square still drawn tight.

He could feel his breath quickening and his pulse pounding as his eyes adjusted quickly to the darkness. He threaded his way through the crowded furniture toward the inner room. "Dr. Sterling?"

The old physician lay sprawled just inside the doorway to the bedroom, his back a ripped, bloody mess, his hands curled up as if he'd been reaching for something as he fell. His old-fashioned powdered wig lay near one shoulder. But his neck ended in a raw, pulpy mess of flesh and bone and sinew.

"Jesus Christ," whispered Sebastian, the gorge rising in his throat as his gaze followed a trail of blood to the bed.

Nestled amidst the pillows, Douglas Sterling's bald head stared back at him with wide, sightless eyes.

"Damn," said Sebastian, wiping the back of one hand across his mouth.

Damn, damn, damn.

"It doesn't make any sense," said Lovejoy, staring down at the aged physician's bloody body.

"No," agreed Sebastian.

Lovejoy rubbed his eyes with one thumb and forefinger and sighed. "When you spoke with him yesterday, he gave no hint of the purpose of his meeting with Stanley Preston last Sunday?"

"None. But something must have happened to frighten him—or at least make him reconsider his silence—because he sent a message last night asking to see me. Unfortunately, it was nearly midnight by the time I received it."

Lovejoy blew out a long, troubled breath. "I wonder what he knew."

Sebastian shook his head. He could see no obvious connection between Sterling and the various individuals he'd come to suspect of involvement in Preston's murder.

"Have you ever heard of a man named Diggory Flynn?" asked Sebastian.

The magistrate looked over at him. "No. Who is he?"

"That's what I'd like to know. He was following me in Houndsditch yesterday. And he may well be the same man Lady Devlin noticed watching her earlier."

Lovejoy frowned. "Lady Devlin? Good heavens. I'll set some of the lads to looking into him. Diggory Flynn, you say?"

"Yes."

"You think he's involved in all this?"

"He might well be."

Lovejoy watched the men from the deadhouse shift Sterling's headless corpse onto the shell they would use to carry the murdered man to Paul Gibson's surgery. "I wonder how long the poor fellow's been dead."

"Some hours, I'd say. Probably since last night."

Lovejoy turned to survey the overcrowded rooms. "No sign of a struggle or forced entry that I can see."

"No. Which suggests he knew his killer. Let him in, then realized his mistake too late and turned to run."

"And was stabbed in the back?"

Sebastian nodded. "Multiple times."

They watched as one of the men from the deadhouse carefully lifted the doctor's head from the pillows and rested it atop his torso.

"Let's hope he was dead before that was done to him," said Lovejoy, pressing his folded handkerchief to his lips. "What I don't understand is . . . *why*. Why cut off their heads?"

"I suspect if we can figure that out, it will tell us who the killer is."

"Perhaps," said Lovejoy, although he didn't sound convinced.

Chapter 27

"*D*r. Sterling? *Dead?*" Anne Preston stared at Sebastian with parted lips, her nostrils pinched, her eyes wide with horror. If it was an act, it was a good one.

He had come upon her walking in the weak, fitful sunshine in her garden, a shawl wrapped around her shoulders and her head bowed as if she were lost in thought.

"I'm sorry," said Sebastian. "Would you like to sit?"

"No," she said, although he noticed the hand holding her shawl clenched into a tight fist, and her chest rose and fell jerkily with her agitated breathing. "He didn't die naturally of old age, did he? Tell me truthfully," she added when Sebastian hesitated.

"No."

She swallowed, hard. "Did the killer cut off his head too?"

When Sebastian remained silent, she let out a soft moan and whispered, "Oh, dear God; he did, didn't he?"

"Are you certain you wouldn't like to sit?" said Sebastian.

She shook her head fiercely.

"At least he died quickly," said Sebastian, although

the truth was, he had no idea how long the aged physician had taken to die. The answer to that question would presumably come from Paul Gibson's postmortem.

They turned to walk together along a sunken, mossy brick path, the hem of her mourning gown brushing the plantings of lavender and rosemary beside them.

"He was a good man," she said, her voice quivering. "I know he could seem cranky and irascible and opinionated. But beneath it all he was gentle and caring and . . . harmless. Why would anyone want to kill him?"

"Did you see him last Sunday when he came to visit your father?"

"Only as he was leaving."

"Do you know why he came?"

"No." She kept her gaze fixed on the weathered wooden gazebo at the end of the path. "I asked Father if he was ill, but he said no. He said Dr. Sterling had only stopped by to talk about old times."

"How did your father seem after the physician left?"

She looked over at him, her brows pinched together with confusion. "I'm sorry; I don't understand."

"Was he pleased to have visited with an old acquaintance? Or upset—perhaps even angry?"

She stared out over the ancient garden toward the new row houses of Sloane Street. "He did seem a bit . . . preoccupied. Even a bit angry. But I don't know why."

"He didn't say anything—anything at all—that might indicate what the two men discussed?"

"No. But it was shortly after that he called for a hackney and went off for a few hours."

"Did he do that often? Call for a hackney, I mean, rather than take his own carriage."

"Sometimes, yes. Often, he'd simply walk into the City, if the weather wasn't too bad."

"He liked to walk?"

"Yes."

"Did he often walk at night?"

"Oh, no; only as far as his pub." A faint smile touched her lips, then faded into something sad and painful. "He was accosted by footpads once as a young man. And while London is considerably safer these days than it was in the last century, he still worried."

It fit with what Knightly had told him. But it made Preston's behavior that fatal night all the more troublesome. "You still can't think of why he might have gone to Bloody Bridge that night?"

"No. I'm sorry."

"Had he said anything to you about his plans to purchase several new items for his collection? Some Stuart relics?"

"No." They'd reached the gazebo at the end of the path, and she turned toward him. "I've had the constables here again, asking about Captain Wyeth. They think Hugh did it, don't they? They think he killed my father."

"They certainly consider him a strong suspect, I'm afraid."

"But I told you, Hugh would never have killed Father! Never."

"Yet they did quarrel."

She sucked in a quick breath. "Hugh told you about that, did he?"

"Yes."

A faint hint of color touched her cheeks. "I . . . I'm sorry I tried to deceive you."

She certainly looked contrite. Yet would she have admitted the deception had she not realized he'd learned the truth?

He doubted it.

He said, "Captain Wyeth also told me that you and he are considerably more than friends."

Her chin came up before she could stop it, and Sebastian knew he'd read her right. She said, "We are, yes.

But Father didn't know that." She gazed at him with wide, still eyes, as if she could somehow will Sebastian into believing her. "I swear it."

He raised one eyebrow in polite incredulity. "You 'swear' it, Miss Preston?"

To his surprise, her lips trembled, and she turned away from him, her eyes blinking rapidly, one fist coming up to press against her mouth.

"Oh, *God*!" she said with a desperation he suspected was all too real. "You must believe me! Hugh did not do this!"

"It might be easier to believe you if you tried being a tad more honest."

She looked at him over her shoulder, eyes swimming with unshed tears. "I'm sorry! It's just . . . I'm terrified Hugh is going to hang for this. And he didn't do it!"

So certain? thought Sebastian. But all he said was, "I'm told your father swore he'd disinherit you if you married Captain Wyeth. Did he issue that threat to you?"

"He did. And I told him I didn't care. I told him there's more to life than wealth and a family's position in society."

"What was his response?"

Her eyes flashed with remembered wrath and indignation. "He said I was too young to know what I was talking about."

"When was this?"

She wiped the heel of her hand across her wet eyes. "Saturday evening."

"And then what happened?"

"He . . . left."

"Is that when he went to confront Captain Wyeth?"

She nodded. "But Hugh didn't kill him. You must believe me." She sniffed rather loudly. "Hugh told you about Father's quarrel with Basil Thistlewood over the Duke of Suffolk's head, didn't he?"

"He did, yes."

"Did you speak to Thistlewood?"

"I did."

"And?"

"He says he didn't kill your father."

"Well, he would say that, wouldn't he?" She leaned toward him earnestly. "It was not their first confrontation, you know. About a month or so ago, Thistlewood acquired a rosary supposedly made from some old saint's bones. He was extraordinarily proud of it. Only, when Father inspected it, he challenged its authenticity. Thistlewood was furious—beyond furious. Swore if he heard Papa was going around telling people the thing was a fake, he'd kill him."

"You mean the St. Anthony of Padua rosary Thistlewood has on display?"

"Yes; that's it."

"And what was your father's reaction?"

"He laughed in Thistlewood's face."

"Yet this was, as you said, a month ago."

"Yes. But don't you see? If Thistlewood was already furious with Father because of the rosary and then realized Father had bested him over Suffolk's head, it might well have driven him to murder."

"Perhaps. Only, what possible reason would Thistlewood have to kill Dr. Douglas Sterling?"

She stared at him. It was obvious the question hadn't occurred to her. "I don't know! But Hugh had no reason to kill Dr. Sterling either."

"So who did have a reason to kill both men?"

She pushed the short curls away from her forehead in an exasperated gesture. "I don't know!"

Sebastian studied her pale, strained face, with its small, delicately molded nose and trembling mouth, and he knew an upsurge of frustration and irritation mingled with no small measure of sympathy.

Anne Preston was so desperate to convince him—and Bow Street—that Captain Hugh Wyeth did not kill her father, she'd say anything.

The problem was, Sebastian suspected she was even more desperate to convince herself.

Chapter 28

Sebastian knew he could in all likelihood discount the vast majority of what Anne Preston had told him. But on the off chance there was something to her accusations, he decided to pay another visit to Basil Thistlewood.

He found the curiosity collector in a lean-to workshop attached to the rear of his Cheyne Walk establishment, a leather apron tied over his old-fashioned clothes. A half-constructed display case stood on the workbench before him.

"Thought you'd be back," said Thistlewood, looking up for only a moment before returning to his task.

Sebastian let his gaze wander around the surprisingly tidy space, with its rows of well-oiled tools and neat stacks of fine wood. "Oh? Why's that?"

"Ain't found Preston's killer, have you?"

"No," said Sebastian, leaning one shoulder against the doorframe. "You didn't tell me you had another conflict with the man just a few weeks ago."

Basil Thistlewood kept his focus on the thin strip of wood he was measuring. "You'd be hard-pressed to find anyone hereabouts that Preston didn't have more than one run-in with. The man was opinionated and quick to take offense."

Sebastian found himself smiling. In his observation, the description could be applied to Thistlewood as easily as Preston. "Tell me about the rosary."

Thistlewood grunted and walked over to select another length of wood from his stack. "Always trying to show off, he was. Acting like he was the big expert because he went to Cambridge and I didn't. I weren't born yesterday, you know. Grew up in the business, I did."

"Preston questioned the rosary's authenticity?"

"He did. 'Cept he only decided it was questionable after I refused to sell it to him. If it weren't authentic, then why'd he want to buy it from me? You answer me that."

"I understand you were rather upset by his claims."

"Course I was. Who wouldn't be? Questioning my judgment and knowledge like that? Cast aspersions on the authenticity of everything in my collection, it did."

"Did it?"

"Of course it did!" Thistlewood pointed one end of the narrow strip of wood at Sebastian. "I can tell you right now, there's more than a thing or two in *his* collection that I wouldn't have in *mine*. Do you have any idea how many folks have stirrups said to have been used by Richard III at Bosworth Field? The man would've needed to be an octopus to have used half of them."

"Did you tell Preston that?"

"I did."

"And?"

"That's when he turned ugly. Called me an impudent jackanapes, like he was some high 'n' mighty lord of the manor, and me no more than a medieval serf tilling his lordship's fields."

"And?"

"I told him—" Thistlewood broke off, his jaw sagging

open in a ludicrous expression as he realized once again where his runaway mouth was leading him. He swallowed, his Adam's apple bobbing visibly up and down, and said more calmly, "A man says things sometimes in the heat of the moment he don't mean."

"Things like, 'I could kill you'?"

"I may've said some such thing. Can't rightly recall it now."

"No?"

"No."

"Ever hear of a man named Douglas Sterling?"

The sudden shift in topic seemed to confuse the coffee shop owner. "Who?"

"Dr. Douglas Sterling."

"Can't say I have. Who's he?"

"An aged physician who lived in Chatham Place. Someone killed him last night. Cut off his head."

Thistlewood carefully set down his strip of wood with a hand that was suddenly far from steady. "An old man, you say? Why would someone want to kill him?"

"Perhaps because he met with Stanley Preston less than twelve hours before Preston was killed."

"And now he's dead too?"

"Yes."

Thistlewood shook his head. "Worrisome, ain't it?"

Sebastian studied the curiosity collector's mobile, almost comical face. "Have you heard about the recent discovery out at St. George's, Windsor Castle?"

"No." An eager gleam crept into Thistlewood's watery eyes. "Has there been some new find?"

"There has. Although I'm afraid I'm not at liberty to go into the details."

Thistlewood nodded. "Heard they've been doing some digging in the crypt. Not surprised they run into something. When they was doing some work a few years back, they found a woman and child wrapped in lead. Obviously wellborn, they were, though nobody ever did figure out who they were. I got a look at 'em, and if you ask me, they dated back to Saxon times—maybe even late Roman. Wouldn't surprise me if there was an older church on that very site."

"How did you happen to get a look at them?" asked Sebastian.

Thistlewood gave a sly smile and winked. "Knows folks, I do."

"Ever hear of a man named Diggory Flynn?"

"Don't think so, no. He dead too?"

"Not to my knowledge. He followed me yesterday evening, after I'd paid a visit to Priss Mulligan's shop in Houndsditch."

Thistlewood made a sucking sound with his tongue against the back of his teeth. "Told you she weren't somebody you wanted to cross."

"She claimed she hadn't seen Stanley Preston for a month or more."

"Huh. She lies for a living, that woman; don't ever forget it. She got a new shipment in just last week, she did. And Preston was always one of the first she let know about it."

"A new shipment from the Continent, you mean?"

"Aye. Told you she was in thick with smugglers, didn't I?"

"So you did." Sebastian touched his hand to his hat. "You've been very helpful."

The curiosity collector's wrinkled face broke into a wide smile. "I try. I do try."

Sebastian stood beside the Thames, his gaze on the swollen brown waters of the river spreading out before him. The newly budding elms that edged Cheyne Walk cast dappled patterns of light and shadow across the greening grass, and the strengthening spring sun felt warm on his shoulders. But the air was cold and damp.

Have I seen you before? Priss Mulligan had said. *You look more'n a bit like that rifleman keeps a tavern just off Bishopsgate. Got those same nasty yellow eyes, he does.*

Sebastian was only too familiar with Jamie Knox, a onetime rifleman who owned the Black Devil near St. Helen's, Bishopsgate. The resemblance between the two men—one an earl's heir, the other the son of a Shropshire barmaid—was as uncanny as it was inexplicable.

Those unfamiliar with the Earl of Hendon might simply assume that Knox must be one of the earl's by-blows. But Sebastian knew better. Knew that Knox was no more Hendon's son than was Sebastian himself.

He narrowed his eyes against the fitful sunlight glinting off the water, felt the breeze off the river, icy against his face. He didn't want to reopen the old wounds, didn't want to confront the unanswered questions associated with the mysterious rifleman. But the ties between Jamie Knox and the world of smuggling were murky but indisputable.

It was past time to pay a visit to the Black Devil.

Chapter 29

The Black Devil stood in a narrow cobbled lane just off Bishopsgate, not far, Sebastian realized, from the Houndsditch shop of Priss Mulligan. Popular with the area's tradesmen and apprentices, it had half-timbered walls, twisted brick chimneys, and a high-gabled roof that marked it as a relic of a bygone era.

He paused for a moment on the far side of the lane, his gaze traveling over the tavern's ancient, diamond-paned windows and the cracked wooden sign depicting a horned black devil dancing against the flames of hell. Then he crossed the street to push open the taproom door.

The interior of the tavern was as little altered as the exterior, its low ceiling supported by dark, heavy beams, its sunken flagged floor strewn with sawdust to absorb spills, the oak-paneled walls blackened by centuries of smoke from the vast stone hearth. The air was thick with the smell of tobacco and ale and workingmen's sweat.

"You," said the lovely dark-haired young barmaid, her exotic, almond-shaped eyes narrowed with animosity as she watched him walk up to her.

"Yes, me," Sebastian said cheerfully, resting one

forearm along the bar's scarred surface as he surveyed the crowded room. Jamie Knox was nowhere in sight. "Where is he?"

"What you want with him? You're trouble, you are. I knowed it from the first time I seen you. You want a pint, I'll give you a pint. Otherwise, why don't you jist take yourself off?"

Sebastian turned his head to meet her angry gaze. "I'll take a pint."

"Make that two pints, Pippa," said Jamie Knox. "And bring them back here, if you will."

Sebastian shifted to find the tavern owner leaning against the doorframe of a small back room that served as a kind of office. He was built tall and leanly muscled, taller even than Sebastian, with hair of a slightly darker shade. But the high-boned cheeks and gently curving lips were eerily the same as Sebastian's, as were the strange yellow eyes.

Like the devil who danced on the tavern's painted sign, he was dressed all in black—black coat and trousers, black waistcoat, black cravat; only his shirt was white. His origins were as murky as his history. The son of a poor, unmarried barmaid, Knox claimed not to know the identity of his father. Once, he'd been a rifleman with the 145th, a man famed for his eerily keen eyesight and animal-like hearing and quick reflexes. Discharged when his unit was reduced after the disaster at Corunna, he'd returned to England, some said to take to the High Toby as a highwayman . . . although there were also those who whispered he'd acquired the Black Devil simply by murdering its previous owner.

The two men had first encountered each other some months before. They had never directly addressed the startling and inexplicable physical resemblance between them, never openly speculated on its possible causes or implications. But the awareness of it was always there, for both men a source of antagonism and an unwanted but undeniable bond.

For Sebastian, it was an unwelcome reminder of a painful truth about his own paternity that had come close to destroying him. Yet it was also, beguilingly, a tantalizing clue to the identity of the unknown man who had bequeathed to him the same golden eyes and uncanny, wolflike senses that Knox possessed.

And Knox himself? Not for the first time, Sebastian found himself wondering how the rifleman viewed the unknown relationship between them.

For one long moment the two men stared at each other. Then Sebastian pushed away from the bar and walked toward the man who might—or might not—be his half brother.

Knox stepped back to allow Sebastian to enter the room. "What do you want?" he asked without preamble.

"How do you know I'm not simply thirsty?"

Knox grunted. "Last I heard, there was no shortage of taverns in the East End."

Sebastian went to stand at the small window overlooking the rear court. The tavern backed up against the wall of St. Helen's churchyard, so that from here he could see the tops of the weathered gray tombs and the winter-bared branches of the elms standing stark against the sky. He said, "It's a melancholy view. I can see it bothering some—such a constant reminder of death."

"Pippa doesn't care for it, that's for sure."

Sebastian turned to look at him. "And you?"

Knox shrugged. "I've seen enough death in my life; I don't need to look out the window to be reminded that life is short and uncertain."

"Shorter for some than others."

"True."

Sebastian leaned back against the windowsill. "There's

a secondhand dealer in Houndsditch named Priss Mulligan. Deals in rare historical objects. I understand you know her."

Knox reached for a clay pipe and began to fill the bowl with tobacco. "Let's just say that I know of her. Why?"

"I'm told a fair portion of her merchandise is smuggled in from the Continent."

"There's heaps of smugglers working the Channel these days," said Knox without looking up from his task.

"I hear she received a new shipment last week. Is that true?"

Knox thrust a taper into the fire on the hearth and watched the end flare. "I didn't have anything to do with it, if that's what you're asking."

"But the shipment did arrive?"

"So I hear." He held the taper to his pipe and sucked on it for a moment before looking up. "I don't do business with the woman myself."

"Any particular reason?"

"The same reason I make it a practice to avoid rabid dogs and vipers' nests."

"She's dangerous?"

Knox blew out a long stream of tobacco smoke. "I think the word you're looking for is 'deadly.' "

The two men's gazes met and held, then broke toward the door as Pippa came in carrying foaming pints of ale. Without even looking at Sebastian, she slammed the tankards down on the simple gateleg table near the window, then left after throwing Knox a long, pregnant glare.

Knox said, "I hear you've had a son. A future Earl of Hendon."

"Yes."

"Congratulations."

"Thank you."

"And yet you're still chasing after murderers?"

"How do you know I'm investigating a murder?"

A gleam of amusement showed in the eyes that were so much like Sebastian's own. "It's the only time you ever come here."

"Huh. Must be something about the people you know."

Knox sucked on his pipe, his lean cheeks hollowing, his expression enigmatic.

Sebastian said, "Ever hear of a man named Diggory Flynn?"

"Can't say I have. Who is he?"

"He doesn't work for Priss Mulligan?"

"Not to my knowledge. But then, I did mention I try to stay away from the woman."

"Yet she knows you."

"What makes you say that?"

"She told me I look like you."

"Ah." Knox reached for his ale and took a long, slow sip. He was silent for a moment, as if thoughtful. Then he said, "I hear someone tried to kill you the other night."

"Where'd you hear that?"

The tavern owner wiped the foam from his mouth with the back of one hand and smiled. Then the smile faded. "Does Priss Mulligan know you're looking into her?"

"She does. Why?"

"There was a smuggler named Pete Carpenter tried to cheat Priss a few years back. He had a wife and two sons. The little boys weren't more than four or five. He came home one day to find them chopped into pieces, with the bits deliberately positioned about the house—a head sitting up on the mantel, a leg on the kitchen table, a hand under the bed—that sort of thing. He never did find his wife."

Sebastian felt the tavern keeper's words wash over

him, raising the hairs at the back of his neck and sucking the moisture from his mouth as the horror of the
tale—and its implications—hit his gut. He focused his
attention on taking a long drink of his ale and swallowed, hard, before saying, "I take it you've heard about
Preston and Sterling?"

"I have." Knox drained his own tankard and set it
aside with a soft *thump.* "Some people are just flat-out
evil. Priss Mulligan is one of them. If I were you, I'd be
careful. Of yourself, and of your family."

Sebastian sat beside his library fire, a glass cradled in
one palm, his gaze on the golden-red glow of the coals
on the hearth. The house lay dark and quiet around him.

He took a sip of the brandy, felt it burn in his throat.
He was drinking too much lately and he knew it—a
slow, dangerous slide back into the self-destructive hell
that had nearly consumed him in the months after he'd
first returned to London.

The clock on the hearth chimed two and then fell
silent. In its wake, the stillness of the night felt like a
heavy presence, oppressive and soul sucking, and he was
aware of the long, grueling hours of darkness stretching
out ahead of him. He'd gone to bed with his wife; made
slow, desperate love to her, then held her in his arms as
she eased peacefully into sleep. He loved her with a
tenderness and a passion that humbled, awed, and
frightened him; he was closer to her than he had ever
been to anyone. Yet in some vital, inexplicable way he
found himself feeling more alone and disconnected than
ever. And so he'd slipped from her side to draw on his
breeches and dressing gown and come here.

He took another sip of the brandy, his unnaturally
acute hearing picking up the sound of her door opening
far above, her light footsteps on the stairs. He held him-

self very still. He did not want her to find him like this. Didn't want her to see his weakness and his fear and his uncertainty.

She came up behind him and leaned over the chair to slip her arms around his neck and rest her linked hands against his chest. "You're thinking about them, again, aren't you?" she said. "The women and children of Santa Iria."

"Yes."

"You need to stop blaming yourself. You've dedicated years to making amends for a wrong that others did. But the past is past, and nothing you can do will ever change that. You can't keep torturing yourself like this."

He tipped back his head to look up at her. Her face was golden in the firelight, the strength of her features accentuated by the shadows and framed by the heavy fall of her dark hair.

He said, "I didn't tell you everything."

She brought up a hand to run the backs of her fingers down his cheek. "I know."

In the silence that followed, he heard the fall of ash on the hearth and the endless tick of the clock. Then she came around to sit on the rug beside him and rest the side of her head against his leg.

He touched her hair, felt it slide soft and silky smooth through his fingers, and expelled his breath in a long, painful rush. "I watched the French kill them."

"You don't need to tell me."

He shook his head, kept his gaze on the fire. "I knew the French captain and his men had left their camp a good half an hour before I managed to escape. But I rode to the convent anyway. It was as if I couldn't believe that I was too late to warn them. To save them."

He felt an ache pull across his chest. "Some of the children had been playing in an orange grove at the end of the valley when the soldiers came up. The French must have galloped at them with sabers drawn, because the earth around them was trampled by the hooves of the horses. And the children . . ."

She touched his hand. "Sebastian . . ."

He swallowed, remembering how he'd stopped and knelt beside each slashed, bloodied little body. "Two of the littlest ones—a boy and a girl—couldn't have been more than five or six; big brown eyes, baby-soft light brown hair. They looked enough alike that they were probably brother and sister—maybe even twins. They were still holding hands. They must have held on to each other when the soldiers rode down on them."

"They were dead?"

"All of them."

"And the French?"

"I could hear horses neighing, men shouting, children screaming, women praying to God to save them. So I rode on. The convent was ancient, surrounded by a high sandstone wall. But the French had left the gates open. I could have ridden inside. I almost did. But at the last moment, I turned into a copse of trees at the edge of the road. I stayed there and watched them kill everything and everyone inside that convent. Babies in their cradles. Cattle. Chickens. Dogs. Everything."

"And if you had ridden in? What do you think you could have done? You'd have been killed in an instant."

"Yes. But it seemed right that I should die with them. I *wanted* to die with them."

"Oh, God, Sebastian; no."

He shook his head. "The only reason I didn't was because I knew that if I stayed alive, I could avenge them. I planned to start with Sinclair Oliphant, but by the time I made it back to headquarters, he was gone—recalled to England on the death of his brother. So I set out after the French soldiers instead. I went back to the convent and tracked the troop that had done it until they were in a vulnerable position. And then I betrayed them to the Spanish partisans. The Spaniards knew what those men had done at Santa Iria. The soldiers' deaths were not easy or quick."

"And the captain?" she asked, her voice cracking.

"I'd meant to let the partisans have him too. But when I saw him again, I couldn't stop myself. I . . . beat him to death." He realized he'd clenched his fist and forced himself to open his hand. "I tell myself he deserved to die. But what I did was little short of murder. And when it was over, I found I had no pleasure in his killing. The truth is, I live with his death and the deaths of his men as surely as I live with the deaths of the innocents of Santa Iria."

"It was war."

"No, it wasn't. It was revenge. Those women and children deserve justice. But there is no real justice in murder."

He saw her sad smile, the almost imperceptible shake of her head. She drew the line between right and wrong in a different place than he. It was one of the ways in which they differed, one of the ways in which she was very much her father's daughter.

He touched her face, ran his fingertips along the curve of her cheek. "I believe those who die violently at the hands of others deserve justice. We owe them that. The problem is, by going after ruthless men—and women—I run the risk of putting you in danger. You and Simon too."

He told her then what he'd learned from Knox, about the threat Priss Mulligan might pose to them all. He said, "Promise me you'll be careful?"

She took his hand in hers, pressed a kiss to his palm. "I knew what you did when I married you, Devlin. It's a part of who you are—a part of what I love about you. I won't try to pretend that I don't worry something might happen to you, because I do—the same way I worry about Simon catching a fever or coming down with the flux. But I refuse to be ruled by my fears." She gave him a lopsided smile. "As for Simon and me . . . we're both constantly surrounded by a small army of servants. I don't think we're exactly vulnerable."

He wanted to say, *Everyone is vulnerable.*

But some fears were best left unspoken.

Chapter 30

Friday, 26 March

*T*he next morning, Sebastian drove toward the Tower of London, to Paul Gibson's surgery.

He left Tom to water the horses at the fountain near the ancient fortress's walls and slipped through the shadowy, narrow passage that led to the unkempt yard at the rear of the Irishman's old stone house. Only, this time, in place of Gibson's throaty tenor warbling some Irish drinking song, he could hear a Frenchwoman's soft, clear voice singing, *"Madame à sa tour monte, mironton, mironton, mirontaine . . ."*

He reached the open doorway to find Alexi Sauvage bent over the naked, eviscerated body of Douglas Sterling laid out on the stone slab before her. She had a leather apron tied over her simple gown and a bloody scalpel in one hand and was singing softly to herself, *"Madame à sa tour monte si haut qu'elle peut—"*

"What are you doing here?" he demanded. He knew she had trained as a doctor in Italy, knew she must have done this sort of thing before. But finding her here was still disconcerting.

A lock of flame red hair fell across her eyes as she

looked up at him. She pushed it back with one bent wrist. "What does it look like I'm doing?"

"Where's Gibson?"

She set aside the scalpel with a clatter. She was an attractive woman, with pale, delicate skin and a high-bridged nose and brown eyes, dark now with an old hatred. Sebastian might have had a good reason for killing the man she'd once loved, but he knew she had never forgiven him for it.

"Gibson is"—she hesitated, then finished by saying— "not well today."

"Meaning what?"

"Meaning, your friend is an opium eater. How he managed to meet his responsibilities with even a semblance of normalcy before I arrived is beyond me. But I don't think he could have kept it up much longer."

Sebastian studied her set, angry face. "You said you could help him. Yet you have not done so."

She reached for a rag and wiped her hands. "As long as he suffers the phantom pains from his missing leg, he will never be able to free himself of the opium."

"You said you can help him with that too."

"Only if he allows it."

"Why would he not?"

"Perhaps you should try asking him that yourself." She picked up her scalpel again. "Although you're not likely to get a coherent response from him at the moment."

Sebastian nodded to the decapitated body between them. "What have you discovered?"

"Not much. For an old man, Douglas Sterling was as healthy as an ox. He'd likely have lived another ten or more years, if someone hadn't stabbed him in the back and cut off his head."

"In that order?"

"Yes."

"You're certain?"

"Are you suggesting I'm incompetent?"

I'm suggesting you're probably not as good at this as Gibson, he thought. But all he said was, "Is there anything that might tell us who did this?"

She gave him a tight, unpleasant smile. "I was under the impression that was your job."

Sebastian shifted his gaze to where Sterling's bloodless head rested in a basin on the shelf, and for a moment, all he could think about was the tale Knox had told him, of the smuggler who'd come home to find his wife missing and his little boys hideously dismembered.

He said, "Where's Gibson?"

She shook her head. "You don't want to see him."

"No. But I think I should."

Her gaze met his, but her eyes were hooded and he could not begin to guess at her thoughts.

Then she said, "He's in the parlor."

He found Gibson sprawled in one of the old cracked leather chairs beside the cold hearth, his coat rumpled, his cravat gone, the collar of his shirt stained with sweat. Sebastian thought his friend lost in an opium-induced stupor. Then the Irishman looked up, his eyes hazy, his smile dreamy.

"Devlin."

Sebastian walked over to pour himself a brandy, then gulped it down in one long pull.

"You're here about this latest headless fellow, I suppose." Gibson waved one hand vaguely in the direction of the yard. "Haven't started yet, I'm afraid."

Sebastian poured himself another drink. "Alexi Sauvage has almost finished the postmortem."

Something flickered across Gibson's features, then faded into bland contentment. "Has she, now? She's very clever. Wish she'd marry me. But she won't."

"She says your leg has been troubling you."

"My leg?" Gibson's fuzzy smile never slipped. "I

think about it sometimes, still over there, doubtless a bare, weathered bone by now. While I'm here. Not yet a pile of bare bones."

When Sebastian said nothing, the surgeon drew in a slow, even breath that eased out like a sigh. "It's a bit like a woman, you know. Opium, I mean. Soft. Caressing . . . Deceptive. A delightful exaltation of the spirit mingled with cloudless serenity. Truly a gift from the gods."

"That can kill," said Sebastian.

Gibson's smile grew lopsided. "The gifts of the gods are often double-edged, are they not?"

"Did you look at Sterling yourself at all?"

"Who?" said Gibson, his head lolling against the back of the chair. "Sometimes I wish I were a poet—or maybe a composer—so I could share this joy and beauty. Everything's so much clearer. Brighter. More intense. Delicious . . ."

His voice faded and his gaze grew unfocused again, his face slack.

A soft step in the passage drew Sebastian's gaze to the doorway.

"He wouldn't have wanted you to see him like this," said Alexi Sauvage, her hands cupping her bent elbows close to her body, her voice low.

Sebastian turned toward her, aware of a powerful rush of fear and guilt all twisted up into a helpless rage that somehow ended up being directed at her. "*God damn you.* Why don't you help him?"

"I told you: He won't let me."

"Why not?"

She shifted her gaze to the man now lost in a cloud of opium-hued bliss. "Fear. Embarrassment. A man's peculiar notion of pride. I don't know. You tell me; you're a man—his friend. All I know is, he can't keep going on like this. It's destroying his mind and body. *Killing* him."

"When will he be . . ."

"Normal?" She shrugged. "He'll sleep for some time now. When he wakes, he'll be listless, depressed. Nauseous. Tomorrow will be better than tonight."

Sebastian set aside his second brandy untouched. "Then I'll be back tomorrow."

Chapter 31

"What we doin' 'ere?" asked Tom as Sebastian drew his curricle to a halt at the side of the lane leading to Bloody Bridge.

The sky was light blue and marbled with ripples of white clouds, the spring air rich with the smell of freshly turned earth and budding leaves and the smoke rising from the chimneys of the nearby cottages. Sebastian handed the boy his reins. "Thinking," he said, and dropped lightly to the ground.

He could feel the drying, muddy ruts of the roadway crumble beneath his boots as he walked toward the bridge, his gaze drifting over the expanse of market and nursery gardens that stretched away to the east. The tolling bell of a small country chapel, its tower barely visible above a distant cluster of trees, was carried on the cool breeze. Frowning, he turned to look back at Sloane Square, now drenched with a rich golden sunlight.

"So whatcha thinkin'?" asked Tom, watching him.

"No one seems to be able to tell me what Stanley Preston was doing here on a rainy Sunday night."

"Some folks just like t' walk in the rain," said Tom. "Never made no sense to me, but 'tis a fact."

"True. Yet Preston was afraid of footpads, and Bloody Bridge has a decidedly nasty history."

Sebastian went to hunker down in the grassy verge where they'd found Preston's decapitated body sprawled on its back. There was no sign now that it had ever been there. He rested a forearm on one thigh. "Molly Watson from the Rose and Crown says Preston's greatcoat was open, with his pocket watch dangling on the grass beside him."

"Ye think somebody was goin' through 'is pockets, lookin' fer somethin'?"

"That's one explanation."

Tom screwed up his face in puzzlement. "There's another?"

"He was stabbed in the back, which suggests he either turned his back on his killer—obviously not a wise thing to do—or he didn't hear the killer come up behind him." Sebastian rose to his feet. "When do people typically look at their watches?"

"I don't know. Ne'er 'ad one, meself."

Sebastian found himself smiling. "Men generally check their watches when they're late for an appointment, or when someone else is late."

"So yer sayin' ye think 'e was 'ere t' meet somebody? Somebody who was late?"

"I think so, yes. And whoever it was, that person was obviously someone Preston was extraordinarily anxious to see."

"How ye know that?"

"Because Preston was afraid of Bloody Bridge at night, yet he still agreed to come here, alone, after dark."

Sebastian stared across the open green of Sloane Square toward Chelsea and the river that flowed out of sight at the base of the hill. Anyone traveling down from Windsor to deliver the stolen royal relics to Preston would in all likelihood have come by the Thames. If he landed at Cheyne Walk, he would need only to come up the short stretch of Paradise Row and skirt the shadowy gardens of Chelsea Hospital and the Royal Military Asylum in order to reach Sloane Square and—just beyond it—the quiet, deserted lane to Bloody Bridge. Above Sloane Square lay the long, straight stretch of Sloane Street and Hans Place, both well lit and heavily traveled. The kinds of places where a man might be seen—and recognized.

So Bloody Bridge was not simply out of the way and little frequented; it was essentially halfway between Alford House and the river.

Sebastian went to stand at the edge of the rivulet where he'd found the ancient inscribed length of lead strapping. He was now fairly certain that Stanley Preston had come here that night to take possession of the relics from a thief whose identity Sebastian still didn't know. Was it a trap? Possibly. If so, who had set it? Priss Mulligan? Thistlewood? Oliphant? Or had the killer simply taken advantage of Preston's unwise decision to venture alone to such a dark, out-of-the-way spot? And what about the thief? Had he arrived before or after the murder? Impossible to say. But the thief had been there; the presence of the coffin strap proved that.

So who was the thief? And where was the King's head?

"What sort of fellow arranges a meeting in a dark, out-of-the-way spot?" said Sebastian.

"Someone who don't want nobody t' see 'im!" said Tom in triumph.

Turning away from that death-haunted bridge, Sebastian went to leap up into the curricle's high seat and take the reins. "Exactly."

"Stop glowering at us, Jarvis," grumbled George, His Royal Highness the Prince of Wales, Regent of the

United Kingdom of Great Britain and Ireland. Swallowing a half-masticated mouthful of buttered crab, the Prince reached for his wineglass and drank deeply. "It's enough to give us indigestion."

They were in one of Carlton House's private withdrawing rooms, the table before the Prince spread with a feast intended to still the hunger pains that so often came upon His Highness in the midafternoon.

"Your meeting with the Russian Ambassador—" Jarvis began.

"Can be put off until tomorrow," said the Prince, negligently waving a delicate silver fork piled with more crab. "The Countess of Hertford should be here any moment. You wouldn't expect me to forgo such a treat, now, would you?" He flashed a smile that was meant to be roguish but came off simply as simpering and foolish.

He was fifty years old and grossly fat, his once handsome features coarsened by decades of dissipation and excess. But in his own mind, he was still the dashing young Prince Florizel who'd charmed the nation that now despised him for his extravagance and his irresponsibility and his breathtaking selfishness.

Jarvis kept his own features bland. One did not reach—or retain—his position of power by indulging in useless displays of annoyance and contempt. "The Ambassador has been waiting three hours."

"Then one would think he'd welcome the opportunity to go home. Tell him to come back tomorrow. And take yourself off as well, before you bring on my spasms."

Any spasms the Prince was likely to suffer would owe considerably more to the pile of crab and two bottles of burgundy he'd already consumed than to the demands of his royal responsibilities. But Jarvis bowed and said, "Yes, sir."

He'd almost reached the door when the Prince said, "Oh, and Jarvis? I trust the arrangements for the formal opening of Charles I's coffin are all in place?"

Jarvis paused. "The opening is scheduled for the first of April, the day following your aunt the Duchess's funeral."

"Excellent." George gave a wide, slightly greasy smile. "What a treat it will be."

Jarvis bowed again and withdrew.

He spent the next half hour soothing the outraged Russian Ambassador's ruffled sensibilities and averting a minor diplomatic crisis. Then, feeling in need of a good, strong drink, he returned to his own chambers to find his son-in-law, Viscount Devlin, leaning against the sill of the window overlooking the forecourt, his arms folded at his chest and his boots crossed at the ankles.

"What the devil are you doing here?" demanded Jarvis, going to pour himself a glass of brandy.

"Have your men made any progress in their efforts to track down Charles I's missing head?"

"They have not. Have you?"

"No."

Jarvis eased the stopper from the crystal decanter and poured a healthy measure into one glass. "I won't offer you a brandy since you're not staying."

The Viscount smiled. "When's the formal opening to be?"

Jarvis set aside the decanter and turned to face him, glass in hand. "Next Thursday."

"How many people know Charles's head is missing?"

"The Dean and the virger of St. George's, and the two men I've tasked with the item's recovery. Why?"

"I assume all have been sworn to secrecy?"

"Naturally."

"I plan to drive out to Windsor Castle in the morning and take a look at the royal vault. It might be helpful if you sent a message instructing the Dean and the virger to cooperate with me."

Jarvis took a long drink, then paused a moment before saying, "You've found evidence to suggest these rather macabre murders are indeed linked to the theft from the royal crypt?"

"Evidence? No."

Jarvis grunted. "I'll send the message. But you will keep me informed." It was not a question.

Devlin pushed away from the window. "Of course."

Jarvis waited until the Viscount had taken himself off. Then he rang for his clerk.

"Send Major Archer to me. Now."

Chapter 32

That evening, Sebastian and Hero were sitting down to dinner when a peal sounded at the front door.

His gaze met hers. "Expecting anyone?"

"No," she said, just as Morey appeared in the doorway with a bow.

"Lord Sidmouth to see you, my lord. I have taken the liberty of showing his lordship into the library."

⁂

Sebastian found the Home Secretary pacing back and forth before the fire, his hands clasped behind his back, his chin sunk into the folds of his snowy white cravat. He wore the silk knee breeches, white silk stockings, and buckled evening shoes of a man dressed for a formal dinner or a ball. But when he turned toward Sebastian, his face was pinched and pale.

"My lord," said Sebastian. "May I offer you some wine? A brandy?"

"Thank you, but no; I won't keep you long. My apologies for interrupting your evening."

"Please, have a seat."

Sidmouth drew up with his back to the fireplace and shook his head. "I looked into the incident in Portugal you told me about—the one involving the convent." He sucked in a quick, jerky breath. "My God. How could anyone do something like that?"

Sebastian had never had much respect for Sidmouth. He was typical of the sycophants who hung around the court: ambitious, venal, and opportunistic. Yet it said something for the man that he still recoiled in horror from an act of such calculated cynicism.

Sebastian walked over to splash brandy into two glasses and held one out to the Home Secretary, who took it without comment and downed half the contents in one long, shaky pull.

Sebastian said, "Tell me what happened between Oliphant and Stanley Preston."

Sidmouth brought up a hand to rub his eyes with one splayed thumb and forefinger. "Most colonial governors find ways to use their positions for personal gain. It's virtually expected, actually. But some . . . some go too far."

"Bribery? Corruption?"

The Home Secretary nodded and blew out a long, harsh breath. "I began hearing about the problems between James Preston—Stanley's son—and the new governor almost as soon as Oliphant arrived in Jamaica. It seemed as if every other week brought a different complaint from Stanley. For the most part I ignored them—you know what Stanley was like. But then, things became more serious. Oliphant confiscated a valuable stretch of the Prestons' largest plantation. He claimed the land was needed to build a public road, although everyone knew the road was solely for the benefit of one individual—a large landowner who paid Oliphant handsomely for his efforts."

"When was this?"

"Last spring."

Sidmouth paused to take another gulp of his brandy. "By that point we'd started receiving complaints from other prominent colonial figures. It was obvious that something needed to be done. But Oliphant has some powerful backers, which limited my ability to act. I told Stanley that if he wanted Oliphant recalled, he needed to find something else—something less personal and more injurious to the interests of the Crown."

"That's when Preston went out to Jamaica himself?"

"Yes. He was determined to dig up something he could use."

"And he found it?"

"He did. To be frank, I could scarcely believe it at first. I mean, bribery and corruption are one thing. But flouting the laws against the slave trade is something else entirely."

"You're saying Oliphant was involved in slave running?"

Sidmouth nodded. "It's become extraordinarily lucrative, now that the slave trade has been shut down."

Sebastian doubted a slave owner like Stanley Preston would have had any personal moral objections to such activities. But the discovery would have served his purposes very well.

"The evidence was damning enough that Oliphant agreed to return to London," Sidmouth was saying. "That should have satisfied Stanley—it would have any normal man. But not my cousin. He was determined to see formal charges brought against Oliphant. Except then . . ." Sidmouth's voice trailed off.

"Yes?" prompted Sebastian.

"Last Saturday—the day before Stanley was killed— I ran into him in St. James's Street. Frankly, I was rather chagrined to see him, since he'd taken to seizing every opportunity—however inappropriate—to pester me about Oliphant. But to my surprise, he said he was dropping the entire affair. I was stunned."

"Did he say why?"

"No. But he was behaving most peculiarly—very unlike himself."

"In what sense?"

"I think he was frightened. Which puzzled me, because Stanley Preston was not a man who frightened easily. But he was afraid that day, and I think he was afraid of Lord Oliphant."

Sebastian studied the Home Secretary's strained features. "Have you ever heard of a man named Diggory Flynn?"

"Who?"

"Diggory Flynn—a rather disheveled individual with an oddly lopsided face. I could be wrong, but I believe he works for Sinclair Oliphant."

Sidmouth's heavy jaw went oddly slack. "A lopsided face, you say?"

"That's right. Have you seen him?"

"No." Sidmouth shook his head. "No. No."

But Sebastian noticed his hand was far from steady as he brought his brandy to his lips and drained the glass.

※

Sinclair, Lord Oliphant, was standing beside the E.O. table in a gaming hell near Portland Square when Sebastian came up to him.

"We need to talk," said Sebastian. "Walk outside with me for a moment."

Oliphant kept his gaze on the spinning ball before him. "I think not. Whatever you have to say to me can be said here."

"You might change your mind when you hear that the topic of conversation is slave running." The E.O. ball fell into one of the bar slots, and Sebastian said, "You lose anyway."

"Actually, I've yet to place a bet." Oliphant's habitual,

faint smile never slipped. But his blue eyes narrowed and hardened, and he turned to walk out of the gaming hell's dim, smoky atmosphere into the startlingly clear, crisp night.

"Now, what is this about?" he demanded as they descended the front steps.

"I've just been listening to an interesting tale—about how you used your position as governor of Jamaica to cheat Stanley Preston out of a valuable section of his land. He swore to make you pay, and he did—by discovering that in addition to the usual bribery and corruption so common amongst Britain's colonial governors, you were also dabbling in the slave trade."

"The accusations were baseless," Oliphant said calmly as the two men turned their steps toward the square, "which is why no charges were ever filed."

"Yet you did return to London."

Oliphant shrugged. "The islands have a certain appeal, I'll not deny. But after a time, ennui sets in. I was more than ready to return to England."

"And Preston had nothing to do with it? Is that what you're saying?"

"That's right."

Sebastian shook his head. "I think Preston wasn't content with having you quietly removed from the governorship. I think he was determined to see you publicly disgraced, and that's why you killed him."

Oliphant gave a brittle laugh and swung to face him. "Do you seriously think I would allow some upstart merchant's grandson to drive me from a post I wished to retain? Me? An Oliphant of Calgary Hall? Hardly. I tell you, the charges were unproven."

"Perhaps. Yet Preston could conceivably have found the proof he needed to make them stick."

"I'm afraid your information is sadly inaccurate, Devlin. Stanley Preston and I had a nice little chat the Friday before he died. And the very next day, he formally retracted his allegations."

"Threatened him, did you? With what? Did you suggest that something vile might befall his daughter, if he continued?"

"Does it matter? The point is, I had no reason to kill him. In fact, I had every reason not to—particularly in such a spectacularly gruesome fashion that could only serve to attract attention to the very falsehoods I wished to quiet."

"He could have changed his mind."

Oliphant gave a low laugh. "The man wasn't that stupid." He started to brush past Sebastian, heading back toward the gaming house.

"Tell me about Diggory Flynn," said Sebastian.

Oliphant hesitated for the briefest instant—so briefly that Sebastian afterward wondered if he might have imagined it. Then he quickly mounted the steps, rapped sharply on the gaming house door, and disappeared inside.

※

That night, Sebastian dreamt of blood-soaked orange blossoms and a laughing man with mismatched eyes in a strangely lopsided face.

He left his bed just before dawn, when the air was tangy and crisp, the dark streets below empty and quiet. He was standing at the window and watching the first hint of light spread across the sky when Hero came to wrap her arms around his waist and press her warm, soft body against his naked back.

She said, "Troublesome dreams?"

He rested his hands on hers. "Yes."

She laid her cheek against his shoulder. "I owe you an apology. I thought you were wrong, you know—that you were allowing your own past with Oliphant to influence your thinking about Stanley Preston's killer. But revenge and fear are powerful motives, and Oliphant obviously possessed both."

Sebastian kept his gaze on the lightening sky above the rooftops. "I could still be wrong. Sometimes I think I keep trying to prove that Oliphant is the murderer just so that I can kill him." He paused as a chorus of morning birdsong filled the air, sweet and bright and achingly clear. "But I'm still missing something—something vitally important. And I'm afraid more people are going to die because of it."

"Perhaps you'll find some hint of what it is at Windsor this morning," she said.

"Perhaps," he said, and turned to take her in his arms.

Chapter 33

Sebastian reached Windsor shortly before ten that morning.

The sky was a limpid blue filled with clusters of white clouds that turned the castle's soaring sandstone walls and towers by turns moody and golden in the fitful spring sunshine. The black-cassocked man who hurried out into the lower court to meet his curricle was tall and rail thin, with greasy, limp hair and an extraordinarily large, toothy mouth. "Lord Devlin!" he exclaimed, bowing nearly double. "This is an honor—truly an honor. Allow me to introduce myself: Rowan Toop, my lord, virger of St. George's. Unfortunately, the Dean had a previous engagement this morning that will preclude him from meeting with you. But he sends his regrets and has instructed me to cooperate with you in every way possible." He laced his long, bony fingers together and rested them against the front of his cassock, his face frozen in an eager grin that was wide enough to look almost painful.

"I understand the burial of the dead is under your charge," said Sebastian, dropping lightly to the ground. He exchanged a meaningful look with Tom, who nodded almost imperceptibly before driving off toward the stables.

Toop's grin faltered. "It is, yes, to be sure, to be sure." He bowed again. "The Dean tells me you'd like to view the newly discovered royal burial chamber."

"That would be helpful, yes."

The virger extended a hand toward St. George's ancient, soot-stained facade. "If you will come this way, my lord?"

They climbed the steps to the grand royal chapel and pushed open one of the heavy, weathered west doors. The soaring, stone-vaulted nave lay hushed and empty in a rich, colorful light that poured in through the high rows of stained-glass windows above.

"I fear this theft has been a shock to Dean Legge. A terrible shock," said Toop as he paused in the narthex to light a simple horn lantern he then carried with them to the padlocked gate in the quire. Setting down the lantern, he fished a large iron key from the depths of his cassock and held it up as if for Sebastian's inspection. "Had this gate specially installed, he did—not that it did much good, unfortunately."

Sebastian studied the stout iron bars and padlocked heavy chain. "When exactly was it installed?"

"Ordered it put in just after Lord Jarvis's first inspection of the tomb, he did."

"Immediately after?"

Toop frowned as he carefully fitted the key into the lock. "Well, we had to have the gate made, of course. So it was a day or two before it was actually in place. That must've been when the thieves struck."

"Thieves? What makes you think there were more than one?"

"Just assumed it, I suppose."

"Did anyone check Charles's coffin at the time of the gate's installation?"

"Well, no. Why would we? I mean, Lord Jarvis left

strict instructions that nothing was to be disturbed again until the Prince Regent's formal examination of the remains. And since we'd replaced the black velvet pall, it would have been impossible to see that the coffin had been tampered with even if we had chanced to look into the vault again—which I don't believe anyone actually did. His lordship is not one you care to cross."

The padlock clicked open, the clanking of the chain sounding unnaturally loud in the stillness of the deserted quire as Toop unwound it from around the bars and swung the gate wide. "If you'll allow me to go first, my lord," he said, reaching for the lantern, "I'll be able to light the way for you. It's rather dark down there."

"Who do you think stole the King's head?" Sebastian asked as he followed the virger down a narrow, sloping passageway, the light from the horn lantern bouncing and swaying over the rough walls.

"Me?" Toop twisted around to stare back at Sebastian with wide, bloodshot eyes. "Good heavens; I can't imagine. We must always be careful with new burials on account of the resurrection men. But no surgeon is going to want a head that's more than a hundred and fifty years old, now, is he? I mean, what could he do with it? I can't imagine who'd want such a thing."

"A collector?" suggested Sebastian.

Toop's large mouth twisted into an exaggerated grimace. "He'd need to be powerfully queer, if you ask me."

"There are those for whom royalty exudes an extraordinary fascination. And there's something about the Stuarts that many find particularly compelling."

The virger sniffed. "I've dealt with the dead for more than twenty years now, from the freshest corpses to musty, thousand-year-old bones. But I certainly wouldn't want some rotting head sitting around my house, king or no king. It's not healthy. It's not right. It's not . . . normal."

They drew up before a rough, man-sized opening in

the passage's wall. "Ah, here it is," he said, stepping back as he held the lantern high. "After you, my lord."

Stooping low, Sebastian entered a barrel-roofed vault lined with unfaced bricks and scarcely wide enough to hold the three caskets that rested on its damp, bare floor. A dusty black velvet pall shrouded the coffin to his left, although the other two were uncovered. The smallest coffin, against the far wall, looked intact. But the largest of the three—well over six feet in length and obviously made broad enough to accommodate a man of enormous proportions—was so shattered that fragments of bone and shreds of discolored, decaying shroud showed clearly through the broken sides and top.

"Any indication that the other two coffins were also disturbed?" asked Sebastian.

Rowan Toop ducked in behind him, the soft glow from his lantern sending their shadows ranging long and distorted across the ceiling and far wall. "Oh, no, my lord. Jane Seymour is still sealed up as tight as you could wish, while old Henry here looked like this when we found him. It was the gasses from his bloated, putrefying body started it, you know—burst the coffin open even before he was laid to rest. His corpse lay for the night in the chapel of Syon Abbey while on its way here for burial, and when they went to collect him in the morning, they discovered the coffin had exploded. Dogs were feasting on the royal remains."

"Divine retribution for the dissolution of the abbeys?"

Rowan Toop gave another of his odd, almost comical grimaces. "Well, that's what they said at the time. Course, I suspect it was only made worse when they stuck Charles in here." Toop lowered his voice to a stage whisper. "Dropped the one king on the other, if you ask me."

"What about the other royal vaults? Have they also been targeted by thieves?"

"Oh, no, my lord. We've checked, and all are secure."

Sebastian let his gaze wander around the crude, low-ceilinged crypt. "Seems an uncharacteristically humble place for a king like Henry VIII to have chosen to rest for eternity."

"Yes, but he didn't choose it, you see. He'd planned a magnificent tomb with white marble pillars and gilded angels and a life-sized equestrian statue of himself beneath a triumphal arch. Except that he didn't like to think about his own death, so only parts of it were finished by the time he went. Both he and Jane were supposed to be in here only temporarily, while the grand tomb was built. But none of his three children ever got around to completing it, and in the end, even those bits that were finished were scattered. They say the bronze effigies of Henry and Jane were melted down during the Civil War. His grand black sarcophagus is now in the crypt of St. Paul's cathedral, with Horatio Nelson inside it."

"At least it was finally put to use."

"True, true."

Sebastian brought his gaze back to the timeworn black pall that draped the simple coffin of the murdered King.

Toop cleared his throat uncomfortably. "Would you like to actually *see* him, my lord? Whoever stole the King's head cut a hole in the top of the coffin. Although I must warn you, it's not a pretty sight."

Sebastian had no desire to view any more decapitated bodies. But he acknowledged the need to verify what he had been told. "Yes," he said reluctantly.

The virger swallowed hard and moved to draw back the old cloth. "He's extraordinarily well preserved. They often are, in crypts."

A heavy stench of decay wafted through the stale air. Sebastian took one look at the moldering King's truncated neck and the discolored depression left by his purloined head, and nodded. "That's good. Thank you."

He ducked back through the opening into the dark

passage while the virger replaced the pall and carefully smoothed its aged folds. "How many people knew of the burial chamber's discovery?"

Toop followed him with the lantern. "Truthfully? I'd say just about everyone in Windsor who isn't deaf or dead. There's no way to keep workmen from talking, I'm afraid. They go home and tell their wives, or their mothers and sisters. And then they go down to the pub and brag about it to their friends, and before you know what's what, the whole town is talking about it."

"Yet it's one thing to know about the vault, and something else again to gain access to it."

"Well . . ." Toop lowered his voice as they retraced their steps toward the surface. "I wouldn't say this in front of the Dean, but the truth is, just about anybody could've got in here before the gate was up, if they'd a mind to do it. The castle might be a royal residence, but St. George's Chapel has always been open to the public."

"Have you had trouble with things being taken before?"

"Now and then, yes," said Toop as they emerged from the dank passage into the incense-scented air of the quire. "Needless to say, the Dean is beside himself over this. He's always nourished ambitions of becoming a bishop, you see. But once the Regent learns of this—as he surely will unless the head is somehow recovered . . ." He gave another of his rubbery-mouthed grimaces.

"How long have you been virger here?" asked Sebastian.

"Me? More than fifteen years now, my lord."

"Since before Dean Legge, then."

"Oh, yes, my lord; long before." His mouth stretched into a wide, toothy grin. "And I'll still be here long after he's moved on to other things—God willing."

Sebastian thanked him and left the virger there, still grinning aimlessly as he rewound the chain around the gated crypt entrance.

He sent a message to the stables for Tom, then walked out the gate to the sunlit terrace overlooking the village and the old royal deer park with its distant, elm-lined Long Walk stretching for miles across the undulating countryside. His visit to Windsor Castle had proved to be frustratingly unenlightening. If Toop were to be believed, virtually anyone could have made away with King Charles I's head and coffin strap. How—or even if—that theft had played a part in Preston's death was still murky.

Sebastian braced his outthrust hands against the stone parapet edging the terrace, his gaze on the wind-tossed shadows of clouds chasing one another across the landscape below. The sense that he was missing something—something vitally important—continued to haunt him.

A flock of pigeons rose in a sudden burst into the sky, wings whirling in alarm and drawing Sebastian's attention to a disheveled, slope-shouldered man standing with his back to the stone wall edging the steep approach to the gate. He caught Sebastian's gaze and nodded, his eyes alight with amusement.

"Why the devil are you still following me?" Sebastian demanded, walking up to him.

Diggory Flynn's full, crooked lips quirked up in a grin. "What makes you think I'm here 'cause of you?"

"You just happened to take it into your head to visit Windsor this morning, did you? Is that what you would have me believe?"

"Sure then, but 'tis more pleasant than a day spent in the likes of Smithfield Market or Covent—"

Sebastian's hand flashed out to close around the other man's neck and shove him back against the low stone wall.

Flynn let out a yelp, fingers digging into Sebastian's forearms as he bent the man backward over the parapet. "Here, what you wanna go and do that for?"

"Let me warn you right now," said Sebastian, keeping his voice low and even. "Follow me if you like; I can deal with that. But if I hear you've been anywhere near my family again, I swear to God, I'll kill you."

The man's face contorted into a parody of pain. "Ouch. It's hurting me, you are."

"Good." Sebastian tightened his hold on the man's throat. "Who sent you?"

"I told you; I don't work for nobody."

"I don't believe you."

Diggory Flynn's eyes rolled sideways as he considered the drop-off behind him, his tongue flicking out to moisten his dry lips. "You can't kill me. People're watching. There's laws agin' murder in this country. Just 'cause you're a viscount don't mean you can go around killin' folk."

"Don't worry," said Sebastian, releasing his grip on the man and taking a step back. "If I kill you, there won't be any witnesses."

"That supposed to reassure me?" Flynn carefully straightened his grimy neckcloth and tugged at the hem of his worn, rucked-up waistcoat. "You're just trying to scare me, you are."

"You should be scared. I mean what I say."

Flynn's mismatched eyes widened ever so slightly. Then he pushed away from the old stone wall and scuttled off, his head down, the tails of his tattered coat fluttering in the breeze.

"Who was that?" asked Tom, drawing the curricle up beside Sebastian.

"I'm not quite certain."

"'E's a real Cap'n Queernabs, he is," said Tom.

"A what?"

"Don't ye know? A Cap'n Queernabs is a cove what's dressed real shabby-like."

"He is that." Sebastian leapt up into the curricle. "Hear anything of interest in the stables?"

"They're all talkin' about how somebody prigged one of the old kings' heads."

"So much for swearing all interested parties to secrecy," said Sebastian, taking the reins. "Anyone have any idea who might be behind the theft?"

"Oh, they got all sorts of ideas. But ain't no two alike." The boy scrambled back to his perch. "What'd you say was the name of that cove?"

Sebastian gave his horses the office to start. "Flynn. Diggory Flynn. Why?"

"Calhoun was talkin' 'bout somebody hangin' around Brook Street the other day—somebody who sounded more'n a bit like yon Cap'n Queernabs."

Sebastian reined in hard and turned to stare at his tiger. "When was this?"

"Dunno. Few days ago. Why?"

But Sebastian only shook his head, the wind cold on his face as he whipped the horses for home.

Chapter 34

"The thing ye gots t' understand," said the costermonger, leaning against the side of a donkey cart piled high with whole, fresh fish still glistening and wet from the market, "is that not ev'rybody sellin' on the streets is a coster."

"Oh?" said Hero, intrigued by the costermongers' determination to hold themselves apart from all other street sellers.

"Course not," said the coster. He was a big man named Mica McDougal, with beefy arms and a wind-reddened face and dark hair covered by a small cap. "Why, the Dutch buy-a-broom girls, the Jew old-clothes men, the pea soup and bread 'n' butter sellers, the wooden-spoon makers—ain't none of 'em proper costermongers."

"So what makes one a 'proper' costermonger?"

"Proper costermongers sell stock we buys at the fruit and vegetable and fish markets. Some of us 'as stalls or stands in the streets, and some of us makes rounds with a barrow or donkey cart. But you'll never find a costermonger sellin' tatted 'air nets or wooden clothes pins." He wrinkled his nose in disdain.

"How far do you travel on your daily rounds?"

"Oh, usually nine or ten miles."

"That's quite a distance to walk every day."

"Nah. Sometimes in the summer, Liz 'n' me'll go on country rounds for as much as twenty-five miles."

"Liz?"

The coster grinned and shifted to lay an affectionate arm across his donkey's withers. "Liz."

The donkey peeled its lips away from its long teeth and let out a loud *hee-haw.*

"Do you live around here?" Hero asked.

"Ah, no; we lives off Fish Street Hill, m'lady. You'll find most costermongers what deals in fish lives thereabouts, so's we're close t' Billingsgate Market."

"You have children?"

"I got three: two boys and a girl. 'Twere five, but two o' the little ones died o' fever afore Christmas."

"I'm sorry."

The costermonger twitched one shoulder and swallowed hard.

Hero said, "Do you think your children will grow up to be costermongers?"

He swiped a meaty hand down over his whisker-stubbled face. "Sure then, we're already sendin' them out to sell nuts and oranges and watercress. The streets teaches 'em what they needs to know. Why, they're as sharp as terriers, little as they are. They 'as t' be; they know better'n t' come 'ome if they ain't done well."

Hero was careful to keep her instinctive reaction to his words from showing on her face. "How old are they?"

"The girl's eight, and the boys is five and seven."

"Your wife is a costermonger as well?"

"Aye. She works Fleet Street. This time o' year she sells flowers all a-growin'. But come June she'll switch t' peas and beans, then cherries and strawberries in July."

Remembering what Mattie Robinson had told her, Hero was tempted to ask if his "wife" actually was his

wedded wife. Instead, she said, "Was your father a costermonger?"

"Oh, aye; and 'is father afore 'im. You'll find most costermongers proper was born into the business. The ones
I feel sorry for is the mechanics and laborers what've lost
their jobs and try turnin' their 'and t' sellin' in the streets.
They think it looks easy, but it ain't, and they almost never
do well."

"Why not?"

"Ain't up t' the dodges, ye see. The problem is, they
go out into the streets with fear in 'ere—" He thumped
one meaty fist against his chest. "They don't know 'ow to
bargain and they ain't good salesmen. Poor buggers—
beggin' yer pardon, yer ladyship—I mean, poor fellows,
they almost always end up losin' everything." He shook
his head sadly. "For them, it's just another way o' starvin'."

The donkey shifted its weight and shook its head,
rattling the harness.

"I gots t' move on, m'lady. Liz 'ere is gettin' restless."

"Thank you for your time," said Hero, handing the
costermonger his shillings.

The money disappeared into one of his coat's deep,
flapped pockets. "Ye really gonna write about the
costers?"

"Yes."

"Why?"

"Because no one ever has."

But Mica McDougal simply shook his head, as if the
ways of the Quality were beyond his comprehension.

Chapter 35

Sebastian arrived back at Brook Street to find Hero still out on her interview and Claire Bisette preparing Simon for an outing in the park.

"Take one of the footmen with you," Sebastian told her, his voice sounding more curt than he'd intended.

Claire stared at him. "A *footman*?"

"Just . . . humor me, Claire."

"I'll get Edward," she said, still vaguely frowning as she turned away, the bundled-up child wide-eyed in her arms.

Sebastian walked into the library, poured himself a drink, and sent for Jules Calhoun.

"Tom says you saw some 'Captain Queernabs' near the house a few days ago," he said when the valet appeared a few minutes later. "Tell me about him."

Calhoun blinked but did not question the request. "Odd-looking fellow, he was—and I don't mean just the way he was dressed. It was as if the two sides of his face didn't belong together; one eye was even a different color than the other. But it was actually his boots that made me notice him at first. His clothes were those of a common workman, but he had a pair of fine new boots that would be the envy of many a Bond Street beau."

"When was this?"

"Monday, my lord."

"Monday?" Neither Sebastian nor Hero had seen Diggory Flynn before Tuesday. "You're certain?"

"Yes, my lord. I noticed him as I was returning from Hobbs. I remember because I'd been telling him how pleased we were with your new beaver hat." A pained expression shadowed the valet's even features. "The same hat someone put a bullet hole through that very night."

"What was the man doing when you saw him?"

"Simply leaning against the corner. But he looked so out of place that I paused to ask if there was something he needed."

"And?"

"He said no. Then he pushed away from the wall and walked off. Whistling."

"If you see him again, let me know about it. But be careful with him. I think there may well be more to the man than meets the eye."

"Yes, my lord." Calhoun gave a neat bow and started to turn away, then paused. "Are you still interested in Captain Wyeth, my lord?"

"I am indeed. Did you have any success at the Shepherd's Rest?"

"Far more than I should have, actually. The staff there are appallingly eager to chat about the inn's residents."

"What do they say about Captain Wyeth?"

"The general consensus is that he's a likeable enough fellow most of the time, although he does have a tendency to be moody and curt when his wounds are paining him. And he has a bit of a temper, it seems."

"Oh?"

"Last Saturday evening, the captain was having a pint down in the public room when Stanley Preston came charging in and threatened to horsewhip him."

"Yes, Wyeth told me of the incident."

"Did he also tell you he threatened to kill the man?"

"Wyeth threatened to kill Stanley Preston?"

"That's right. I thought at first the barman who told me the tale might be exaggerating a touch. But two of the other lads backed him up."

"What was Preston's reaction?"

"I gather he simply said, 'You don't scare me,' and left."

Sebastian glanced at the clock. "I think perhaps I need to have another chat with our gallant captain."

Sebastian found Captain Hugh Wyeth standing beside the ring of the Life Guards riding school, his arms looped over the top rail of the fence and his gaze following a half dozen new recruits being put through their paces. The air was thick with the smell of saddle leather and horse sweat and a fine dust that shimmered in the spring sunshine.

"So what do you think?" asked Sebastian, coming to stand beside him, his gaze on the horses and riders in the ring before them.

"They're green. But they're willing and able. They'll get there." He glanced over at Sebastian. "Ever miss the Army?"

"Sometimes."

"Why'd you sell out?"

Because I realized I wasn't fighting on the side of good against evil, thought Sebastian, still watching the men in the ring. *Because my own colonel sent me off with falsified dispatches and then betrayed me to the French. Because I trusted the wrong people, and dozens of innocent women and children died as a result.*

But all he said was, "I grew tired of killing men who were much like me, except they spoke a different language and owed allegiance to a different country."

Wyeth was silent for a moment, his hands tightening over the top rail, the smile lines fanning his eyes etched deep, although he was not smiling. "Those are not comfortable thoughts."

"No."

The captain narrowed his gaze against the dust. "Why are you here?"

"I'm wondering why you didn't tell me that when Stanley Preston threatened to take a horsewhip to you, you swore you'd kill him."

Wyeth blew out a long, painful breath.

Sebastian said, "It did happen, didn't it?"

The captain nodded, his lips pressed into a tight line. Then he threw Sebastian an assessing, sideways glance. "You trying to convince me you never threatened to kill anyone? It's the kind of thing a man says in anger—'I could kill you.' Or even, 'I swear to God, I'll kill you.'"

Sebastian thought about the number of times he'd sworn to kill his own father-in-law, but remained silent.

Wyeth said, "I won't deny I wanted to kill the bastard. But I couldn't have done it—even if he had tried to take a horsewhip to me. Don't you understand? He was Anne's father! She loved him, and his death has devastated her. I could never have done that to her."

Sebastian studied the younger man's handsome, earnest face. It was hard not to like Captain Wyeth. But Sebastian had known other handsome, seemingly charming men who were extraordinarily adept at projecting an intense impression of affability and sincerity when the reality was something quite different entirely.

"Tell me again what happened last Sunday night," he said.

Wyeth shrugged. "There's not much to tell. Anne wrangled an invitation for me to Lady Farningham's musical evening. But she had Miss Austen there with her, and we found it impossible to have any real private conversation together. So in the end, I left."

"You're saying Miss Preston spent Sunday evening in the company of Jane Austen?"

"That's right. Why?"

Sebastian shook his head. "I hadn't realized it. Go on."

"That's it, really. I left around ten. Only, I wasn't in the mood to come back to the inn and drink with the lads, so I went for a walk."

"Where?"

"Along Knightsbridge, mainly. I was just . . . walking."

"See anyone?"

"No one I knew."

"What about when you returned to the inn? Did anyone see you then?"

"No. I told you, I wasn't in the mood to be sociable. I went straight up to my room. Why?"

Sebastian had asked the question because whoever killed Stanley Preston would surely have been splattered with blood. But all he said was, "Ever meet an elderly physician named Douglas Sterling?"

"The one who was found dead yesterday?" Wyeth shook his head. "No." He stared off beyond the barracks, toward the park. "I've had the constables here again, questioning me. They think I did it, don't they?"

"I'm afraid so. You've a powerful motive, no alibi, and considerable practice lopping off people's heads."

Wyeth gave a soft, rueful laugh. "They think I'm some sort of fortune hunter—like that fellow Wickham. Or Willoughby."

The names sounded vaguely familiar, but Sebastian couldn't place them. "Who?"

"From *Sense and Sensibility* and *Pride and Prejudice*."

"Don't tell me you read romance novels too?"

Wyeth laughed. "Only the ones Miss Austen writes. They're very clever—especially this last one."

Sebastian stared at him. "Jane Austen is the author of this new book that's taking the ton by storm?"

Wyeth pulled a face. "I forgot I wasn't supposed to say anything. You won't tell anyone, will you?"

Returning to Brook Street, Sebastian found Hero writing up her interview notes at the library table, their infant son dozing contentedly in a basket beside her and the black cat she'd named Mr. Darcy lying stretched out like a dog nearby.

"How was your interview?" he asked, going to pour himself a glass of wine.

"Informative. This fellow has a donkey cart, which places him amongst the most prosperous of all costermongers." She laid aside her quill and leaned back in her chair. "Care to tell me why you saw the need to send a footman to the park with Claire and Simon this morning?"

Sebastian came to stand beside the fire, his gaze on his sleeping son's peaceful, innocent face. "A man who sounds like Diggory Flynn has been seen watching the house. I don't know who he is or what he wants, but I'd feel better if you and Simon both kept someone with you."

Hero stared at him for a long, quiet moment. "What makes you think he's a threat to us? Not you, but us?"

Sebastian took a slow sip of his wine. "I keep thinking about the tale Jamie Knox told me, about the smuggler who ran afoul of Priss Mulligan and came home one day to find his wife missing and the dismembered bodies of his children strategically displayed around the house."

"So you're back to thinking Flynn works for Priss Mulligan?"

"I don't know for certain who he works for. But I don't want to take any chances."

Beside them, Simon stretched and let out a soft gurgle.

Hero stared at Sebastian for a long, quiet moment, then went to lift the child from his basket and hold him in her arms, the blue wool skirts of her walking dress swirling about her ankles as she swung him gently from side to side and said, "Well, good afternoon, young man."

Simon cooed and laughed in response, and for one long moment, Sebastian lost himself in looking at them. Then he said, "Tell me about this character in *Pride and Prejudice*—I think his name is Wickham."

She glanced over at him with a soft, startled laugh. "George Wickham? Whatever for?"

"Because everyone seems to keep referencing him, and I've just discovered Miss Jane Austen is the book's author."

"You can't be serious. Who told you that?"

"Captain Wyeth. Ordinarily, I'd be inclined to question his reliability, but it makes sense of something Henry Austen said to me the other day."

Hero brought Simon up so she could rub noses with him, her gaze on the laughing child. "George Wickham is an officer in the militia who is stationed near the Bennetts—they're the family at the center of the story. At first he's portrayed as handsome and charming and excellent in every way—except of course for his sad lack of fortune. But the reader gradually begins to realize that he is in truth a cunning and unscrupulous liar who uses others for his own ends without conscience or regret." Simon gurgled happily, and she shifted the child's weight, his eyes big and wide and golden as he grinned at Sebastian over her shoulder. "You think Captain Wyeth could be another George Wickham?"

"I'm told Jane Austen fears he might be. So who is Willoughby?"

"I suppose you could call him the villain of *Sense and Sensibility*—or one of them, at any rate. Like Wickham, he is charming, handsome, and impoverished, as well as being deceptive and breathtakingly selfish. Although I don't think Willoughby is quite as conscienceless or calculating as Wickham. Needless to say, neither comparison reflects well on Captain Wyeth."

"No. Which makes me wonder why he mentioned them."

Wide-awake now, Simon reached out to close his tiny first around the thick silver chain at Hero's neck and pulled hard.

"Ouch," she said, laughing as she tried without success to loosen his hold on the necklace. "Your son has a shockingly strong grip."

Sebastian set aside his wine. "Here; let me help." It wasn't until he came closer that he got his first good look at the intricately worked chain and the pendant that nestled at the base of her throat.

"Where did you get this?" he asked, his voice sounding odd even to his own ears.

"My father gave it to me some time ago. Why?"

Sebastian carefully loosed his son's hold on the centuries-old necklace. "I've never seen you wear it."

"The catch was faulty. I only recently had it mended." The frown lines were back between her brows. "Is something wrong?"

"No. Of course not." He reached out, hesitantly, to touch his fingertips to the smooth bluestone disk with a closed silver triskelion set against it. And for one heart-wrenching moment, he imagined he could feel the familiar pulse of its legendary, inexplicable power.

She said, "Have you spoken to Miss Jane Austen about any of this?"

"What? Oh; no." He dropped his hand and turned away to retrieve his glass.

"Would you like me to talk to her? After all, I have read the books."

"It might be better."

She tilted her head to one side, as if both puzzled and concerned by something she saw. "Sebastian, are you all right?"

"Yes, of course," he said, and drained the rest of his wine in one long, burning pull.

Chapter 36

*M*iss Jane Austen was in the elegant parterre garden at the rear of her brother's house, deep in earnest consultation with an aged, gnarled gardener who was gesturing wildly with his hands, when Hero arrived at Sloane Street.

"I'm interrupting you," said Hero when a flustered young housemaid showed her to the terrace. "I do beg your pardon."

"No, please," said Miss Austen, hurrying forward to offer Hero a seat at a wrought-iron table positioned to catch the warmth of the rare spring sunshine. She wore a faded bonnet and a plain, old-fashioned gown, had a faint smudge of dirt across one red cheek, and was utterly unruffled. "Jenkins simply wanted my approval of some new plantings for the parterres. The garden is my cousin Eliza's design, you know. She spent many happy years in France, before the Revolution, and I think it reminds her of those days."

"It is lovely," said Hero, unfurling her parasol against the sun's rays. "How does your cousin?"

"Not well, I fear." Jane Austen's dark eyes pinched with a deep, quiet sorrow kept carefully tucked away.

"I'm sorry."

Her hostess nodded, her face held tight against a threatened upsurge of emotions. "She's lived a marvelously adventurous life, you know—born in India, then living through the Revolution. She's always been so vibrant, so full of life. To see her like this is . . . painful."

"It must be very difficult for your brother."

"It is, yes. He has loved her almost his entire life." She carefully smoothed the skirt of her faded gown. "Please tell me you aren't here because Lord Devlin still thinks Henry had something to do with Stanley Preston's death."

The truth was, Devlin hadn't ruled out anyone at this stage. But Hero simply adjusted the tilt of her parasol and said, "Actually, Devlin is interested in certain aspects of your novels."

"My . . ." Miss Austen's naturally ruddy cheeks darkened ever so slightly. "Who told you? My brother?"

"Indirectly—along with Captain Wyeth."

"Ah." She paused while the young housemaid reappeared bearing a hastily assembled tea tray, the delicate, rose-strewn china cups and plates clattering as the girl dumped the tray on the table. "Throughout history, we women have been endlessly scorned for our supposed readiness to reveal things which ought by rights to remain private. Yet I find that, in practice, men are equally—if not more—inclined to indiscretion."

Hero laughed. "I suspect you are right. Although the truth is, your novels have excited so much interest in fashionable circles that I doubt you'll be able to remain anonymous much longer."

It was a thought that did not appear to trouble the author overly much, and Hero suspected the choice to publish anonymously had been prompted less by a desire to remain unknown than by the realization that society would condemn any spinster vicar's daughter who appeared to be chasing fame and recognition.

Miss Austen eased the cover from the teapot and

began to pour. "Surely Lord Devlin can't think my novels have anything to do with this murder."

"No, of course not. But your brother says you think Captain Wyeth might be another Wickham or Willoughby, and I assume it isn't simply because the three men's names all begin with the same consonant."

Miss Austen kept her attention on the task of pouring the tea. "It would be more accurate to say I *worry* that he might be. Have you met him?"

"No."

"He comes across as an agreeable, sensible man with good understanding and a warm heart. A man of strength and principle."

"But?" prompted Hero.

Miss Austen looked up from the tea. "Who can answer for the true sentiments of a clever man?"

"Is he clever?"

"Very."

Hero took the teacup handed her. "Has he given you reason to suspect his sincerity?"

"Truthfully? No." Miss Austen took a sip of her own tea and stared out over the sun-warmed, French-style garden. "Eliza—my cousin—believes that Anne's love has proven itself so enduring that she ought to be allowed to marry her captain, although of course she worries what sort of future lies ahead for them. We've all known young women who married poor men for love, only to live a life of regret. Poverty can be so terribly grinding."

Hero studied her hostess's even, carefully composed features and found herself wondering about this woman's own romantic past. How much of the author's own life experiences, Hero wondered, had made their way into her books?

"Yet she won't be poor," said Hero, choosing her words carefully. "Stanley Preston's death means that Anne is now free to marry her impoverished young captain *and* keep her inheritance from her father."

Miss Austen raised her gaze to Hero's face. "I may have questioned Captain Wyeth's sincerity, but I never would have believed him capable of—of—"

"Murder?"

"Especially one of such savagery."

"He's spent the last six years at war. That sort of experience can brutalize some men."

"Most men, I should think," said Miss Austen quietly.

Hero took a sip of her tea and shifted her gaze to where the old gardener, Jenkins, was forking over the earth of one of the parterres. "I understand Miss Preston attended Lady Farningham's musical evening in your company."

"She did, yes. My cousin had hoped to be able to go with her, but I'm afraid Eliza rarely leaves her room these days."

"Did you know Captain Wyeth would be there?"

Miss Austen expelled her breath in a kind of a sigh. "No. Although I realize in retrospect that Anne obviously knew it. No simple musical evening could have inspired the level of excitement and anticipation she displayed. Unfortunately, she and the captain had words during the break, and he left almost immediately afterward."

"They quarreled?"

"Yes, although I couldn't tell you the reason for the disagreement. Anne refused to discuss it, and I had no desire to press her. We ourselves left not long afterward. She pled a sick headache and wanted to go home."

"So she was home before ten?" *A good half hour before her father's murder,* thought Hero, although she didn't say it.

"Yes."

"Interesting. I don't believe that was made clear to anyone."

A vaguely troubled look came over Miss Austen's features. But she simply picked up the plate of biscuits from the tray and held it out to Hero. "Please, have some."

"Thank you."

"That's an interesting necklace you're wearing," said Miss Austen, adroitly shifting to a safer topic of conversation as she set the plate between them. "It looks quite ancient."

Hero touched her fingertips to the bluestone and silver triskelion at her neck. "I believe it is, yes. Although I must confess, I don't know its history."

"I saw something quite like it once while visiting friends near Ludlow. We were invited to dine one evening at Northcott Abbey, and Lady Seaton showed us the portrait gallery. There was a painting of a woman wearing an almost identical piece. I remember it because the family legend attached to it caught my imagination. According to the story, the necklace had the power to choose its next owner by growing warm to that person's touch. It seems Lord Seaton's great-great-grandmother was a natural daughter of James II, and the necklace was his gift to her on her wedding day."

Hero was suddenly, intensely conscious of the pendant lying warm against the flesh of her throat, and of the inscribed initials entwined on its back.

A.C. and J.S.

"There was some tragedy involved," Miss Austen was saying, "although I must confess I don't recall all the details. I believe she married a Scottish lord who treated her abysmally after her father the King lost his throne. In fiction, we can mold reality to our will and make all rich men as worthy and handsome as anyone could wish. But life is unfortunately far less tidy. Wealthy men are often silly, insufferable bores—or worse—while far too many handsome men with good hearts have everything to recommend them except a comfortable independence."

"So is Captain Wyeth a particularly vicious version of George Wickham, or a sadly impoverished Mr. Darcy?"

Miss Austen's worried gaze met Hero's. "I wish I knew."

※

Hero was perched halfway up the library ladder, a copy of *Debrett's Peerage* open in her hands, when Devlin walked into the room.

"What are you doing?" he asked.

"Trying to find the name of the Scottish lord who married one of James II's natural daughters," said Hero, still flipping through the pages.

"Why?"

"I saw Miss Austen this afternoon."

"And?"

"You were right; she does indeed worry that Captain Wyeth might not be as amiable or openhearted as he takes pains to appear. She also tells me that Anne and her captain quarreled halfway through Lady Farningham's musical evening, at which point Anne pled a sick headache and went home. Before ten."

She looked up then to find him frowning. He said, "I don't like the sound of that."

"No; I didn't think you would."

He nodded to the book in her hands. "What does James II's natural daughter have to do with anything?"

"She doesn't. But Miss Austen was intrigued by my necklace. She said it reminded her of a piece she'd once seen in a portrait of a woman reputed to be the daughter of James Stuart by one of his mistresses. Which is fascinating because on the back of this necklace are two sets of entwined initials—"

"A.C. and J.S."

Hero stared at him. "How did you know?"

He turned away and went to where the brandy stood warming by the fire. She could see the rigid set to his shoulders, hear the tension in his voice. "The necklace once belonged to my mother," he said, easing the stopper from the decanter. "She was wearing it when she was lost at sea the summer I was eleven."

Hero felt a yawing ache open up inside her, the ache she always felt when she thought of the losses suffered by the boy he'd once been. In one hot, unforgettable summer, he had lost both his older brother Cecil and his mother.

There was a portrait of Sophia, the Countess of Hendon, that hung over the fireplace in the drawing room, and Hero often found herself studying it. The Countess had been a beautiful woman, her hair the color of gold guineas, her features exquisitely molded, her eyes clear and sparkling with intelligence and humor and a wild kind of thirst, as if she yearned for something missing in her life. And then one sunny August day, she'd sailed away from Brighton on a friend's yacht for what was supposed to be a few hours' pleasure cruise, and she'd never returned.

Lost at sea, they told the world—told Sebastian, even though he refused to believe it. Day after day he stood on the cliffs, looking out to sea, waiting for her to return, convinced that she couldn't be dead. Convinced that if she were dead, he'd know it—feel it. In time, he had come to accept that they told the truth, only to learn as a man grown that it was all lies. She had simply left the Earl—the man he had falsely believed to be his father.

Left *him.*

Sebastian had shared with Hero many of his darkest, most painful secrets. But the truth about his mother— that she still lived—Hero had learned only from Jarvis. And she had never told Devlin what she knew.

Now she watched him splash brandy into his glass and said softly, "Except that she wasn't really lost at sea, was she, Devlin?"

He looked at her over his shoulder, the decanter held forgotten in his hand, his face a mask of control. "Jarvis told you?"

"Yes."

"Did he also tell you that she ran off to Venice with her latest lover—a handsome young poet a good ten years her junior?"

"No." Hero set aside the book and stepped off the ladder, her gaze never leaving his face. "How did my father come to have the necklace?"

"It reappeared two years ago, around the neck of Guinevere Anglessey's dead body."

"But . . ." She shook her head, not understanding. He'd solved Guinevere's murder, as he had solved so many. But that had been before Hero's life became inextricably merged with his. "Where did she get it?"

"It seems my mother gave it to her years ago, when they met briefly in the South of France after the Peace of Amiens. Guinevere was still a child at the time, while my mother . . ." He replaced the stopper in the decanter and set it aside. "My mother was the mistress of a French general."

Hero studied his tightly held face. "Do you know where she is now? Lady Hendon, I mean."

He shook his head. "I've hired men to look for her, but the war does rather complicate things."

Why? Hero wanted to ask. *Why are you so desperate to find the mother who sailed off and left you when you were so young? Left you with a man she knew was not your father?*

But she realized she knew the answer: He searched for the beautiful, laughing Countess because he still loved her, despite the hurt and anger and sting of betrayal. And because he wanted to ask her which of her many unnamed lovers had fathered the man now known to the world as Viscount Devlin.

"I still don't understand how Jarvis came to have the necklace," said Hero.

"I gave it to him. I had no desire to see it again."

Reaching up, she loosed the necklace's clasp and held it out to him. "I'm sorry I wore it. I didn't know."

He made no move to take it from her. "The portrait Jane Austen told you about; did she mention where she'd seen it?"

"A place called Northcott Abbey, near Ludlow."

"Ludlow?"

"Yes. Why?" she asked. And then, as soon as she said it, she realized why: Jamie Knox, the Bishopsgate tavern keeper who looked enough like Devlin to be his brother, was from Ludlow.

Devlin simply shook his head, obviously unwilling to put his thoughts into words. But when she laid the necklace on the table beside him, he picked it up.

Chapter 37

Jamie Knox was stripped down to his shirtsleeves and chopping kindling in the ancient courtyard at the rear of the Black Devil when Sebastian walked up to him.

He glanced over at Sebastian but kept at his task, the muscles in his back bunching and flexing beneath the linen of his shirt as he swung the axe. "Still looking for your murderer, are you?"

"Yes. But that's not why I'm here."

"Oh?"

Sebastian held up the silver and bluestone necklace so that the pendant dangled from its chain. "Have you ever seen this before?"

Knox paused to swipe one forearm across his sweaty forehead, then reached out and cupped the pendant in his left palm, his yellow eyes narrowing. "Not to my knowledge. Why?"

"I'm told it can be seen in a seventeenth-century painting that hangs in the portrait gallery of Northcott Abbey, near Ludlow."

Knox gave a soft grunt. "And you're thinking that because I'm from Shropshire, I might've seen this painting? It's a grand place, Northcott Abbey. Last I heard, Lord and Lady Seaton were more than a bit choosy

about who they invited inside. Or do you suspect me of
having prigged the bobble at some point in my long and
varied career?"

"Actually, it once belonged to my mother. An old
Welshwoman gave it to her before I was born."

Knox reached for a pitcher of ale that rested atop a
nearby stretch of stone wall, and drank heavily. Then he
stood for a moment with his hands on his hips, his breath
coming heavy from his labors, his gaze thoughtful on
Sebastian's face. "You ever been to Shropshire?"

Sebastian shook his head. "Not since I was quite
young."

"You have people there?"

"Not to my knowledge."

A breeze gusted up, filled with the rattle of dead
leaves across the ancient paving and the whisper of
unanswered questions that had never been asked.

Knox wiped his sleeve across his forehead again.
"When I was sixteen, I couldn't get away from there fast
enough. Took the King's shilling and marched off to see
the world, convinced I'd never want to go back. But
lately I find myself thinking Shropshire wouldn't be such
a bad place to raise a family."

"You could still go back. They have pubs in Shropshire."

Knox's teeth flashed in a smile as he hefted his axe.
"So they do."

Once, the tavern keeper had told Sebastian that his
mother was a young barmaid who'd named three men
as the possible father of her child: a Gypsy stable hand,
an English lord, and a Welsh cavalry officer. But she died
before she was able to tell anyone which of the three the
boy resembled.

For Sebastian, the desire to know the truth—the truth
about the mysterious man who may have sired them
both, the truth about the shared blood that in all likelihood flowed through their veins—was like an open,

festering wound. As a boy, he'd grown up with two brothers—or rather, two half brothers, sons of the Earl of Hendon and his unfaithful Countess. Both were long dead. Now Sebastian looked at Jamie Knox and wondered if he were looking at another brother, a third half brother he'd never known he had. It was, Sebastian knew, the real reason he kept coming back here. The real reason the two men kept circling around each other, for he didn't need to be told to know that Jamie Knox was as puzzled and intrigued as he.

"I heard an interesting tale last night," said Knox as he turned back to his work, his axe blade biting deep into a new length of wood.

Sebastian watched him free the axe and swing again. "Oh? What's that?"

"Seems a month or so ago, your Stanley Preston bought a medieval reliquary from Priss Mulligan. Paid a pretty penny for it, he did, only to discover just last week that it's a fake. And that Priss knew it all along."

"So what did he do?"

"Went charging over to Houndsditch and demanded his money back. Even threatened to expose Priss to the authorities."

"When was this?"

"Last Saturday."

"The day before he was killed?"

"That's right."

"How reliable is your source?"

Knox paused to look at Sebastian over one shoulder, his lean face slick with sweat, his expression unreadable. "Very."

"And how did Priss Mulligan respond to Preston's threat?"

"She swore that if he so much as thought about going to the authorities, she'd send her lads to strangle Preston with his own intestines and feed what was left of him to the dogs."

"Colorful," said Sebastian.

Knox sank his axehead deep into the chopping block and straightened. "She is that—and more."

Priss Mulligan was winding the key of a mechanical nightingale when Sebastian pushed open the battered door and walked into her shop.

Despite the brightness of the afternoon, the interior was gloomy, the small panes of the front windows thick with the accumulated grime, cobwebs, and entombed dead insects of centuries. Rather than look up, Priss simply kept winding the gilded, jewel-encrusted trinket, and he realized she must keep lookouts posted on the street outside, because she'd obviously known he was coming.

"Back again, are you?" she said, setting the trinket on the counter between them. The nightingale began to sing melodiously, its delicate, gilded wings beating slowly up and down, its tiny beak opening and closing, the jeweled collar around its neck glittering with simulated fire.

"Interesting," said Sebastian, watching it.

"Ain't it just? And the jewels are real rubies and sapphires too—no paste."

"Of course they are," said Sebastian.

Rather than take offense, she laughed out loud, her small beady eyes practically disappearing into her fat face.

He nodded to the mechanical bird between them. "Where does it come from?"

"Persia. Or maybe China. Does it matter? Sings as sweet and sunny as an angel of the good Lord, it does."

The clear notes began to slow down, the key cleverly concealed in the bird's tail feathers turning slower and slower, the wings seeming to grow heavier and heavier with each flutter.

He said, "I've discovered you've been less than honest with me."

She gave him a look of shocked innocence. "You don't say?"

"Last Saturday, Stanley Preston came charging into your shop and accused you of cheating him. He threatened to turn you in to the authorities as a fence, whereupon you threatened to strangle him with his own intestines and feed what was left of him to the dogs."

"Nah, that weren't it. Don't know who you been talking to, but I said I was gonna strangle him with his own *guts* and feed his *privates* to the dogs."

Sebastian studied her broad, still smiling face. "Yet you told me you hadn't seen the man in a month or more."

She shrugged. "Reckon I forgot."

"You forgot."

"Got a terrible memory, I do."

"You do realize, of course, that his threat to turn you over to the authorities gives you a powerful motive for murder?"

"It might—if I'd thought he meant it. Only, he didn't."

"So certain?"

"Course I'm certain. Everybody cheats each other in this business—when they can. And the buyers is as guilty as the sellers. You such a flat as t' think Preston cared whether the stuff he bought here was stolen or not? He couldn't expose me without exposing himself, now, could he?"

"He could claim not to know the origins of your merchandise."

"To be sure, he could. But then, so could I, now, couldn't I?" She poked one short, fat finger toward him. "If he'd been strung up by his own innards and gelded, you might be able to pin this on me. But he weren't. So get out of me shop."

Sebastian nodded to the now silent bird on the counter between them. "How much is the nightingale?"

She snatched it up and cradled it against her massive bosom as if it were something rare and precious to her. " 'Tain't for sale. Not to you."

Sebastian kept his gaze on her face. "Ever have dealings with anyone from Windsor Castle?"

Her unexpected, slow smile betrayed not a hint of either recognition or alarm. "I told you, I only deal in human heads if they're gilded and studded with jewels."

"I don't recall saying anything about a head," said Sebastian, and walked out of her shop.

The sun was sinking low in the sky when Sebastian joined Gibson for a pint at an ancient, half-timbered tavern near the Tower. The Irishman's eyes were hollow and bruised-looking, and there was a decidedly green tinge to his face.

"You think it was a trap?" said Gibson, wrapping his unsteady hands around his tankard. "That Priss Mulligan used the King's head as bait to lure Preston to Bloody Bridge and then kill him?"

Sebastian leaned his shoulders against the worn, high back of the old-fashioned settle. "I think it's a strong possibility, yes."

Gibson drained the rest of his ale and set aside the empty tankard. "How do you know your unknown thief himself isn't the killer? Maybe he decided to kill Preston, steal whatever money he'd brought, and then sell the head to Priss Mulligan."

"That's also a possibility."

"But you don't think so?"

"Why would a simple thief go to all the trouble of cutting off Preston's head and setting it up on the bridge?"

"Why would anyone who wasn't more than a wee bit crazy?"

"True." Sebastian signaled the barmaid for two more pints. "There is a third possibility."

"There is?"

"Preston could have been at the bridge to meet whoever stole the royal relics. Only, someone else followed him to the bridge and killed him."

"Someone like Wyeth or Oliphant?"

"Or even Henry Austen. After all, we only have his word as to the nature of their quarrel."

Gibson grunted. "What I don't understand is how this old physician—Sterling—fits into anything. Why kill him?"

"My guess is he figured out who killed Preston, or at least had a pretty good idea." Sebastian frowned. "Although there could always be another link that I'm missing entirely."

Gibson swiped a shaky hand down over his pale, clammy face. "Alexi says she gave you the results of Sterling's autopsy."

"She did, yes." Sebastian studied his friend's heavy-lidded, bloodshot eyes. "Did you ever get a chance to look at the body yourself?"

Gibson shook his head, his gaze sliding away.

"How's your leg now?" Sebastian asked gently.

"Better."

Sebastian remained silent, but Gibson seemed to know the direction of his thoughts, for he said, "It's barmy, if you ask me—thinking you can get rid of the phantom pains from a man's missing leg with nothing more than a box and mirrors."

"We don't understand much about the mind or how it functions, do we? Madame Sauvage seems to think it could work. So why not try it? What have you to lose?" *Besides your pain and an opium addiction that's going to kill you,* Sebastian thought, although he didn't say it.

Gibson set his jaw and shook his head, and Sebastian knew his refusal was all tied up with his pride, and a fear of looking foolish or weak, and a host of other emotions Sebastian couldn't even guess at and suspected Gibson himself had no desire to probe.

The surgeon waited while the buxom young barmaid set two new tankards on the table, then said, "So where's this king's head now, do you think?"

"I suppose that depends on whether the thief and the killer are the same person. But if the thief *isn't* the killer, then I'm afraid he's probably in danger—and I suspect he knows it."

Gibson stared at him. "How you figure that?"

"One of two things: either the killer used the King's head to lure Preston to Bloody Bridge, in which case the thief knows who the killer is, or the thief had nothing to do with the murder but arrived at the bridge in time to see something."

"What makes you think he saw something?"

"Because someone—either the thief, the killer, or Preston himself—dropped that inscribed lead strap beside the stream. And if it was the thief, then he must have been too rattled—or afraid of being seen—to take the time to look for it in the dark. Otherwise, why leave something that valuable—especially something that has the potential to tie him to murder?"

Gibson leaned forward. "Maybe that's why Sterling was killed. He was a physician, after all. Most of them are more interested in drinking urine and dispensing potions than in studying anatomy, but some do. Could be he had ties to the resurrection men working out at Windsor and figured out who your thief was."

Sebastian paused with his tankard lifted halfway to his mouth. "Do you know any of them?"

Gibson shook his head. "Resurrection men are fiercely territorial, and the lads I deal with tend to stick to the churchyards of the City or Mayfair. But I'll bet that virger you talked to could give you their names. He might not have ever managed to catch them red-handed, but he knows who they are—you can count on that."

"Actually, he was at pains to convince me that virtually anyone in Windsor could have accessed the crypt—something I suspect the Dean would be shocked to hear."

Gibson grunted. "Sounds like he probably deals with them himself. God knows he wouldn't be the first."

Sebastian tried to picture toothy Rowan Toop surreptitiously leaving greased gates unlocked in anticipation of the stealthy midnight visits of body snatchers, or offering to sell choice items lifted from the crypts under his care.

And Sebastian found he had no difficulty imagining either scenario.

Chapter 38

Sunday, 28 March

The next morning, Sebastian drove out to Windsor Castle to find the Right Reverend Edward Legge pacing back and forth before the chapel steps, his full cheeks flushed with annoyance. The morning had dawned cool and damp, with a fine mist that drifted across the lower court and hung in the half-dead trees near the cloisters.

"I don't know where the fool has taken himself off to," snapped the Dean when Sebastian introduced himself and asked for the virger. "He wasn't here for morning services. And I'm to meet with the Canons in less than ten minutes. He's supposed to be there! The interment of Princess Augusta is this Wednesday."

Sebastian studied the Dean's plump, self-absorbed face. "Have you sent to make inquiries at his lodgings?"

"Of course I've sent to make inquiries," said the Dean. "What sort of imbecile do you take me for? His wife claims he went for a walk and never came back."

"When?"

"How on earth would I know?"

Sebastian shifted his gaze to a castle guard who was trotting across the court toward them. The Dean turned, following Sebastian's gaze.

The guard was young and fresh faced and breathing heavily, and he had to pause to suck in a few gulps of air before saying with a gasp, "He's dead, Reverend."

Legge stared at him. "*Toop?* Are you saying Toop is *dead*?"

"Yes, sir. They . . ." The young guard paused to swallow hard. "They found him down by Romney Island. In the river."

"What did the fool do? Fall in and drown?"

"I don't think so, sir. His head's all caved in."

※

A long, narrow stretch of wooded land in the middle of the Thames, Romney Island lay just below the old wooden bridge that connected Windsor to the town of Eton on the north bank of the river. That morning, a gap-toothed, tow-headed boy of twelve had rowed his skiff from Eton out to the island and was just dropping a fishing line into the water when he noticed the black cloth of the virger's cassock floating amidst the exposed roots of a willow at the river's edge.

By the time Sebastian reached the island, a constable and the keeper from the nearby lock had already hauled the sodden body up onto the gravel bank. The virger lay on his stomach, his arms sprawled stiffly out from his sides, his head turned so that one glassy eye seemed to stare at Sebastian in startled horror as he hunkered down beside the body. From the looks of things, the man had probably been dead a good eight to ten hours, although Sebastian could never remember if cold water sped up or slowed down the processes of death.

He looked up at the constable. "Do you know when he was last seen?"

The constable—a brawny, middle-aged man with a heavy morning stubble of dark beard—wiped the back of one hand across his nose and sniffed. "His wife says he took the dog for a walk last night around half past eight. Gone a good while, he was, before she realized he hadn't come back. Had her sister visiting, and they was busy chatting, you see. Wasn't till the dog come barkin' at the door that she knew something was amiss."

"How big is the dog?"

The constable looked at Sebastian as if that were just the sort of daft question one might expect from some bloody London lord they'd been ordered to cooperate with. "Little gray thing about the size of a cat. Why?"

If the constable couldn't fathom the significance of the size of the dog, Sebastian didn't have time to explain it to him. Then he realized the constable wasn't thinking in terms of murder.

"The fog come up real bad just after dusk last night," said the constable. "Looks to me like the virger must've taken his dog for a walk along the river, slipped, hit his head on somethin', and fell in the river and drowned."

"That's certainly one explanation," said Sebastian, studying the ugly gash on the side of the virger's head. The water had washed away all trace of blood, although the wound had undoubtedly bled profusely; he could see shattered bone amidst the pulpy flesh. "If that's the case, it shouldn't be difficult to find the spot where he came to grief; his blood should be smeared all over whatever he hit."

"I suppose so, my lord. But . . . what difference does it make?"

"I'm afraid there's a very good chance your virger had some help going into the river."

The constable shook his head. "I don't understand. Help from who?"

Sebastian pushed to his feet. "From whoever killed him."

Sebastian's desire to have the dead virger sent to Paul Gibson for autopsy was met with predictable resistance from Dean Legge.

"Send the body for a postmortem?" said the Dean with an indignant squeak. "All the way to London? When the fool simply tumbled into the river? What an unconscionable waste of funds."

Sebastian kept his own voice calm and even. "I don't think we're dealing with an accident."

"You can't be serious. Who would want to kill a simple virger? No, no; I can't authorize it. Even if a postmortem were necessary, Windsor boasts any number of competent medical men who are more than capable of performing the task."

Sebastian stared off across the misty court and uttered those magic words "Jarvis" and "King Charles's head."

The Dean closed his mouth, turned a sickly shade of gray, and bustled off to make the arrangements without further argument.

The virger's lodgings lay to the west of the chapel in that part of the castle known as Horseshoe Cloister. A quaint old house of timber framing filled in with brick noggin, it dated back to the fifteenth century, with delicate window tracery and a second story that jutted out over the ground floor.

Sebastian found Rowan Toop's widow seated in a small but surprisingly fine parlor and surrounded by a bevy of somber-faced women who stared at him as if he were a crow who'd alit in the midst of a covey of mourning doves. He wouldn't have been surprised if the grieving widow had simply buried her face in the depths of her black linen handkerchief and used her grief as a reason not to speak with him. Instead, she excused herself to the ruffled ladies and withdrew with Sebastian through a low door into an adjoining dining room.

"They mean well, I know," she said, closing the door to the parlor with a sigh of relief. "It's just that, sometimes, sympathy can be more oppressive than grief."

It certainly appeared to be so in this case, Sebastian thought, studying her self-composed features and noticeably dry eyes. Either that, or the Widow Toop was extraordinarily successful at hiding her feelings.

She was a startlingly plain woman, built tall and as bony thin as her late husband. But she was better born, and lost no time in letting Sebastian know she was the daughter of one of St. George's former Canons. She was also, he suspected, better educated and more intelligent than Toop. Yet it was not at all difficult to understand how she had ended up married to a mere virger. Intelligent she might be, and gently bred, but she had a most unfortunate face, with a small squashed nose and no chin and bad teeth.

She fixed Sebastian with a steady gaze. "You're here because of the death of my husband?"

"Yes. I'm sorry."

She nodded. "Rowan told me you'd been asking about the missing relics."

"Can you tell me if he stayed home last Sunday evening? Or did he go out?"

The question didn't seem to surprise her, although he noticed her gaze slid away. "He was out, yes."

"Long enough to make it to London and back?"

She nodded quietly and went to fiddle with an expensive-looking silver epergne on the sideboard. Like the parlor, the dining room was small but exquisitely furnished, with a cabinet of fine French china and gilded sconces dripping cascades of faceted crystals. Some items were undoubtedly her own pieces, inherited from her mother, the Canon's wife. But not all.

"Do you know where he went?" asked Sebastian. "Or why?"

"No."

Somehow, Sebastian couldn't bring himself to come right out and ask this recently widowed woman if she'd known her husband was a grave robber. So he said instead, "Did your husband ever mention a woman named Priss Mulligan? She owns a secondhand shop in Houndsditch."

"I don't believe so, no. But then, Rowan knew I had no interest in . . . in some of the things he did."

That's one way to put it, Sebastian thought. Aloud, he said, "How did he seem when he came home Sunday night?"

"Truthfully? I'd never seen him in such a state."

"In what sense?"

"It's almost as if he were . . . frightened. Yes, that's it; frightened. Terrified, actually."

"Of what? Do you know?"

"No; I'm sorry. He said he didn't want to talk about it and went to bed."

"Was he carrying anything when he returned?"

"No." The question obviously puzzled her. "Whatever do you mean?"

Sebastian simply shook his head. "What about last night? Was he frightened when he took the dog for its walk?"

"I don't think so, no. They've been busy planning Princess Augusta's funeral, you know, and he always enjoyed royal affairs at the chapel."

"Can you think of anyone who might have wanted to harm your husband?"

Her eyes widened. "No, but . . . I thought they said he simply fell into the river?"

"Perhaps. Perhaps not. Your husband never told you anything about what happened Sunday night? About who he was going to meet, or why?"

"No."

Sebastian studied the widow's plain face, the delicate gold locket nestled at her throat, the fine muslin gown her husband had doubtless purchased with money gained from dealing with resurrection men or selling trinkets snatched from the dead.

She was no fool. He had no doubt she had long ago guessed where the extra money came from to buy the fine china, the fashionable gowns, the expensive carpets on her floors. But she had simply accepted it all as her due while remaining nominally ignorant of the activities that made it possible. And for the first time, Sebastian found himself almost feeling sorry for Toop, married to this plain, wellborn, unhappy woman who still felt nothing but contempt for him, no matter how hard he had tried to please her.

He wondered why she had agreed to speak to him when she basically had nothing to tell him. Then he saw the spasm that passed over her features as her gaze wandered to the closed door to the parlor, and he thought he understood. The women who had come to "comfort" her—the wives and daughters of the Canons of St. George's—still belonged to the world from which she had been demoted. And he had no doubt they were adept at subtly reminding her of her lowered station in life.

He said, "Where will you go now?" This house would be given to the new virger of St. George's, whoever he might be.

"My widowed sister has a cottage in Eton. I'll live with her." A small, wirehaired gray dog came trotting in from the passage that led to the kitchen, and she bent to scoop it up into her arms.

"Please accept my condolences," he said with a bow. "If you think of anything—anything at all—that might help make sense of what happened to your husband, you will let me know?"

"Yes, of course," she said.

But he knew she would not.

What mattered to her was that Rowan Toop's death meant she was now utterly responsible for her own maintenance in a world that was not at all kind to plain, gently bred, impoverished women.

Chapter 39

Sebastian returned to Brook Street to find Sir Henry Lovejoy on the verge of descending the house's front steps.

"Sir Henry," said Sebastian, handing Tom the reins and hopping down from the curricle's high seat. "I'm glad I caught you. Please, come in."

He led the way to the drawing room, ordered tea for Lovejoy, poured himself a brandy, and told the magistrate the results of his trip to Windsor.

"Merciful heavens," said the magistrate after listening to the circumstances surrounding Toop's death. "You don't think it possible the virger simply slipped into the river and drowned?"

"It would be a startling coincidence if he did. But we'll know more once Gibson gets a look at him."

Lovejoy sipped his tea for a moment in thoughtful silence. "If it was murder, then why didn't the killer cut off Toop's head, as he did with the others?"

"That, I can't answer." Sebastian cradled his brandy in one palm and went to stand before the fire. "Were you coming to see me for a particular reason?"

"I was, yes. It may be unimportant, but you'll recall that Stanley Preston went off somewhere in a hackney the day he was killed? Well, we've finally located the jarvey involved."

"And?"

"The jarvey remembers the fare quite clearly, for he found it rather peculiar." Lovejoy set aside his teacup and leaned forward. "Preston asked to be put down at the entrance to Bucket Lane, on Fish Street Hill."

"Good God; whatever for?" A thoroughfare linking London Bridge to Gracechurch Street and Bishopsgate, Fish Street Hill was the center of a poor, overcrowded area inhabited mainly by those connected in some way with the fish market of Billingsgate, which lay just to the west of the bridgehead. Sebastian could think of nothing that might have taken Preston to the area.

"That we've yet to ascertain," said Lovejoy. "Miss Preston says she has no notion what her father could have been doing there."

"You believe her?"

Lovejoy looked at him in surprise. "You don't?"

"I think Miss Anne Preston is being less than honest with us about a number of things."

"Oh, dear; I hadn't realized that." The magistrate looked thoughtful for a moment.

"What?" said Sebastian, watching him.

"Only that the constable who questioned Preston's servants reported the staff were not as forthcoming as they might have been. You think they could be protecting Miss Preston for some reason?"

"It's possible. You might have one of your lads take another go at them."

Lovejoy nodded. "I'll have Constable Hart talk to them again. I sent him out to Bucket Lane, by the way. Unfortunately, he was unable to locate anyone who would admit to knowing Preston or even remembered seeing him."

"I'm not surprised." People who lived in places such as Fish Street Hill weren't exactly known for their friendliness to constables. "Your constable was lucky to get out of there alive."

"That's what he said. And he's refusing to go back again."

Sebastian was rubbing a nasty mixture of bacon grease and ashes into his hair when Hero came to stand at the entrance to his dressing room. "Seven Dials?" she asked, watching him. "Or Stepney Green?"

"Billingsgate."

"Really? Whatever for?"

He told her.

She said, "Why Billingsgate? It makes no sense."

"I know." He paused to slip his small double-barreled pistol into the pocket of one of his most old-fashioned and ill-fitting Rosemary Lane coats. "That's what makes it so intriguing."

Chapter 40

A pungent seaweed-like odor permeated the air around London Bridge, taking on the more distinct smell of fish the closer Sebastian came to the bridge and its adjacent fish market.

For as long as anyone could remember, the bridge-head had been dominated by the fishmongers of Billingsgate. This was an area of brawny women in aprons shiny with fish scales, of men in slime-stiffened canvas trousers or the red-worsted caps of sailors. The tangled rigging of oyster boats showed in the breaks between the tightly packed buildings, and seagulls wheeled overhead, their plaintive cries mingling with the shouts of *"Plaice alive, alive, cheap,"* and *"Mussels, a penny a quart."*

The stretch of the bridge approach known as Fish Street Hill was crowded with shops selling everything from cod and periwinkles to stores of wine, pitch, and tar. But in the warren of narrow lanes and mean courts to the west lived the fishmongers themselves, along with the costers who bought the fish of Billingsgate to sell on the streets of London.

Sebastian arrived by hackney, slipping easily into the persona he had chosen to adopt: Silas Nelson, a

somewhat mentally deficient bumpkin from a small village in Kent. By the time he paid off his hackney at the
entrance to the narrow passage leading to Bucket Lane,
all trace of the self-confident viscount had vanished.
His shoulders slumped, and he walked with his head
thrust forward, his gaze flitting nervously from side
to side, a foolish half grin plastered on his slack features.

It was a trick his former lover, Kat Boleyn, had taught
him long ago, when she was first making her mark on
the stage and he was an idealistic youth just down from
Oxford. "It's not enough simply to dress the part of a
character," she'd told him. "You need to let their per-
sonality infuse every fiber of your being—the way you
walk and talk, your attitude toward yourself and others,
even life itself."

The lesson had served him well during the war, when
he'd operated as an exploring officer in the mountains
of Italy and the Peninsula. . . .

But he slammed his mind shut against those memories.

Now, shuffling along with an awkward gait, he cut
through the passage to find himself in a dim lane of
bleak, dilapidated houses that seemed almost to touch
overhead, shutting out all sunlight. Tattered laundry
hung from upper-story windows, while vacant-eyed children and half-starved, snarling dogs clustered in the
narrow stretch of mud and steaming garbage that passed
for a street. The air was thick with the smell of decay
and excrement and the inescapable, oppressive odor of
fish.

He knocked on the first door to his right and waited,
still vaguely smiling.

No one answered.

Tipping back his head, he peered up at the cracked,
grimy windows of the overhanging second story. He

could feel the inhabitants inside, hear their soft whispers and furtive movements. But the door remained closed.

He moved on to the next house and rapped loudly on the worn, weathered door.

Silence.

"Hey!" he hollered. "Anybody home?"

Farther down the lane, a door opened and an old man came out leaning on a cane, a cap pulled low over his ears and a tattered scarf wrapped thick about his neck.

"Excuse me," called Silas Nelson, hurrying toward him. "Can I talk to you?"

The man glanced once at Sebastian, then turned to walk in the opposite direction, his cane gripped tightly in his fist.

"Hey! I'm lookin' for Mr. Stanley Preston; you know him?"

The man kept walking.

Silas Nelson drew up, his shoulders slumping more than ever. "Why won't anybody talk to me?" he asked of the now empty street. Even the children had disappeared.

"Who're you?" demanded a voice behind him.

Sebastian spun around.

A woman stood in the center of the muddy, refuse-strewn lane, her arms crossed at her chest, her head thrown back as she stared at him with narrowed, startlingly turquoise eyes. She looked to be somewhere in her thirties and was stunningly beautiful, with smooth café au lait skin and rich dark hair that peeked from beneath the red kerchief she wore around her head. She was built tall and slender, with a graceful long neck and high cheekbones and full lips.

"You deaf or somethin'?" she asked when he didn't answer. "I said, who are you?"

"Silas Nelson, ma'am," said Sebastian, snatching off his moth-eaten cap and executing a jerky bow.

The woman sniffed. "Ne'er seen you before. What you doin' here?"

"Beggin' your pardon, ma'am, but I'm lookin' for Mr. Preston—Mr. Stanley Preston. Would you know him, by chance?"

"Ain't no one by that name lives round 'ere."

"I'm told he was here last Sunday."

"Who told you that?"

It had occurred to Sebastian that Lovejoy's constable had probably agitated the neighborhood to the extent that any stranger suddenly appearing in their midst that day would be immediately suspect. So he twisted his cap in his hands and said, "Constable, ma'am. Well, I s'pose I should say, the innkeeper of the Red Fox, what had it from the constable. That's where I'm stayin', you see—at the Red Fox, on Fish Street Hill. When the inn-keeper heard I'd come t' town lookin' for Mr. Preston, he said, 'That's right queer, for we had a constable here just this mornin' askin' about him. Said he'd been in Bucket Lane.'" Sebastian's Silas Nelson leaned forward eagerly. "Have you seen him, then? Oh, please say you have."

Her expression turned from one of suspicion to mild disgust. "Who are you?"

"I'm Silas Nelson, ma'am."

"You already told me that. What I mean is, where you come from? What you want with Preston?"

"I'm from Dymchurch, ma'am, down in Kent. I come up to London because my sister's been takin' care of me. But she done gone and died, and now what'm I to do? I remembered her husband had some dealin's once with Mr. Preston, so I come to town, hopin' maybe he could find somethin' for me to do. I hear he's powerful rich. Only, I don't know his direction and London is ever so big. I'd no notion; it's nothing like Dymchurch, you know. I was puzzlin' on how to even begin lookin' for him when the innkeeper tells me about Bucket Lane." Sebastian gave a broad grin. "So here I am."

"You're an idiot." It was said more as a statement of fact than as an insult.

Sebastian widened his grin. "Yes, ma'am."

She pushed out her breath between her teeth and shook her head. "Your Mr. Preston don't live 'ere. He lives in a grand house out Knightsbridge way. Or I suppose I should say, he did. He's dead."

"Dead?" Sebastian let his face fall ludicrously.

"That's right."

"But . . . what'm I to do?"

"Go back to Kent?" she suggested.

"But . . . you did know Mr. Preston, yes?"

She didn't deny it, but simply stared at him, waiting for him to finish.

He leaned forward. "Maybe . . . maybe you know somebody could find me work? I may not be smart, but I am strong. Sorta."

"Sorry." She threw an expressive glace at the surrounding squalor. "Take a look around. People here have a hard enough time feedin' themselves, let alone findin' work for others. And you're wrong; I didn't know Preston." Her upper lip curled in disgust. "The only people like me that man ever knew was workin' in his sugarcane fields and callin' him massa."

Sebastian looked confused. "Ma'am?"

"Never mind." She jerked her head toward the passage leading back to Fish Street Hill. "Just . . . get out of here before somethin' happens to you. This ain't no place for the likes of you."

"Ma'am?"

"You heard me. Take yourself off. Now."

Sebastian pulled his cap down on his head with both hands and allowed his whole being to sag with dejection and despair as he turned back toward Fish Street Hill.

He paused at the dark mouth of the passage to look back.

She still stood in the middle of the muddy lane, her arms crossed at her chest, her gaze narrowed as she watched him. Although whether she watched to keep him from harm or to make certain he actually did leave, he couldn't have said.

※

Sebastian settled against the worn squabs of the hackney carrying him back to Brook Street, his gaze on the tumbledown buildings and ragged, desperate people that flashed past on the far side of the carriage window. The farther west they traveled, the finer the shops and houses became, the wider and better paved the streets, the better dressed—and better fed—the people, until it seemed to him that he might have entered a different land.

Their society was one of infinitesimally exact gradations, with each individual acutely aware of his or her own place in relation to all others. Grand nobles such as Sebastian's aunt Henrietta were casually contemptuous of mere landed gentry such as Stanley Preston. Yet Preston had considered himself fully justified in despising—and protecting his daughter from—the likes of Captain Hugh Wyeth, who might be gently born but was nevertheless woefully impoverished.

Intelligence, moral fiber, education, talent—all counted for little without birth and wealth. What mattered in their world was a carefully calibrated interplay of those two vital attributes. It was a delicate equation that would no doubt baffle an outsider, but never those who lived within it, who grew up instinctively attuned to the implications of their subtlest gradations.

And then there were those without either birth or land, those engaged in that shameful thing called *trade*.

Make enough money and a man could buy an estate and in a few short generations convince his peers to forget his plebian origins, his ties to that great horde who actually worked for a living. Yet even the common multitude had their own distinct gradations in rank. Merchants, craftsmen, innkeepers, laborers, costermongers, prostitutes—all knew their exact place in society and considered themselves superior to those ranked below them. Even the thieves had their elites and their dregs, with highwaymen looking down on the housebreakers, who in turn despised the mere cutpurses and pickpockets.

By all reports, Stanley Preston had been both painfully aware and deeply resentful of what he saw as his own inadequate position in the grand scheme of things. Desperate to claw his way higher up the social ladder, he had married a lord's daughter and fought hard to secure advantageous marriages for his children, all the while surrounding himself with artifacts of the great nobles and kings and queens of the past. And yet fewer than twelve hours before someone cut off his head and set it up on the parapet of Bloody Bridge, he'd traveled across London to a mean lane off Fish Street Hill to interact in some unknown way with a tall, dusky-skinned woman with turquoise eyes who despised him.

Why?

She was no simple prostitute; of that Sebastian was fairly certain. The neighborhood was one favored by costermongers, who tended to cluster together close to the markets they visited at dawn to buy their stock. From her dress, Sebastian suspected the unknown woman of Bucket Lane was a coster herself, while her appearance and remarks suggested that at least one of her grandparents had been of African blood. Was that significant?

Perhaps.

A new theory was forming in his imagination, outlandish, improbable even, and yet . . .

What he needed, he realized, was to speak to someone who knew Preston well. Really knew him. And that meant not his daughter, Anne, but his longtime friend, Sir Galen Knightly.

Chapter 41

*N*ewly changed into doeskin breeches and a well-tailored dark blue coat, with his hair still damp, Sebastian knocked on the door of Sir Galen Knightly's town house in Half Moon Street to find the Baronet standing in the stately, old-fashioned hall with his gloves in one hand and a walking stick tucked up under his arm.

"I beg your pardon," said Sebastian. "Have I caught you on the verge of going out?"

Sir Galen looked vaguely chagrined. "Well . . . actually, yes. Did you need something?"

"I had a few more questions about Preston I was hoping you might be able to answer."

The Baronet glanced at the hall clock. "Would you mind walking with me toward Bond Street?"

It was Sir Galen's practice, Sebastian recalled, to dine at Stevens every Wednesday and Sunday at half past six. "Of course," said Sebastian, and the older man's face cleared.

Sebastian let his gaze drift around the hall while Knightly conferred for a moment with his butler. From the looks of things, the house had been little altered since the days of Sir Galen's grandfather. The Baronet's tragic young bride, who had survived her wedding by only ten months before dying in childbirth, hadn't lived long enough to make many changes, and her grief-stricken widower had obviously been content to leave things as they were.

"Have you made some progress in your investigations?" asked Sir Galen as they descended the front steps and turned toward the east.

"Some. I was wondering if you know what might have taken Stanley Preston to Fish Street Hill last Sunday—to a wretched alley called Bucket Lane."

"Fish Street Hill?" Knightly glanced over at him in surprise. "Good heavens; no. I can't imagine. You're certain?"

"Yes."

"How very odd."

"Is it?"

"Very. Stanley had what you might call an aversion to those of low birth. In general, he avoided them as much as possible."

"Low birth and low means?"

"Well, yes. Of course."

Sebastian paused to hand a penny to the young crossing sweep who was busy clearing manure from the intersection with a ragged broom. "It's been how long since Preston's wife died?"

"Eight years, I believe. Why?"

"He was still a fairly young man at the time of her death. Yet he never remarried."

"No. But then, he was sincerely attached to his late wife. I honestly don't think he ever looked at another woman—before or after her death. He worshipped her."

"No mistresses?"

"No. Never. And if you're thinking that might be what took Stanley to this Bucket Lane, then I'm afraid you really don't understand the man who was Stanley Preston. If Stanley had been inclined to take a mistress— which he never did, of course, but if he had—he would never have chosen some common Billingsgate trollop. I remember hearing him say once that for a gentleman to lie down with a baseborn wench was tantamount to miscegenation."

Sebastian thought of the Bucket Lane woman's flawless, dusky skin and exquisite bone structure and wondered if Sir Galen actually knew his old friend as well as he thought he did. "An interesting choice of words," said Sebastian. "Miscegenation. Do I take it he never had any interest in the enslaved women who worked his plantations in Jamaica either?"

"Good God, no!"

"Yet it's not uncommon, is it?"

"It is amongst gentlemen of honor."

Sebastian watched a ponderous coal wagon making its way up the street and said nothing.

Sir Galen cleared his throat. "To my knowledge, Stanley Preston seldom ventured east of Bond Street except on business at the bank or exchange. I can't imagine what might have taken him to an area such as Fish Street Hill."

"Yet he did business with the likes of Priss Mulligan."

Knightly's brows drew together in a puzzled frown. "Who?"

"Priss Mulligan—a decidedly unsavory woman who keeps a secondhand shop in Houndsditch."

"Ah, yes; I remember hearing him speak of her. But then, I suspect Stanley would have ventured into Hades and done business with Satan himself if the devil happened to possess something Stanley wanted for his collection." The Baronet's eyes widened as if inspired by a sudden thought. "Perhaps that's what he was doing in this Bucket Lane. Buying some relic or another."

"The area's inhabitants are costers and fishmongers. Not thieves and fences."

"Some costers have been known to deal in stolen goods."

"Stolen hams and bolts of cloth, perhaps. Not priceless relics."

"Perhaps one got lucky."

"Perhaps. Only, how would he know to offer it to Preston?"

"True; I hadn't thought of that." He shrugged. "Then I'm afraid I have no explanation." He hesitated a moment, then said, "Are you no closer to discovering who might have killed him?"

"I'm afraid not."

Knightly pushed out a long, pained sigh. "And now Dr. Sterling is dead too. It's beyond ghastly."

"You were acquainted with Sterling?"

Knightly shrugged. "Jamaica is a very small island."

Sebastian stared at him. "Are you saying Douglas Sterling spent time in Jamaica?"

"Yes. You didn't know?"

"When?"

"He practiced there as a young man. And he still goes out every few years to visit a daughter who married a merchant in Kingston." Knightly paused. "Although I suppose I should say he *used to go.*"

"That's a long voyage for a man of his age."

"It was, yes. But he always claimed the sea air was good for him—that it more than made up for the fatigue of the journey. Said it was the London fog that was going to kill him." Knightly shook his head sadly at the implications of his own words.

"When was Sterling last in Jamaica? Do you know?"

"Recently, I believe. Although I couldn't say precisely when."

"During Sinclair Oliphant's period as governor?"

"It must have been, I suppose." Knightly drew up on the footpath before the Stevens. "You think that's significant?"

"It may be. I don't know."

Knightly nodded, then glanced surreptitiously at his

watch as a nearby clock tower chimed the quarter hour. "Would you care to join me for dinner?"

"Thank you, but I'm afraid I have a previous engagement."

It was only partially a lie. Sebastian's engagement was with Sinclair Oliphant.

The colonel just didn't know about it yet.

Dressed now in satin knee breeches and an evening coat, with a chapeaux bras and a silver-headed walking stick that concealed a sharp, deadly dagger, Sebastian trolled the pleasure grounds of London's haut ton: the gentlemen's clubs and gaming rooms and glittering, elegant ballrooms that provided evening entertainment to the city's most bored, most pampered residents. He finally came upon his quarry at the highly fashionable ball being given by Lady Davenport.

Lord Oliphant and his slim, blond wife were in her ladyship's supper room enjoying their hostess's lemon ices. Lady Oliphant was younger than her husband, probably no more than twenty-five or thirty. One of six daughters of an impoverished squire, she was an attractive woman, although her face and nose were considered too long, her mouth too small and prim, her chin too pointed, for her to be acknowledged a beauty. When she first married Oliphant, he had been a mere Army officer, destined for a life in that second tier reserved for younger sons. But the death of his childless elder brother had changed all that, bringing Oliphant a title, estate, wealth, and status. Watching her, Sebastian found himself wondering if she knew of the things her husband had done in the war, before he'd become Lord Oliphant and governor of Jamaica. Would she care if she did?

For some reason he could not have explained, Sebastian found himself doubting it.

He pushed away from the doorframe and walked

toward them. He knew exactly when Oliphant became aware of his presence, knew it by the subtle shifting of the man's posture and the faint glitter that leapt into his eyes. But Oliphant continued eating his ice with an assumption of insouciance.

Or perhaps it wasn't an assumption, Sebastian thought, watching him. In Sebastian's experience, men like Oliphant were made fundamentally different from their fellow beings. It was as if they'd been born immune not only to empathy and compassion, but to worry and self-doubt and fear as well.

"Again?" said Oliphant when Sebastian drew up, the groaning expanse of Lady Davenport's heavily laden supper table between them.

"Again." He tightened his grip on the head of his sword stick. "I'm told you knew Dr. Douglas Sterling."

"I did, yes." Oliphant's eyelids drooped slightly as he sucked on a spoonful of lemon ice. "As did any number of other people, I'm sure."

"True. But that number narrows considerably when one eliminates those who did not also know Stanley Preston."

Lady Oliphant paused with her spoon hovering above her lemon ice, her entire being stiff with outrage. "Surely you're not suggesting my husband has anything to do with these dreadful murders?"

"Yes," said Sebastian.

Her long, thin nose quivered with scorn. "The very idea is beyond preposterous. A lord of the realm!"

"Did your husband ever tell you about Santa Iria?" he asked, watching her closely.

She gave him a blank look. "What?"

"Santa Iria. It is—or perhaps I should say, was—a convent in the mountains of Portugal. A place of refuge for simple, devout women and the war orphans they cared for."

She looked uninterested. "And what has this to do with anything?"

"The abbess of Santa Iria was the daughter of a local grandee—a prominent landowner who was reluctant to be seen taking sides against the French for fear his people would suffer reprisals should the British be defeated. So your husband came up with a way to persuade him."

She threw Oliphant an admiring smile. "Sinclair is very inventive."

Oliphant bowed but said nothing.

"He is that," agreed Sebastian. "He sent out a courier carrying false dispatches—dispatches suggesting the abbess of Santa Iria was acting as a spy for the British. Then he tipped off a French troop in the area, so that they were able to capture the courier. Needless to say, the French believed the dispatches to be genuine."

"That was clever," said Lady Oliphant.

"The courier didn't think so."

She shrugged.

Oliphant sucked on another spoonful of ice. "Do finish your story. I suspect my wife will enjoy it."

She looked at Sebastian expectantly.

He said, "The French attacked Santa Iria at dawn. The convent was burned, the women and children all killed. Not even the smallest of babes were spared. The abbess—who was no British spy but an innocent nun— was repeatedly violated and tortured in an effort to make her talk. She died in agony."

"And her father? The dithering grandee? Was he persuaded by this French outrage to finally turn against Napoléon?"

"Actually, no. He was so horrified by what had been done that he suffered a seizure and died."

"Hmm. Pity. Still, you must admit it was an ingenious plan."

"Dozens of innocent women and children died, needlessly."

"Yes. The French have perpetrated many such outrages across Europe. Which is why, with the grace of God, they will soon be defeated."

A gleam of amusement shone in her husband's light blue eyes.

Sebastian said, "I don't think God had anything to do with what happened at Santa Iria."

"The good Lord works in mysterious ways."

Sebastian studied her smug, self-satisfied face. He'd often wondered what sort of woman could be content married to a man like Oliphant.

Now he knew.

Oliphant said, "One of these days, Devlin, you really must move beyond the events of that spring in Portugal. War is war; dreadful things happen. But do you think a London ball is the proper place to be dredging up the gruesome details?"

"When people are still dying—here, in London? Yes."

"I take it you're referring to this tiresome matter of Preston?"

"And Sterling."

Oliphant sighed and handed his empty ice cup to a hovering waiter. "Shall I give you a little hint? Yes; I do believe I shall."

"Sinclair is always most generous," said Lady Oliphant.

Oliphant gave a small bow. "You are aware, of course, of the star-crossed love affair between Miss Preston and a certain hussar captain?"

When Sebastian remained silent, Oliphant said, "Of course, Preston and his son did an admirable job of hushing up the elopement six years ago. But somehow, whispers always seem to get about; have you noticed? I tend to blame the servants."

Had Hugh Wyeth and Anne Preston attempted an elopement in the past? Sebastian wondered. If so, this was the first he'd heard of it. He kept his voice sounding bored. "This is your hint?"

"Oh, no; I assumed you already knew about the young captain. But are you aware, I wonder, that there are interesting links between the captain and Dr. Sterling?" Oliphant's face creased into an indulgent smile. "Do you know where Captain Wyeth's regiment was stationed before their transfer to Portugal?" He leaned forward and whispered loudly. *"It was Jamaica."*

When Sebastian made no response, Oliphant's lips pursed into a simulated moue of concern. "I'm afraid your obsession with the past is not only unhealthy, but is also negatively impacting your goal of catching this killer." He raised one eyebrow in mocking inquiry. "At least, I assume that is your goal. Is it not?"

With a petulant frown, Lady Oliphant set aside her ice cup and shook out the skirts of her elegant satin ball gown. "Come away, Sinclair; do. I want to dance."

Oliphant took her hand in his and rested it on the crook of his bent arm. "Of course, my dear." He nodded casually to Sebastian. "Devlin."

Sebastian watched them thread their way through the growing crowd of guests filtering into the supper room from the ballroom above. He watched as Lady Oliphant, a smile now plastered on her face, curtsied low to a dowager countess while Oliphant laughed heartily at a few pleasantries exchanged with her son, a cabinet minister.

The conviction that Oliphant was hiding something remained. But all the old doubts came crowding back as Sebastian acknowledged the possibility that maybe— just maybe—he was allowing the events of the past to color his interpretation of the present.

And because of it, men were still dying.

Chapter 42

*C*aptain Hugh Wyeth was throwing darts by himself in the Shepherd's Rest public room, pitching one after the other at a battered board hanging against a pock-marked wall. He hardly seemed to be focusing or even looking, and yet his aim was true every time.

"You're good," said Sebastian, coming to lean against a nearby wall.

"I've had a lot of practice lately. There's not much else to do."

"When do you rejoin your regiment?"

Wyeth let fly another dart. "According to the doctors, not as soon as I had hoped."

"Who were you with?"

"The Twentieth Hussars."

"The Twentieth Hussars used to be stationed in Jamaica."

Wyeth looked over at him, puzzled. "We were, yes. Why?"

"Did you ever meet Dr. Sterling there?"

"Not to my knowledge. Was he in Jamaica?"

"As it happens, yes."

The captain sent his last dart flying at the target. "You look like you're dressed for a ball."

"I am."

Wyeth grunted and went to retrieve his tightly clustered darts. He no longer wore his sling, but Sebastian noticed he held his right arm stiffly against his side.

Sebastian said, "You told me you didn't know Sinclair Oliphant. Yet he seems to know you."

Wyeth looked around in surprise. "What?"

"He's the one who told me you were stationed in Jamaica—presumably to shift suspicion away from himself and onto you."

"Did it work?"

When Sebastian returned no answer, the captain gave a soft, humorless laugh and said, "I suppose the fact that you're here tells me all I need to know." He walked back to the throwing line, then paused, weighing his first dart. "Why would I kill some old doctor? Tell me that."

"I don't know. But then, I can't figure out why anyone would want to murder him—unless it was because he knew something worrisome about whoever killed Stanley Preston."

Wyeth threw his dart and practically missed the target entirely.

Sebastian said, "Ever hear of a man named Rowan Toop?"

"No. Why? Is he dead too?"

Sebastian nodded. "They found him this morning, at Windsor."

"Someone cut off his head?"

"No, actually; he drowned."

"You think I did that?"

"You wouldn't happen to know what might have taken Stanley Preston to Bucket Lane last Sunday, would you?"

"Where?"

"Bucket Lane. Off Fish Street Hill, near London Bridge."

"No. Don't tell me someone's died there too?"

"Not to my knowledge."

Wyeth threw the rest of his darts at the target, one after the other in rapid succession. This time, they were spread all over the round wooden board in a chaotic pattern.

Sebastian said, "Last Sunday at Lady Farningham's musical evening, you and Miss Preston quarreled. That's why you left early, isn't it? In fact, Miss Preston herself left not long after you did."

"So?"

"Why did you quarrel?"

"Does it matter?"

"You tell me. Does it?"

The captain twitched one shoulder and said nothing.

Sebastian studied the younger man's angry, tightly held features. "Sinclair Oliphant told me something else. He says that six years ago, you tried to elope with Miss Preston. Only, her father and brother caught up with you and brought her back."

Sebastian watched the blood drain from the captain's face. "How the devil did he know that?"

"Stanley Preston made himself Oliphant's enemy, and Oliphant is the kind of man who makes it his business to know his enemies' most dangerous secrets. So it's true?"

Wyeth swallowed hard. "Yes. Look—I'm not proud of what we did, but . . . we were both very young and desperate, and . . . we didn't understand the gravity of what we were doing."

"It certainly does much to explain Preston's animosity toward you."

Wyeth tightened his jaw and said nothing.

"Miss Preston is of age now. Yet most women are reluctant to marry without their father's blessing." *Particularly when there's a potential inheritance involved,* Sebastian thought. "Would she have married you, do you think, if her father continued to withhold his consent?"

"Stanley Preston was never going to change his mind, believe me."

"So would she have married you anyway?"

Wyeth swung to face him, his hands curling into fists at his sides. "You think I would have done that to her? Married her without his blessing? Preston would never have forgiven her. He swore he'd cut her off without a penny and never speak to her again, and he meant it. Yet you think I would have married her anyway? Taken her away from a life of comfort to make her follow the drum and live in poverty? My God; what kind of man do you take me for?"

"You were certainly ready to elope with her six years ago."

"I was eighteen! I told you, I'm not proud of what happened six years ago. But I know better now."

"She wouldn't have been completely penniless," said Sebastian. "She'd still have had her mother's portion."

"Her mother's portion amounts to even less than my annual pay. Enough to help buy a few promotions, perhaps, and ease the worst hardships that come with life in the Army. But without her inheritance from Preston, I could never have given her anything like the kind of life she's always known."

"Is that so important?"

"You know it is. I've seen what poverty can do to a gently reared woman. My grandfather was never as wealthy as Preston, but my mother still grew up surrounded by servants, with a carriage and her own pony and summers spent at the seaside. With five daughters and an estate entailed to the male line, my grandfather couldn't give her much of a dowry, but she was pretty enough that he hoped she'd attract suitors anyway. And she did—the grandest being a man worth ten thousand pounds a year."

"She turned them all down to marry your father?"

Wyeth nodded. "My father's living was worth barely two hundred pounds a year." He gave a ragged laugh. "Once, she'd worn ball gowns worth nearly that much."

"Were they happy?"

"They were happy with each other, yes. But her life was . . . hard. She'd cry sometimes, when she didn't know I could hear her. She worried constantly, about where they were going to find the money to fix the vicarage roof, or pay my school fees, or provide for my three sisters. All that worry and fear . . . In the end, it killed her. That's when I realized how selfish I'd been, asking Anne to marry me, expecting her to endure a different version of the kind of life that killed my mother."

"You're saying that when faced with a choice between love and wealth, a woman should choose wealth?"

"No. But—"

"You think your mother would have been happier married to a man with ten thousand pounds a year whom she didn't love?"

"No. But—"

"And if your father had made the choice for her by walking away, would she have been happy?"

Wyeth glared at him. "God *damn* you. Who are you— an earl's son, heir to a grand fortune—to presume to pass judgment on me? What do you know of the kind of choices the rest of us must make?"

"More than you might think," said Sebastian.

He was turning away when Wyeth's fist caught him high on the side of his cheek.

❧

"You let him hit you?" said Hero, holding a twisted cloth filled with ice against the rapidly purpling bruise.

"Not exactly," said Sebastian, wincing. "But I did provoke him. It didn't seem right to hit him back."

"You're going to end up with a black eye."

"It won't be the first."

She made an incoherent noise deep in her throat and went to refill her cloth from the bucket of ice provided by Calhoun. "If he were clever, Captain Wyeth would be trying to convince you that Preston had agreed to let him marry Anne. Instead, he insists Preston would never have consented, then goes on to detail why a man of honor would never marry Anne without her inheritance. It's as if he were determined to tie a noose around his own neck and hang himself."

"I know. Which, ironically enough, makes me think he probably *didn't* kill Stanley Preston." Sebastian went to peer at his discolored face in the washstand mirror. "I wish I could say I felt the same way about Miss Anne Preston."

Hero turned to look at him, the ice-filled cloth held slack in her hand. "You can't be serious."

"Oh, I don't mean that she personally stabbed Preston and Sterling and cut off their heads. But she wouldn't be the first woman to hire someone to do her dirty work for her. Someone such as, say, Diggory Flynn."

"Surely she can't be that diabolical? To kill her own father . . ."

Sebastian shrugged. "Patricide, matricide, fratricide: They seem so unnatural that we're repelled by the very thought. Yet they happen—often enough that we've even coined words for them. Anne Preston wanted Captain Hugh Wyeth, but she knew he'd never marry her without her inheritance. Not because he's a greedy fortune hunter, but because he saw what poverty did to his mother and he's too noble to do that to a woman he loves."

"So she removes Stanley Preston, and now she's free to marry her captain *and* receive her inheritance? Is that what you're suggesting? His noble qualms are stilled, and she never needs to worry about having to wash her own clothes in a muddy stream in some backward part of the world? Yes; it makes sense—if she's that shockingly selfish and coldhearted. But it doesn't give her a reason to kill Douglas Sterling."

"Just because we don't know of a reason doesn't mean one doesn't exist."

Hero set aside the ice-filled cloth. "Why order the killer to cut off his victims' heads?"

"Perhaps that was his own embellishment. Or perhaps she thought a more gruesome killing would help deflect suspicion from her."

"Surely she can't be that . . . evil."

"I wouldn't have said so. But I've been wrong about people before." He took the ice-filled cloth and carefully pressed it against his face. "The problem is, it still doesn't explain why Stanley Preston made a most uncharacteristic visit to Bucket Lane just hours before he was killed."

"That could be entirely unrelated to anything."

"It could be," said Sebastian, remembering the dusky-skinned woman with the long neck and the strange, turquoise eyes. "But I doubt it. And if it is related, then whoever Preston went to see that day might very well be in danger—although they probably don't know it."

Hero went to hunker down beside the black cat curled up before the dressing room fire. "One of the costermongers I interviewed lives near Fish Street Hill," she said, her hand trailing down the cat's back. "I could ask him to look into it. They all seem to know each other." She shifted her hand to scratch behind the cat's ears. "And Rowan Toop? How do you think he fits into all this?"

"I think he stole the royal relics from the crypt and was selling them to Preston. They'd arranged to meet at Bloody Bridge, except by the time Toop arrived, Preston was already dead. Toop was probably so horrified by what he discovered that he ran off—dropping the inscribed coffin strap in the process. It's hard to say whether or not he saw—or knew—something that could have identified the killer. But the killer obviously thought he did. And killed him too."

Hero kept her gaze on the cat. "Or Toop could have been so rattled by recent events that he simply slipped in the mud while taking his dog for a walk and pitched into the Thames—without anyone's help."

"True." Sebastian set aside the melting ice and reached for a clean cloth to dry his face. "I'm hoping Gibson will have an answer when I see him tomorrow."

If he's not lost in an opium-induced fog, thought Sebastian.

Chapter 43

*A*fter some thirty-six hours, Rowan Toop's corpse had taken on the vague odor of rotting fish.

Naked and eviscerated, it lay on the stone table in the outbuilding at the base of Paul Gibson's unkempt yard. The Irishman was there, cold sober and cranky. He was not singing.

"I was wondering when you'd show up," he said when Sebastian came to stand in the doorway.

"Good morning," said Sebastian.

The surgeon grunted. "Nice black eye."

"Thank you."

Sebastian took one look at what was left of Toop, then looked elsewhere. "So did he drown? Or was he murdered?"

"Maybe both. Maybe one, maybe the other. It's hard to say."

"It is?"

"It is." Gibson set aside his knife with a clatter and reached for a rag to wipe the gore from his hands. "He could have been hit over the head, then thrown into the river, whereupon he drowned. Or he could have fallen and hit his own head, slipped into the river, and drowned. He could even have slipped into the river, hit his head on something, and then drowned."

"But you're saying he was alive when he went into the water?"

"Not necessarily. He could also have been hit on the head, died, and then been tossed into the river. That's a nasty blow he's got there—nasty enough to kill him without any help from the river."

"Was there water in his lungs?"

"There was. Water, sand—even a few bits of grass."

"So he must have breathed all that stuff in. Right?"

"No. If there hadn't been any water in his lungs, then I could tell you, yes, he was probably dead when he hit the water. But the action of the river could have driven water into his lungs even after he was dead." Gibson picked up his knife and pointed at what Sebastian realized must be Rowan Toop's lungs, sitting on a rusty tray parked on a nearby shelf. "See that white foam?"

"Yes," said Sebastian, who had no desire to peer too closely.

"You often find a fine white froth like that in the lungs of drownings pulled from the Thames. But you also see it in the lungs of men whose hearts have failed, or who've hit their heads. Now, your Rowan Toop's heart was just fine. But you obviously can't say the same thing about his head."

Sebastian blew out a long, frustrated breath. "So you can't tell me *anything*?"

"No. Only thing remotely queer about any of this is that they found him so fast. A freshly dead body'll usually sink like a rock. They don't typically come up again until enough gas builds in their guts to float them to the surface. And this time of year, that usually takes about five days."

"Five days? So why was Toop found on Romney Island less than twelve hours after he disappeared?"

Gibson shrugged. "Must've been something about the way he went in the water. Trapped air in his cassock. It happens. He floated down to the island and got caught in the trees before he had a chance to sink."

Sebastian braced his hands against the stone table and stared at the dead man's pale, bony face. "I can't believe he just slipped and hit his head. Somebody killed him."

"Probably," agreed Gibson. "But unless they find a bloody cudgel by the side of the river, you'll never be able to prove it."

Later that morning, Sebastian joined Sir Henry Lovejoy at a coffeehouse just off the Strand.

"I've had the lads looking into this Diggory Flynn you were asking about," said Lovejoy, taking a cautious sip of his hot chocolate. "Unfortunately, they haven't been able to find a trace of him."

"It could be an assumed name." Sebastian wrapped his hands around his own steaming coffee. "I've just come from Gibson's surgery."

"And?"

"He says Toop's postmortem is inconclusive; the virger may have been killed, or he may simply have slipped and fallen in the river."

Lovejoy looked thoughtfully at Sebastian's discolored eye. But all he said was, "Perhaps that explains why Toop's head wasn't cut off—because he wasn't actually murdered."

"He was murdered," said Sebastian.

"Then how do you explain the differences in both the method of murder and the treatment of the body?"

"It could be because the killer didn't have time to be more grisly. Or perhaps he didn't want us to realize that Toop's death was connected to those of Preston and Sterling. Or . . ."

"Or?" prompted Lovejoy.

Sebastian rested his elbows on the table. "Ask yourself: Why would a killer cut off his victims' heads?"

"Because he's mad."

"That's one explanation. But there are others. The killer's purpose could be to create fear—either in the community at large, or in one specifically targeted individual who knows he's next."

"Such as who?"

Sebastian shook his head. "I don't know." From the distance came the *rat-a-tat-tat* of a military drum and the tramp of marching feet.

"Either way," said Lovejoy, "it's still the work of a madman. No sane individual goes around cutting off people's heads."

"I think most of us are a bit mad, each in our own way."

"But . . . to cut off a man's head?"

Sebastian stared out the bowed window at a street filled with stout matrons and City merchants and all the usual bustle of a London morning. But he wasn't seeing any of it. He was seeing another time, another place. "It happens in battle," he said. "More often than you might think. It's as if the act of killing taps into something primitive within us—a deep and powerful rage that finds expression in the mutilation of a dead enemy."

"You think that's what we're dealing with here? Rage? But . . . over what?"

"I still don't know. But I suspect that rage was directed at Preston and Sterling, whereas Toop . . . Toop was killed simply out of concern he might have seen something."

"What a disturbing thought." Lovejoy sat for a moment in silence. Then he cleared his throat and said, "I've had some of the lads interviewing the regular patrons at the Monster, as you suggested. They located a solicitor who was seated at a table near Henry Austen when Preston came into the tavern last Sunday night. He says the way Preston was yelling made it virtually impossible not to hear everything that was said."

"And?"

"It seems that, amongst other threats, Preston swore he was going to withdraw his funds from Austen's bank."

"Did Preston bank with Austen?"

"He did. Indeed, his deposits were quite substantial. And here's another interesting thing: Dr. Douglas Sterling was also a subscriber."

"What does Henry Austen say about all this?"

"He claims his bank is strong enough to withstand the defection of a dozen such subscribers."

"Is it?"

"Who can say? But this doesn't look good for him. It doesn't look good at all."

※

Sebastian found Henry Austen coming out of a small brick chapel tucked away off Brompton Row. This was a part of Hans Town as yet unspoiled by London's creeping sprawl, where budding chestnut trees swayed gently in the breeze and vast fields of market gardens stretched away to the east. The day had dawned gloriously warm, with the sky a rare, clear blue and the air fresh with the promise of spring.

Sebastian paused his curricle across from the chapel, the brim of his hat tipped against the strengthening sun, and watched Henry Austen walk out the chapel door, eyes blinking against the sudden fierceness of the light. His gaze focused on Sebastian and he momentarily froze before turning to speak to the two women who accompanied him: his sister Jane and their friend, Miss Anne Preston.

Jane Austen looked up, smiled, and nodded to Sebastian. Anne Preston stared at him, but she did not smile or acknowledge him in any way.

"That younger gentry mort don't appear to like ye overly much," observed Tom from his perch at the rear of the curricle.

"She doesn't, does she?" agreed Sebastian.

Leaving the two women to walk on alone, Henry Austen crossed the street toward Sebastian, then drew up while still some feet away. "How did you find me?"

"Your clerk told me you were helping Miss Preston finalize the details of her father's funeral."

Austen nodded, his arms hanging loosely at his sides. "I know why you're here."

"I figured you would. Climb up. Tom will get down and wait for us."

Austen hesitated a moment, then leapt into the high seat as Tom scrambled down.

"I won't be long," Sebastian told the tiger, and gave his horses the office to start.

"Fine pair," said Austen, his gaze on the chestnuts' sun-warmed hides as they bowled up the lane toward Fulham.

"They were bred on my estate down in Hampshire."

Austen turned his head to look at Sebastian. "I take it you find my failure to tell you of Preston's threat to my bank suspicious."

"Should I?"

"Bow Street does."

"Perhaps that's because they don't understand the important part that confidence plays in the stability of a bank. I'm not surprised you chose to keep it quiet. Or as quiet as you could after Preston shouted his intentions in a crowded tavern."

When Austen remained silent, Sebastian said, "Could your bank have withstood Preston's withdrawal? And before you answer, I should warn you that I have the resources to verify your answer."

"Then why bother to ask?" snapped the banker.

Sebastian kept his attention on the road.

After a moment, Austen said, "Yes, the bank is solid, damn you. Preston was a large investor; I won't deny that. But not by any means the largest."

"Do you think he would have carried through on his threat?"

"Honestly? I don't know. He was always flying off the handle and saying wild things, only to later calm down and reconsider."

"And Douglas Sterling? Would he have followed his old friend's lead and also removed his funds from your bank?"

Austen looked genuinely surprised. "Sterling? Of course not. Why would he?"

"Because of the friendship between them?"

Austen shook his head. "They knew each other, of course—had known each other for years. But I'd characterize them more as acquaintances than what you might call friends. Apart from the difference in their ages, Sterling was a physician from a relatively humble background, whereas Preston had grand ambitions of taking his place in Society. He was always talking about his late wife the Baron's daughter, or his cousin the Home Secretary. Another man might have ignored the disparity in their rank and wealth. But not Preston."

"Was Preston ill, do you think?" Sebastian asked, guiding his horses around an empty farm wagon.

"Not to my knowledge. But then, as I said, Preston and I weren't exactly great friends either."

"From the sound of things, he wasn't intimate with many people."

"In my experience, people who view others as social or financial assets rarely do accumulate close friends."

"True," said Sebastian. "You wouldn't by chance happen to know what took Preston to Fish Street Hill last Sunday, would you?"

"Fish Street Hill? Good heavens; no."

"Ever know Preston to keep a mistress?"

Austen's eyes widened at the question. "No. He was genuinely, madly in love with his wife and never got over her death."

"What about when he was a very young man? Say thirty or thirty-five years ago, when he was in Jamaica?"

Rather than answer immediately, Austen studied Sebastian from beneath half-lowered lids. "What are you suggesting?"

"Any possibility Preston could have had a child by one of the slave women on his plantations?"

"You can't be serious."

"Is it so improbable?"

"Let's just say that if you'd known Preston, you'd understand just how improbable it is. His belief in the superiority of the English was intense and unshakable. I mean, the man could never forgive my wife for once having married a *Frenchman*. And while I wasn't acquainted with him thirty years ago, the mind frankly boggles at the thought of him raping one of his slave women—if that's what you're suggesting."

"Those who rail the loudest against 'racial impurity' are often those who feel they have something to hide. Something that violates their own twisted moral code."

Austen thought about it a moment, then blew out a long breath. "I suppose it's possible, but . . . Whatever gave you such an idea?"

"I have a very active imagination."

Austen gave a startled laugh. "You must. I'm not convinced even my sister Jane could have come up with that one." The banker stared off across a sunlit pasture dotted with grazing brown cows. His eyes narrowed, as if he were struggling to come to some sort of decision. Then he said, "Jane told me something the other day that might interest you, by the way."

"Oh? What's that?"

"You know that fellow who keeps a curiosity shop in Chelsea?"

"Basil Thistlewood?"

"That's him. Well, it seems that when she arrived at Alford House to take Anne up in my carriage, Preston and Thistlewood were standing in the middle of the street, shouting at each other. She didn't think too much of it at the time—Preston was always squabbling with someone, you know. But while she has no desire to say something that might throw suspicion on an innocent man, she's begun to wonder if perhaps you shouldn't know about it."

"This happened last Sunday evening?"

"Yes; around nine," said Austen. "That surprises you; why?"

Sebastian swung his horses in a wide loop at the crossroads and headed back toward Brompton Row. "Because Thistlewood claims he never left his coffeehouse that day at all."

Chapter 44

*B*asil Thistlewood was standing beneath the elms lining the Thames at Cheyne Walk and throwing chunks of bread to a gathering of some half a dozen ducks when Sebastian walked up to him. The spring sunlight glimmered on the wide stretch of river beside them, and the limbs of the budding trees overhead throbbed with birdsong.

The curiosity collector cast a quick, sideways glance at Sebastian, then went back to pitching bread. "Didn't expect to see you again."

"You should have," said Sebastian, watching the ducks dart after the bread, their feathers iridescent in the sunlight. "When you stand in the middle of the street shouting at someone who turns up dead later that very evening, you have to expect that sooner or later someone is going to remember it."

"How'd you hear about that?"

"Does it matter?"

"S'pose not." Thistlewood tore off another chunk of bread and pitched it at the ducks.

"Care to tell me about it?"

Thistlewood twitched one shoulder. "Not much to tell. Friend of mine's got a shop in Knightsbridge. I was walking back from visiting him and just minding my own business when Preston comes barging out of his house and chases after me, accusing me of all sorts of outlandish stuff."

"What sort of outlandish stuff?"

"Watching his house."

"Were you watching his house?"

"Well, I may've stopped and looked at it. But I weren't *watching* it. I was coming back from having a game of chess with Rory. You can check; he'll tell you—Rory Lemar, lives over his tobacco shop in Knightsbridge. You ask him, and he'll tell you I was there."

"You told me you never left your coffee shop that Sunday."

Thistlewood sniffed. "What you think? That I'm gonna step forward and volunteer the information that Preston and me had words an hour or two before he got himself killed?"

"It does rather make it look as if you have something to hide."

"Just 'cause I hid the fact I saw him that day don't mean I killed him!"

"Some might interpret it that way."

The curiosity collector pressed his lips together and thrust them out in a way that made him look somewhat like a disgruntled turtle.

Sebastian said, "It was Rowan Toop who showed you the lead-wrapped bodies of the woman and child you told me about; wasn't it?"

Thistlewood's eyes widened. "I read about what happened to him in the papers. What are you saying? That I maybe killed him too? I didn't."

"But you did know him."

"I knew him. Never bought nothin' from him, though. I told you before—I can't afford to pay for the things I put on display."

"And Toop wanted to be paid?"

"He did indeed."

"Did Toop ever sell items to Stanley Preston?"

"I can't say for certain, but I 'spect so." The curiosity collector shot Sebastian another one of his sideways glances. "You think whoever lopped off Preston's head also done for Toop?"

"I think it more than likely."

"Well, all I know is, it weren't me. Ask anyone, they'll tell you: I'm not a violent man."

"Despite your fascination with swords and headsmen's axes and executioners' blocks?"

"You don't find 'em fascinating?"

"In a macabre sort of way, I suppose I do. But they also repel me."

Thistlewood tore off another piece of bread and chucked it at the ducks. "I reckon we're all afraid of death. We know we're gonna die, but none of us wants to." He gave a strange, watery chuckle. "Some folks, they've got this notion that if they think about death, they're inviting it closer. So they don't want to be reminded of it in any way. But then there's others who think that by gettin' close to death—by staring it in the face, so to speak—we make it less scary."

"I take it you fall into the latter category?"

Thistlewood gave another of his odd chuckles. "Reckon I do. And you too."

"Me?"

"Why else would you do what you do? Look for murderers, I mean."

Sebastian started to deny it. If asked, he'd have said his dedication to finding a measure of justice for the victims of murder had far more to do with guilt and a need for redemption than with a fear of death. And yet . . .

He watched as the curiosity collector crumpled the last of his bread and scattered it in the water. The branches of the elms overhead cast shifting patterns of light and shade across the waves washing gently against the riverbank; the air smelled of damp earth and the wild mint that grew in the hollows between the gnarled roots. He listened to the splash of a wherryman's oars farther out on the Thames, heard the squeals and laughter of children playing in a nearby pasture. And he was forced to acknowledge that, in a sense, Thistlewood was right. Except it wasn't his own death Sebastian feared but the death of those he loved, lest they be forced to pay with their own lives for the lives of the women and children he'd failed to save.

"Have you ever killed anyone?" Thistlewood asked suddenly. "Surely you have—you being in the Army and all."

"Why do you ask?"

"I attend the hangings at Newgate, sometimes. I watch the hangman pull that lever and I think, What must it feel like, to kill someone? To know that one minute they're living and the next they're not, and it's *you* who's done that." He looked at Sebastian expectantly, his lips pulled back in a hopeful, almost eager half smile.

But Sebastian only shook his head, unwilling to satisfy the man's ghoulish curiosity.

Until that moment, Sebastian would have said he doubted that Thistlewood had anything to do with the recent string of murders. Despite Thistlewood's lies, despite the public arguments and intense professional and personal jealousy, Sebastian had largely discounted him as a suspect, instead becoming more and more convinced that the grisly killings were the work of someone hired by Sinclair Oliphant or Priss Mulligan, or perhaps even by Preston's own daughter, Anne.

Now he wasn't so sure.

❧

Mica McDougal leaned against his donkey cart, his beefy arms crossed at his chest, first one cheek, then the other puffing out with air as he stared thoughtfully at Hero.

"Stanley Preston? Ain't 'e the cove what got 'is 'ead cut off out at Bloody Bridge?"

Hero nodded. "He visited Bucket Lane just hours before he was killed. I'm trying to find out why he went there and whom he saw."

McDougal squinted up at the thick gray clouds scuttling in overhead to rob the day of its promise of warmth and sunshine. A cold wind had kicked up, ruffling the feathers of the gulls screaming overhead and intensifying the odor of raw fish that rose from both the man and his cart. "Ye thinkin' maybe some coster done fer 'im?"

"No; not at all. But two other people who knew Preston and saw him that day are now dead too. Which means that whoever Preston visited in Bucket Lane could very well be in danger. Only he—or she—might not know it."

McDougal brought his gaze back to her face. "Well, I can look into it, m'lady. But I can't guarantee they'll be willin' t' talk t' ye."

"I know. Just . . . whoever it is, please try to help them understand that their lives might be threatened. If they know anything—anything at all—it's important for them to come forward."

He rasped one palm across the several days' worth of beard shading his jaw. "I'll try, my lady. I'll try."

The rain was already beginning to fall by the time Hero made it back to Brook Street, a fine but hard-driven rain that swirled in wind-whipped eddies between the tall town houses and stung the tender bare skin of her face.

She had just stepped from her carriage and was about to mount the front steps when she saw Devlin round the corner from Bond Street, the capes of his black greatcoat flapping in the wind, his hat tipped low against the downpour.

"Devlin," she called, and he looked up, his face lean

and unsmiling. Then his strange yellow eyes widened, his body jerking as the crack of a rifle shot reverberated between the tall row houses.

A shiny wet stain bloomed dark against the darkness of his coat.

"*No!*" Hero screamed.

The bullet's impact spun him around. He grasped the iron railing of a nearby house's area steps. Tried to stay upright. Crumpled slowly to his knees.

"Oh, my God." Hero ran, hands fisted in her skirts. Her world narrowed down to a gray wet canyon where the only sound was a desperate gasping she dimly recognized as her own, and the only color the red splash of Devlin's blood.

"Sebastian."

She dropped to her knees beside him, hands reaching for him. He lay curled on his side away from her, the rain washing over his pale face. She touched his shoulder and he turned toward her. She saw the confusion in those familiar yellow eyes, the pain that convulsed the features that were so like Devlin's. But it wasn't Devlin.

It was Jamie Knox.

Chapter 45

Sebastian reached home just as Pippa, the barmaid from the Black Devil, was coming down the front steps. She had a paisley shawl drawn up over her head and a child of perhaps a year on her hip. At the sight of Sebastian she paused, her arms tightening around the child, so that he squirmed in protest.

"It's your fault!" she screamed, tears mingling with the rain on her face. "I told him no good would come of it, but would he listen to me? No. He never listened t' me."

Sebastian stared at the child in her arms. It was a boy, with fine-boned features and a small, turned-up nose and the same yellow eyes that stared back at Sebastian from his own mirror.

From his own infant son.

"What are you talking about?" he said.

Her laugh was raw, torn; not really a laugh at all. "You sayin' you don't know? He's layin' up there in one of your own fancy beds, dyin' because of you, and *you don't know*?"

He grabbed her arm more roughly than he'd intended. "Knox?"

She jerked away from him. "You tell him— You tell

him, I won't stay and watch him die." And she pushed
past him, her head bowed against the rain, her shoulders convulsing with her sobs as the boy gazed back at
Sebastian with a solemn, intense stare.

Gibson was coming out of the guest bedroom at the
end of the hall when Sebastian reached the second floor.

"How is he?"

The surgeon rubbed his eyes with a spread thumb
and forefinger. "I've done what I can. The bullet ripped
through his lungs and lodged beside his heart. He's
bleeding inside, and there's no way to stop it. At this
point, it's just a matter of time."

"Surely there's some hope—a chance—"

Gibson shook his head. "Lady Devlin thinks whoever shot him mistook Knox for you."

Sebastian felt an aching hollowness open up inside
him, carved out by denial and rage and a hideous,
familiar sense of guilt. "Where was he?"

"Just steps from your front door." Gibson started to
say something else, then stopped.

"What?" asked Sebastian.

"It's just . . . the resemblance is uncanny."

"Yes," said Sebastian, and turned toward the bedroom.

He found Knox lying with his eyes closed, so ashen and
still that for a moment Sebastian thought him already
dead. Then he saw the rifleman's bare, bandaged chest
jerk, heard the labored rasp of a dying man's breath.

Hero sat nearby, her fingers laced together in her lap,
her eyes sunken and stark, as if she'd just been given a
glimpse into the yawning mouth of hell. "He was coming to see you," she said softly.

"Do you know why?"

She shook her head. "He tried to say, but it didn't make any sense. And then he lost consciousness."

Sebastian stared down at the pale face that was so like his own. And he knew a renewed surge of anger and regret and a panicked sense of impending loss that he could do nothing—nothing—to avert.

Knox drew another ragged breath and opened his eyes. "It's bad, isn't it?" he said, his voice a hushed quaver.

Sebastian felt his throat seize up, so that for a moment all he could do was set his jaw and nod.

"You asked . . . You asked about Diggory Flynn."

"Never mind about Flynn. You need to save your breath."

A ghost of amusement flitted across the former rifleman's features. "Save it for what? It's probably Flynn who killed me. They say . . . he's a good shot."

"Who is he?"

Knox's head moved restlessly against his pillow. "He doesn't . . . really exist. But there's . . ." His breath caught on a cough, and a line of blood spilled from the corner of his mouth.

Sebastian reached for his handkerchief and carefully wiped away the blood.

Knox licked his dry lips "They say there's a Buckinghamshire vicar's son . . . served as an exploring officer in the Peninsula . . . likes to use that name."

"Who told you this?"

"Doesn't matter. She doesn't know . . . any more." Knox's hand came up to grasp Sebastian's wrist. "Tell . . . tell Pippa . . . I'm sorry. The boy . . ." He drew in a noisy, oddly sucking breath. "Should have married her. Know what it's like . . . growing up the bastard son of a barmaid. Now . . . too late."

"No." Sebastian took Knox's hand in both of his and gripped it with a determined fierceness. "It's not too late. I can find a vicar. Get a special license and—"

But Knox's hand lay limp in Sebastian's grasp. And as he watched, the eyes that were so much like his own grew unfocused and empty, and the bandaged chest lay ominously still.

"Breathe, damn you!" Sebastian sank to both knees, the rifleman's hand still clenched tightly between his own as he watched, waited for the next breath.

"Breathe!"

He was aware of Hero coming to stand beside him, felt her touch on his shoulder although he did not look up. She stood beside him as the minutes stretched out, until the absence of life had shifted from a dread to an undeniable certainty.

Finally, she said, "I am so sorry, Devlin."

He suddenly felt bone tired, his eyes aching, a tight band squeezing his chest as he shook his head slowly from side to side. "I don't even know who he was. Don't know if I just lost a brother, or not."

"Does it matter?"

"On one level, no. But . . . I should know." *A man should know his own brother,* thought Sebastian.

His own father.

She turned toward him, cradling his head in her palms to draw his body against her soft warmth. The only sounds were the patter of the wind-driven rain striking the windowpanes, the fall of the ash on the hearth, and his own anguished breath.

"I thought he was you," Hero said to Sebastian later as she sat by the fire in the library, a forgotten cup of tea on the table at her side. "I saw him coming around the corner from Bond Street as I was stepping down from the carriage. I called to him—called your name. And then I saw the bullet hit his chest and I thought you were dead. I thought I'd lost you and . . ."

She swallowed, her voice becoming shaky. Hushed. "I

didn't know I could hurt that much inside. Then I realized it wasn't you, it was Knox, and I was glad because it meant you were still alive." Her face took on a stark, fierce look. "God help me, I was glad."

He knelt at her feet, his hands entwined with hers in her lap. He'd seen her shoot an attacker in the face and bash in a murderer's head without losing her composure or equanimity. But what had happened today had obviously shaken her badly; he could feel the fine trembling going on inside her still.

She said, "And then that poor woman—Pippa— came, and even though I felt sorry for her, all I could think was how relieved I was that it was her man who was dying. I knew it was wrong, but I couldn't help it. Because if I lost you . . . I don't know how I'd bear it."

His hands tightened on hers. He understood how she'd felt because he'd known the same helpless despair when he thought he was about to lose her in childbirth. He said, "I'm sorry, Hero. I'm so sorry. But . . . I can't stop what I do, if that's what you're asking me."

She loosed her hands from his grip to press her fingers against his lips. "I'm not asking you to stop. I won't pretend I don't fear for you—I fear for *myself*, because I know my love for you makes me vulnerable. But I know too that what I feel is the same fear endured by every woman whose man ever marched off to war; every wife who watches her son or lover sail to sea or go down in a mine to earn his bread. Risk is a part of what it means to be alive. We can't live our lives in a constant, paralyzing fear of death."

"Some do," he said, his lips moving against her fingers.

A fierce light shone in her eyes. "Yes. But I refuse to."

Her words echoed something Kat Boleyn had said to him once, long ago. He shifted his hands to Hero's shoulders, leaned forward until his forehead was pressed against hers. "I will be careful. I can promise you that."

Once, he had been careless with his life, heedless of whether he lived or died.

That was no longer true.

She gave him a sad smile. "I know."

He kissed her, hard, on her mouth, then rose to unlock the upper right drawer in his desk and withdraw a sleek, walnut-handled dueling pistol. This was not the small, double-barreled flintlock he often carried, which was easily concealed but accurate only at close range. This pistol was made with a long, lightly rifled barrel that made it deadly even at some distance.

"You think the shooter was Diggory Flynn?" she asked, watching as Sebastian set about loading and priming the pistol.

"I'd say it's more than likely, yes. I think he was watching the house, waiting for me. He saw Knox, and like you, he assumed Knox was me." Sebastian paused, his hands stilling at their task as the bitter truth of it all washed over him anew. "Knox died because he looked like me. He died in my place."

She rested her hand on his arm. He thought she was going to tell him it wasn't his fault, that he couldn't keep blaming himself for deaths caused by others. Instead, she said, "Will you kill him?"

"First, I'm going to find out who hired him." Sebastian slipped the pistol into the pocket of his caped greatcoat. "And then I'm going to kill him."

Chapter 46

Sebastian spent the next hour or so frequenting taverns favored by ex-military men, particularly those who'd served as exploring or observing officers.

Most such men rode a war-torn countryside wearing their British uniforms, lest they be caught and ignobly hanged as spies. But there were some who knew how to blend in with the local populace, to slip behind enemy lines and return again with none the wiser. It was frowned upon, of course—for a gentleman to use subterfuge and deception. Yet for thousands of years, generals had relied upon those with such skills.

Their motives differed. Some risked everything out of love of country, or for the sake of the men with whom they served, or because the vicissitudes of life had eroded their attachment to the things most other men held dear. But there were some who acted solely for the thrill of it all, for the joy of deception and the opportunities it offered.

Sebastian suspected Diggory Flynn fell into the latter category.

It was in a smoky, run-down inn off Cursitor Street that Sebastian found the old acquaintance he was looking for: a one-legged former lieutenant named Dillon

Rutherford, who peered at him over the rim of a brandy glass and said, "Diggory Flynn? What do you want with him?"

"I want to kill him," said Sebastian, taking the seat opposite the lieutenant.

A soundless chuckle shook the lieutenant's thin chest. "You and a fair number of other people. Unfortunately, he's not all that easy to kill."

Rutherford was one of those men who looked as if he could be anywhere between thirty and fifty. Of medium height and slim build, with a gaunt face and thinning brown hair, he'd been born the youngest of a country squire's five sons. When he was sixteen, his family scraped together enough money to purchase his first pair of colors. But in more than ten years of service he'd managed to save enough to buy only one promotion. And after losing a leg and the use of his right arm at Medina de Rioseco, he'd been invalided out. He now survives by tutoring small boys from a rented room near the Inns of Court.

"Where can I find him?" asked Sebastian.

Rutherford licked his lips. "Flynn isn't his real name."

Sebastian ordered two brandies and slid one across the table toward Rutherford. "What is?"

"He's used so many over the years that I have a hard time keeping them all straight. Barnes? Brady? Something like that."

"His father was a vicar?"

"So they say." The lieutenant sipped from his new glass of brandy.

"Did he ever serve under Colonel Sinclair Oliphant?"

The lieutenant widened his eyes. "You don't know?"

"Know what?"

"It was Oliphant kept him from being hanged, when Wellesley was all for stringing him up in Lisbon, back in 1808."

That would have been not long before Oliphant was

made colonel of Sebastian's regiment. He said, "What had Flynn done?"

"Killed a fellow officer in a fight over a woman. Flynn was the type best kept behind enemy lines. He had a habit of falling into trouble when left with too much time on his hands."

"What does he do now?"

"I don't know. Heard he found himself in a bit of an awkward spot in Jamaica."

"He was in Jamaica? With Oliphant?"

Rutherford gave a shrug that could have meant anything. "Oh, not officially, of course. But a man like Diggory Flynn can be useful, if you know what I mean."

"Where can I find him?" Sebastian asked again.

The lieutenant fingered his empty glass.

Sebastian ordered another.

Rutherford waited until the brandy appeared and took a drink before saying, "I honestly don't know where you might find him. The fact is, you could run into him in the street and not recognize him. He's that good."

"What does he look like? I mean, really look like."

The lieutenant frowned with the effort of memory. "Red hair. About my size, maybe a bit fleshier these days. He's got one of those faces that blends easily into a crowd, although he's right clever at shifting the way he looks. Don't know how he does it. Only really distinctive thing about him is his eyes, and there's nothing he can do about them."

"His eyes?"

The lieutenant held up two fingers and pointed to his own somewhat bloodshot eyes. "One's blue and the other's brown. It's the queerest thing I've ever seen."

Sinclair, Lord Oliphant, entered his elegant, book-lined library and closed the door behind him. He carried a brace of candles, the flames flaring as he walked across the room to set it on the mantel. Then, as if becoming aware of another presence in the room, he froze.

"Turn around very carefully," said Sebastian, thumbing back the hammer on his flintlock. "And keep your hands where I can see them."

Oliphant pivoted slowly, his habitual, faintly contemptuous smile firmly in place, his hands spread out at his sides. "Who let you in?"

"Do you really need to ask?"

"Nice black eye."

"Thank you."

Oliphant's gaze drifted to a nearby window, where the heavy velvet drapes shifted in a draft. But all he said was, "May I offer you a drink?"

"Thank you, but no."

"Mind if I have one?"

"Not as long as you keep your hands in sight. And remember: I'd love an excuse to shoot you."

"And hang for murder?"

"If necessary. The only reason you're not dead already is because I want Diggory Flynn. And because as much as I might suspect you're the one controlling him, I can't prove it. Yet."

Oliphant moved to where brandy and a set of glasses waited on a table beside the fire. His movements were deliberate but seemingly untroubled, as if he were still utterly in control of the situation.

"Diggory Flynn," Sebastian said again. "I want him."

Oliphant's attention was all for the task of pouring his brandy. "Who?"

Sebastian found his finger tightening on the trigger and had to force himself to relax. "Allow me to refresh your memory: former exploring officer; hails from a vicarage in Buckinghamshire by way of Lisbon, where he should have hanged but, thanks to your intervention, did not."

Oliphant set aside his decanter with a soft *thump*. "You've been very busy."

"So has Flynn—or Barnes, or Brady, or whatever his real name happens to be. Except that rather than murdering me as intended, he shot and killed a Bishopsgate tavern owner who happens to look a fair bit like me."

"Oh? Now, there's a pity."

"That an innocent man is dead? Or that I'm still alive?"

Oliphant turned to face him, the brandy cradled in one hand. "As it happens, an exploring officer who liked to use the name Diggory Flynn did once serve under me. But I haven't seen him since I left Jamaica."

"Why was he there?"

"In Jamaica?" Oliphant shrugged. "How should I know? Needless to say, we didn't exactly move in the same social circles. In fact, Preston *père et fils* accused him of working with a gang of slave runners operating in the area."

"The same allegations were made against you."

"Nasty lies, of course. Unfortunately, in Flynn's case I suspect the accusation may well have been true. He was arrested and sentenced to hang, only somehow managed to escape."

"One of his talents."

"Oh, he's very talented." Oliphant took a slow sip of his brandy. "My point is, the man you call Diggory Flynn had a powerful grudge against the Prestons."

"You're suggesting Flynn had his own reasons for killing Stanley Preston, are you?"

"The man always did have a tendency to carry a grudge."

"What's his real name?"

Oliphant huffed a laugh. "I honestly can't remember."

"Where would I find him?"

"I haven't the slightest idea. He's fallen in with some

rough elements since leaving the Army—not only slave runners, but smugglers as well."

Sebastian rose to his feet, the pistol still in his hand. "If I discover proof that you're lying, I'll kill you."

Oliphant raised one eyebrow in polite incredulity. "And risk leaving your young wife a widow and your newborn son an orphan? I think not."

Sebastian paused at the door to look back at him. "You and I both know there are ways to kill without being caught."

Oliphant paused with his brandy lifted halfway to his lips. "Are you saying you'd commit cold-blooded murder? For the sake of a common tavern owner?"

"For Jamie Knox, and for the women and children of Santa Iria."

"The French killed the women and children of Santa Iria."

"So they did," said Sebastian, and walked out of the library and out of the house.

Chapter 47

*P*ippa was filling three pewter tankards with ale when Sebastian pushed open the door to the Black Devil's taproom.

The tavern was crowded with its usual evening assortment of tradesmen, apprentices, and laborers. The smell of spilled spirits hung heavy in the smoky air and bursts of hearty laughter punctuated the soft roar of men's voices. As the door closed behind him, she looked up and saw him, and for a moment she froze. Then she swallowed hard and went back to her task.

"Is he dead, then?" she asked as Sebastian walked up to the counter, her attention seemingly all for the tankards of ale.

"Yes."

He saw a quiver pass over her features, but she simply set her jaw and said nothing.

He said, "The boy—Knox's son. If he should ever require anything, I want you to know that all you need do is ask."

She looked up then, her eyes glazed with unshed tears, her face tight with anger. "What's he to you, anyway?"

Sebastian met her furious gaze. "I honestly don't know."

She hefted the three tankards with practiced ease and carried them to the men at a nearby table. When she came back, she grabbed a cloth and set about wiping the surface of the bar as if indifferent to Sebastian's presence.

He said, "What do you know of Knox's family in Shropshire?"

She twitched one shoulder, her fist clenching on the cloth. "What's there t' know? His mum died when he was just a wee babe."

"Who raised him?"

"His nana."

"His grandmother? Is she still alive?"

"Last we heard. Just this afternoon, he was talkin' about maybe goin' t' see her soon. Had somethin' he wanted to give her."

"What?"

She threw the cloth aside and disappeared into the back room to return in a moment with a gilded mechanical nightingale that she slammed down on the counter before him.

Sebastian picked it up with a hand that was not quite steady, the jewels in its collar flaming with color as they caught the firelight. "Where did this come from?"

"Got it off Priss Mulligan, he did. Said his nana was always partial to nightingales."

"Knox went to Houndsditch this afternoon?"

He watched as a fearful light came into Pippa's eyes. She said, "You know he did."

He hadn't known it. In fact, it made no sense, although he remembered the rifleman saying, *She doesn't know any more.* "What can you tell me about a man named Diggory Flynn?"

Pippa wrinkled her nose and shook her head. "Ne'er heard of him."

"Knox didn't mention him?"

"No."

He studied her closed, resentful face. She had always regarded him with both animosity and suspicion, instinctively knowing him for a threat even as his resemblance to Knox confused and frightened her. Now the father of her son was dead, and she held Sebastian responsible. And the truth was that if Sebastian had never come into their lives, Jamie Knox would still be alive.

He set the mechanical nightingale on the counter between them. "I'm sorry."

She shoved the gilded bird toward him. "Take it. I don't want it. I never want t' see it again."

"You could send it to his grandmother," he suggested. Yet even as he said it, he knew she never would.

She stared at him, her eyes glittering with raw hatred.

He picked up the nightingale. "What's her name?"

"Heddie. Heddie Kincaid. Lives in a village called Ayleswick, just outside o' Ludlow."

He slipped an envelope thick with banknotes from his pocket and laid it before her. No amount of money could compensate for the loss of her son's father. But it would make her life—and the boy's—easier. "I'll let you know when the funeral arrangements have been made," he said.

He thought she might object, might even throw his money in his face.

But she didn't.

Sebastian was sitting beside the library fire, the mechanical nightingale in his hands, his gaze on the coals glowing on the hearth, when Hero came to stand in the room's entrance.

"Did you kill him?" she asked, pausing with one hand on the doorframe beside her.

He looked up at her. "If you mean Diggory Flynn, the answer is no; I haven't been able to find him. And if you mean Oliphant, I'm afraid the answer is still no. I'll admit I came damned close, but you were right; I can't be completely certain that Oliphant is the one controlling Flynn."

"Still?"

"I know Flynn was an exploring officer under Oliphant and that both men were in Jamaica together, but . . ." He held up the gilded bird. "I'm puzzled by this."

"What is it?"

He wound the key and set the nightingale on the table beside him, the clear, heartbreakingly beautiful notes filling the air as the bird's mechanical wings rose and fell. "It appears that Knox learned of Flynn's identity from Priss Mulligan. According to Oliphant, Flynn has been using his talents in a variety of nefarious pursuits, from slave running to smuggling."

"Smuggling? Well, you did first see him in Houndsditch."

"I did."

"So he could work for Priss Mulligan."

"He could indeed." He watched the mechanical toy slowly wind down and stop. "It seems as if just when I think I'm beginning to understand what happened to Preston and Sterling and Toop, everything shifts and I realize I don't understand anything at all."

Hero walked over to pick up the mechanical nightingale and wind the key. Then she set it on the table and together they watched the gilded wings beat slowly up and down in the glow of the firelight.

Chapter 48

*T*he next morning dawned cold and misty, with a bitter wind blowing down out of the north. Priss Mulligan was wrapped in a heavy shawl and poking around the jumble of old glass and metal items displayed on a Houndsditch street stall when Sebastian walked up to her.

"I understand you know Diggory Flynn," he said.

She looked over at him, her lower lip distended by a plug of tobacco, her beady black eyes widening ever so slightly. "Oh? And how ye know that?"

"Deduction."

"Ain't ne'er heard of nobody named Dee Duckshun," she said with a sniff and returned her attention to the secondhand stall.

Sebastian watched her pick up a tarnished old candlestick and squint at it. He said, "You heard Knox is dead?"

"Aye." She heaved a heavy sigh. " 'Tis a pity. He was a good-lookin' lad, that one."

"I think Diggory Flynn killed him."

"Now, what would he want to go and do that for?"

"Because he mistook Knox for me."

Priss Mulligan stared thoughtfully at Sebastian, then turned her head to shoot a stream of tobacco juice into the gutter. "Aye; 'tis possible, I s'pose. There's no denying the two of you is as alike as a couple o' pups out the same litter."

Sebastian said, "I think Flynn is working for you." *Or Sinclair Oliphant. Or Anne Preston,* he thought, watching her carefully.

She used her tongue to shift the wad of tobacco to her cheek. "Sure then, but Flynn ain't ne'er worked for me. *With* me, meybe, from time to time. But ne'er for me."

"And why should I believe you?"

She shrugged. "Ask anybody knows him."

"I could ask him myself if I knew where to find him."

Her lips pulled into a wide grin that showed her small, tobacco-stained teeth. "Ho; you think I'm gonna tell you, do you? Not likely." She winked. "Fact is, I couldn't even if I wanted to. He contacts me; not t'other way around."

He watched her set aside the candlestick and reach for a small glass figurine. He said, "You're Irish, aren't you?"

The question obviously took her by surprise, because she hesitated and looked up at him again. "What's that got t' do with anythin'?"

"Have you ever heard of a Dullahan?"

"Course I have. Why?"

"Tell me about it."

She dropped her voice low and waved one small, childlike hand through the air like a storyteller conjuring an image. "Keeps his own head tucked up under one arm, he does. Oh, he's a fright to look at: little black eyes always dartin' this way and that, with a grinnin' mouth as wide as his skull and skin like moldy cheese. Carries a whip made from a dead man's backbone, and when he calls your name, it's your turn to die. Ain't nothin' you can do to stop him. You can try barring your gate and lockin' your door, but they'll just open for him, like magic."

"He rides a horse?"

"Sometimes. Sometimes he drives a carriage." She sniffed. "Why you wanna know about the Dullahan? He don't like bein' watched, you know. You try watchin' him, and he'll pluck out your eyes with his whip. That, or throw a bucket o' blood on you, markin' you as the next to die."

"I hear there's one thing that will scare him away."

She gave a breathy laugh, her small eyes practically disappearing in the fat of her face as she fished beneath her shawl and came up with a bored gold coin tied around her neck by a leather thong. "Sure then, 'tis gold. Why you think the rich don't die as often as the poor?"

"Lots of food. A warm fire. A solid roof over their heads."

"Maybe," she said with a sniff. "Though I still don't see what the Dullahan's got to do with nothin'."

"Perhaps it doesn't," said Sebastian, and walked away, leaving her staring after him, the glass figurine held forgotten in one fist and her eyes narrowed with malevolent suspicion.

Chapter 49

$\mathcal{T}$he little girl clutched the rusty tray of nuts against her thin chest. She was a tiny thing, with spindly arms and legs, a pale, wind-chapped face, and lifeless hair the same dull brown as her eyes. She told Hero her name was Sarah Devon. She was nine years old, and she'd already been selling nuts for three years.

"I didn't start on the streets till after Papa died," she told Hero. "He was a whitesmith, you know—sold tin and pewter. For a while, Mama tried to keep us on what she makes selling oranges, but it weren't enough. So she took to sending me out with six ha'pennies' worth of nuts. I'm supposed to bring back sixpence."

"What happens if you don't?"

The little girl's gaze slid away. "She don't usually beat me. Only when she's been drinking. And she don't drink more'n once a week. Usually."

Hero's sympathy for the struggling widow instantly vanished. "You always sell your nuts here, in Piccadilly?"

"Mostly, m'lady. Although sometimes I goes into the public houses. I like the taprooms; it's warm in there."

Hero looked up from scribbling her notes. "You sell your nuts in taverns?" She tried to keep the shock off her face, but she must not have entirely succeeded because Sarah took a hesitant step back.

"I usually only goes into the Pied Duck," said Sarah, shifting nervously from one foot to the other. "The barman used to be a friend of Papa's, and if he's there, he doesn't let the men be rude to me."

"Are the men rude?"

The little girl hung her head. "Sometimes."

Hero's fist clenched around her pencil so hard she heard it crack.

"Here," she said, pressing two shillings into the little girl's hand. "Only, don't give it all to your mother at once or she's liable to drink it up."

Sarah's fingers closed around the coins, her eyes going wide. "I thought you said you'd give me a shilling if I talked to you. So why're you giving me two?"

Because you're so thin and frail it breaks my heart, thought Hero. *Because I don't want you to have to worry about being beaten when you go home. Because little girls shouldn't need to sell nuts in taverns to survive.*

But all she said was, "Because you've been so very helpful."

Sarah tipped her head to one side. "You really gonna write about us costers in the newspapers?"

"Yes."

She looked thoughtful. "I don't mind going out in the street to sell, you know. It's better'n staying inside without a fire and with nothing to do."

Which was, Hero decided as she walked back to her carriage with the two footmen Devlin had insisted she bring with her, a consolation of sorts.

But only if she didn't think too much about it.

Chapter 50

"I don't understand why we keep comin' 'ere," said Tom, standing beside the chestnuts' heads at the edge of the lane while Sebastian walked over to study the narrow, moss-covered arch of Bloody Bridge.

"Because I know I'm missing something."

"What makes ye think it's 'ere?"

"It may not be," said Sebastian, which only served to make Tom look more puzzled.

Sebastian stared off across the rolling green expanse of market gardens still half-hidden by lingering wisps of the morning's fog. "Think about this: The Friday before he is killed, Stanley Preston has an unpleasant encounter with the former governor of Jamaica. We don't know exactly where this meeting takes place or what is said, but knowing Oliphant, I suspect it involves some nasty and rather explicit threats against Anne Preston. Whatever it is, it frightens Preston enough that the next day he tells his cousin the Home Secretary that he has given up his determination to see Oliphant ruined."

"So that means the gov'nor didn't have no reason to kill him no more. Right?"

"Perhaps," said Sebastian. "Unless for some reason Preston changed his mind. At any rate, later that same day—Saturday—he charges into Priss Mulligan's shop in Houndsditch and threatens to turn her over to the authorities, at which point she threatens to have him gutted, strangled, and gelded."

"Does that scare him?"

"From all I know of Priss Mulligan, it should have. But even if it does, he's obviously still feeling cantankerous because—"

"Can—what?"

"Cantankerous. It means foul tempered. Testy. Bloody-minded."

"Oh."

"Because he then goes storming into the Shepherd's Rest and threatens to horsewhip the impecunious Captain Wyeth, at which point Wyeth, in turn, threatens to kill him."

"'E was a right ornery fellow, this Preston. What'd ye call it?"

"Cantankerous," said Sebastian, his gaze following the course of the narrow rivulet that ran under the bridge. "Now, the next morning—Sunday, the day of the murder—Preston receives a visit from Dr. Douglas Sterling. The doctor claims the visit is for medical reasons, although no one close to Preston seems to know he's ill in any way. And after the physician leaves, Preston calls for a hackney and drives off to Bucket Lane for reasons that seem to escape everyone. He returns home several hours later and putters about with his collections until shortly before nine, when he looks out his window to see Basil Thistlewood staring at his house. Preston charges out to indulge himself in a decidedly uncouth shouting match in the street. Then, sometime after that, he leaves the house again and walks to the Monster, where he berates Henry Austen for what he sees as the Austen women's tendency to encourage Anne's romantic notions."

"And then 'e comes 'ere?" said Tom.

"He does. Presumably to meet Rowan Toop, who is selling the purloined head and coffin strap of King Charles I. Preston is standing here"—Sebastian stepped onto the grassy verge beside the lane—"with his watch in his hand, undoubtedly gazing back toward Sloane Square in anticipation of Toop's arrival, when—" Sebastian turned so that he was facing the square, and frowned.

"What?" said Tom as Sebastian swung around again to study the overgrown thicket of shrubbery that choked both banks of the stream to the north of the bridge.

"Preston was stabbed in the back. That means that he either deliberately turned his back on his killer—which is unlikely if that person had recently threatened to kill him—or the killer crept up behind him. I've been thinking the killer probably followed Preston from the Monster. Except that, if he had, Preston would surely have seen him as he stared back toward the square, watching for Toop. Which means that whoever killed Preston must have known he was planning to meet Rowan Toop at Bloody Bridge that night and was already here waiting for him, probably in the shadows of that shrubbery."

The tiger's face lit up with quick comprehension. "So who knew Preston was gonna be 'ere?"

"It's possible Thistlewood learned of the meeting from Toop, but I doubt it. I also find it unlikely that Henry Austen was privy to Preston's clandestine activities. Preston's daughter, Anne, claims she had no idea what he was doing at Bloody Bridge that night but could easily be lying."

"So she could've told Cap'n Wyeth?"

"She could have. Although I think it more likely she hired Diggory Flynn and sent him to kill Preston."

Tom's jaw sagged. "Ye think she done fer 'er own da? *Gor*."

"She's definitely been moved into the suspects' column," said Sebastian. "But men like Diggory Flynn are trained to learn other people's secrets. So it's conceivable that Flynn could have found out about the assignation even if he was working for Priss Mulligan or Lord Oliphant."

Sebastian's gaze returned to the square, where a gentlewoman had emerged from Sloane Street to turn along the side of the square and enter the lane leading to the bridge. She wore a plain brown pelisse and a sensible hat, and her gait was the strong, easy stride of someone accustomed to walking miles along country lanes and across fields. She had her head bowed and appeared lost in thought. But when she looked up and saw him, she smiled.

"Lord Devlin," said Jane Austen. "I wasn't expecting to meet you again."

He moved toward her. "Miss Austen. What brings you this way?"

"I try to take a walk every morning, either to the river or through Five Fields. There's a small country chapel, just there, with a lovely churchyard." She nodded toward the bell tower barely visible above the distant clump of trees. Then her gaze fell on the bridge, and a shadow crossed her small, even features. "It was one of Anne's favorite walks as well. But I doubt she'll ever want to come this way again."

"And how is Miss Preston?" he asked.

The question was not as idle as it seemed.

"To be frank, she's making herself ill with the fear you mean to see Captain Wyeth hang for her father's murder."

"I don't believe Captain Wyeth killed Stanley Preston," he said, studying the novelist's round, small-featured face. He wished he could say the same thing about Anne, but he kept that thought to himself.

"May I tell her that?" said Miss Austen.

"Of course. Although I obviously don't speak for Bow Street."

"I think Anne is more afraid of you than she is of the authorities."

"Oh?"

"That surprises you? My cousin Eliza likewise fears that you may still suspect Henry."

"I don't think your brother has anything to worry about either," he said. "How is Mrs. Austen today?"

A pinched, bleak light came into Miss Austen's face. "I'm afraid it's only a matter of time."

"I'm sorry."

She blinked rapidly and nodded, her throat working as she swallowed.

He said, "You wouldn't by chance know a man named Diggory Flynn—a somewhat disheveled character with an oddly crooked face?"

"I don't believe so, no. Why? You think he could be involved in what happened here?"

"He may be."

She tipped her head to one side. "May I ask why you've changed your mind about Captain Wyeth?"

"Largely because I've come to believe he is precisely the honorable, conscientious man he appears."

"That is good to hear," she said with a soft smile. "Anne deserves to be happy."

"Let's hope she will be," he said, just as the bells of the distant country chapel began to toll.

Chapter 51

Sebastian's next stop was the Rose and Crown, where he discovered that Cian O'Neal had never returned to work in the stables.

He finally found the former stableboy hoeing rows of newly sprouting vegetables in the kitchen gardens of Chelsea Hospital. At the sight of Sebastian, he froze, his fists tightening around the handle of his hoe and his chest jerking on a quickly indrawn breath.

"What ye want wit' me?"

"I need to ask you a few questions," said Sebastian, pausing some feet away when the boy looked as if he might bolt.

"I already told that other feller, I didn't see nothin'. Nothin'!"

Sebastian studied the lad's tight, strained face. "What other fellow?"

"The feller from Bow Street."

"The one who spoke to you before?"

"No. A different one."

"Did he ask about the Dullahan?"

Cian stared at him, eyes wide and afraid.

"You saw it, didn't you?" said Sebastian.

"Nobody sees the Dullahan and lives."

"So perhaps what you saw wasn't the Dullahan. Perhaps it was simply a man."

"But he was carryin' a h—" Cian broke off and dropped his gaze to the ground, his cheeks flaming with his shame.

"A head? Is that what you saw? Not the severed head at the end of the bridge, but another head?"

The boy wiped one ragged cuff across the end of his nose and nodded. "Won't nobody believe me, but 'tis true."

"I believe you," said Sebastian. "Where was this man when you saw him?"

Cian kept his gaze on his feet, his voice barely more than a whisper. "The other side of the bridge. Not far from the barn we was goin' to."

"What did he look like?"

"I dunno. It was dark, and he was wearin' some sort of flowin' black robes with a floppy hat on his head."

"You mean, on the head attached to his own shoulders? Not on the head he carried?"

The color in the boy's cheeks deepened. "Aye."

"So it couldn't have been the Dullahan. It was simply a man dressed in a black cassock and carrying a head."

The boy looked up, his features contorted with a swirling inner agony of confusion and a nameless fear that wasn't going to go away. "But whose head? You tell me that. Ain't no other body missin' a head that I heard of."

"Did you see anyone else at the bridge that night? Perhaps nothing more than a shadow moving in the shrubbery edging the stream?"

The boy took a step back, then another. He was sweating now, although the day was cold, the wind flattening the thin cloth of his smock against his chest. "I don't know what I seen no more! I told that fellow from Bow

Street: It was dark, and the wind was blowin' the trees somethin' fierce."

Sebastian frowned. "This man from Bow Street; when was he here asking you questions?"

"I dunno. Some days ago."

"What did he look like?"

"Dressed fine, he was, like a gentleman. Not flashy; but real fine."

"How old?"

The boy shrugged. "Older'n you, I s'pose. But not by too much."

"Dark or fair? Tall or short? Thin or fleshy?"

The lad's features contorted with the effort of memory. "'Bout as tall as me and dark headed, but I wouldn't say he was either overly thin or fleshy."

Sebastian knew all of Lovejoy's constables, and the boy's description fit none of them. "He told you he was from Bow Street?"

"Aye."

"Did he ask you anything else?"

"Only if Molly seen anythin'."

"What did you tell him?"

"I said no. If she'd seen what I seen, she wouldn't be laughin' at me. She wouldn't be goin' around tellin' folks I'm simpleminded."

"I don't think you're simpleminded. But the man who asked you those questions wasn't from Bow Street."

The boy's face went slack. "What you sayin'?"

"I'm saying that if you see him again, you need to be careful."

"But . . . who is he?"

"I think he may very well be the killer."

Sebastian arrived back at Brook Street to be met by Morey wearing a disapproving face.

"A lady to see you, my lord," said the majordomo. "Miss Anne Preston. I told her both you and Lady Devlin were out, but she insisted on waiting." His frown deepened. "I've put her in the drawing room."

"Thank you," said Sebastian, handing Morey his hat and walking stick as he headed for the stairs.

She was sitting stiffly upright on one of the cane chairs by the bow window, her hands clenched in her lap, her face a tight, unsmiling mask of control. At the sight of Sebastian, she thrust up from the chair, her arms held stiffly at her sides. "I'm here because of Jane—Miss Austen," she said without preamble.

"May I offer you some tea, Miss Preston?"

"No, thank you; your majordomo already did." She drew in a deep breath and said in a rush, "I—I'm afraid I haven't been exactly honest with you about some things."

Sebastian suspected she hadn't been honest with him about a number of things. But all he said was, "Please, have a seat."

"No." She jerked away to stand at the window, looking out at the scene below. "Bow Street thinks Hugh killed Father. But Jane—Miss Austen—tells me you don't agree with them."

Sebastian studied her tightly held profile. "Exactly what are you trying to tell me, Miss Preston?"

She kept her gaze on the carts and carriages filling the street. "Hugh had this idea that if he could meet with Father—talk to him, man to man—then maybe he could convince Father to change his mind about our marriage."

"Was this before or after your father stormed into the Shepherd's Rest and threatened to horsewhip him?"

She sucked in a quick breath that flared her nostrils and caused her chest to jerk. "After."

"So, Sunday?"

"Yes. I told Hugh he was mad, that Father would

never agree. But Hugh said he was honor-bound to formally ask for my hand in marriage."

"Admirable."

She gave a small, ragged laugh. "Admirable, perhaps. But mad, nonetheless."

"So what happened?"

She ran her fingers down the curtain beside her to smooth it, although it was already hanging straight. "A predictable disaster. It probably didn't help that Hugh arrived at the house just after Douglas Sterling had been there. I don't know what Dr. Sterling told Father, but whatever it was, it left him in an odd humor. He took one look at Hugh and flew into a rage—right there in the hall in front of Chambliss, our butler."

"You obviously have very loyal servants," said Sebastian. "None of them breathed a word of Captain Wyeth's visit to the constables."

"I begged Chambliss to keep it to himself. It was wrong of me, I know. But I feared Bow Street would put the worst possible construction on Hugh's visit. I mean, Father was standing in the hall, shouting that he'd see me die an old maid before he'd allow me to align our house with some penniless vicar's son."

"You were present at their meeting?"

"Not at first, no; Hugh had thought they'd do better alone. But the way Papa was shouting, it's a wonder they didn't hear him in the next county. I tried to stay away, but I finally couldn't bear it any longer and came downstairs. I told Papa that if I couldn't marry Hugh, I *would* die an old maid, and that if he was opposing the match in the hopes that I would become Lady Knightly instead, then he was living in cloud-cuckoo-land."

She paused, her face wan and tired. "That's when Papa said the strangest thing. You must understand that he'd been wildly enthusiastic at the prospect of a match between Sir Galen and me. But when I mentioned Knightly's name, Papa flew into such a rage, he was shaking. Said he'd rather see me married to some English chimney sweep than Sir Galen. He rounded on Chambliss, who was still standing there with a wooden face— it was most mortifying—and told him that if Sir Galen ever came to the door again, he was not to be admitted. Then Papa grabbed his hat and stormed off."

"In the hackney?"

"Yes. Bow Street says he went to Fish Street Hill, although I can't for the life of me imagine what could have taken him there."

Sebastian now thought he had a fairly good idea what might have driven Stanley Preston to the streets surrounding Billingsgate Market. But all he said was, "When you quarreled with Captain Wyeth at Lady Farningham's, was it over that morning's confrontation with your father?"

"Not exactly." A touch of color crept into her face. "If you must know, I wanted Hugh to agree to elope. I knew Father would fly into one of his rages over it, but I was convinced he'd eventually calm down and accept our marriage, particularly if for some reason he'd given up his dream of seeing me as Lady Knightly."

"But Captain Wyeth refused?"

The color in her cheeks darkened. "Yes."

Sebastian said, "What made you decide to tell me this now?"

"It was something Jane—Miss Austen—said. She said I was wrong to keep back anything that happened that day. That each event by itself might not seem to mean anything, but that when taken together with everything else, it might very well provide the key you need to understand what happened to Father."

She tented her hands over her nose and mouth, her eyes squeezing shut a moment before she said, "I didn't tell you of it before because I was afraid it would make you even more convinced that it was Hugh who'd killed

Papa. But he didn't! You must believe me. He's not some conniving fortune hunter; he's a worthy, honorable man—far more noble and high-minded than I am. He didn't kill my father."

"No," said Sebastian. "But I think I know who did."

Chapter 52

Sometimes, solving a murder could be as simple as asking the right questions. Except that in this case, Sebastian hadn't been asking the right questions.

At least, not about the right person.

He spent the next several hours visiting those London coffeehouses and pubs favored by men with extensive connections to the West Indies. The conversations were oblique, the queries carefully worded, the answers often guarded or merely suggestive.

But in the end, the information he gleaned was damning.

Hero was strolling the rear gardens with a bundled-up Simon in her arms when Sebastian walked up to her. Her cheeks were pleasantly flushed by the cool air. But her eyes were troubled, and he knew that whatever costermonger's story of hardship and deprivation she'd heard that morning still haunted her.

He said, "Difficult interview?"

She drew a deep breath and shifted Simon's weight so that she could press her cheek against the child's. "A little girl. She sells nuts in taverns. Alone."

He wanted to say, *Why don't you stop doing this to yourself? Why torment yourself with the ugly realities of a part of London life of which most gentlewomen remain blissfully ignorant?* But he knew that was precisely what she wanted to change; she wanted the spoiled, complacent, self-satisfied residents of the West End to know what life was like for those less fortunate. In her own way, she was as driven as he.

The baby fussed, and she loosened her hold on him, saying, "I've heard back from my Fish Street Hill costermonger. He contacted me after I talked to Sarah."

"And?"

"He says Stanley Preston was in Bucket Lane to see a woman. Unfortunately, she refuses to speak with us, although he did accidentally let slip a name: Juba."

Juba. It was an African name, often given in the American colonies to girls born on a Monday morning. Sebastian suspected it belonged to the beautiful, duskyskinned woman who had confronted him in the lane.

"You think this Juba could be Preston's daughter?" said Hero.

"Actually, I think it far more likely her connection is to Sir Galen Knightly."

"Knightly?" Hero stared at him. "Are you serious?"

She listened while he told her of the sudden aversion to Knightly that Preston had expressed the morning of his murder, of the dark-haired gentleman who had questioned Cian O'Neal, and of Sebastian's own conversations with various West Indies planters.

"Knightly told me once that he inherited his plantations and slaves," said Sebastian. "He claimed to be a kindly master who would gladly free all of his slaves if the law didn't make it so onerous. But none of that is true. He's actually extended his holdings of both land and slaves in the years since his great-uncle's death. And while there isn't a planter in Jamaica who doesn't make use of the whip, I'm told Knightly's punishments can be unusually brutal—particularly if he's enraged. They say he doesn't lose his temper often, but when he does, he's vicious. He once personally slashed a slave's throat with a cane knife when the man mishandled a favorite mare."

"Killed him?"

"Yes. Practically took off the poor man's head—although of course they made up some tale for the authorities."

"So what do you think Stanley Preston and Douglas Sterling could have done that drove Knightly into a murderous rage?"

"I think Sterling must have told Preston something that Sunday morning, something that convinced Preston he didn't want his daughter to marry Knightly and that sent him to talk to Juba in Bucket Lane."

"But Preston knew Knightly well. He had to know of his temper and his treatment of his slaves. So what could Sterling possibly have said that would suddenly turn Preston against the man?"

"Knightly told me once that Preston had a horror of miscegenation. And Juba is part African."

"You think she could be Knightly's daughter?"

"No; she's not young enough for that. But she could very well have had a child by him."

"Dear God," said Hero softly. "Would he kill her too, do you think? If he thought she was a threat to him?"

Sebastian reached out to lift his son from her arms and hold Simon close. "This is a man who owns other human beings and has them whipped when they refuse to work. Who's capable of slitting a helpless slave's throat for mishandling a horse and who probably bashed in the skull of Rowan Toop on the off chance the virger might have seen something that could incriminate him. So yes, I think he'd kill her if he thought she might betray him.

"Her and her child both."

Chapter 53

It was early afternoon by the time Sebastian reached Fish Street Hill. The crowds had thinned, the cries of the sellers in Billingsgate Market largely stilled.

Leaving the curricle with Tom, he cut through the noisome alley to Bucket Lane. The sky had grown increasingly dark and heavy with clouds, the light thin and white and flat, the lane deserted except for a knot of ragged children playing some game with broken pieces of brick.

Sebastian walked up to one of the lads, a delicately boned, brown-eyed boy of perhaps ten or twelve, and held up a coin. "I'm looking for Juba. A shilling if you lead me to her."

The boy stared at Sebastian with a hard, emotionless face. Then he made a quick grab at the coin.

"Ah-ah," said Sebastian, lifting the shilling out of his reach. "You'll get it, but not until you've led me to Juba."

The boy's expression never altered. Then his gaze broke to someone behind Sebastian.

"It's you, ain't it?" said a familiar voice.

Sebastian turned to find the woman called Juba standing in the middle of the lane, her fists on her slim hips, her head thrown back as she stared at him with suspicion and hostility and what he recognized as a touch of curiosity.

"Yes," he said.

"Who are you? Really."

"Lord Devlin. I want to know why Stanley Preston came to see you last Sunday."

"He didn't come to see me."

"Then who did he see?"

She shook her head. "First you want me t' believe you're an idiot, and now you're pretending t' be some grand lord?"

"I am a lord. Not exactly what I'd call 'grand,' but a lord, nonetheless."

She huffed a scornful expulsion of air. "And what're you claiming is your interest in Preston this time? *My lord.*"

"I'm trying to figure out who killed him, and why."

He saw the sudden leap of fear in those turquoise-hued eyes. "I didn't kill him," she said huskily. "I had no reason to kill him."

"I know."

"What difference it make to you, who killed this Preston, or why?"

"I happen to have a moral objection to people getting away with cold-blooded murder."

"Sure then," she said, her lip curling. "Rich man gets hisself killed, ev'rybody from Fleet Street to Bow Street is interested in finding who done it. But let somebody stab an old fishmonger in the back, and ain't nobody cares."

Sebastian shook his head. "I don't understand."

"Come. I'll show you."

She turned and strode toward a nearby battered door without waiting to see if he followed, as if whether he did so or not were a matter of supreme indifference to her.

He found himself in a narrow, dilapidated corridor smelling strongly of fish, thanks to the dripping pile of baskets and hampers stacked near the street. She pushed open the first door to the left, revealing a room that was small and meanly furnished but clean, with a scrubbed trestle table and crude benches and two pallets laid out near the cold hearth. On one of the pallets lay the body of an old woman, her face pale and waxy with death.

She looked to be perhaps sixty years old or more, her café-au-lait skin wrinkled and sunken with age, her hair steel gray and thin. But once she must have been beautiful, for the exquisite, regal bone structure she had bequeathed to her daughter was still clearly visible despite the ravages of age and mortality.

Sebastian raised his gaze from the dead woman to Juba. "When was she killed?"

"Last night. They be comin' anytime now to sew her int' her shroud."

"Tell me what happened."

"Ain't nothin' to tell. She went out t' fetch water, only she never come back. Banjo went lookin' and found her not five feet from the pump. Breathed her last in his arms."

"Banjo?"

"My boy." She jerked her head toward the street. "That's him you was talkin' to just now."

Sebastian studied her beautiful, tightly held face and read there a powerful mixture of grief and shock and fury. He said, "Tell me why Stanley Preston came here a week ago Sunday."

She stared back at him. "Why should I?"

"Because whoever killed your mother also killed Stanley Preston—and at least two other men. And because if he feels threatened, he may not stop there; he may decide he needs to eliminate you and your son as well."

A pulse had begun to beat wildly at the base of her long, elegant neck. But a lifetime of suspicion and resentment held her silent.

"Tell me," he said softly.

She went to stand before the cold hearth, where a few chipped cups and plates rested on a rough shelf.

He said, "I'll see that you come to no harm."

She gave a harsh laugh. "Why should I believe you?"

"Do you have a choice?"

She stared back at him, her hands fisting in her apron, her strangely hued eyes wide with fear and mistrust.

"Tell me," he said again.

Slowly, haltingly, she began to talk. And as he listened, Sebastian came to realize that he had misjudged Knightly's motives entirely, that the secrets the man had killed to protect were far more dangerous than Sebastian had ever imagined.

When she finished, he said, "I want you and your boy to come away from here, come with me so that I can keep you safe until this is all over."

"No."

"Don't you understand—"

"What you think?" She took a quick step toward him, one arm slashing through the air as she cut him off, her features stiff with an anger born of a lifetime of slights and insults. "That I'm a fool—or as much of an idiot as your Silas Nelson? No. I ain't puttin' our lives in your hands. This is our home. Here, we surrounded by people knows us. People we trusts. Costermongers always take care of their own. You got what you come for. Now, get out of here."

He drew a calling card from his pocket and held it out to her. "If you change your mind, or if anyone should threaten you in any way, come to me. Number forty-one Brook Street."

She made no move to take the card, and it occurred to him she probably couldn't read it if she did. Hero had told him that fewer than one out of ten of the city's costermongers were literate.

He laid the card on the trestle tabletop. "I'm sorry about your mother," he said.

But she only stared back at him, her face hollow with grief and eyes cold with resentment.

Sebastian's next stop was Blackfriars Bridge, where he had a short conversation with the owner of Douglas Sterling's favorite coffee shop. Then he drove to Park Lane, where he found his aunt Henrietta's shiny carriage drawn up outside her town house and the Dowager Duchess herself smoothing on a pair of elegant kid gloves in the grand entrance hall.

"I don't have time to talk to you now, Devlin," she told him, still busy with her gloves. "I'm on my way to Sally Jersey's."

"This won't take long. I want to know what you can tell me about the birth of Sir Galen Knightly."

"Knightly?" She looked up at him. "Good heavens. Has someone killed *him* now?"

"No."

She stared at Sebastian, her blue St. Cyr eyes going wide and still with comprehension. Then she glanced at her wooden-faced butler and said, "Tell Coachman John I shan't be but a moment."

She led Sebastian to a small withdrawing room.

Sebastian said, "That bad, is it?"

"Well, it's certainly not a tale I'd care to relate in front of the servants. Sir Galen's father was Beaumont Knightly, eldest son of the old baronet, Sir Maxwell Knightly, and as dissolute a young man as ever joined the Hellfire Club—which is truly saying something, I'm afraid. Gambling, drinking, women, dueling—the usual, only far, far worse. If even half the tales told of his conduct were true, he must have cost his father a fortune. In the end, old Sir Maxwell shipped him off to a maternal uncle who owned plantations in the West Indies."

"Jamaica?"

"Yes. Most people thought old Sir Maxwell was

hoping the yellow fever would carry the reprobate off, so that a younger brother could inherit."

"Only, no such luck?"

"Not quickly enough, at any rate. The young man hadn't been on the island a month before he seduced the daughter of a local plantation owner. As I understand it, the girl's father was on the verge of shooting the ne'er-do-well when she announced she was with child. So Beau Knightly was allowed to live, on the condition he make an honest woman of the foolish chit."

"Doesn't sound like anyone I'd want as a son-in-law," said Sebastian.

Henrietta shrugged. "Perhaps the girl's father intended to shoot the rascal after the child was born. But in the end, he didn't need to. Both Beau Knightly and his bride died of the fever less than a year later."

"What happened to the child?"

"He also fell ill with the fever, but obviously survived. He was eventually brought to England to be raised by his grandfather. Carelessly conceived the boy may have been, but he was still old Sir Maxwell's heir, after all."

Maybe, thought Sebastian. *Or maybe not.* "Tell me about this maternal uncle."

"Kitch McGill? Good heavens; why do you want to know about him?"

"Humor me."

"Well, let's see. He was a younger son, of course. The family sent him off to Jamaica after he half killed some constable with his bare hands. He did quite well for himself there, in the end. But he's been dead twenty or thirty years now. Never did have any children of his own—leastways none he could acknowledge. His wife was barren, which is how he ended up making Sir Galen his heir."

"Did he ever come back to England?"

Henrietta frowned. "Only once, if I remember correctly. I believe he brought the child and his nurse back to Sir Maxwell, after Beau Knightly's death." She fixed him with a hard glare. "And now, not another word do you get out of me until you tell me what this is all about."

But Sebastian simply gave her a resounding kiss on one powdered and rouged cheek and said, "Thank you, Aunt. Enjoy your visit with Lady Jersey."

Chapter 54

The bell towers of the city were striking four when Sebastian watched Sir Galen Knightly tuck a silver-headed walking stick up under one arm and pause to purchase a paper from one of the newsboys on St. James's Street. A dark, angry storm was sweeping in on the city, the air heavy with the scent of coming rain.

"Walk with me a ways, if you will, Sir Galen?" said Sebastian, stepping forward as the Baronet turned toward the entrance to White's.

The laugh lines beside the Baronet's eyes creased as he seemed almost to wince at the suggestion he depart from his comfortable daily routine. "Well . . . I was just on my way to the reading room," he said, his gaze drifting longingly toward his club's stately facade.

"I know; I'm sorry. But I'd like your opinion on a tale I've just been told, and to be frank, I'd rather not repeat it where we might be overheard."

Knightly hesitated, then shrugged. "As you wish."

They walked down the hill toward the high, soot-stained brick walls of St. James's Palace and the Mall beyond it. Lightning flickered across the roiling underbelly of the clouds, and the air filled with dark, swirling flocks of birds coming in to roost.

Sebastian said, "I had an interesting conversation this afternoon with the owner of a coffee shop frequented by Dr. Douglas Sterling. He tells me Sterling spent all of last year in Jamaica and returned only a few weeks ago."

"Oh?" said Knightly. "I had no notion it was so recently."

Sebastian studied the older man's hard-boned profile. "I think I know why both he and Stanley Preston were killed."

Knightly glanced sideways at him. "Do you? Why is that?"

"It all goes back to a deception carried out some forty years ago."

"Forty years?" Knightly gave a brittle, forced laugh. "You can't be serious."

"I'm afraid I am. You see, forty-odd years ago, a certain Hertfordshire baronet shipped his young, excessively profligate heir off to a maternal uncle in Jamaica. The idea was to remove the heir from the influences of his boon companions, who by all accounts were a rather unsavory lot. Only, things didn't go quite according to plan."

"They rarely do," observed Knightly, swinging his walking stick back and forth.

"True," said Sebastian. "It seems that shortly after his arrival in Jamaica, our young heir impregnated and was forced to marry the daughter of a prominent local landowner. Unfortunately, the young man barely lived long enough to see his son take his first steps before succumbing with his bride to a yellow fever epidemic."

"Yes, I'm afraid yellow jack has long been a terrible scourge in the warmer American colonies. But . . . is there a point to this tale?"

"There is. You see, the father's death meant the orphaned babe was now the Baronet's new heir. The grandfather wanted the child raised in England, and the uncle finally agreed to bring him."

Knightly kept his gaze on the wind-tossed trees in the park beyond the palace, his jaw set hard, and said nothing.

"The child had lost his wet nurse along with his parents," said Sebastian, weaving together what he'd learned from Juba with what he'd been told by the Duchess of Claiborne, "and was being nursed by one of the uncle's own slaves—a pale-skinned quadroon named Cally whose babe had died in the same epidemic. Cally was by all accounts a beautiful woman, so beautiful the uncle was rumored to have made her his mistress. When the uncle and the child set sail for England, Cally came with them."

Knightly pursed his lips in a way that sucked in his cheeks, his gaze fixed relentlessly straight ahead.

"Now, here's where it gets interesting," said Sebastian. "Before he died, Douglas Sterling told Stanley Preston that he believed the real heir to the baronetcy had actually died in the epidemic along with his mother and father. That the child brought to England was in fact the child of the slave woman, Cally, and the uncle—"

"It's a lie!" Nostrils flaring with the agitation of his breathing and both fists tightening on the handle of his walking stick, Knightly drew up abruptly and swung to face Sebastian. "You hear me? It's all a lie."

Thunder rumbled long and ominously close as Sebastian studied the older man's rigid, angry face. "It may well be. But Dr. Douglas Sterling was a physician, which meant he was in a position to know if something irregular had occurred. I can't explain why he kept silent all these years—perhaps he only suspected a switch had been made and was unable to prove it. But when he arrived back in London after a lengthy visit to his daughter to find Stanley Preston anxious to marry his daughter to that very child—long since grown to manhood and now in possession of a baronetcy to which he might actually have no real claim—I think Sterling decided to share his suspicions with Preston. Preston, of course, reacted to the tale with all the horror to be expected of a man obsessed with wealth and birth—not to mention a biblically inspired conviction in the superiority of the European race. It was you, after all, who told me of Preston's aversion to miscegenation. Remember?"

Knightly fingered the catch on his walking stick—a walking stick that in all likelihood concealed a long, thin sword.

Watching him carefully, Sebastian said, "That morning, shortly after the doctor left, Preston called a hackney and went to Fish Street Hill. That's where the old woman who'd once served as the child's nurse now lives, you see; in Bucket Lane. When the child's uncle returned to Jamaica, he left Cally behind to care for the boy. Only, when the lad was just three years old, Sir Maxwell dismissed her." Sebastian paused. "If the child truly was hers, the separation must have caused her unimaginable agony. Although perhaps she consoled herself with the thought her son was growing up the heir to a baronet."

"It's not true," said Knightly, his features dark and twisted with rage. "You hear me? None of it is true."

"I hope not," said Sebastian. "Because if it is true, then when you killed the old woman, Cally, you killed your own mother."

The twin rows of Pall Mall's lampposts lent a golden cast to the strengthening rain. Knightly stared straight ahead, his jaw clenched tight.

Sebastian said, "She denied it, you know. When Preston came to see her that day, Cally swore you were Beau Knightly's son. That it was her own child who'd died in the yellow fever epidemic. And after Preston left, when the daughter she'd had by a London costermonger questioned her, she still denied it. So perhaps it is nothing more than an old doctor's muddled suspicions. But three people are still dead because of it—four if you count the virger, Toop, who simply had the misfortune to be in the wrong place at the wrong time."

The rain was falling harder now, large drops that pinged on the iron handrail beside them and ran down the Baronet's hard, sun-darkened cheeks. "You're mad. Do you hear me? Utterly mad."

Sebastian shook his head. "When he left Bucket Lane, Stanley Preston went to confront you, didn't he? I've no doubt you denied it all to him, just as you're denying it to me now. Why didn't you kill him then, I wonder? Did the conversation take place somewhere too public? Is that why you decided to wait and kill him later that night when he went to meet Rowan Toop at Bloody Bridge? You did know of that meeting, didn't you?"

Knightly gave a harsh, ringing laugh. "Try telling this tale to the magistrates and see how far you get without any proof. You have none. You hear me? You have nothing." The laugh ended abruptly, his face twisting into something ugly as he brought up one hand to point a warning finger at Sebastian over the silver head of his swordstick. "But you breathe one word of this nonsense in the clubs—*one word*—and I swear to God, I'll call you out for it."

Sebastian studied the other man's angry, pinched face, looking for some trace of the elegant bone structure that the old slave woman, Cally, had bequeathed to her daughter and grandson. But he could see only the slab-like Anglo-Saxon features of a typical Englishman. "You're right; I don't have any proof yet. But I will."

And then he walked away, leaving the Baronet staring after him, the silver-headed walking stick gripped tightly in his hands.

⚜

"What precisely are you trying to do?" asked Hero, later, staring at him. "Provoke Knightly into killing you?"

Sebastian walked over to where a carafe of brandy

stood warming beside the library fire. "I'm hoping he'll try. Because he's right; I can't prove he killed Preston. I can't prove he killed any of them. The only thing I can do is rattle him enough that he does something stupid."

"And if he should by some strange, inexplicable chance succeed in killing you?"

He looked over at her with a crooked smile. "Then you'll know I was right."

She made an inelegant noise deep in her throat and rose from the library table where she'd been working on her article. "If you are right about Knightly—which at this point is still an *if*—then how do you explain Diggory Flynn?"

Sebastian poured a measure of brandy into a glass and set aside the decanter. "I think Oliphant decided he needed to kill me as soon as he returned to London, and he hired Diggory Flynn to do the job."

"Because he thought you intended to kill him?"

"Yes." He went to stand at the library window, his brandy cradled in one hand as he stared out at the storm. "And if I had killed the bastard, Jamie Knox would still be alive today."

A jagged sizzle of lightning lit up the nearly deserted wet street and silhouetted the dark rooftops of the opposite houses against the roiling underbelly of the storm clouds overhead. He could see a workman struggling to lash down the tools in his handcart, the lightning limning a pale, rain-washed face cut by the strap of an eye patch as the old man squinted up at the sky. Then the flash subsided, leaving the scene in near total darkness, and Sebastian realized the gusting wind must have blown out most of the oil lamps on the street.

Hero said, "Oliphant should have known that's not your way."

"I think you give me too much credit."

"No."

Light footsteps sounded in the hall, and Hero turned

toward the door as Claire came in carrying Simon. "Awake, little one?" she said with a smile. "And not screaming yet?"

Sebastian watched her move to take the child into her arms, saw the toothless grin that spread across his son's face as she lifted him up. And he knew a jolting frisson of alarm as the significance of the workman's eye patch suddenly hit him.

"Hero," he said, starting toward her. . . .

Just as the windowpane beside him shattered and a roll of thunder mingled with the crack of a rifle.

Chapter 55

 $\mathcal{T}$ he globe of the oil lamp on the table near the door exploded in a shower of glass.

"Get down!" shouted Sebastian, lunging toward Hero and Simon as he saw her fall.

"*Hero* ..." Crouching low, he caught her up in his arms, ran his hands over her and felt the warm stickiness of blood. "Mother of God, you're hit. Where? Simon—"

"We're all right," said Hero, her eyes dark and wide, the now screaming child cradled close. "It's just cuts from the flying glass."

He looked over at the Frenchwoman huddled behind a nearby chair. "Claire?"

Claire's terrified gaze met his, and she nodded.

He pushed up. "Stay here."

"Devlin!" he heard Hero shout as he tore across the entry hall and wrenched open the front door.

A cold, wind-driven rain stung his face and whipped at the tails of his coat as he pelted down the wet front steps. He could see the aged workman pushing his cart toward Bond Street, head down against the storm, the wheels of the cart bouncing over the paving stones. Then he must have heard Sebastian's running footsteps, because he threw a quick glance over his shoulder. His hair had been liberally smeared with gray ashes, and the oddly lopsided grimace he'd once affected was gone, leaving him almost unrecognizable.

"Flynn!" shouted Sebastian.

The one-eyed man reached beneath his coat.

Sebastian dove sideways behind the front steps of the house beside him as Diggory Flynn ripped off his eye patch and brought up a long-barreled pistol to fire. The shot ricocheted off the iron railing beside Sebastian's head, sparks showering the night.

"You son of a bitch," swore Sebastian, scrambling to his feet again.

Flynn abandoned the workman's cart and took off running.

Sebastian tore after him.

The former observing officer was both shorter and older, and Sebastian gained on him rapidly. Reaching out with his left hand, he grabbed Flynn's right shoulder and spun him around to drive his fist into the middle of the man's face, feeling bone and teeth give way in a blood-slicked crunch.

"You bastard," swore Sebastian. *"You could have killed my wife and son."*

"You moved!"

Without losing his hold on the man's shoulder, Sebastian buried his fist in Flynn's gut, then caught him under the chin with a punishing right hook.

Flynn's head snapped back, the force of the blow wrenching his coat from Sebastian's grasp. The man stumbled, tripped on the kerbstone, and went down hard on his rump.

Sebastian slipped his knife from his boot and advanced on him. "The same way you killed my brother."

"Brother?" Flynn scrambled backward on his hands and buttocks, his face smeared with blood. "What brother?" His shoulder bumped against the area railing of the house behind him and he reached to haul himself up.

"Jamie Knox," said Sebastian, grabbing a fistful of the man's coat front and swinging him around to slam his back against the house wall.

"But I—"

Sebastian pressed the knife blade against his throat.

Flynn's eyes widened and he swallowed hard, blood dripping off his chin from his broken nose and mouth. "Don't kill me."

Sebastian shook his head, his lips curling away from his teeth. "Name one good reason why I shouldn't."

Flynn's chest jerked on a ragged, quickly indrawn breath. "I can give you Oliphant."

The French overture to Haydn's last piano sonata thundered with an energetic and passionate verve as Sebastian threaded his way through Lady Farningham's crowded reception rooms. It was her second musical evening of the Season, and it seemed that all of fashionable London had come to hear her latest Italian virtuoso. The more intent listeners were seated in the rows of gilded chairs drawn up before the pianoforte. But most of the guests circulated freely, drinking and eating and chatting in small clusters.

Sinclair, Lord Oliphant, was standing beside one of the ornate pilasters in the drawing room, his gaze fixed on the pianist, when Sebastian walked up behind his former colonel and said quietly, "I have Diggory Flynn. He's willing to testify that you paid him to kill Jamie Knox."

Oliphant kept his eyes on the musician, not even bothering to turn his head as he said, "I never did any such thing."

Lady Oliphant was too far away to hear their words, but she looked over at Sebastian and frowned pointedly.

Sebastian kept his voice low. "True; you paid him to kill me. But Knox died."

"Diggory Flynn is scum. No one will believe him. Do you honestly think a jury would take the word of a smuggler against that of a peer of the realm?"

"Perhaps. Perhaps not." Like Oliphant, Sebastian kept his attention seemingly focused on the performer. "The thing is, you see, your man shot at me tonight with my wife and son standing beside me. *Jarvis's daughter and grandson.* The only reason I haven't already killed you is because they weren't hurt. But don't expect Jarvis to be swayed by such technicalities. You'll be lucky if you live long enough to stand trial." He watched as that perpetual, confident smile slid slowly from Oliphant's face. "I suppose you could try to run. But I don't think you'll get far."

He bowed his head toward Oliphant's scowling wife. "My lady," he said, and turned to walk out of the room and out of the house.

As he descended the front steps, he noticed one of the tall, dark-haired former hussar officers employed by Jarvis waiting across the rain-drenched street. For a moment, their gazes met. Then he heard Tom's shout.

"Gov'nor! Oy, gov'nor."

He could see the tiger threading his way through the crowd of gawkers that always formed around such events.

"Gov'nor," said the boy, struggling to catch his breath as he skidded to a halt at the base of the steps. He held out a somewhat grubby calling card. "A lad just brung this from Bucket Lane!"

It was one of Sebastian's own cards. He flipped it over to see that someone had written on the back in a childish hand.

Plees help. Juba

"I think it's a trap," said Tom.

They were in a hackney headed toward Fish Street Hill. The rain had eased up for the moment, but water still dripped from the eaves of the mean houses and shops they passed, and a cold wind buffeted the old carriage.

"Of course it's a trap," said Sebastian, his gaze on the soaring tower of the church of St. Magnus that loomed over the bridgehead and Billingsgate Market. He'd expected Knightly to try to silence him. And he had worried about the safety of Juba and Banjo. What he hadn't foreseen was that the killer would use the woman and child to bait a trap for Sebastian.

He wondered if life really spun in circles, or if it was simply some trick of the human mind that made people see patterns where none truly existed. The last time women and children had been put at risk because of him, he had failed to save them. He'd spent the last three years seeking some sort of redemption for that failure and had found a measure of solace in his efforts on behalf of other victims of human evil.

But now it was happening all over again.

Tom shook his head. "So why ye goin' there?"

"Because if I don't, Juba and her son will die."

Lit only by the occasional glimmer of a tallow candle showing through a grimy window, Bucket Lane lay dark and wet and deserted beneath the stormy sky.

"What we gonna do?" whispered Tom as they slipped down the lane to draw up in a shadowy doorway.

Centuries old, Juba's house had only two stories and was built so that the upper floor jutted out over the lower. It contained just two rooms per floor, with a different family living in each room. The front room of the upper story was dark. But the flickering, smoky light of a tallow candle showed through the thin, ragged curtain of the ground-floor room.

"I want you to go inside, slowly count to ten, and then knock on the first door to your left. Just be certain to flatten yourself against the wall before you reach over to knock, and jerk your hand back quickly. I wouldn't put it past Knightly to shoot through the door rather than open it."

"And then what?"

"And then I want you to run into the street and keep running, no matter what happens."

"But . . . gov'nor!"

"You heard me."

The boy hung his head. "Aye, gov'nor."

Sebastian watched the tiger let himself in the house's battered street door, and began to count.

One, two . . .

A single large shadow seated at the trestle table near the door showed through the worn cloth of the curtain. Knightly? Probably. But if so, then where were Juba and Banjo?

Three, four . . .

He told himself the woman and boy couldn't already be dead. Surely Knightly would leave them alive until he had Sebastian?

Five, six . . .

Leaping up, Sebastian caught hold of one of the beams supporting the cantilevered upper story where it jutted out above the window.

Seven, eight . . .

Kicking his legs, he began to swing back and forth, gathering momentum.

Nine, ten.

He heard the tiger's knock, heard the sound of a bench being pushed back, saw the shadow rise to its feet. Then he kicked back hard with his legs and let go of the beam as he swung forward again toward the house.

He crashed through the window feetfirst in a shower of broken glass and shattered framing. Coming down hard on his feet, he lost his balance and fell to his knees. He saw Juba crouched on the pallet near the hearth, her son clutched in her arms. Saw Knightly spin toward him, the barrel of a flintlock pistol wavering as he brought up his other hand to steady it.

Sebastian threw himself sideways, jerked his own pistol free as he fell, and fired.

In the confined space of the small room, the pistol's report was deafening, an explosion of smoke and flame and blood. Juba screamed. Knightly staggered back, slammed into the table, and crumpled slowly to the floor.

The door from the hall burst open and Tom catapulted into the room.

"Bloody hell; I told you to run," swore Sebastian.

Tom drew up short, his eyes wide, his breath coming hard and fast. Swiping one sleeve across his nose, he edged closer to Knightly's now still body. "Gor. Ye plugged 'im right through the eye, ye did. Is 'e dead?"

Sebastian pushed to his feet, brushing broken glass from his clothes as he walked over to stare down at the Baronet's slack face. "Yes."

He bent to pick up the dead man's pistol, then went to hunker down beside Juba and Banjo, still pressed up against the corner by the hearth. "You both all right?"

She nodded, her face slack, her pupils wide with terror. "I didn't want to send you that note. But he said he'd kill Banjo if I didn't."

Sebastian shook his head. "Don't blame yourself. I'm the one who inadvertently put you at risk."

She gazed beyond him, to where Sir Galen Knightly

lay sprawled with one carefully manicured hand flung out so that it lay curled against the worn paving stones of her house.

She said, "Is he really my half brother?"

Sebastian shook his head. "I'm not sure we'll ever know."

Chapter 56

"*N*one of this can be allowed to get out, naturally," said Jarvis, his hands clasped behind his back as he stood before the drawing room's bowed front window. Jarvis seldom came to Brook Street, but he had arrived that morning shortly after dawn.

"Of course not," said Sebastian. "Wouldn't do to have the lower orders start thinking us their equals in depravity and violence."

Jarvis glanced over at him. "I take it you are being facetious." He reached for his snuffbox. "The morning papers will carry the shocking news that Sir Galen Knightly has fallen victim to footpads whilst venturing unwisely into one of the more insalubrious areas of the city. A Bethnal Green navvy who killed and dismembered his wife several days ago has confessed to also murdering Stanley Preston and Dr. Douglas Sterling. Unfortunately, he has since succumbed to some sort of fatal seizure, so there will be no trial."

"Unfortunate for him, certainly. But no great loss to society, from the sounds of things."

"More levity," said Jarvis, lifting a pinch of snuff to one nostril.

Sebastian smiled. "Any luck yet finding King Charles's head?"

Jarvis inhaled so sharply he sneezed.

"Bless you," said Sebastian as his father-in-law sneezed again and reached for his handkerchief. "When is the Regent's formal opening of the vault to be?"

Jarvis glared at him over the folds of his handkerchief. "Tomorrow."

"Not much time left."

"I take it you've no idea what's happened to it?"

"Sorry."

Jarvis tucked away his handkerchief. "I assume my daughter and grandson are in the nursery?"

"Yes."

"Hero tells me you encourage her in this barbaric nonsense of refusing to hire a wet nurse."

"I support her, yes. But the decision is hers and hers alone."

"What drivel." Jarvis turned toward the door. Then he paused to look back and say, "Oh, by the way; Lord Oliphant has inexplicably disappeared. Speculation of an accident or foul play will likely appear in tomorrow's papers, but I'm told the body shouldn't surface for another four or five days, depending upon the weather. At that point it will be concluded he must have slipped and fallen into the river during Tuesday night's storm. And if he had succeeded in harming either my daughter or my grandson, you would be dead by now as well."

The two men's gazes met and held.

Then Jarvis nodded and walked out of the room.

After the previous night's storm, the day had dawned clear and sunny, with the streets washed clean by the rain.

Driving himself in his curricle, Sebastian curved along the southern edge of Hyde Park toward Knightsbridge and Hans Town. His first stop was Sloane Street, where he found Miss Jane Austen walking in the gardens of Cadogan Square. She wore an old-fashioned round bonnet and her sensible brown pelisse, and her cheeks were ruddy with the cool, fresh air.

"Lord Devlin," she said when she saw him coming toward her. "You've read the news in this morning's papers?"

"Yes."

Her eyes narrowed as her intense gaze searched his face. "And none of it's true, is it?"

"No."

"I didn't think so. But that can only mean . . . The killer was *Knightly*? Why?"

"Because he feared Preston and Sterling were in possession of information he was desperate to keep from becoming known."

"And so he killed them? And cut off their heads in his rage? Who could have believed him capable of such viciousness?"

"A wise woman once noted that it is difficult to know the true sentiments of a clever man."

Her small, dark eyes shone with amused delight. Then she shook her head. "Not so wise, given that I thought him another Colonel Brandon—staid, steadfast, and boring."

"And how did Miss Preston receive this morning's news?" asked Sebastian as they turned to walk along the garden path. "Do you know?"

"I don't think she believes the reports in the newspapers either. But she is understandably relieved. She and Captain Wyeth plan to be wed as soon as possible, rather than wait for the passage of the customary twelve months of mourning."

"Sensible. They've waited enough years already."

Miss Austen glanced over at him. "I hear Lord Oliphant has disappeared."

"So he has."

"And you're not going to explain any of it to me, are you?"

"No," he said. "But I'm confident in your ability to use your imagination."

Continuing down Sloane Street toward Chelsea, Sebastian turned his curricle to run along the square, then drove into the lane that led toward Bloody Bridge.

"What we doin' 'ere *again*?" said Tom.

The chestnuts snorted and tried to shy as Sebastian guided them across the bridge and into the fields that stretched away on either side of the rutted road. "I have an idea."

He drove through market gardens fresh and green after the previous night's rain, toward the tower of the small country chapel that rose above the elms and hawthorns of its churchyard. The way he figured it, Rowan Toop must have come upon Preston's body not long after the killing and, in his terror, accidentally dropped whatever satchel contained the King's head and coffin strap. The virger had obviously managed to retrieve the severed head. But he must have still been flailing about trying to find the coffin strap when he heard the approach of the young couple from the Rose and Crown. At that point, he had abandoned his search and—with the King's head tucked under one arm—run in the only direction possible: across the bridge into Five Fields. Rattled by what he'd seen and terrified of being caught in possession of relics plundered from the royal chapel, Toop's first instinct, surely, would have been to hide the item he'd hoped to sell to Stanley Preston.

And where better to hide a dead man's head than in a churchyard?

A small, neoclassical structure, Five Fields Chapel was not old, having been built in the previous century. But its churchyard was already overflowing, for there never seemed to be enough room to bury London's endless supply of dead.

After reining in beside the lych-gate, Sebastian handed Tom the reins and dropped lightly to the ground. "I won't be long."

Wandering paths overgrown with weeds and rampant ivy, past rusting iron fences and weathered headstones crusted with lichen, he found what he was looking for not far from the road: a neglected, crumbling tomb so old it was collapsing badly at one end.

Crouching down beside it, Sebastian peered into the tomb's dank, musty interior. He could see decaying wood and the dull gleam of weathered bone, and a canvas sack thrust hurriedly out of sight by a frightened man who hadn't lived long enough to retrieve it.

He lifted the sack from its hiding place to find the cloth wet from the previous night's storm and stained a nasty greenish red. Working carefully, he untied the thong fastening. Then he hesitated a moment before peeling back the canvas to reveal an ancient severed head, the skin of the eerily familiar, oval face dark and discolored, the pointed beard still showing reddish brown.

But the hair at the back of the neck was stained black by old, dried blood and cut short in anticipation of the executioner's blade.

Thursday, 1 April

"This is so *exciting*," said the Prince Regent, shivering with a combination of delicious anticipation and bone-numbing cold. He stood with Dean Legge, his brother the Duke of Cumberland, and two boon companions in the newly constructed passage that led down to the royal vault beneath St. George's Chapel in Windsor Castle. "But . . . are you quite certain I won't fit inside the vault itself?"

Charles, Lord Jarvis, stood near the crude entrance to Henry VIII's small burial chamber. "I'm afraid not, Your Highness. The tomb is less than five feet in height and only seven by nine and a half feet wide. And with three burials—one of them extraordinarily large—there is barely enough room for Halford and the workman cutting an opening in the coffin's lid."

"They should have thought to build a larger chamber," grumbled the Prince. Then excitement overcame the minor bout of petulance, and he brought up his clasped hands to tuck them beneath his chin. "Oh, I do hope the body is complete."

"I fear the chances of that are unfortunately slim, Your Highness," said Jarvis. "You must prepare yourself for the possibility that Charles's head was in all likelihood not buried with his body."

He nodded to Sir Henry Halford, the president of the Royal College of Physicians and a fawning sycophant who knew precisely where the real power in the realm lay.

The laborer—well paid to keep the truth of that day's events to himself—stood back.

"I do believe . . . Yes, I do believe . . . ," said Halford, prolonging the suspense as he carefully separated the sticky folds of the coffin's cerecloth.

"Yes?" Eager to see, the Prince thrust his head through the vault's entrance, his bloated body effectively blocking everyone else's view of the proceedings. "Is it there? Is the head there?"

"It's here, Your Highness. Just look!" said the physician, smiling in stunned triumph as he held aloft the unexpectedly wet, dripping head of the long-dead King.

They buried Jamie Knox on a misty evening in the elm-shaded, medieval churchyard of St. Helen's, Bishopsgate, in the shadow of the moss-covered wall that backed onto the yard of the Black Devil.

Afterward, Sebastian stood alone with Hero beside the stark, turned earth of the new grave, his hat in his hand and his head bowed, although he did not pray. He could hear the raucous call of a blackbird somewhere nearby, smell the pungent odor of damp loam and old stone.

He said, "I've been thinking of making a trip up to Shropshire, to take the mechanical nightingale to Knox's grandmother." There was no need to state the other reason—perhaps the main reason—for his desire to visit the place of Knox's birth.

Hero looked over at him, her eyes solemn and knowing. But all she said was, "I'm sure she would like that."

He reached out to take her hand. "Will you come with me?"

"If you want me to."

"I want you," he said, his throat tight with emotion as a gust of wind shuddered the trees overhead and sent a scattering of leaves spinning down to lie pale and shriveled against the cold, dark earth.

Author's Note

The discovery in early 1813 of the "lost" burial vault containing the coffins of Henry VIII, Jane Seymour, and Charles I was real and excited considerable popular attention. At the time, Byron wrote of the discovery, "Famed for contemptuous breach of sacred ties, / By headless Charles see heartless Henry lies," while Cruikshank produced a satire of the event called *Meditations amongst the Tombs*. The caricature portrays the effeminate, unhappily married Prince Regent as envious of Henry VIII's success in ridding himself of so many wives, while Charles sits up in his coffin holding his own detached head in silent warning.

Cruikshank's cartoon considerably exaggerates both the size and the grandeur of the crude vault, which was indeed less than five feet high and ten feet wide. My description of the burial vault and the formal opening of Charles I's coffin comes largely from the account written by Sir Henry Halford, one of the Regent's personal physicians who was present for the opening and was responsible for the removal of several items, including a piece of the severed vertebrae and a tooth. When these items were returned to the vault in 1888, a still extant watercolor sketch was made that shows the interior of

the tomb and the disposition of the coffins. That watercolor can now be found online.

There is some dispute as to the wording of the inscription on Charles's coffin strap. Sir Henry Halford reports
that the lead strap was inscribed with the words, "King
Charles, 1648." Later writers, including Guizot, who
wrote a *History of the English Revolution* in 1838, claim
the strap read "Charles, Rex, 1648." Another nineteenth-
century writer named Sanderson claims it read, "Charles
King of England." Clarendon Fuller says it was a plate
of silver, not a lead strap, and was inscribed "King
Charles I," while John Ashton goes with Halford's version, "King Charles, 1648." Since Halford was there and
wrote his account shortly after viewing the coffin, I have
used him as my authority.

For the execution and burial of Charles I, see *Mem-
oirs of the Last Two Years of the Reign of King Charles
I*, written by Sir Thomas Herbert, who was present at
the hurried burial of the executed King. Although his
account plus a letter written by Herbert to Sir William
Dugdale in 1681, which also detailed the burial of the
King, were in existence in 1813, both were forgotten
and the location of Charles I's body was considered a
mystery. Although I have omitted it to avoid confusion,
there was actually a fourth burial found in the vault: A
small mahogany coffin covered with crimson velvet and
containing the stillborn child of Queen Anne was found
resting atop Charles's coffin (which tells us that at the
time of Queen Anne, the exact location of Charles I's
body was known).

The description of what happened to the remains of
Edward IV when his tomb was discovered in St. George's
Chapel in 1789 is based on fact; even Horace Walpole
bragged about having managed to snag a lock of the
King's hair.

For the colorful history of Oliver Cromwell's head, see
Beales, *The Posthumous History of Oliver Cromwell's*

Head, and Howard, *The Embalmed Head of Oliver Cromwell*. Cromwell's head was recently reburied; the fate of the rest of his body is unknown.

For the history of Henri IV's head, see Gabet and Charlier, *L'énigme du roi sans tête*. Henri IV was originally buried at Saint-Denis, but his head was reputedly stolen in 1793 when the revolutionaries broke into the royal tombs and tossed the Bourbons' bones into a common grave. When that grave was opened in 1817, Henri IV's head was indeed found to be missing. Forensic reconstruction of a head currently held in a Parisian bank and long believed to be the one taken from the grave confirmed that it belonged to Henri. Recent DNA testing on the same head cast doubt on that authentication, as its DNA reportedly did not match that of a living Bourbon who provided a sample. However, the paternity of a number of Bourbons has always been cloudy, and the accuracy of the test is also in dispute.

Henry Addington, First Viscount Sidmouth, was a former Prime Minister and Home Secretary in 1813. His father was indeed a simple physician, although of course he had no cousin named Stanley Preston.

The Irish Dullahan is essentially an embodiment of death and is most likely derived from some forgotten, ancient god placated with human sacrifices in which the victims were decapitated.

Lord Mansfield's famous decision in the 1772 Somersett case is generally considered to have essentially ended chattel slavery in England and Wales, although emancipation came gradually enough that advertisements for "runaway slaves" were still occasionally seen into the late 1780s. The decision did not apply to Scotland, where colliers and salters were still held in conditions of slavery until 1799. Although Britain abolished the slave trade in 1807, slavery still flourished in its colonies, and there was little opprobrium attached to those—such as Sir Galen Knightly and Stanley Preston—who owned slaves. The wealthy family in Jane Austen's *Mansfield Park* owned plantations worked by slaves.

The number of works written about Jane Austen is staggering. For my portrayal of Austen, I have relied, among others, on Le Faye's *A Chronology of Jane Austen and Her Family*; Byrne's *The Real Jane Austen: A Life in Small Things*; Honan's *Jane Austen: Her Life*, and of course Austen's own letters and novels. The biographical information given for Jane Austen's brother Henry and her cousin and sister-in-law, Eliza, is largely taken from those works. Eliza Austen died of breast cancer on 25 April 1813.

There really was a Bloody Bridge that spanned the small rivulet running along Five Fields. There was an ancient tavern in the area called the Monster, a corruption of the Monastery, but it was not precisely where I have placed it. The Twentieth Light Hussars served in both Jamaica and the Peninsula, although not precisely in the years I have used here. Basil Thistlewood's coffeehouse in Cheyne Walk is patterned on the very real curiosity shop in Chelsea owned by a man who called himself Don Salerno.

While today we tend to think of butter as a luxury item, the poor of London actually ate a great deal of bread and butter; the fat it provided was an important part of what kept them alive. Hero's articles on the poor of London are inspired by a similar work carried out several decades later by Henry Mayhew, and Mayhew is the source for Hero's interviews with the various costermongers.

Having traveled with his wife, Hero,
to Shropshire in hopes of learning more
about his own parentage, Sebastian St. Cyr
is caught up in an investigation into the
apparent suicide of a solitary young woman.
Soon, the peaceful, pastoral village where
he is staying is revealed to be a place
of dark tragedy and long-held secrets.
Don't miss the next taut, compelling
new mystery in the exciting
Sebastian St. Cyr series,

WHEN
FALCONS FALL

Available from Obsidian in hardcover
and e-book in March 2016,
and in paperback in March 2017.
An excerpt follows. . . .

Chapter 1

Ayleswick-on-Teme, Shropshire
Tuesday, 3 August 1813

*I*t was the fly that got to him.

In the misty light of early morning, the dead woman looked as if she might be sleeping, her dusky lashes resting against cheeks of pale eggshell, her lips faintly parted. She lay at the edge of a clover-strewn meadow near the river, the back of her head nestled against a mossy log, her slim hands folded at the high waist of her fashionable dove gray mourning gown.

Then that fly came crawling out of her mouth.

Archie barely made it behind the nearest furze bush before losing the bread and cheese he'd grabbed for breakfast.

"There, there, now, lad," said Constable Webster Nash, the beefy, middle-aged man who also served as the village's sexton and bell ringer. "No need to be feeling queasy. Ain't like there's a mess o' blood."

"I'm all right." Archie's guts heaved again and his thin body shuddered, but he swallowed hard and forced himself to straighten. "I'm all right." Not that it made any difference, of course; he could say it a hundred times, and word would still be all around the village by noon, about how the young Squire had cast up his accounts at the mere sight of the dead woman.

Archie swiped the back of one trembling hand across his lips. Archibald Rawlins had been Squire of Ayleswick for just five months. It was an honor accorded his father, and his father before him, on back through the ages to that battle-hardened esquire who'd built the Grange near the banks of the River Teme and successfully defended it against all comers. One of the acknowledged duties of the squire was to serve as his village's justice of the peace or magistrate, which was how Archie came to be standing in the river meadow on that misty morning and staring at the dead body of a beautiful young widow who had arrived in the village less than a week before.

"'Tis a sinful thing," said Nash, tsking through the gap left by a missing incisor. "Sinful, for a woman to take her own life like this. The Good Book says, 'If any man defile the temple of God, him shall God destroy; for the temple of God is holy, which temple ye are.' And I reckon that's as true for a woman as for any man."

Archie cleared his throat. "I don't think we can say that yet—that she took her own life, I mean."

Constable Nash let out a sound somewhere between a grunt and a derisive laugh as he bent to pick up the brown glass bottle that nestled in the grass at her side. "Laudanum," he said, turning the bottle so that the POISON label faced Archie. "Emptied it, she did."

"Yes, I noticed it."

Archie stared down at the woman's neatly folded spencer. It lay to one side with her broad-brimmed velvet-trimmed straw hat, as if she had taken them off and carefully set them aside before stretching out to— what? Drink a massive dose of an opium tincture that in small measures could ease pain but in excess brought death?

It was the obvious conclusion. And yet . . .

Archie let his gaze drift around the clearing. The meadow was eerily hushed and still, as if the mist drifting up from the river had deadened all sound. The young lad who had stumbled upon the dead woman's body at dawn and led them here was now gone; the creatures of forest and field had all fled or hidden themselves. Even the unseen birds in the tree canopy above seemed loath to break the silence with their usual chorus of cheerful morning song. Archie felt a chill dance up his spine, as if he could somehow sense a lingering malevolence in this place, an evil, a disturbance in the way things ought to be that was no less real for being inexplicable.

But he had no intention of uttering such fanciful sentiments to the gruff, no-nonsense constable beside him. So he simply said, "I think you should put the bottle back where it was, Nash."

"What?" The constable's jaw sagged, his full, ruddy cheeks darkening.

Archie tried hard to infuse his voice with a note of authority. "Put it back exactly as you found it, Constable. Until we know for certain otherwise, I think we should consider this a murder."

Constable Nash's face crimped. His small, dark eyes had a way of disappearing into the flesh of his face when he was amused or angry, and they disappeared now. But he didn't say anything.

"There's a viscount staying in the village," said Archie. "Arrived just yesterday evening. I've heard of him; his name is Devlin, and he works with Bow Street sometimes, solving murders. I'm going to ask for his advice in this."

"Ain't no need to go troublin' no grand London lord. I tell ye, she killed herself."

"Perhaps. But I'd like to be certain."

Archie readjusted the tilt of his hat and smoothed the front of his simple brown corduroy coat. Standing up to the village's loud, bullying constable was one thing; Archie had only to call upon some six hundred years of Rawlins tradition and heritage.

But approaching the son and heir of the mighty Earl of Hendon and asking him to help a simple village squire investigate the death of a stranger was considerably more daunting.

Chapter 2

A picturesque cluster of half-timbered and stone cottages huddled in the shadow of a squat, timeworn Norman church, the Shropshire village of Ayleswick lay just to the southwest of Ludlow, near the banks of the River Teme. Once, it had been the site of the Benedictine priory of St. Hilary, famous along the Welsh Marches as a pilgrimage destination, thanks to its possession of an ancient wooden statue of the Virgin said to work miracles.

But the priory was long gone, its famous statue consigned to the flames and many of the stones from its sprawling monastic complex sold or hauled up the hill to build a grand Tudor estate known as Northcott Abbey. The once-bustling village had sunk into obscurity and now boasted only one decent inn, the Blue Boar, a rambling, half-timbered relic that fronted both the village green and the narrow, winding high street.

Sebastian St. Cyr, Viscount Devlin, stood at the window of his chamber at the inn, his view of the misty green below rippled by the casement's ancient leaded glass. The impression was one of bucolic peace, of innocence and harmony and timeless grace. But Sebastian knew that all is often not as it seems, just as he knew that those who probe the secrets of the past risk hearing truths they might wish they'd never learned.

He dropped his gaze to the mechanical nightingale he held in his hands. It had been purchased for an old woman Sebastian had never met, by a man who was now dead. And so Sebastian had come here, to the old woman's village, to deliver her dead grandson's gift.

He heard the soft whisper of fine muslin skirts as Hero came to slide her arms around his waist and rest her dark head against his. Tall, statuesque, and striking, she'd been his wife for a year now. Their infant son slept peacefully in his nearby cradle, and Sebastian loved both mother and child with a passionate tenderness that awed, humbled, and terrified him.

She shifted to take the nightingale from his hands, wound the key cleverly concealed in its tail feathers, and set the bird on the deep windowsill before them. The nightingale's gilded wings beat slowly up and down, the jewels in its collar sparkling in the early-morning sunlight as a cascade of melodious notes filled the air.

She said, "Shall I come with you?"

He hesitated, his attention caught by a young country gentleman in an unfashionable corduroy coat who was striding toward the inn's door. "You don't think a simple, aged countrywoman might find a visit from the two of us a bit overwhelming?"

"Probably," she said, although he saw the faint frown that pinched her forehead. She knew that the nightingale was only part of what had brought him to this small Shropshire village, just as she knew that what quickened his pulse and tore at his gut was the possibility that the unknown elderly woman might possess the answer to a question that had shattered his world and forever altered his understanding of who—and what—he was.

An unexpected knock at the chamber door brought his head around. "Yes?"

A spry middle-aged chambermaid with a leprechaun's face and wild iron gray hair imperfectly contained by a mobcap opened the door and bobbed a quick curtsy. "It's young Squire Rawlins, milord. He says t' beg yer lordship's pardon, but he's most anxious to meet with you, he is." She dropped her voice and leaned forward as she added, "I'm thinkin' it's on account of the lady, milord. Heard Constable Nash tellin' Cook about it, I did."

"What lady?"

"Why, the one they done found down in the water meadows, just this mornin'. Dead, she is!"

He and Hero exchanged silent glances.

On the windowsill, the mechanical nightingale wound down and stopped.

C.S. Harris

WHEN FALCONS FALL
A Sebastian St. Cyr Mystery

Ayleswick-on-Teme, 1813. Sebastian St. Cyr,
Viscount Devlin, has come to this seemingly
peaceful Shropshire village to honor a slain friend
and on a quest to learn more about his own
ancestry. But when the body of a lovely widow is
found on the banks of the river Teme, a bottle of
laudanum at her side, the village's inexperienced
new magistrate turns to Sebastian for help.

Almost immediately, Sebastian realizes that Emma
Chance did not, in truth, take her own life.
Sebastian's investigation takes on new urgency when
he discovers that Emma was not the first, or even
the second, beautiful young woman in the village to
die under suspicious circumstances. As he faces his
most diabolical opponent ever, he is forced to
consider what malevolence he's willing to embrace
in order to destroy a killer.

"Harris is a master of the genre."
—*The Historical Novels Review*

ALSO AVAILABLE

FROM NATIONAL BESTSELLING AUTHOR

C.S. Harris

The Sebastian St. Cyr Mysteries

"[The] best historical thriller writer in the business...the entire series is simply elegant."
—*New York Times* bestselling author
Lisa Gardner

What Angels Fear
When Gods Die
Why Mermaids Sing
Where Serpents Sleep
What Remains of Heaven
Where Shadows Dance
When Maidens Mourn
What Darkness Brings
Why Kings Confess
Who Buries the Dead

Available wherever books are sold or at
penguin.com

facebook.com/TheCrimeSceneBooks